Captured by the Billionaire

ROBYN DONALD

BARBARA DUNLOP

LUCY KING

Published in Great Britain 2014
by Mills & Boon, an imprint of Harlequin (UK) Limited,
Eton House, 18-24 Paradise Road, Richmond, Surrey, TW9 1SR

CAPTURED BY THE BILLIONAIRE © 2014 Harlequin Books S.A.

Brooding Billionaire, Impoverished Princess, Beauty and the Billionaire and *Propositioned by the Billionaire* were first published in Great Britain by Harlequin (UK) Limited.

Brooding Billionaire, Impoverished Princess © 2010 Robyn Donald
Beauty and the Billionaire © 2008 Barbara Dunlop
Propositioned by the Billionaire © 2010 Lucy King

ISBN: 978-0-263-91207-4
eBook ISBN: 978-1-472-04502-7

05-1114

Harlequin (UK) Limited's policy is to use papers that are natural, renewable and recyclable products and made from wood grown in sustainable forests. The logging and manufacturing processes conform to the legal environmental regulations of the country of origin.

Printed and bound in Spain
by CPI, Barcelona

BROODING BILLIONAIRE, IMPOVERISHED PRINCESS

BY
ROBYN DONALD

Robyn Donald can't remember not being able to read, and will be eternally grateful to the local farmers who carefully avoided her on a dusty country road as she read her way to and from school, transported to places and times far away from her small village in Northland, New Zealand. Growing up fed her habit. As well as training as a teacher, marrying and raising two children, she discovered the delights of romances and read them voraciously, especially enjoying the ones written by New Zealand writers. So much so that one day she decided to write one herself. Writing soon grew to be as much of a delight as reading—although infinitely more challenging—and when eventually her first book was accepted by Mills & Boon she felt she'd arrived home. She still lives in a small town in Northland, with her family close by, using the landscape as a setting for much of her work. Her life is enriched by the friends she's made among writers and readers, and complicated by a determined corgi called Buster, who is convinced that blackbirds are evil entities. Her greatest hobby is still reading, with travelling a very close second.

CHAPTER ONE

NARROW-EYED, Alex Matthews surveyed the ballroom of the palace. The band had just played a few bars of the Carathian national folk song, a tune in waltz-time that was the signal for guests to take their partners for the first dance of the evening. The resultant rustle around the margins of the room flashed colour from the women's elaborate gowns and magnificent jewellery.

Alex's angular features softened a little when he saw the bride. His half-sister outshone any jewel, her blazing happiness making Alex feel uncomfortably like an intruder. Quite a few years younger, Rosie was the daughter of his father's second wife and, although they'd become friends over the past few years, he'd never had a close relationship with her.

Alex transferred his gaze to his brother-in-law of a few hours, the Grand Duke of Carathia. Gerd wasn't given to displays of overt emotion, but Alex blinked at the other man's unguarded expression when he looked down at the woman on his arm. It was as though there was no one in the room but the two of them.

It lasted scarcely a moment, just long enough for Alex to wonder at the subtle emotion that twisted inside him.

Envy? No.

Sex and affection he understood—respect and liking also—but love was foreign to him.

Probably always would be. The ability to feel such intense emotion didn't seem to be part of his character. And since breaking hearts wasn't something he enjoyed—a lesson he'd learned from a painful experience in his youth—he now chose lovers who could accept his essential aloofness.

However, although he couldn't imagine that sort of emotion in himself, he was glad his half-sister loved a man worthy of her, one who not only returned her ardour but valued her for it. Although he and Gerd were distant cousins, they had grown up more like brothers—and if anyone deserved Rosie's love, Gerd did.

Couples began to group around the royal pair, leaving them a space in the middle of the ballroom.

The man beside him said, 'Are you planning to sit this one out, Alex?'

'No, I'm pledged for it.' Alex's blue gaze moved to a woman standing alone at the side of the room.

Elegant and smoothly confident, Princess Serina's beautiful face revealed nothing beyond calm pleasure. Yet until Rosie and Gerd had announced their engagement, most of the rarefied circle of high society she moved in had assumed the Princess would be the next Grand Duchess of Carathia.

Regally inscrutable, if Serina of Montevel *was* secretly grieving she refused to give anyone the titillating satisfaction of seeing it. Alex admired her for that.

During the last few days he'd overheard several remarks from watchful wedding guests—a few compassionate but most from people looking for drama, the chance to see a cracked heart exposed.

Made obscurely angry by their snide spite, Alex mentally shrugged. The Princess didn't need his protection; her impervious armour of breeding and self-sufficiency deflected all snide comments, denied all attempts at sympathy.

He'd met her a year ago at Gerd's coronation ball, introduced by an elderly Spanish aristocrat who had formally reeled off her full complement of surnames. Surprised by a quick masculine desire, Alex had read amusement in the Princess's amazing, darkly violet eyes.

A little sardonically he'd commented on that roll call of blood and pride, power and position.

Her low amused chuckle had further fired his senses. 'If you had the same conventions in New Zealand you'd have a phalanx of names too,' she'd informed him with unruffled composure. 'They're nothing more than a kind of family tree.'

Possibly she'd meant it, but now, possessed of disturbing knowledge about her brother, Alex wasn't so sure. Doran of Montevel was only too aware that those names were embedded in European history. Did the Princess have any idea of what her younger brother had got himself mixed up with?

If she did she'd done nothing about it, so perhaps she also wanted to see herself back in Montevel, a true princess instead of the bearer of a defunct title inherited from her deposed grandfather.

And Alex needed to find out just what she did know. He set off towards her.

She saw him coming, of course, and immediately

produced an irritatingly gracious smile. The smoky violet of her gown echoed the colour of her eyes and hugged a narrow waist, displaying curves that unleashed something elemental and fierce inside Alex, an urge to discover what lay beneath that lovely façade, to challenge her on the most fundamental level—man to woman.

'Alex,' she said, the smile widening a fraction when he stopped in front of her. 'This is such a happy occasion for us all. I've never seen such a blissful bride, and Gerd looks—well, almost transfigured.'

A controlled man himself, Alex admired her skill in conveying that her heart wasn't broken. 'Indeed,' he responded. 'My dance, I believe.'

Still smiling, she laid a slender hand on his arm and together they walked into the waiting, chattering circle around Rosie and Gerd.

Alex glanced down, a phrase from childhood echoing in his head. *White as snow, red as blood, black as ebony.* Snow White, he remembered.

And Serina was an almost perfect snow princess.

Exquisite enough to star in a fairy tale, she radiated grace. Her black chignon set off her tiara and classical features perfectly, contrasting sensuously with the almost translucent pallor of her skin.

She'd passed on one part of the description, though; her lips were painted a restrained shade of dark, clear pink. A bold red would be too blatant, too provocative for this Princess.

But they were tempting lips…

A hunting instinct as old as time stirred into life deep within Alex. He'd wanted Serina Montevel ever since he'd first seen her, but because he too had wondered if she was wounded by dashed hopes he'd made no move to attract her attention. However, a year had passed—enough time to heal any damage to her heart.

He stopped with Serina on the edge of the crowd of dancers and sent a flinty territorial glance, sharp as a rapier, to a man a few paces away eyeing Serina with open appreciation. It gave him cold pleasure to watch the ogler hastily transfer his appreciative gaze elsewhere.

The band swung into the tune and the crowd fell silent as the newlyweds began waltzing. Softly the onlookers began to clap in time to the beat.

Serina glanced up, tensing when her eyes clashed with a sharp blue gaze. Her breath locked in her throat while she wrestled down an exhilarating excitement. Tall, dark and arrogantly handsome, Alex Matthews had a strangely weakening effect on her.

Warily, because the silence between them grew too heavy, almost significant, she broke into it with the first thing that came into her head. 'This is a very pretty tradition.'

'The Carathian wedding dance?'

'Yes.'

Neither Rosie nor Gerd smiled; eyes locked, it was as if they were alone together, absorbed, so intent on each other that Serina felt a sharp stab of—regret?

No, not quite. A kind of wistful envy.

Just over a year previously she'd decided to make it clear to Gerd—without being so crass as to say the words—that she wasn't on the market to become Grand Duchess of Carathia. Such a union would have solved a lot of her problems, and she admired Gerd very much, but she wanted more than a *convenient* marriage.

Just as well, because shortly afterwards Gerd had taken one look at the Rosie he'd last seen as a child and lost his heart.

What would it be like to feel that herself? To be loved so ardently that even in public their emotions were barely containable?

Keeping her eyes on them, she said quietly, 'They fit, don't they.' It wasn't a question.

Alex's enigmatic glance, as polished as the steel-sheen on a sword blade, brought heat to her skin. What a foolish thing to say about a couple who'd just made their wedding vows!

Of course they fitted. For now, anyway, she thought cynically. Somewhere she'd read that the first flush of love and passion lasted two years, so Gerd and Rosie would enjoy perhaps another year of this incandescent delight in each other before it began to fade.

'Perceptive of you,' Alex commented in a level voice. 'Yes, they fit.'

The music swelled, accompanied by a whirl of colour and movement as everyone joined in the dance, swirling around the absorbed couple.

Serina braced herself. Nerves taut, she rested one hand on Alex's shoulder and felt his fingers close around the other as he swung her into the waltz. Anticipation sizzled through her—heady, compelling, so unnerving that after a few steps she stumbled.

Alex's arm clamped her against his lean, athletic body for breathless seconds before he drawled, 'Relax, Princess.'

His warm breath on her skin sent tiny, delicious shudders through her, a gentler counterpoint to the sultry heat that burgeoned deeply within her at the intimate flexing of his thigh muscles. Shocked by the immediacy of her response, Serina pulled herself a safe distance away and forced herself to ignore the sensual tug until her natural sense of rhythm settled her steps.

This acute physical response—jungle drums of sensation pounding through her—had sprung into action the first time she'd met Alex. Gritting her teeth, she resisted the tantalising thrill, sharp and adrenalin-charged as though she faced a sudden danger.

Did he feel the same?

She risked an upward glance, heart racing into overdrive when she met searing, disturbingly intent eyes. His grip didn't tighten, but she sensed a quickening in him that he couldn't control.

Yes, she thought triumphantly, before a flurry of panic squelched that intoxicating emotion.

Swallowing, she said in her most remote tone, 'Sorry. I wasn't concentrating.'

Then wondered uneasily if the admission had hinted at her body's wilful blooming.

Rapidly she added brightly, 'This has been one of the most charming weddings I've ever attended. Rosie is so happy, and it's lovely to see Gerd utterly smitten.'

'Yet you seem a little distracted. Is something worrying you?' Alex enquired smoothly.

Well, yes—several things, in fact, with one in particular nagging at her mind.

But Alex wasn't referring to her brother. He'd have noticed that plenty of eyes around the ballroom were fixed on her, some pitying, others malicious. Of the two she preferred the spite, although a hissed aside that had been pitched carefully to reach her ears still stung.

'It must be like eating bitter aloes for her,' a French duchess had said.

Her blonde companion had returned on a laugh, 'I'll bet the brother's furious—once she failed to land Prince Gerd they lost their best chance of clawing their way out of poverty. And losing out to a nobody must be bitter indeed.'

Not everyone was as catty, but she'd noticed enough abruptly terminated conversations and parried enough speculative glances to know what many of the guests were thinking.

Let them think what they liked! Pride stiffening her spine, she smiled up at Alex. Oh, not too widely, in case those watchers suspected her of acting—but with a slow, amused glimmer that should give some of the eager gossipers a few seconds of thought.

'I'm not distracted, and nothing's wrong,' she told him, her tone level and deliberate.

His black brows climbed for a second. 'As you've probably noticed, quite a few people here are wondering whether you're regretting a missed opportunity.'

At least he'd come out and said it. She tilted her head and met his calculating scrutiny with unwavering steadiness, praying he couldn't see how brittle she was beneath the surface self-possession.

'About as much as Gerd is,' she returned coolly, hoping she'd banished every trace of defiance from her voice.

Alex's mouth—unsoftened by its compelling hint of sensuality—relaxed into a smile that was more challenge than amusement. 'Indeed?'

'Indeed,' she returned, infusing the word with complete assurance.

'Good.'

She shot him a questioning glance, parrying a look that sent a quiver the full length of her spine. He let his gaze wander across her face, finally settling it on her lips. A voluptuous excitement smouldered through her.

Surely—yes, she thought with a triumph so complete she could feel it radiating through her—he was *flirting* with her. And she was going to respond.

But first she had to know something. That suspect recklessness gave her the courage to say, 'I'm surprised you're alone this week.'

His latest reputed lover was a gloriously beautiful Greek heiress, quite recently divorced. Rumour had it that Alex had been the reason for the marriage breakup but Serina found that difficult to believe. He was noted for an iron-bound sense of integrity, and it seemed unlikely he'd let a passing fancy for a beautiful woman compromise that.

However, she thought with another spurt of cynicism, what did she really know about him? Nothing, except that he'd used his formidable intelligence, ruthless drive and an uncompromising authority to build a worldwide business empire.

Besides, his fancy for his Greek lover might not be passing.

Alex's tone was matter-of-fact. 'Why? I have no partner or significant other.'

So that was that. *Neither have I* seemed far too much like a bald, much too obvious invitation.

Serina contented herself with a short nod, and kept

her eyes fixed on the throng whirling behind him. He was an excellent dancer, moving with the lithe, muscular grace of an athlete, and wearing his formal clothes with a kind of lethal elegance that proclaimed the powerful body beneath.

'So what's ahead for you?' Alex asked coolly. 'More of the same?'

'More weddings? No one else I know is getting married in the immediate future,' she returned, deflecting the query.

He met her glance with a glinting one of his own. 'You're happy just doing the social round?'

A little shortly, Serina replied, 'Actually, I'm planning to go back to school.'

Alex's gaze sharpened. 'You surprise me. I thought you'd settled into being Rassel's muse.'

'We decided he needed a new one,' she told him without rancour.

Her time with the up-and-coming Parisian fashion designer had been stimulating but, although losing the very generous salary was a blow, she'd been relieved when he'd decided he needed someone more edgy, more in tune with his new direction.

She had no illusions. Rassel had originally chosen her because she had the entrée to the circles he aspired to. The fact that she both photographed well and possessed the body to display his clothes superbly had helped him make the decision. It had always been a problematic relationship; although Rassel referred to her as his muse he'd expected her to behave like a model, and had only reluctantly accepted any input from her. Now that he'd made his reputation he didn't need her any more.

And she didn't miss his monstrous ego or his insecurity.

Alex asked, 'So what are you going to study? Horticulture?'

Did he know she wrote a column on gardens?

'Landscape architecture.'

She was so looking forward to it. She'd just come into a small inheritance from her grandfather, the last King of Montevel. Added to the money she earned for the column, the bequest would provide enough money for Doran to finish university as well as pay her tuition fees and living expenses.

It would mean an even more rigorous routine of scrimping, but she was accustomed to that.

'I suppose that figures. Will you continue writing your garden column for that celebrity magazine?' Alex's dismissive tone made it quite clear what he thought of the publication.

'Of course.' Loyalty to the editor made her enlarge on her first stiff response. 'They took a chance on me and I've always done my best to live up to their expectations.'

Why on earth was she justifying herself to this man? She tried to ignore a turbulent flutter beneath her ribs when she parried his enigmatic gaze.

'Why landscape architecture? It's a far cry from writing about pretty flowers and people who never get their hands dirty.'

Allowing a hint of frost to chill her words, she said, 'Apart from admiring the beauty of what they achieve, I respect the hopeless, impossible ambition of gardeners, their desire to create a perfect, idealised landscape—to return to Eden.' Crisply she finished, 'And I'll be good at it.'

'Your title and social cachet will see that you succeed.'

The comment, delivered in a negligent voice, hurt her. Especially since she knew there was an element of truth to it.

Serina hid her stormy gaze with long lashes. 'It will help. But to succeed I'll need more than that.'

'And you think you have whatever it takes?'

'I know I have,' she said calmly.

For answer he pulled her hand into a suitable position for inspection. 'Perfect skin,' he murmured on a sardonic note. 'Not a scratch or stain anywhere. Immaculately manicured nails. I'll bet you've never got your hands dirty.'

The corners of her mouth curved upwards and her eyes glittered. 'How much will you wager?'

Alex's laugh smashed through defences already weakened by the feel of his arms around her and the subtle connection with his body, the brush of his thighs against her, the barely discernible scent that seemed to be a mixture of soap and his own inherent male essence.

'Nothing,' he said promptly, returning her hand to its normal position. 'If you want to gamble you shouldn't show your hand so obviously. Did you have a flower garden as a child?'

'I did, and a very productive vegetable plot. My mother believed gardening was good for children.'

His expression gave nothing away. Hard-featured, magnetic, he was far too handsome—and Serina was far too aware of his dangerous charisma.

He said, 'Of course, I should have remembered that your parents' garden on the Riviera was famous for its beauty.'

'Yes.' Her mother had been the guiding light behind that. Working in her garden had helped soothe her heart whenever her husband's affairs figured in the gossip columns.

The property had been sold after her parents' deaths, gone like everything else to pay the debts they'd left behind.

The music drew to an end, and Alex loosened his strong arm about her, looking down with a smile that was pure male challenge. 'You should come to New Zealand. It has fascinating plants, superb scenery and some of the best gardens in the world.'

'So I believe. Perhaps one of these days I'll get there.'

'I'm going back tomorrow. Why not come with me?'

Startled, she flashed him a glance, wondering at his unexpectedly keen scrutiny. Why on earth had he suggested such a crazy thing? Yet she had to resist a fierce desire to take him up on his offer—and on whatever else he was offering.

Just pack a small bag and go...

But of course she couldn't. Reluctantly she said, 'Thank you very much but no, I can't just head off like that, however much I might want to.'

'Is there anything keeping you on this side of the world? An occasion you don't dare miss?' He paused before drawling, 'A lover?'

Colour flared briefly in her cheeks. A lover? No such thing in her life—ever.

'No,' she admitted reluctantly. 'But I can't just disappear.'

'Why not? Haruru—the place I own in Northland—is on the coast, and if you're interested in flora there's a lot of bush on it.' When she looked at him enquiringly he expanded, 'In New Zealand all forest is called bush. And in Northland, my home, botanists are still discovering new species of plants.'

He smiled down at her with such charm that for a charged moment she forgot everything but a highly suspicious desire to go with him.

It was high summer, and the small, cheap apartment in the back street of Nice was stuffy and hot, the streets crowded with tourists… Photographs she'd seen of New Zealand had shown a green country, lush and cool and mysterious.

But it was impossible. 'It sounds wonderful, but I don't do impulse,' she returned lightly.

'Then perhaps it's time you did. Bring your brother, if you want to.'

If only! Temptation wooed her, fogging her brain and reducing her willpower to a pale imitation of its normal robust self.

A trip to New Zealand might divert Doran from his increasingly worrying preoccupation with that wretched video game he and his friends were concocting. Prone to violent enthusiasms, he usually lost interest as quickly as he'd found it, but his fascination with this latest pursuit seemed to be coming worryingly close to an addiction. Serina had barely seen him during the past few months.

A holiday could wean him away from it.

It suggested a way for her to avoid the frustration of these past months, too. The sly innuendoes and unspoken sympathy, the rudeness of media people demanding to know how she felt now that her heart was supposedly shattered, the downright lies written about her in the tabloids—it had all been getting to her, she admitted bleakly.

If she went to New Zealand with Alex Matthews her world would assume they were lovers. How she'd enjoy hurling a supposed affair in every smug, avid face! A sharp, clamouring excitement almost persuaded her to agree.

For a moment she wavered, only to rally at the return of common sense. Just how would that prove she wasn't hiding a broken heart or shattered hopes?

It wouldn't. The gossips would accurately peg it as bravado, and therefore further confirmation of their suspicions.

'That's very kind of you,' she said carefully, 'and I'm sure Doran would love to visit New Zealand.'

'But?' Alex said ironically.

'We can't afford a holiday right now.'

Broad shoulders lifted in a slight shrug, but his gaze didn't waver. 'I share a jet with Kelt and Gerd, so transport won't be a problem. And I have an appointment in Madrid in a month's time, so I could drop you both off at Nice on the way there.' He looked down, eyes glinting, and challenged softly, 'Scared, Princess?'

'My name is Serina,' she stated, tipped off balance by the cynical note in his voice. 'What reason do I have to be afraid?'

Apprehensive, yes. Her stomach felt as though she were standing on the edge of a high cliff. Alex Matthews was way out of her league. Yet Doran…

She looked across the ballroom to her brother,

laughing with a group of young men, one of whom was his greatest friend, the son of an old associate of her father's, another exile from Montevel. It was young Janke who'd introduced Doran to the excitement of computer gaming. Together they'd come up with the idea of creating their own game and making a fortune by selling the rights.

It would be a huge success, Doran had told her enthusiastically, and sworn her to secrecy in case any other video game creator got wind of their idea and stole it.

At first she'd dismissed it as an amusing fantasy on their part—until the project had taken over Doran's life.

A month on the other side of the world might just break the spell.

Alex said bluntly, 'You have nothing to fear from me.'

Colour heated her skin. 'I know that,' she said on a note that probably sounded a bit equivocal.

As though she hadn't spoken, he went on, 'And accommodation won't be a problem—I live in a huge old Victorian house with enough bedrooms for a huge Victorian family. As well as being beautiful, Northland is interesting in itself—the first place where Maori and Europeans met and mingled and clashed.'

The hairs on the back of her neck lifted in a primitive reaction to…what?

Nothing, she told herself curtly. Although Alex's tone was pleasant, it was also impersonal, and his offer to host Doran as well meant he didn't expect her to fall into his bed.

Well, not right away…

Nerves zinging, she said, 'It's just not possible,' and dismissed the subversive thought that a month in New

Zealand would provide her with photographs and information for quite a few columns.

But Alex must have noticed that moment of weakness because he said, 'Why not?' And when she hesitated he went on, 'Why don't you ask your brother how he feels?'

He'd refuse, she was sure. 'OK, I'll do that.'

She sent another look across the room, intercepted by her brother, who strode across to them, lean and athletic-looking for someone who'd spent most of the past six months in front of a computer.

When Alex casually mentioned his suggestion Doran responded with his usual enthusiasm. 'Of course you must go, Serina!'

'The invitation is for you too,' Alex said pleasantly.

Excitement lit up Doran's mobile face, then faded. He glanced at Serina before saying, 'I wish I could, but...you know how it is.' He spread his hands and finished vaguely, 'Appointments, you see.'

Alex said, 'I believe you're interested in diving.'

'Well, yes.' Doran's eager response was a sharp contrast to his previous tone.

'New Zealand has some fantastic sites—in fact, there are two magnificent wrecks not far from Haruru, but friends of mine are going up to Vanuatu in the Pacific to dive the reefs. If you're interested I'm sure I could get you a berth.'

Doran's look of extreme longing increased almost comically when Alex added, 'They're talking about diving the Second World War wrecks there, as well.'

Serina said quickly, 'Wouldn't you have to be an experienced diver to deal with those?'

'Serina—'

Doran's protest was overridden by Alex's voice. 'So what are your qualifications, Doran, and where have you dived?'

Doran launched into his CV and, when he'd run down, Alex said, 'That sounds good enough.' He looked at Serina and added with a smile that held more than a tinge of irony, 'And, just to reassure your anxious sister, my friends are responsible and expert divers and I'm sure you're sensible.' He mentioned the name of a family famed for their exploration of the seas and the subsequent prize-winning television programmes.

'Wow! And I'm a very cautious diver!' Doran said, clearly forgetting that he'd refused the trip. He flashed an indignant glance at his sister. 'You know that, Serina.'

She blinked. She'd had to learn thrift since her parents' death, so that now the easy way the very rich moved around the world startled her, and the smoothly masterful way Alex had taken control of the situation made her feel the ground had been cut from under her feet.

'Of course you are,' she said, 'but you'd have to get to Vanuatu, and we can't possibly impose—'

Alex cut her short. 'Doran won't be imposing. My friends are taking up a yacht.' He glanced at the man beside him. 'You'll probably have to work your passage.'

Cheerfully, Doran said, 'That's no problem.'

Without looking at Serina, Alex said casually, 'I'll be leaving tomorrow morning. Let me know when you've made up your mind. And now, if you'll excuse me, I'd better go and see whether Gerd needs me for anything.'

CHAPTER TWO

BARELY waiting long enough for Alex to walk out of hearing, Doran said defiantly, 'Serina, don't be so damned *responsible*. I'm an adult, you know, legally and in every other way. The diving in Vanuatu is absolutely fantastic, and since you let Gerd slip through your fingers this will probably be the only chance I'm ever likely to get to see it.'

Serina returned acidly, 'I thought you were going to make your fortune with your wretched game!'

And could have kicked herself for letting his angry response get to her. Her brother loved her, but he needed a more mature figure in his life, someone he would respect and listen to.

Shamefaced, he admitted, 'OK, I was completely out of order and unfair. I'm sorry. But...' The words trailed away.

'Anyway, you told Alex you couldn't go,' she reminded him.

He sent her a look of mingled exasperation and embarrassment. 'It's too good a chance to miss. I can organise it.'

Relieved, she retorted, 'In that case, you'd be mad not to take Alex up on his offer.'

'So would you,' he said.

They measured glances. It looked as though he'd refuse if she did.

Surrendering, Serina shrugged and said lightly, 'Fair enough. I've always wanted to see New Zealand, and it would be a fantastic opportunity to find material for the column.'

'Oh, for heaven's sake, Serina, loosen up a bit! Forget the column and being a big sister—just have a proper holiday. Give Alex Matthews a chance to show you how much easier life can be when you're not trying so hard to be a role model.'

That hurt, but she smiled and said coolly, 'Perhaps I might.'

Watching him stride away, she asked herself why she wasn't exulting that—thanks to Alex's unexpected offer—things had fallen into place so easily.

Instead, she found Doran's final comment running around in her mind.

Fun? With Alex Matthews? She looked across to where he stood talking to the royal couple. Her gaze roved his face, unconsciously noting the strong framework, the lean body in superbly tailored evening clothes, the formidable, arrogantly effortless impact of his presence.

Tingles of sensation shortened her breath and hastened her pulse. He impressed her altogether too much, and that could be dangerous.

Of course, on closer acquaintance they might decide they didn't like each other...

Serina dragged in an unsteady breath, feeling as

though she'd been caught up in a storm, tossed and tumbled by strong winds until she didn't know where she was going. *Liking* had nothing to do with the stark fact that whenever she saw Alex Matthews—or even thought of him—something shifted in the pit of her stomach and she felt a strange mixture of wariness and elation as her hormones raged out of control.

If she went to New Zealand she suspected she'd be even more vulnerable. Could she subdue this elemental response, leash it so she'd return unscathed after a month of close contact?

Put like that, it sounded idiotically Victorian—just like the mansion Alex lived in.

She didn't have to go. Doran had clearly decided to take up his offer. She could turn his invitation down, retreat to normality…

And spend the rest of her life wondering if she'd been a complete coward.

Controlling an urge to gnaw her lip indecisively, she greeted an approaching couple with relief. But later in the evening she found herself face to face with someone she'd successfully avoided until then. Superbly dressed, the older woman was still beautiful enough to dazzle.

As she had dazzled Serina's father.

Her mother's anguish only too vividly remembered, Serina masked her dislike and contempt with a calm smile as the woman cooed, 'My dear girl, this must be *such* a difficult time for you.' Her words oozing an odious sympathy that clashed with her avid scrutiny, she went on, 'I do so admire your courage in coming here.'

Serina held onto her temper with a stoic determination she hoped didn't show in her face. 'You are too complimentary—I can assure you it took no courage.'

The older woman sighed. 'Such noble defiance,' she said patronisingly. 'So like your dear father—he clung to that magnificent aristocratic pride even when he'd lost everything. One could only admire his spirit in the face of such tragedy, and wish that he had been rewarded for it.'

Furious at the mention of her father, Serina couldn't trust herself to speak, so raised her brows instead.

The older woman went on, 'And for you, I hope that soon the pangs of being rejected will ease. A broken heart is—' She broke off abruptly, her gaze darting behind and above Serina.

The back of Serina's neck prickled and she had to stop herself from twisting around. She knew who'd come up behind her.

A warm smile pulled up the corners of the older woman's impossibly lush mouth. 'Mr Matthews,' she purred, 'how lovely to see you.' Her tone was deep, slightly husky, and somehow she imbued the meaningless words with an undercurrent of sexuality.

A sizzle of emotion tightened Serina's face, caused by something that came humiliatingly close to jealousy. She half-turned and met Alex's hard blue gaze. After a second he looked away and greeted the older woman with aloof courtesy.

Her father's mistress cooed, 'As I was about to tell the Princess, repining is such a waste of time, but I see I have no need to bore her with lessons learnt over a lifetime. Clearly she has already packed away the past and is looking to the future.'

Serina met her smug smile with a stiff movement of

her head. 'So kind of you to take an interest in my life,' she said, disgust and anger edging her words. How dared the woman insinuate that she was chasing Alex?

Smoothly, Alex said, 'I'm sure you'll excuse us, madam. The Grand Duke and Duchess wish to speak to the Princess before they leave.'

As they walked away Serina said stiffly, 'You didn't need to rescue me; I can cope.'

'I'm sure you can,' he said, a sardonic smile tilting his hard, beautiful mouth, 'but I dislike vultures on principle. They foul the atmosphere.'

Serina gave a shocked gasp, followed by a choke of laughter. 'She's a horrid woman, but that's really too harsh.'

'It's not. You are far too polite.'

A raw note in the words made her look up sharply. After the slightest of pauses he went on, 'I like that little gurgle of laughter. I don't think I've heard it before.'

'I don't do it to order,' she retorted, furious because she was flushing. What was it about this man that turned her into some witless idiot?

'Careful,' Alex warned, his voice amused. 'The mask is slipping.'

Serina faltered. The hand beneath her elbow gripped hard enough to keep her upright, and for a second she wondered if she'd have bruises there tomorrow.

'The mask?' she enquired stiffly.

'The one you wear all the time—the perfect-princess mask that hides the puppet behind,' he returned with cool insolence, relaxing his grip.

Was that how he saw her—a lifeless *thing* hiding behind a disguise?

Squelching a foolish stab of pain, she stated, 'I'm not really a princess—Montevel is now a republic so it's just another empty title. And surely you must know that nobody is perfect.'

'So what's behind that utterly poised, totally collected, exceedingly beautiful face?'

Her startled glance clashed with an assessing scrutiny that sent a shiver scudding down her spine. 'A very ordinary person,' she countered, hoping she sounded more composed than she felt.

A very ordinary person still fuming over the exchange with her father's mistress—and secretly thrilled by Alex's cool summary of her attributes.

Thankfully they'd reached the royal couple, and Alex drawled, 'Rosie, Gerd, tell Serina she'll love New Zealand. I don't think I've entirely convinced her that it's worth crossing half the world to see.'

The brand-new Grand Duchess smiled up at Serina, her vivid face alight. 'Of *course* you'll love it,' she said, her pride in her country obvious. 'It's the most beautiful country in the world—apart from Carathia. And as a Northlander born and bred, I'm convinced that Northland is the best part of it.'

'Everyone says it's glorious,' Serina said, very aware of Gerd's speculative glance.

Enthusiastically, Rosie continued, 'And Haruru is just—magical. Huge and green and with beaches that match anything the Mediterranean offers.' She and her new husband exchanged an intimate smile that indicated a shared experience.

Serina stifled another pang of envy.

Blandly, Alex said, 'Gerd, perhaps you can reassure

the Princess that she'll be perfectly safe staying with me.'

Embarrassed by his bluntness, Serina sent him a furious glance and blurted, 'I didn't think—' She caught herself and finished more sedately, 'Of course I know that!'

Gerd's brows lifted and the two men exchanged a look, a masculine thrust and parry that made Serina wonder. Although Alex and the Grand Duke didn't look alike, for a second the resemblance between them outweighed the differences.

Then Gerd said levelly, 'You can trust Alex.'

'I'll second that,' Rosie said with conviction, adding with a wry laugh, 'Even when he's being a pain in the neck—actually, *especially* when he's being a pain in the neck—he's utterly staunch.'

Grabbing at her composure, Serina said, 'I'm quite sure he is.' She took in a swift breath and managed to smile. 'I'm just not accustomed to making such quick decisions.'

They spoke for a few more minutes, then she wished them all happiness, and Alex escorted her back. Halfway across the expanse of floor, he said, 'So are you coming to New Zealand or not?'

'Yes,' she snapped, making up her mind with jarring suddenness.

Lapis lazuli eyes held hers for a tense moment before Alex nodded. 'You'll enjoy it—and think of the columns you'll be able to source. I'm leaving at ten tomorrow morning, so I'll see you get a wake-up call in time.'

Serina's fingers trembled as she fastened her seat belt. She'd used cosmetics to hide the toll a sleepless night had taken on her face, but nothing could smooth away the turmoil of thoughts and emotions knotting her stomach.

The previous night, raw from her encounter with her father's mistress and Doran's words, it had been easy to be defiant, but once the ball was over and Rosie and Gerd had been farewelled in showers of rose petals, she'd gone to her room wondering why on earth she'd let her dislike of the woman manoeuvre her into a decision she might come to regret.

And there had been a couple of shocks since then, the first when Alex had told her that Doran had left for Vanuatu halfway through the night.

'Why?' she demanded in the car that was taking her and Alex to the airport.

'When I contacted my friends last night they told me they were already there, and almost ready to leave for the diving sites, so I got Doran to organise his own journey. He managed to talk himself onto several flights that will get him there within their deadline.'

She gave him a look of astonishment mingled with indignation. Doran had always relied on her to organise any travel arrangements. And who was paying his fare? A sick apprehension clutched at her.

As though he could read her mind, Alex said blandly, 'Don't worry about finances. Doran and I worked it out between us.'

'How?' she demanded.

'He's going to spend his holidays for the next year working for me,' Alex told her calmly.

'Working for you?' This time she felt a mixture of bewilderment and relief. If Doran was working for Alex he wouldn't have time to sit in front of a computer dreaming up fairy-tale fantasies of derring-do that might—but probably wouldn't—earn him a fortune.

'There's always something to be done in an organisation like mine,' Alex told her.

She eyed him sharply. 'Why are you doing this for him?'

'He was desperate to get to Vanuatu, and this seemed the best way to achieve that.'

'It's very kind of you,' she said with reserve.

'I'm not particularly kind,' he corrected her, 'but I don't like to make an offer and then have to retract it. This way he'll get the holiday he wants, and he'll also see a bit of the world. As for working for me—I assume he's going to have to earn his living?'

'Of course.'

'Then the experience will give him an idea of how the corporate and business worlds are organised.'

Serina had barely digested this when she discovered that Gerd's brother Kelt and his family weren't travelling with them.

Surprised anew, she said, 'I thought—somehow I assumed they were going home with us—with you.'

He shook his head. 'They're flying to Moraze to spend some time with his in-laws.'

She'd watched Alex with his cousin's small children, surprised and rather touched by their patent pleasure in his company. And his obvious affection for them hinted at a softer side to the man.

She'd looked forward to seeing more of them. But she and Alex would be alone—or as alone as anyone could be on a plane that boasted more flight crew than passengers.

A rebellious excitement welled up, so keen she could feel it thrilling through every cell. She, Serina Montevel, who'd never done a reckless thing in her life, was heading for a holiday on the other side of the world with a man she found wildly attractive.

Although *attractive* was far too pallid and emotionless a word. A sensible woman would have refused his invitation—would have kept on saying no until Alex decided she was more bother than she was worth…

Serina realised she was exceedingly glad that she wasn't that sensible woman.

Alex broke into her scattered thoughts with a question. 'Are you a nervous flier?'

'No,' she told him decisively, adding, 'This is all new to me. I've never been in a private jet before.'

A black brow climbed. 'You surprise me.'

'Why?'

He leaned back and regarded her with enigmatic eyes. 'I had the impression you spent a lot of time jetting around the royal circuit.'

'Usually I drive,' she told him evenly. Sometimes she used trains. It irritated her—no, it *hurt*—that he should despise her without bothering to take the trouble of finding out anything about her.

She went on, 'And I've never crossed the world before. Is jet lag as bad as they say?'

'Some people find it very difficult to deal with. I don't.'

'Ah, an iron man,' she said sweetly.

His smile was swift and unexpected, sending a reckless shiver of pleasure through Serina.

'Did I sound smug?' he asked. 'I'm fortunate, but I do take precautions.'

'Such as?'

'I always change my watch to the time of my destination.' He extended an arm to show her.

Automatically, Serina noted the watch—a superb brand, classic and without ostentation. She dragged her gaze from that sinewy wrist, rejecting the memory of how strong it was. When she'd faltered he'd held her upright without any visible effort. And yes, he'd marked her. The bruises were faint and would soon fade, but she felt oddly as though she'd been branded.

'New Zealand is nine hours ahead of us, and from now on we'll be eating at that time,' Alex told her. 'If you can relax enough to sleep later, you'll have adjusted to the local time when we arrive in Auckland.'

Sleeping wouldn't be difficult. She'd spent a lot of last night staring into the darkness and wondering what on earth she'd agreed to.

Nothing, she told herself again. After all, Alex's attitude, as well as his remark to Gerd and Rosie the previous night, had made it obvious that he was fully in control of his physical urges. Which had to be a good thing...

It was a pity she couldn't quite feel any gratitude for his unspoken promise of restraint.

She bent her head and altered her watch to match his, saying, 'Rosie says she drinks gallons of water and tries to spend at least ten minutes every hour walking or doing exercises.'

She'd been grateful for that information; at least striding around the cabin would give her something to do, something to concentrate on.

Not that drinking a lake of water or walking the

whole way to New Zealand would slow the pace of her heart, or stop her from being so acutely, intensely aware of Alex she felt as though she was inhaling his essence with every breath she took.

'Keeping away from alcohol and caffeine seems to help too,' Alex told her laconically.

'That won't be a problem.'

However, when the engines changed note and they began to pick up speed down the runway, Serina decided she could use something strong and sustaining. Dry-mouthed, she peered out at the mountains of Carathia rapidly speeding past as the jet broke free of the earth and started to climb.

A weird, baseless panic clenched her stomach muscles. Deliberately, carefully, she relaxed them and kept her eyes fixed on the view outside.

Never in all her life had she behaved so impetuously. *Never.* Thinking back, she couldn't remember when she'd decided that the best way to meet life was with restraint and cool composure. Possibly she'd just been born sensible and prosaic.

Whatever the cause, having been her mother's confidante in the continuing saga of unfaithfulness and despair that had been her parents' marriage, she'd vowed that she wasn't going to endure pain like that. So far, no man had ever been able to test that decision.

Yet Alex's caustic comparison of her to a puppet had been the final impetus that stung her into jettisoning caution and common sense to take this wild step into the unknown.

Alex leaned back in his seat and smiled at her. Her heart jumped and she relished an intoxicating sense of freedom. Half scared, half excited, she admitted that Doran had been right.

Unless she wanted to wear the princess mask for the rest of her life, she needed to break out and find out who the real Serina was. Restraint and reserve could go hang. While she was in New Zealand she'd be the perfectly ordinary woman she'd told Alex she was.

A sudden lightness, almost a feeling of relief, sent her spirits soaring. All her life she'd been an appendage to something or someone else—the daughter of her parents, Doran's sister, the last Princess of Montevel, cousin to every royal family in Europe.

Even her career… Although she'd proved she was a good writer with a gift for painting the essence of a landscape in words, it had been her title—and the entrée it gave her—that got her the chance to write her first column.

Keeping her eyes fixed on the view through the window, she watched as, still climbing steeply, the plane wheeled and turned away from the Europe she knew so well, heading towards unknown, more primal shores on the other side of the world.

When the seat belt light flicked off Alex touched her arm—the lightest of touches, yet it ran like wildfire through her.

He said, 'I have work to do. If you need anything, ring for the steward.'

She nodded, watching him surreptitiously as he moved across to a desk that had clearly been set up for business. Tall and rangy, the chiselled planes and angles of his face strong and disturbingly sensual, he dwarfed the cabin, diminishing the luxurious interior into insignificance by the sheer force of his personality.

What would he be like as a lover? Tender and thoughtful, or wildly passionate, as masterful as he was sexually experienced?

Her breath came faster and, to her shock, a languorous heat flowed through her, melting her bones and setting her nerves dancing in forbidden anticipation.

What did she know about loving, about lovers? If Alex made a move she wouldn't know what to do.

He'd probably find that off-putting.

Or laughable.

Fortunately, the steward came silently through with a selection of magazines—including, she noticed, the one she wrote for.

Dragging her mind away, she checked her column, frowned at a sentence she could have framed better, then turned over a few more pages and tried to concentrate on the latest fashions.

Rassel had been right to sack her, she decided, frowning at one photograph. He was heading into punk, and she'd look ridiculous in his latest creations. She didn't suit an edgy, rebellious look—her face and persona were too conventional to cope with the wild side.

Her gaze drifted across the opulently furnished cabin to Alex, dark head bent slightly as he read his way through a mountain of papers. He must have taken a speed-reading course, she thought idly, then forced her eyes back to her magazine.

Feverishly, she pretended to examine a tall redheaded model clad in scraps of gold leather and tried to concentrate on the text beneath, but the words jerked meaninglessly in front of her eyes.

After several minutes she relaxed enough to be able

to breathe easily. Her lashes drooped. The hum of the engines and last night's sleepless hours were a strong sedative. She opened her eyes and stared out the window, only to feel her skin prickle.

Was Alex watching her?

No, of course not. Disciplining herself not to glance his way, she looked down at the page again. The print blurred in front of her.

'You're tired.'

Alex's voice made her jump and the magazine slid from her lap onto the floor. She scrabbled for it but the seat belt held her fast, and helplessly she watched his lean brown hand pick the magazine up and put it down on the seat beside her.

'You might as well use the bedroom over there.' His voice was level as he nodded towards a door off the cabin. 'You'll be more comfortable there.'

Because the thought of him watching her while she slept in the seat was unbearably intimate, she nodded and unclipped her belt, only to stagger slightly when she stood up and the plane tilted a little.

Alex's eyes narrowed and his hand shot out to grip her shoulder. 'It's all right—we're crossing the mountains, and this is minor turbulence. As soon as we hit cruising altitude things will settle down.'

Automatically, Serina straightened. 'I'm not afraid, but thank you,' she said. 'I just wasn't expecting it.'

Immediately his grip loosened. 'OK now?'

'Yes. Fine.'

She headed across to the bedroom, wanting nothing more than to put some distance—and a door—between them. His touch had scrambled her brain and alerted unknown hidden pleasure points in her body, sending secret pulses of sensation through every cell.

If this uncontrollable response was desire, she not only didn't know how to deal with it, she found it downright embarrassing.

Her breath eased out in a long jagged sigh once she'd shut the door behind her. The huge bed was opulent, the cabin decorated for sleep, relying on subtle colours and the cool play of linen against gleaming silk, the soft luxury of a caramel cashmere throw. Her gaze fixed onto the plump pillows that called to her with a siren's lure.

Yet more alluring, more compelling, was that unbidden hunger for something she'd never experienced, something she was afraid of—the reckless, dangerously fascinating clamour of her body for a fulfilment she didn't dare seek.

'So forget about it and start behaving like a sane person,' she commanded beneath her breath.

She sat down and eased off her shoes, then swung up her legs.

But as her eyes closed she found herself wondering how many women had shared this bed with Alex.

CHAPTER THREE

THAT unwelcome query translated into Serina's dreams, darkening them with images of pursuit. She was being chased by something darkly ominous, something that intended to kill her... Although she ran until her breath came in great sobbing gasps she couldn't outpace her pursuer. A thin cry forced itself past her lips.

And then she was shaken so vigorously her teeth chattered.

'Wake up, Serina,' a deep, hard voice commanded. 'Come on, Princess, you're having a nightmare. Wake up and it will be over.'

Still in thrall to the dream, she huddled away from the imperative hand on her shoulder and catapulted towards the other side of the bed, only to be imprisoned by long fingers fettering her wrist.

Her lashes flew up; she stared at Alex Matthews' grim face and, to her horror and shock, tears burned behind her eyelids.

'It must have been a stinker,' he said harshly, his arms tightening around her so that she was hauled up into the refuge of his powerful body, her cheek against the open neck of his shirt.

Warmth enveloped her, and his faint sexy fragrance. Gratefully, she curved into him, soaking up the bone-deep security of his vitality. She could hear his heart, fast and heavy, and anticipation burst into full flower inside her, so shameless and sudden she shuddered at the intensity of it.

Until she realised he was as aware of her as she was of him. Shocked, she jerked upwards, and this time Alex let her go.

'Oh, good lord,' she muttered, despising her lack of self-control. 'Sorry—I didn't mean to disturb you.'

And then her words registered. Heat washed her entire body in a flood of colour, and she had to stop her instinctive dive under the nearest pillow. Instead, she stared belligerently at him.

'It's all right,' he said shortly. He got to his feet and looked down at her. 'Do you have nightmares often?'

Serina managed to rally enough fragments of her usual composure to say in a voice that was almost level, 'Occasionally—but doesn't everyone?'

Not Alex Matthews, she'd be prepared to wager.

He said, 'Want to talk about it?'

'No,' she returned abruptly, then flushed. 'Sorry again; that was rude of me.'

'Sometimes talking about something will banish the fear.'

He sounded only mildly interested but after one rapid glance at him she looked away, her nerves stretched so taut she could feel them twanging.

However, he had comforted her so he deserved some sort of explanation. Reluctantly, she said, 'I think it's a standard nightmare—I was being chased, running like crazy but not being able to escape whoever or whatever was after me. I can never see what it is I'm afraid of, which is idiotic.'

If only she could see it she'd be able to face it and deal with it, but the terrifying menace had never revealed itself to her.

She should have outgrown it years ago. Her mother had told her it was a growing-up dream, a fear of leaving childhood behind and becoming an adult, but Serina no longer believed that. She'd had to grow up the year she'd turned eighteen, the year her parents had died.

'Expecting dreams to follow any sort of logic sounds like a recipe for futility,' Alex said casually.

She tried a pale smile. 'Oh, well, it's over. Thank you very much for rescuing me.'

There was no immediate answer, and she looked up again to catch a frown before he asked in the same impersonal tone, 'Can you think of any reason for having it now?'

With an attempt at her usual crispness she said, 'No. But then, as you've just pointed out, dreams don't necessarily have a reason.'

His brows smoothed out, leaving his bold face unreadable. 'A meal will be ready soon. If you'd like a shower, feel free to use the bathroom.'

'I'd like that very much.' As he turned to go, she added, 'Thank you. You've been very kind.'

'No problem,' he said over his shoulder as he left.

For a few seconds Serina sat very still, deliberately allowing her shoulders to sag while she breathed slowly and steadily in an attempt to relax.

What a fool she'd been! Dear heaven, the moment

Alex lifted her she should have pulled away and found the self-control to reject his well-meant comfort politely but definitely.

Instead, she'd snuggled—yes, *snuggled*—into him as though he were her last refuge in a dangerous world.

And it had been wonderful—strong arms around her, that faint disturbing scent that was his alone, his body quickening into life against hers…

Until she'd realised what she was doing—what she'd been begging for.

Humiliation roiled through her in a sick flood. Biting her lip, she opened the door into the small, luxurious bathroom and turned the shower onto cold.

Alex looked up when she emerged, every hair in place, cosmetics subtly renewed. The mask was back, he thought sardonically, and this time set in concrete. A piercing twist of hunger took him by surprise. Irritated, he tried to banish it.

Why did she exasperate him so much? Because she'd turned a defunct royal connection into a lifestyle? A clearly profitable lifestyle, if her wardrobe was anything to go by.

No, that was unfair; her clothes were almost certainly advertisements for the designer she'd been a muse for.

What the hell did a muse do? Nothing, he suspected, beyond attracting attention and showing off the couture clothes made for her. If so, the designer had chosen well; Serina of Montevel had connections to royalty all over Europe, and she looked superb in the subtly sensuous clothes that draped her elegant body.

Which didn't alter the fact that Alex despised people who played on their heritage, their title or their position.

Yet he didn't seem to be able to despise Serina—

Princess Serina, he reminded himself. He'd not only invited her to stay with him, he'd organised a holiday for her brother to keep him out of mischief, and promised him holiday work for a year.

So why was he pushing his way into her life? Because she was a challenge?

He dismissed that thought; he'd never regarded women as trophies, the harder to win the more prestigious. As for her kid brother—well, he quite liked the boy, and keeping him away from the pack of wolves he'd inadvertently fallen in with would be to Gerd and Rosie's advantage because Montevel and Carathia shared a border.

And the Princess? She intrigued him.

Reduced to the most basic level, he wanted her. And it cut both ways—he was too experienced to misread the quick fluctuations of colour in her exquisite skin, the subtle alterations in her breathing, the tiny physical signals she couldn't control.

Fight it with everything she had—and she was certainly doing that—the elegant Princess Serina couldn't hide her response to him. Yet she'd made it plain she resented the mindless tug of desire and had no intention of acting on it. Which probably meant that just as the attraction was mutual, so was the exasperation.

It seemed a waste, but it was her decision to make.

He glanced at her serene face as she lowered herself gracefully into the chair and picked up a magazine.

Last night the woman who'd finally wrecked her parents' marriage and possibly caused their deaths had insinuated that Serina was on the lookout for a rich husband. He despised the woman—and himself for not being able to banish her words from his mind.

Perhaps Serina was saving herself for marriage, although he'd heard rumours of a couple of serious relationships. Since when had he allowed himself to worry about rumours? The elegant, intelligent, exquisitely mannered Princess with social kudos to spare would be the perfect wife for any man who could afford her.

With Gerd's marriage a sure thing, had Serina seen Rosie's half-brother—certainly not royal, but rich and well-connected—as a possible second-best?

And if Serina knew more about her brother's conspiracy than Gerd's security men had been able to uncover, then a wealthy, besotted husband would be a definite asset in their plans.

Mentally he shrugged. It wouldn't be the first time a woman had pursued him for reasons of her own, and he doubted if it would be the last. And if Princess Serina thought she could manipulate him into anything with coyness she was hugely mistaken.

He might find her very attractive, but he was fully in control of his sexual urges.

If she *had* wondered whether he was good husband material, she was clearly now having second thoughts. On that bed she'd catapulted out of his arms as though he'd been the unknown, terrifying pursuer of her dream.

Or perhaps, he thought cynically, she'd decided that giving in too soon would lower her value in his eyes…

He was surprised at his relief when the arrival of the steward offering drinks before the meal interrupted his thoughts.

After she'd eaten Serina opened her elderly laptop to map out several future columns. The previous night she'd spent some of her sleepless hours on the Internet researching New Zealand and its plant life.

'Anything I can help you with?' Alex asked casually.

'I don't know.' But he seemed interested, so she went on, 'I emailed my editor, and she's quite excited about my visit to New Zealand. Europeans know all about formal and English country gardens, but she and I are sure the readers will enjoy something different and new.'

Alex said, 'Most of the gardens will be very *in*formal, and you won't be able to give your readers a titillating glimpse into the private lives of the aristocracy. We don't have one.'

'Really?' Serina didn't try to repress her sarcasm. Was he being deliberately insulting? OK, so he had a point; on occasion she'd inserted innocuous information about the owners in her column, but she hoped that wasn't the main reason for her readers' loyalty.

'Actually,' she purred sweetly, 'if you'd ever read my column you'd know that the gardens are the stars, not the people who own them. And to make sure I haven't inadvertently invaded the owners' privacy I show them the copy before it goes to the editor.'

'So it's a collaborative enterprise?'

Repressing an unusual impulse to snap back, she returned, 'Besides, if I relied on gossip to sell my work I'd soon find my choice of gardens drying up. I've done some research, and it seems that in Northland alone there are several magnificent places that I'm sure would interest my readers.' Her smile didn't reach her eyes. 'How about yours?'

'I like it,' he said neutrally, his eyes hardening. 'But I won't allow anyone to write about it.'

'Fine,' she said, showing her teeth as she bit out the word.

Arrogant man! She hoped very much he wasn't going to be like this the whole time she was in New Zealand.

However, for the rest of the trip he was thoughtful and pleasant—and extremely stimulating, she thought gloomily as she gazed through a window at the city of Auckland sprawled out across a narrow isthmus.

She'd read, written, taken frequent walks around the cabin that eased the stiffness of the long journey, but refused to nap again in the luxurious sleeping cabin. Awash with industrial quantities of water, she was looking forward to fresh air, and a night in a bed that was firmly anchored to the ground.

She risked a glance at Alex beside her. That now familiar slow burn of sensation in the pit of her stomach made her hesitate a half-second before she said, 'It's beautiful—a splendid setting. I hadn't realised the city was so big.'

He shrugged. 'New Zealanders like living on their own land. And while we might have only four million inhabitants, a million of them live in Auckland. In area the country's almost as big as Italy.'

'How far away is Haruru?' She pronounced the word carefully.

'Well done,' he said, his smile quickening her pulse. 'It's half an hour's flight north. I'm afraid I have a function to attend in Auckland tonight, so we'll spend the night at my apartment here, then head home tomorrow morning.'

Serina thought she'd hidden her surprise, but a black brow lifted and he said dryly, 'Perhaps I should have mentioned that before.'

Chagrined, she shook her head and made a mental memo to watch her expression more closely. 'Of course not,' she said in her most practical tone.

'I'm sorry to have to leave you alone for your first night in New Zealand.'

She laughed. 'Nonsense. The last thing I want to do is go out for the evening.'

For most of the journey he'd worked solidly, except when he joined her for meals. She'd insisted he take the bed when he decided to sleep, pointing out that as she was shorter she'd be more comfortable in the reclining chair. He'd politely accepted.

If he'd been trying to convey his total lack of interest in her, he'd succeeded.

Serina despised the pang that thought produced.

She was far too conscious of Alex to be comfortable in his presence. He made the world seem a larger, more intriguing place, stirring her senses into hyperdrive and awakening reactions—both physical and mental—that were not only inconvenient but scary.

She must have been mad to agree to come, but four weeks wasn't too long. She'd cope.

She hoped...

The plane eased down to a smooth landing at an airport near one of the city's two harbours. Customs and immigration formalities quickly over, she walked beside Alex to a waiting car.

The driver, a tall, solidly built man, olive-skinned and with finely chiselled features, greeted Alex with a smile. 'Good trip?' he asked.

Alex's return smile made him younger and more approachable than Serina had ever seen him.

'Excellent, thanks, Craig. How's the family?'

Craig beamed. 'Brilliant.' He took Serina's bag and manoeuvred it into the boot before announcing, 'The boy's walking.'

Alex laughed. 'So you don't know what's hit you?'

'He's a hell-child—into everything. It's total mayhem,' Craig told him, his proud smile contradicting his words.

Alex introduced Craig Morehu to her. They shook hands and Serina asked, 'How old is your son?'

'Ten months,' Craig said with even more pride, and grinned at her surprise. 'Yes, apparently he's advanced for his age.'

Alex said, 'Serina, if you don't mind, Craig and I need to talk business so I'll sit in the front seat with him.'

'Of course I don't mind,' she said politely, and during the journey kept her gaze to either side of the car, ignoring the width of Alex's shoulders and the incisive tone of his voice as he and the driver spoke together.

Auckland was leafy and green and busy, the motorway bordered by shrubs and trees, many of which she didn't recognise. Small volcanic cones, most covered in brilliantly green grass, seemed to pop into view wherever she looked, and the twin harbours wove in and out of the land so that each change of direction revealed a new vista.

Alex's apartment was richly welcoming, a big penthouse in a solid nineteenth-century building that had been turned into a hotel. Furnished in traditional style with huge timber-framed windows that took in magnificent views of the harbour and cityscape, the rooms were warmed by flowers.

Serina didn't know what she'd expected—something uncompromisingly minimalist to go with what she knew of Alex's character?

But the decor had probably been produced by a decorator. All Alex would have had to do was throw money at it.

Then she saw the telescope aimed at the harbour. Her father had had one just like it; it still stood in the tiny back street apartment in Nice she shared with Doran when he was home.

She repressed a swift pang of homesickness as Alex showed her into a large bedroom with its own bathroom. This was more feminine, the comfort factor still very evident.

Alex said, 'If you need anything let me know, or ring the bell. I'll be with Craig for another half an hour, and after that we could fill in time by either swimming or playing tennis on the residents' court. Which would you prefer?'

'Tennis,' she said instantly, repressing a forbidden image of him stripped down and glistening...

She suspected he was surprised, but could read nothing in his angular face as he said, 'Then tennis it will be.'

After she'd unpacked she set up her laptop and sent an email to Doran to tell him she'd arrived; he'd already sent one to her, brief but enthusiastic. Clearly, he was enjoying himself.

Spirits rising, she spent a long time in the shower, her dry skin luxuriating in the cool water. The shorts and T-shirt she changed into were neat and practical, although when Alex saw her she was suddenly—foolishly—too aware of her bare legs and arms.

He was wearing shorts and a shirt too, and something very odd happened in the pit of Serina's stomach. Lean and tanned, the lithe power of his body revealed without the sophisticated covering of his more formal clothes, Alex was—overwhelming.

Serina swallowed, heartily glad she'd chosen tennis. If he had this impact on her fully clothed, she'd probably have fainted at the sight of him in swimming trunks, she thought disparagingly.

'What standard do you play?' he asked as they went down to the court.

'Average. You?'

He shrugged. 'Lousy, I imagine—I haven't played for years.'

Possibly not, but the powerful coil and flow of muscle beneath his shirt told her he exercised in some way. And she soon discovered he played a fierce game, revealing a natural athleticism that forced Serina onto the defensive. Fully extended, she set her lips firmly and fought back, determined not to let him win easily.

As they walked back to the penthouse after her honourable defeat, he commented, 'You're a fighter.'

Was that a note of surprise in his voice? *Good*, she thought.

'I try very hard not to lose,' she told him, conscious of her T-shirt clinging to her damp skin and knowing she badly needed another shower.

But she'd enjoyed the hard physical tussle, and the fact that she'd made Alex work for his victory. One of her mother's favourite sayings had been that a man needed to know he was stronger than the woman in his life. Her mother had been wrong. It might apply to men who were fundamentally weak, but Serina didn't believe Alex would have been shattered if he'd been beaten. His innate self-confidence came from something much more firmly based than a constant need to prove himself a winner.

'I don't know of anyone who likes losing,' he said thoughtfully. 'I certainly don't.'

It could have been a warning, but she was oddly warmed by his considered response. It seemed to indicate a relaxation of the formidable authority she found so intimidating.

She said, 'It must be a characteristic of the men in your family. Kelt and Gerd are both win-at-all-costs men.'

'Do you think so?' He frowned. 'We like to win— we work hard at doing just that—but I wouldn't have said that any of us see victory as a goal worth achieving no matter what the cost.'

For once she'd let her tongue run away with her. 'I overstated the case,' she agreed. 'Winning is important to them, though.'

'And to the men in your family too, I understand. So do you think your brother has any chance of getting back the Montevel throne?' he asked, his tone unchanged.

Stunned, Serina stared at him. He was watching her closely, and something about his total lack of expression chilled her. She asked incredulously, 'What on earth are you talking about?'

'Come on, Princess, surely you knew your brother and a bunch of other exiled Montevellans are plotting to regain the throne?'

They had stopped at the elevator that led to the penthouse. As she stepped inside, Serina's brain came up with the answer and she started to laugh.

'You're talking about their computer game, aren't you?'

'Is that what it is?' His tone was neutral, at variance with his probing gaze, hard as quartz.

He pressed the button and the elevator whooshed upwards, leaving her stomach behind. 'How did you hear about it?' she asked.

'News gets around.'

She frowned. 'They'll be worried about that. Doran said the gaming world is really cut-throat, and they don't want anyone to know what they're working on until it's ready for production.' She looked up at Alex. 'Do you have any interests in that area?'

'No,' he said bluntly. 'And I think you've just insulted me. Even if I did have a financial interest in the creation of video games, I wouldn't steal other people's ideas.'

Serina flushed. This man had a seriously weakening effect on her normal good manners, and his reputation for integrity gave Serina no reason to disbelieve him.

Nevertheless, she asked, 'How did you get to hear about it? Doran only told *me* about it because I was angry at the amount of time he was spending on the computer, and even then he swore me to secrecy. He said they were all being really close-mouthed about it.'

'Tell me about this game,' Alex said dryly.

When she hesitated he continued with a flick of hauteur, 'Of course, if you think I can't be trusted—'

'I'm sure you can be,' Serina said, making up her mind, and rather glad to confide in someone. 'It started just before the end of last year. One of Doran's friends is an ardent game player, and apparently when they were talking about Montevel one night he thought of using Montevel itself, and the idea of restoring the monarchy, as the basis for a world-building game. They've all become fascinated by it.' Her smile was a little lopsided. 'Partly because they hope that if it takes off they'll become instant millionaires. Doran's had a lot of fun working out what he'll do with his share.'

Alex lifted an eyebrow. 'And that is?'

'Sail around the world in a super yacht to all the really good diving spots,' she told him wryly.

'So what's your part in it?'

The elevator stopped and the doors slid open. She said, 'None—unless you count nagging Doran about staying up all night when he's working out more tricks and turns to the game. His latest idea is the introduction of a nest of vampires in the mountains on the border of Carathia and Montevel.'

Alex unlocked the door to the penthouse. Should she tell him she was starting to get seriously concerned about Doran's obsession with the game?

No. Loyalty to her brother and a lifetime of keeping her own counsel warned her to stay silent.

Alex stood back to let her into the apartment. She walked through into the living room and stopped by the window, looking out at the view.

The sounds of the city were muted by the glass and the wide terrace outside and, although she couldn't see Alex, she could feel his presence behind her.

It was thanks to Alex that her brother was in Vanuatu—and she hoped he was enjoying himself so much that when he came back the game would no longer have such a grip on him.

Alex said evenly, 'So it's just a fantasy war game

concocted by a group of kids brought up on stories of
the good old days in Montevel?'

Serina turned. Her heart missed a beat. He was
watching her mouth and a glint in the dark, unreadable
blue of his eyes set her pulse skyrocketing.

'What else could it be?' Her voice shook a little, and
her hands were too tightly folded—almost clenched at
her sides. Deliberately, she relaxed them, producing a
coolly amused smile. 'Has someone been feeding you
stories of a bunch of battle-hardened revolutionaries?'

Something about Alex's answering smile—a hint of
ruthlessness—sent tiny cold shivers down her spine.

But his voice was calm and reasonable. 'One of my
security men heard something about their activities—
but didn't realise it was a video game. Because Montevel
is on Gerd's borders, he knew I'd be interested.'

'Ah, I see.' So had he offered the trip to Vanuatu—
and this holiday to her—so he could find out what he
wanted to know?

The suggestion had no right to hurt, but it did. She said
crisply, 'Then you'll be able to reassure him—and Gerd,
because I'm sure you've told him about it—that it's just
a group of romantic kids play-acting rather obsessively.'

He said, 'But you're worried about it.'

Infusing her tone with a false lightness, Serina
evaded, 'Irritated, actually. Doran's spending far too
much time working at it—time he should be studying.
I'm hoping this diving trip will give him something else
to think about.'

'From the tone of your voice, I'd say you've quar-
relled about it.'

He saw too much. 'I have to admit I was glad when

you suggested the trip to Doran. The time he's spending on the game is showing in his college results.' She hesitated before adding, 'I've read about young people who become addicted to video gaming…'

'*Playing* the games, not creating them,' Alex said levelly.

'That's true,' she conceded, feeling a little foolish and over-protective, 'and Doran is inclined to be very one-tracked with every new interest. It's just that this one has lasted a lot longer than any other.'

She smiled up at him. 'But, as for him and his friends being any sort of threat to Carathia or Montevel—no, they're not that far removed from reality, even if they have made grandiose plans for spending the money when they all become instant millionaires! They're all bright young men—'

'Bright young men of Montevellan descent who've been brought up with a somewhat skewed view of the country as it used to be for the upper classes before they were thrown out.'

She folded her arms. 'Did you invite Doran and me out here so you could find out more? If so, I'm afraid it's been a waste of money and time. I've no doubt that if you'd approached him while we were in Carathia for the wedding, he'd have told you all about the game.'

Alex said softly, 'Ah, but then I'd have missed the pleasure of your company.'

His words fell into a deepening pool of silence. The sounds of the city faded so that all Serina could hear was the beating of her heart.

Hurrying into speech, she said briskly, 'And no doubt that would have been a tragedy.'

'Fishing, Princess?'

Before she could answer she felt the lightest touch of his hand on her shoulder. Obeying it, she turned and looked up into a face set hard, narrowed eyes intent and crystalline.

Excitement bumped her already heavily beating heart into overdrive. Suddenly dry-mouthed, she swallowed, but words still wouldn't come. Her dilated gaze fixed on a pulse beating in his jaw, and she clenched her fist to stop herself from reaching up and touching it with a fingertip.

'Alex?' she said uncertainly.

CHAPTER FOUR

ALEX'S lips barely moved when he said, 'Serina,' and traced the outline of her mouth with a lean, gentle forefinger.

Colour burned up through her skin and her heartbeats drummed in her ears, awareness tingling through every cell and filling her with longing. Incredulously, she realised she was holding her breath, unable to summon her wits to move. Drowned in the burnished blue of his eyes, she clung single-mindedly to the simple concept of staying upright.

Then he said, 'You must know already that I'm glad you came.' And stepped away.

Serina fought to hide a fierce disappointment, keen as a knife blade. What had gone wrong? Why had he decided against...?

Against *what*, exactly?

Against kissing her.

Humiliation drove a desperate desire to gloss over the violence of her response. She said on a breath jagged enough to be painful, 'I wasn't fishing for any compliment. I was actually being slightly sarcastic.'

He hadn't answered her question so she still didn't

know whether he'd invited her to New Zealand to find out what Doran and his friends were doing. Had he deliberately engineered that touch, that convincingly intense gaze, to fog her brain with sensual expectation so she wouldn't push for an answer?

If so, he knew now she wanted him more than he did her. Her response gave him power; he'd been able to pull away while she'd been frozen.

Pride came to her rescue. Stiffening her shoulders, she lifted her chin and kept her gaze level and slightly ironic. After all, it wasn't as though she'd never been kissed.

However, past kisses had been pleasant, only mildly stimulating, about as far removed as anything could be from the jolting, heady anticipation she'd experienced when Alex touched her.

What was the difference?

No other man had stirred her as Alex did, arousing a need she'd never felt before, as potent and clamorous as hunger. He was the only man able to set her hormones surging in that delicious, terrifying flood of anticipation…

Cool it, she warned her body staunchly, but she had to wait a few seconds before her voice was steady enough for her to observe in a casual tone, 'I hope you manage to convince Gerd that his concern about trouble on his borders is baseless.'

Alex's expression gave nothing away, but her skin tightened when her eyes met his, unyielding and austere.

'I'll tell him you said so,' he said, then glanced at his watch. 'I've rung the organiser of the fund-raising dinner I promised to attend tonight, and she's quite sure that if you want to come she can arrange that.'

'No, no,' she broke in. The surge of response ebbed

rapidly, leaving her lax and enervated. 'I think jet lag must have struck—I wouldn't be entertaining company tonight.'

Black brows drawn together, he scrutinised her face. 'I should have realised you'd feel the effects—I'm sorry for wearing you out at tennis.'

'You didn't,' she said promptly. 'All I need is a good night's sleep and I'll be fine.'

He nodded. 'I'll be back well before midnight. When you want to eat, use the telephone to call the restaurant and order a meal.'

Serina was relieved when he left, although the big penthouse seemed to echo emptily without his vibrant presence. After she'd eaten an excellent meal, she explored the bookshelves in a room that combined the functions of a library and media area, strangely delighted to find several well-read books she'd enjoyed too. But she couldn't settle and although she was tired enough to feel drowsy it took her a long time to get to sleep.

In fact, she didn't manage it until she heard sounds that indicated Alex had returned.

When she woke, a glance at her watch revealed she'd slept only four hours. City noises floated up to the penthouse—traffic, the distant clamour of a siren, a squeal of brakes from the street below…

Just like all other cities, she thought wearily. And, to take her mind off wondering whether Alex had really intended to kiss her, she tried to imagine what she'd hear in the countryside where he lived.

It was a lost cause. Her wilful memory kept returning to those electrifying moments when he'd touched her mouth. Dreamily, she recalled the look on his face, the charged intensity about him that had awakened her equal untrammelled response.

He *had* wanted to kiss her.

So why had he pulled back? He was experienced; she knew of at least two long-term affairs he'd had. Surely he'd read the signals clearly enough to know she wouldn't slap his face and storm out of the room?

Perhaps he'd decided it was too soon. Which was amazingly considerate of him…

And quite correct. However, there were four weeks ahead for them both to find out more about each other.

Smiling languorously, she turned over, closed her eyes and slid into sleep, waking to a morning as crisp and welcoming as a summer's day. After showering and pulling on a pair of well-cut trousers and a paler blue silk shirt that intensified the colour of her eyes, she opened the curtains and gazed out at a radiant sky beaming over the city, the harbour glinting in the sunlight and dotted with islands that danced clear and bright in the vivid sea.

On the terrace outside her bedroom window flowers bloomed in a small garden; Serina opened the door that led out onto it and on a little exclamation of surprise and pleasure bent to smell one particular potted rose, sinfully crimson with a heart as darkly potent as forbidden love.

'A rose for a rose.'

Alex's voice brought her upright so suddenly her head swam.

'Are you all right?' A second later, his hands clamped around her upper arms, 'Is there something I should know about? This must be the second or third time you've stumbled.'

Shamefully, Serina would have liked nothing more than to rest her head on that broad chest and stay there, but an instinctive self-protection made her stiffen. 'I didn't stumble—I just missed a step each time. And I'm fine, thank you. I just straightened up too quickly.'

Alex looked down at her, a faint smile curving his mouth. For a moment Serina thought her heart stood still.

Hastily, so conscious of his hands on her skin that her thoughts dissolved under a heady burst of sensation, she finished, 'And probably a bit drunk on that gorgeous perfume. Do you know what the rose is called?'

'No, but I can find out.' He sounded abstracted, but he stepped back and when she risked an upwards glance she saw his eyes narrow, become intent and smoky. 'Did you sleep well?'

'Yes, thank you. How…how did the charity function go?'

'Very well.'

Meaningless stuff, she thought, caught in a bubble of stillness. She was babbling, and he—he wasn't concentrating on her words…

A chasm opened up in front of her. If she jumped, it would be into the unknown. She might crash—or she might find some unexplored place ablaze with possibility. Whatever, she'd never be the same again.

Much safer to stay where she was, step back, smile at him, go on talking meaningless platitudes—and leave New Zealand after four weeks, the same person she'd always been.

A coward.

Her heart began to race. Banishing fear, she lifted a hand to touch his cheek.

His smile became set, his gaze piercing. 'Sure, Princess?'

'My name is Serina,' she said, holding his eyes.

She wanted him to kiss the woman she was, not the public persona—serene princess, daughter of a long line of monarchs, scion of a defunct throne.

Serina read comprehension in his eyes, and knew that for some reason he didn't want to make the small surrender. She didn't even know why it was so important to her.

Tension sparked the silence between them, turning it heavy with desire.

'Do you know what you're asking for?' he said, a raw note altering the timbre of his voice and sending little shudders down her spine.

'Yes,' she said. 'Yes, I know. But what do *you* want?'

Something flickered in the burnished blue of his eyes and brought a half-mocking smile to that wicked mouth, with its narrow top lip buttressed by a sensuous lower one. 'A kiss,' he said. 'And I'm not asking, Serina—I'm taking what you've been silently promising me since we danced together at the wedding.'

He drew her towards him. She put a hand on his chest, looking up into an intense chiselled face. On a thrill that was half fear, half voluptuous anticipation, she thought he looked like a hunter.

Buoyed by a sudden, rather shameless relief, she nodded. Yet when he made no move she was assailed by shyness. Hot and embarrassing, colour stole along her cheekbones, but she met his eyes without wavering.

Although his eyes were still fiercely predatory, his voice became gentler. 'All right?'

'Yes.'

And when he bent his head and claimed her mouth with his own she yielded, leaning into him as he gathered her against him. White-hot sensations swamped her in a rush of adrenalin—his hard male contours, the taste of him, the faint barely-there fragrance that was his alone.

Her knees buckled and he tightened his grip, bringing her even closer to his powerful, fully aroused body.

Alex lifted his head and looked down into eyes that were slumbrous, almost dazed with passion, their violet-blue depths mysteriously dark. Gritting his teeth against a hungry surge of triumph, he fought back the primitive impulse to carry her across to the lounger a few metres away and take her then and there.

It was too soon, too public, and she deserved better than a hasty, violent consummation.

But he couldn't resist the enticement of her soft lips. When he lowered his head and claimed them again, she melted into him without resistance, her open, sensual surrender setting off a torrid chain effect that affected his every clamorous cell.

He managed to call a halt, to look into her huge eyes and say in a voice that probably sounded as taut and explosive as he felt, 'Serina—we have to stop this right now or it will be too late.'

Her lashes fell slowly, trembled against skin as translucent as the finest silk, but when she lifted them again she was once more in command of herself.

'So we stop,' she said, a husky note in her voice giving her away.

Alex found himself wishing he'd taken the chance.

For the first time ever he'd lost control, been tempted to follow his desires and damn the consequences.

Mastering his hunger, he released her and tried to summon his usual detached attitude. The aftermath of a carnal storm unlike anything he'd ever experienced made it near impossible.

Who'd have thought the gracious, reserved Princess would show all the instincts of a courtesan?

No, most courtesans had their eyes firmly on their bank balances, bargaining sex for security. Serina had offered herself ardently and without reserve.

And then he wondered whether she'd have been so passionately willing if they hadn't spoken about her brother.

Even as the thought formulated, he knew it wasn't likely. She seemed convinced that Doran and his friends were designing a video game, so why would she be concerned? She also guessed he'd warned Gerd about the possibility of trouble on his borders.

However, he had to assume that she might have been lying. An inner revulsion at the thought forced him to realise how much he wanted to trust her. The computer game story was a brilliant subterfuge, entirely believable. Pity it wasn't true. Young Doran and his band of romantic, eager conspirators had no idea what they'd got into.

He looked down into her face and saw with savage satisfaction that she too was struggling for control. The ache in his groin intensified into a plea, a demand— almost a command. He fought it back because he didn't dare give his innermost instinct free rein.

He'd be betraying Gerd and Rosie if he didn't make every effort to find out whether Serina knew anything— any small scrap of information that could lead them to the people who were backing her brother and his friends. In spite of their efforts, he and Gerd still weren't sure who was pulling the strings, or why, although they had their suspicions. If the Princess had any inkling, he was honour bound to find out.

And if that meant seducing her into pillow talk, then it would have to be done. It was, quite literally, a matter of life and death, not only for her brother and his friends, but for many other people.

Serina looked up, catching a glimpse of something harsh and grim in his eyes. Chilled, she masked a shiver by turning away so she could pretend to examine the rose again.

'I'm sorry,' he said evenly.

'Why?' She even managed a smile. 'I know the tabloids call me the ice princess, but surely you don't believe them? I have been kissed before.'

His brows rose and he surprised her by stooping to snap off the bloom and hold it out to her. In a wry voice he told her, 'I'm sorry because I stupidly made the arrangement for our flights without thinking that we might want to prolong our stay here.'

Colour heated her skin. Now—or *never,* she thought, wondering if he could hear her heart thudding so heavily in her chest.

Now. Because she wanted to know what making love to Alex was like infinitely more than she wanted to obey the strictures drummed into her by her mother and her governess. For the first time in her life she realised how potent desire could be...

'I—thank you,' she said, and answered his unspoken proposition by lifting the flower to her lips, still tender from his kisses. The petals were warm and smooth and she inhaled their sweetly provocative perfume.

Hastily, she said, 'I don't think I've ever seen a rose exactly this shade of red before. And, as it seems perfectly happy growing in a pot, I'd like to buy one for myself when I get back home. It should enjoy living on my balcony, and it would be a charming reminder of my visit here.'

'If you want a true reminder of New Zealand, a native plant might be more appropriate. You can buy sealed packets of seeds that are acceptable to most countries now.'

How could he switch so abruptly—from the passionately demanding kisses of a few minutes ago to this pleasant, conversational courtesy?

With ease, clearly. Emotion and sensation were still churning through her, but Alex was once more fully in control.

'I'll look out for them.' She turned to go, but remembered something. 'What time do you plan to leave this morning?'

He paused, as though remembering something. 'There's been a change of plan—if you're happy with it. I met friends at the dinner last night who live not far north of here in a vineyard. Their garden is beautiful— a showpiece. Today they're launching their latest red with lunch and a reception there. They invited me and, when I mentioned you were with me, they extended the invitation to you.'

'That's very kind of them,' she said uncertainly.

His brows lifted. 'How is it that in your conversation I so often hear a *but* coming?'

The ironic question brought a smile. 'I'd love to meet them, and the launching of a new wine is a very special occasion...'

Her voice trailed away. How could she explain that she didn't want to appear to his friends as his latest conquest, arm candy for a successful man?

Before she could go any further, he said, 'New Zealanders are notoriously informal, and I can promise you the invitation is genuine. Aura suggested we come for lunch and look around their garden as that's your interest.' And, when she hesitated anew, he added, 'She recognised your name and has read some of your columns.'

Somehow that appeased her uncertainty. 'I'd love to go,' she said quietly.

He glanced at his watch. 'Then we'd better move. Breakfast will be in about twenty minutes.'

'I'll be there,' she promised and headed back into her bedroom.

Once inside, she stood still in the middle of the room and took several deep breaths, trying to clear the fog of confusion and frustrated desire from her brain.

The perfume from the rose drifted up, softly seductive, and she said beneath her breath, 'That's enough of that, thank you! I need a clear head right now.'

She filled a glass with water and popped the flower into it, ruefully examining a tiny bead of bright blood where a thorn had broken the skin on her thumb.

For some reason she didn't want to analyse what had happened out there on the terrace. Tiny tantalising prickles of sensation ran across her skin as she remembered...

Stop it, she commanded her wayward mind. So she

enjoyed Alex's kisses—too much—and, judging by his initial reaction, he'd enjoyed her response.

And then he'd shut down. Again.

Why? And where—if anywhere—did they go from here?

She stared at the mirror, absently taking in the luxurious cream and gold opulence of the bathroom. Very feminine. And she'd better not forget that other women would have used this room.

The thought tarnished the residual excitement of his kisses, her pleasure in the day, in the rose.

Once she'd been the unwilling witness to a scene between her mother and her father, when her father had said impatiently, 'It means nothing, my dear. You are and will always be the only woman I love—any others are mere entertainment.'

Her mother had asked wearily, 'Do all men feel that way?'

And her father, probably made uncomfortable by his wife's unspoken grief, had blustered a little before replying, 'Yes. All the ones I have met, anyway. It is simply the way men are.'

Serina's experience had backed up her father's words. Many men—and women—didn't need to love, or even *like* someone to want them.

Serina knew she wasn't that sort of person. She'd promised herself that she'd wait for someone special, someone who would make her feel things she'd never felt before, someone she could respect…

And a year ago that imaginary *someone* became concrete when she'd met Alex. Now she understood that her wildfire physical response to him had made that decision, rather than anything she knew of his character. In danger of letting passion override everything else, she needed to be absolutely sure of her feelings. And to do that she'd have to learn more about him, respond to him intellectually and emotionally as well as with this consuming, elemental hunger.

Only then could she take the next step.

And by then, she thought with an inward quiver of excitement, she'd understand what that next step should be.

In the meantime, she'd better work out what she should wear to a lunch and reception to launch a new wine.

She chose a sleek, sophisticated suit of fine wool in a deep crimson.

When she emerged in it Alex looked at her and asked, 'Did you choose that to match the colour of the wine?'

'It never occurred to me,' she said, half-laughing.

They drove to the vineyard, where his friends made her welcome. The Jansens were a few years older than Alex, and they lived with their four children in a magnificent house overlooking a wide valley braided with vines that ran down to an estuary. They were a striking couple, interesting and informative, and their garden was superb, a blend of native plants and subtropical exotica that transfixed Serina.

The guests at the launch were an equally international selection; Serina enjoyed chatting with the local residents, and was delighted to see an old friend, daughter of the royal house in a Mediterranean island, now living in a vineyard in the South Island with her handsome husband.

There were others she recognised too. As she sipped an exquisite champagne-style wine at the reception, she caught the eye of another old friend making his way towards them. The handsome scion of a famous French champagne house, Gilberte swooped on her, kissing her on both cheeks.

'Dearest Serina,' he said extravagantly, 'what on earth are you doing here in the uttermost ends of the earth?'

'She's with me,' Alex said from behind her.

Smile widening, Gilberte looked up. 'Ah, Alex, I should have known you'd be with the most beautiful woman here—apart from our hostess, of course!'

Serina laughed. 'Same old Gilberte—a compliment for every woman,' she said affectionately, aware of a prickle of tension that had nothing to do with Gilberte. 'What are *you* doing in the den of the opposition?'

'Oh, Flint and I are old friends,' he told her, 'and I come often to New Zealand—just to keep a watch on what they are doing, you understand, but also because I love the place. And because we still sell a lot of champagne here.'

Later, she looked from the window of the small commercial aeroplane as they flew the length of the long, narrow spine of Northland.

Beside her, Alex said, 'Admit it—you were surprised by the people you met at Flint and Aura's launch.'

'A little,' she admitted reluctantly. 'Because New Zealand is so far from anywhere—and looks so small on the map, lost in a waste of ocean—I suppose I'd expected a very insular group, although I'd heard that New Zealanders are extremely friendly.'

'Well-travelled too,' he drawled. 'And accustomed to overseas visitors—we get a lot of them.'

She flashed him a rueful smile. 'All right, I will admit

that the very cosmopolitan guests at the launch surprised me. Apart from the lovely people, the whole occasion was like something out of a dream—the valley with vines braiding the hills and the lovely glimpse of sea, that beautiful house and the wonderful gardens, and some truly fabulous clothes.'

'I'd have thought you were accustomed to occasions like that,' Alex observed, his tone ambiguous.

'It was—' Serina stopped herself from finishing with *special*. Because, although she'd thoroughly enjoyed the occasion, it had been made special by Alex. She ended lamely, '—lovely. So friendly and warm and—well, just plain fun! The setting was exquisite. I liked your friends very much, and the wine they produce is an inspiration.'

Alex said, 'I asked Aura and Flint if you could feature their garden.'

'I—thank you so much,' she said, more than a little surprised, and touched too. Because they were his friends, she hadn't ventured anywhere near that subject. 'That was very kind of you.'

He said, 'They're happy for you to do that, but not immediately—it's holidays next week so they're taking the children to the Maldives. When they come back they'll get in touch and we'll go down in the helicopter.'

'You have a helicopter?'

'I share one with Kelt, who lives not far away.'

Well, what had she expected? He shared a private jet with Kelt and Gerd, and as a businessman with worldwide interests he'd need to travel a lot.

She turned her head to scan the two separate seas that gleamed on either side of a green land folded into hills and valleys.

'The Pacific Ocean on the right,' Alex told her, pointing out an island-studded coast where beaches gleamed golden and white. He indicated the other side. 'And the Tasman Sea on the left.'

The Tasman coast was wilder, more rugged, with no islands and long stretches of cliff-bound shore. Rows of breakers marched onto black glistening beaches that swept for miles. Between the seas were farmlands, small villages, the dark sombreness of vast tracts of pine plantations, and mountains covered in a dense cloak of trees.

'It might look pristine and untouched, but most of it was milled for kauri during the nineteenth century,' Alex said when she remarked on the huge areas of forest. 'Originally this was a land of bush, insects and birds, many of them flightless. The only mammals here were three species of bats, plus the seals and sea lions and dolphins and orca and whales in the seas around the coast.'

She said wistfully, 'It must have been breathtaking to be the first person to step on its shores.'

He regarded her with a slight smile. 'An explorer at heart, Serina?'

'Not until now,' she said, wondering if he might read the underlying meaning in the words.

If he did, he didn't respond. 'The Maori colonised New Zealand from tropical islands. They brought kiore—Maori rats—and dogs that started the destruction of the native wildlife, and of course fire and stone axes travelled with them as well. Yet, even after eight hundred or more years of occupation, the birdlife was enough to make the first Europeans marvel at the dawn chorus. Apparently it was so loud they could hardly hear each other speak.'

He pointed out a swathe of silvery trees marching across hills by the sea. 'Olives—a very successful crop here. And those darker trees are avocados.' He settled back in his seat. 'More predators arrived with the European colonists. Apart from a few visionaries well ahead of their time, people have only recently realised how much has been lost, and started working to bring back some of the glories of the past.'

Fascinated, Serina asked, 'How are they doing that?'

He lifted a brow. 'If you're really interested, I'll take you to see something I'm connected with.'

His sceptical tone irritated her. Did he think she was foolish enough to pretend an interest just to match his?

Probably, she thought realistically.

And why not? He was rich, well-connected and handsome—and, even more than that potent package deal, he possessed a charismatic presence, his combination of effortless male sexuality and compelling authority making him stand out in any company. He probably had gorgeous women flinging themselves at him all the time, wide-eyed with anticipation.

Like several at the launch that afternoon...

The smile she gave him was cool with an edge. 'Oh, I couldn't think of taking up your valuable time,' she said sweetly. 'If you give me a map, I'll check it out.'

'No,' he said calmly. 'It's on my land. I'll take you. We've predator-fenced an area of bush, and when we've trapped the rats and weasels and possums and feral cats inside, we'll return some of the birds that no longer live there.'

Her mother had always said the way to interest a man was to let him talk about himself. Deliberately ignoring the maternal instructions, Serina said, 'I'd love to see it. What's the name of that town beneath us?'

'Whangarei,' he said. 'Northland's only city.'

She looked down. 'It has a glorious setting—those amazing mountains reaching out into the coast, and the harbour curling up into the heart of the town. But then, everything I've seen so far is breathtaking.'

'There are ugly parts too, of course,' he said judicially. 'Some of our towns are old and tired, and some have been built with no regard for the countryside that surrounds them.'

Clearly he loved this part of New Zealand. She said, 'I've read and heard quite a bit about the South Island, but not very much at all about the north.'

'The South Island is magnificent; we'll see whether we can get you there before you go back. But I was born and bred in the north—it's always been home, so to me it's the most beautiful place in the world.'

Without thinking, she said, 'It must be wonderful to feel that way about a place.'

'You don't?'

'No,' she said, wishing she'd stayed silent. 'My parents were Montevellan, and they continually longed to go back. Nice—the Riviera—was only ever a temporary base for them. I think I was born homesick for a place I've never known. I've always felt alien.' She shook her head, meeting hooded blue eyes with a tingle of sensation. 'No, alien is too strong a word; dislocated would be better.'

'You speak English like a native,' he commented idly.

She shrugged. 'Doran and I shared an English nanny and then a governess from Scotland until I went away to school.'

He didn't seem overly interested—and why should he be? But he asked, 'You've not been to Montevel?'

'We can't go. The government banned any member of the royal family from returning.'

'Ever felt like taking another identity and slipping in to find out what it's like? Seeing it might wipe out that inborn nostalgia; few places live up to the praise of the people who love them.'

'I've got the same face as my grandmother,' she said dryly. 'I don't think I'd get in. Anyway, I don't have the courage—or feel the need so badly that I'd break the law to do it.'

'Does your brother feel the same way?'

Alex watched the expression flee from her face; not a muscle moved, but he felt her resistance as palpably as though she'd shouted it at him.

'I think so,' she said remotely, turning her head so that he couldn't see her face.

He settled back into his seat. Whether or not she knew about Doran's plotting, she was worried about him. Which probably—no, *possibly*, Alex corrected himself—meant she did know. Perhaps, in spite of her apparent resignation to her fate, she did crave being a princess of Montevel, in fact as well as in title. He toyed with the idea of asking her directly, but decided against it.

She turned back, and his gut tightened in spontaneous homage. However hard he tried to rationalise his reaction to Serina—and he'd tried damned hard for a fair amount of the previous night—the moment her fingertips had caressed his cheek, such hunger had clamoured through him that he'd forgotten all those excellent reasons for not getting too emotionally involved with her.

Kissing her had been a revelation.

And watching young Gilberte kiss her cheeks had been like a call to arms, a primitive response that negated his understanding that it was nothing more than a greeting between friends. For a moment he'd had to rein in an urge to knock the man away from Serina.

His body clenched. Ruthlessly, he pushed the memory to the back of his mind. Gerd needed information—information he wouldn't get if Alex let his rampant hormones fog his usually logical mind.

Had Serina decided to deflect his interest by pretending to be interested in him?

Two, he thought succinctly, could play at that game.

And if he hurt her?

She might be hurt, he conceded, hardening his resolve, but if her brother went ahead with his plans she'd grieve infinitely more, because it was highly unlikely Doran would survive a foray into Montevel.

Alex made up his mind.

CHAPTER FIVE

THE plane began to descend. Serina swallowed, looking down at a large valley with two small rivers winding through it. They joined to make a lake-like estuary separated from the sea by a gold and amber sandbank. Green and lush, the valley looked remote, like some enchanted place cut off from the rest of the world.

Intrigued, she leaned forward and watched the ground rush to meet them as they banked over another range of hills towards a small airfield. Several private planes were lined up outside a hangar, and she noted two helicopters to one side, as well as a quite large parking area outside another building.

Not exactly the back of beyond, as her nanny used to say.

From beside her, Alex said, 'Ohinga,' pointing to a coastal village tucked away beside another, much bigger river, its banks lined with trees. 'Our nearest shopping centre.'

Catching the shimmer of water beneath foliage, Serina said in surprise, 'Those trees seem to be growing in the water.'

'They're mangroves. They prefer brackish water like tidal rivers and estuaries.'

Mangroves? Serina digested this as the engines changed pitch and they slanted down towards the runway. The excitement she'd been controlling ever since she arrived in New Zealand began to bubble, mixed with a trace of apprehension.

It was sheer overheated fantasy to feel that Alex's searing kisses had pushed her into unknown territory and changed her life for ever. She wasn't the sort of person such dramatic, unlikely experiences happened to—and they were only kisses, for heaven's sake. Not exactly a novelty!

But if his kisses could do that, what would she feel if he touched her even more intimately?

Heat suffused her as her body reacted to that highly subversive thought with brazen excitement.

Even with her eyes fixed onto the scene below, she could sense him beside her—as though he'd imprinted on her at some cellular level, made an indelible impression she'd never be rid of, for ever a part of her…

Oh, calm down and stop being an idiot, she told herself trenchantly. He's very sexy, very sure of himself, very experienced and he kisses like a god, but he's just a man.

Once they were safely down she swallowed hard, cast a glance his way and managed to say staidly, 'I thought mangroves were tropical trees.'

'They are, but New Zealand has the furthermost south of all mangroves. They grow along estuaries in the northern half of the North Island.'

'I wonder how they got here?' Mangroves were safe. If she concentrated on them she wouldn't be tempted to allow her eyes to linger on his formidably masculine features. 'I know the seeds float, but there's a lot of sea between here and the tropics.'

He smiled. Serina's treacherous heart somersaulted.

'One suggestion is that seeds could have drifted across from Australia, but I believe the latest theory is that New Zealand and New Caledonia were once connected by a ridge of land or possibly a chain of islands, so the mangroves could have island-hopped south.'

Serina wrinkled her brow, feverishly trying to recollect where New Caledonia was.

'A large island well to the north and west of us,' Alex provided helpfully.

She nodded as the mental image of the map clicked into place. 'Colonised by France?'

'Yes, and still proudly French.'

Don't look at him—think trees. 'So the mangroves would have had to adapt to a colder climate here?'

'Unless they came south during a warmer era and adapted as it slowly got cooler.'

'Fascinating.' But she couldn't think of anything further to say about mangroves. Now what? she thought desperately.

His expression revealed a certain wry amusement. 'I doubt if many people other than botanists would agree.'

That made her sound like some nerd.

Fortunately, the pilot announced their arrival and everyone stood, the bustle of disembarking saving her the necessity of having to reply.

OK, so nerd she was. That had to be an advance on considering her just another effete aristocrat trading on a title to earn a living.

Anyway, she thought stoutly, I don't care what he thinks. And knew she lied.

Again, a car was waiting for them on the ground but, instead of a well-dressed businessman, this driver was a woman a few years older than Serina, clad in jeans and a woollen jersey that didn't hide any of her admirable assets.

'Hi, Alex,' she greeted him cheerfully. 'Good trip?'

To Serina's surprise, Alex bent his head and dropped a swift kiss on her cheek before saying, 'Serina, this is Lindy Harcourt, who manages Haruru's finances for me. Lindy, Princess Serina of Montevel.'

'Just Serina, thank you,' Serina emphasised, and held out her hand. 'How do you do, Lindy.'

Lindy's grip was strong. 'Oh, good, I was wondering if I'd have to call you Your Highness.'

'Not if you want me to answer,' Serina said forthrightly.

The other woman bestowed a smile on Serina that held no more than a hint of speculation. 'That's all right, then.' She glanced down at Serina's suitcase. Clearly she'd expected more because she commented, 'I needn't have brought the Land Rover, after all.'

Which made a foolishly sensitive Serina wonder if Alex's female visitors usually arrived with a vast wardrobe. Assuming she'd have no need for them, she'd sent most of her formal clothes back to Nice.

Too late now, she decided pragmatically, shrugging off the thought.

Alex picked up his and Serina's bag and headed through the small arrivals area. She was intrigued when various people there nodded to him; clearly he was liked, but an element of respect in their attitudes impressed her. These people, like the guests at the wine launch, instinctively recognised his formidable strength.

Out in the car park, Alex said to Lindy, 'The keys, please.'

'Oh, sorry.' She handed them over and once the vehicle was unlocked slipped into the back seat.

Alex swung the bags into the boot, then held open the door to the front passenger seat and Serina got in, wondering about Lindy Harcourt. There was an easy camaraderie about her interaction with Alex that spoke of something more than simple friendship.

To her shock, Serina realised she was prickly as a cat, tense and smouldering with a completely unrealistic jealousy. The kisses they'd exchanged didn't give her any claim on Alex.

As he set the Land Rover into motion Lindy leaned forward and asked, 'So how did Rosie's wedding go?'

'Very well,' Alex said briefly.

Lindy's laugh held a note of amused resignation that should have soothed Serina's feelings. 'And that's all you're going to say about it, I suppose. Serina, you'll have to tell me everything.'

'I'd be glad to,' Serina said. She added, 'I don't think I've ever seen anyone look so completely happy.'

'Rosie does radiance very well,' Lindy said.

Serina bristled. It seemed an odd thing to say in front of Rosie's brother. 'She looked utterly exquisite and yes, very happy, but I was actually referring to Gerd. They made a magnificent couple.'

Surely that would put an end to any conjecture about whether or not her heart was broken. Almost certainly she was being absurdly—and uncharacteristically—

oversensitive; nobody here could possibly be interested in gossip from half the world away!

Her eyes drifted to Alex's hands, lean and competent on the wheel as he manoeuvred the Land Rover onto the road. Adrenalin tore through her, clouding her brain and fuelling a nerve-racking increase in heart rate.

She twisted to look out of the side window. How could a glimpse of his hands do that? It was almost indecent.

Valiantly, she kept her eyes fixed on the countryside sliding past them—lush green pastures backed by ranges tinged a soft silver-blue as they disappeared into the distance.

Trees, she thought, remembering the mangroves.

She swallowed and said briskly, 'What are those trees? The ones so shamelessly flaunting their autumn leaves? I didn't expect autumn colour here—I had the impression the climate was almost subtropical.'

'Not quite—warm temperate is the official classification,' Alex told her, turning off the bitumen onto a narrow road that immediately began to twist its way up into the hills. 'Which means we can ripen certain sorts of bananas here. The liquid ambers you noticed are some of the few that do colour up in the north, along with persimmons and Japanese maples.'

From the back Lindy asked, 'Are you interested in gardening, Serina?'

'Very,' Serina told her.

'The Princess writes a column for one of the European glossies,' Alex said. He sent a sideways glance at Serina. 'Although it's more about gardens than gardening, I assume.'

Keeping her voice cool, she said, 'Yes.'

Lindy said, 'Then you'll love staying with Alex. His garden is magnificent.'

'I'm looking forward to seeing it,' Serina responded.

The narrow road became a drive, winding down a hill through vast trees. Noting a fantastic oak that would have been several hundred years old in Europe, she realised that northern hemisphere trees must grow much more rapidly in Northland.

And Lindy was absolutely correct—they were magnificent. A great buttressed mound of foliage caught her attention and she twisted in her seat as they passed by it.

'A Moreton Bay fig from Queensland in Australia,' Alex told her. He slanted a glance her way. 'Unfortunately, the fruit isn't edible.'

'Sad,' she returned lightly. 'I love figs. Oh!'

She leaned forward to examine a clump of jade-green trees that turned into one massive tree.

'Puriri,' Alex said. 'They're actually a bush tree, but they don't seem to mind living in paddocks.'

'If they were any happier they might take over the country,' Serina said, amusement colouring her tone.

And then they drove through a grove of different trees and up to a house set in a great sweep of lawns.

'Oh,' Serina breathed on a long exhalation.

Alex's home was glorious. He stopped the vehicle in a gravelled forecourt and, while Serina was still gazing at the long façade of the big house, Lindy came round and opened the front passenger door for her.

Feeling awkward, Serina said, 'Thank you,' and stepped out onto the gravel.

Alex collected the bags from the boot. Putting them on the gravel, he said, 'Thank you, Lindy—I'll see you later.'

Lindy's smile remained firmly in place, but a certain stiffness about the set of her shoulders made Serina wonder again at their relationship.

'No problems,' the other woman said cheerfully. She bestowed that determined smile on Serina. 'I'm sure you'll enjoy your stay here.'

Once she was out of earshot, Alex said, 'Welcome to my home, Serina.'

'It's amazing,' she told him. 'I don't think I've ever seen anything like it.' His friends lived in a sophisticated modern house—Alex's home was clearly a relic of the colonial period.

'High Victoriana,' he explained easily. 'It was built in the late nineteenth century for an Anglo-Indian who exported horses from here to India. Verandas were fashionable then, and he rather went overboard on them.' He bent to pick up their bags.

'I can carry mine,' Serina said, reaching for it. Their hands collided and she jerked back.

Alex straightened with both bags. Eyes gleaming, he said, 'My touch isn't poisonous.'

'I know that,' she blurted, for once unable to think straight. She added, 'Neither is mine.'

They measured glances for a moment and reckless excitement welled up inside her in a warm, heady flood.

Alex said deliberately, 'Lindy is the daughter of the woman who used to be our housekeeper. She's dead now, but Lindy and I more or less grew up together until I was sent away to school. In many ways she's as much of a sister to me as Rosie.'

He was telling her that Lindy meant nothing to him—well, nothing emotional, Serina amended.

Actually, he probably meant nothing emotional in a sexual way, because he was clearly fond of the other woman.

In spite of her efforts, Serina found she couldn't be adult and sophisticated about Alex and the way she felt. The sensations coursing through her suffered a far-from-subtle transmutation into a rising tide of anticipation.

Trying to quell it, she asked, 'How old were you then?'

'Seven.' He headed up the steps and onto the stone-floored veranda.

Horrified, Serina followed. She'd heard of small English children being sent off to school, but she had no idea New Zealanders did the same. Before she could formulate some meaningless comment, Alex looked down at her.

'After my mother died, my father married again. His new wife found a noisy, grubby, resentful child too much to handle, so off I went to school. Which is why Rosie and I have a rather distant relationship for sib-lings—we only spent time together in the holidays.'

Serina ached for the child he'd been, a small boy sent away from the only home he'd known, away from his playmates, from his father and the housekeeper—and the little sister—who'd been the only constants in his life.

She said, 'I'm so glad my parents waited until Doran and I were in our teens before they banished us to school.'

He opened the front door. 'I think Rosie had the worst of it. I settled into school quite well, but when Rosie was born her mother discovered she was no more maternal with her than she had been with me. And since my father, an archaeologist, was rarely here, Lindy's mother was the only reliable motherly figure Rosie ever really had. And then she died when Rosie was eight.'

Serina's heart was touched anew. Her parents' marriage hadn't been a comfortable one, but at least they'd been there for her and Doran. 'I had no idea. Still, she's got Gerd now, and I can tell he adores her just as much as she loves him.'

She wondered then if Alex might think she was hinting about being someone like that for him. Nonsense, she thought stoutly. You're being ridiculous again!

Alex said calmly, 'Yes, I believe they'll make each other happy.'

The wide, high-ceilinged hall was superbly furnished with antiques, mostly English from the Georgian period. A superb wooden staircase, exquisitely carved in some golden wood, wound its way up to another floor.

'Your bedroom is here,' Alex said once they'd climbed it, and opened a door, standing back to let her go in.

The room was big and airy, dominated by a wide bed. French windows led out onto another wide veranda; beneath and beyond it stretched lawns and a haze of flowers and palms against a background of those splendid trees.

After a quick glance around, Serina smiled. 'I can see why you decided on this room for me. You're determined to make sure I learn something about New Zealand's plants, aren't you?'

'My grandmother was a botanical artist,' he told her as she walked across to examine a series of exquisite watercolours. 'These are some of hers.'

'She was an exceptionally good one,' Serina said seriously. She peered at the signature, and said in a hushed voice, 'Oh—*Freda Matthews!* She's acknowledged as one of the greatest botanical artists of the twentieth century. And she's your grandmother!'

It was foolish to feel that somehow this forged a fragile link between them, but she couldn't hide the pleasure that the slight connection gave her.

'She died before I was born so I never knew her.' He dropped her bag onto a low stool.

'She left a superb legacy,' Serina said earnestly, examining each image with intent appreciation.

'Thank you. I think.'

His voice was grave but a note in it caught her attention. She turned her head, caught a betraying glint of amusement in his eyes and laughed up at him, her tension easing. 'Oh, you and Rosie as well, of course!'

'There's that little catch of laughter again. Do you know how infectious it is?'

Something had happened—an unspoken exchange of potent meaning that drove every trace of amusement from her.

And from Alex.

A heady awareness sizzled between them, blocking the breath in her throat. Serina's eyes widened endlessly as he came towards her with the lithe, purposeful gait of a hunter.

Almost silently, he said, 'It's also very, very sexy. And when you look over your shoulder there's something—I don't even know what it is, but you look fey.' His voice deepened. 'And maddeningly irresistible.'

Serina swallowed to ease her suddenly dry mouth. Part of her wanted desperately to defuse the situation, to let him know that she didn't…wasn't yet ready…

And then he turned her to face him, and she looked up mutely into a face drawn and arrogant with desire. Her instinctive, protective resistance crumbled under the impact of a hunger so consuming she sighed as he fitted her into his arms and kissed her.

At first he didn't give her the passion she craved; his mouth touched hers gently, almost tenderly, so that she wanted to stand on tiptoe and *insist* he satisfy the need he'd roused in her.

Yet a slow, languorous heat melted her bones until she could do nothing but accept that silky caress.

Against her lips, he said, 'Is this what you want, Serina?'

'You know it is,' she whispered, unable to temporise, to hedge, even though some distant area of her brain was struggling to send out an All Systems alert.

He gathered her more closely into him, his mouth crushing down on hers in a kiss so ruthlessly demanding her knees almost gave way. And then she wasn't aware of anything but the wild reaction of her eager body, a surrender that overrode every sensible limit she'd lived by until then.

When at last he lifted his mouth, Serina realised he was every bit as aroused as she was. She thrilled to the harsh indrawn breath he took and the urgent lift of his chest, the tense flexion of his arms around her.

And the hard, leashed power of him against her hips.

Yet, despite all the turmoil of thwarted passion, she'd never felt so safe, so wonderfully secure.

And that was the danger, she thought, confusion tumbling around her brain as her breathing slowed into harmony and his arms relaxed.

'Serina,' he said quietly, resting his cheek against her forehead. 'That will have to be enough for now.'

A chill shuddered through her, and she had to stifle a small sound of protest. As though he understood how shaken she still was, he held her for several seconds more until she was able to straighten and trust her knees enough to pull away.

She could read nothing in his face; the dense, crystalline blue of his gaze hid his thoughts, his emotions.

Words falling into the stiff silence like pebbles in a pond, she said through slightly swollen lips, 'I'm going to be crass and ask why.'

Alex's twisted smile held more ruefulness than amusement. 'Because it's almost dinner time, and my housekeeper will wonder what the hell we're doing if we don't arrive for it.'

Her laughter sounded almost like a sob. Hastily, she controlled it, veiling her turbulent gaze with her lashes while she tried to sort out what she wanted to say.

Alex finished, 'And because you're not ready.' He paused. 'A year ago we looked at each other and wanted each other, but the time wasn't right. I don't know if it is yet. I sense some sort of restraint in you.'

His tone was neutral, but his keen scrutiny unnerved her. Not restraint—no, not that. What he sensed was shyness, the modesty of a woman who was still a virgin.

Should she tell him? No.

She bit her lip. 'I didn't come here hoping for—*in-tending*—any sort of—of…' Her voice trailed away.

'Relationship? I despise that word.' His tone was cool, almost mocking. 'Affair? Not much better. What exactly did you come here not expecting?'

Serina's brows lifted and she said with a cutting edge to each word, 'I don't like *relationship* either, but it will suffice.'

She stopped because she didn't know what to say next.

He was silent, his face expressionless, and then to her shock he linked his fingers around her wrist so that his thumb rested on the vulnerable pulse that beat there.

Sheer astonishment held her frozen, but to her dismay she felt the answering leap of her heart at that almost casual grip.

'Whatever you hoped or intended or resisted,' he said, holding her eyes with his own, 'your response tells me—and should convince you, however much you'd like to deny it—there already *is* a relationship.' He emphasised the word enough to lift the hairs on the back of her neck.

'I don't—'

Alex cut in ruthlessly, 'What you decide to do about it is up to you, but don't deny it's there.' He released her. 'And you're not in any danger. I can control my urges, and I'm sure you can too.'

His detached tone and ironic eyes set a barrier between them that hurt when it should have reassured.

After a glance at his watch he said, 'Dinner will be ready soon. I'll come and collect you in about twenty minutes.'

Once he'd left, the memory of the kiss hung in the room like the rose she'd packed so carefully—so foolishly—in her luggage. She opened her bag and picked up the bloom, limp and already fading in the tissue she'd wrapped around it, and made to throw it into the rubbish bin.

But something stayed her hand. Smiling wanly at her weakness, she put it back into the case.

'A shower,' she told herself.

As though she could wash away the memory of their kisses! She had a feeling they'd stay with her all her life—the first time she'd discovered such a depth of passion in herself that she literally had no control over her emotions.

The en suite bathroom was small but superbly fitted, and again she wondered how many women had been accommodated in this room, this house—in Alex's arms.

He certainly wasn't considered a playboy but, apart from Ms Antonides, his name had been linked with several other women, all beauties, and mostly women with high-flying careers in various fields.

About as far removed from her as anyone could be, Serina thought, turning off the water with a vicious twist of her wrist.

Then she shook her head. OK, so she didn't have a proper career, but she'd had to put any hopes of that on hold when her parents had been killed. Left with an estate that was a total mess, she'd salvaged what she could, ruthlessly selling everything of any value so Doran could finish his education at his expensive school. And becoming Rassel's muse—backed by years of serious scrimping—had provided her with enough to pay for his university studies.

Which was why she found his near-obsession with that game so infuriating. Once, when she'd taxed him with it, he'd told that one day he'd be looking after her and, although she was touched, she tried to convince him that it wasn't likely. Some research on video gaming had convinced her it was big companies who came up with profitable new franchises, not rank amateurs.

But Doran was clearly having a fabulous time in Vanuatu, so she could stop worrying about him. For the moment, anyway.

She paced around the room, admiring the delicate, exquisitely precise watercolours on the walls. Alex's grandmother had had huge talent, and her heart warmed at this further evidence of his thoughtfulness.

Her gaze drifted to the laptop. After dinner she'd make notes about what she'd seen so far while the memories were fresh.

Her heart raced when someone tapped on her door. Bracing herself, she opened it and found Alex, his expression coolly non-committal as he gave her a swift glance that encompassed her bare arms and throat.

'You might want a wrap or a cardigan.'

'I'll get one,' she said, wishing she'd thought of it herself. That impersonal survey had hurt a vulnerable part of her she'd never known she possessed.

Collecting a light wrap, she thought indignantly that being kissed by Alex had somehow turned her into a different person—a woman irritatingly sensitive to his every look, to every inflection in his deep voice. A woman who found herself sighing over the way the corners of his mouth turned up whenever he smiled— even the shape of his ears and the fact that the sun struck glints of red from his black hair!

Neither she nor Alex wanted a drink before dinner, so they went straight in to their meal. The woman who brought in the dishes was introduced as Caroline Summers, the housekeeper. In her mid-thirties, she had a pleasant smile and a briskly competent manner that Serina liked.

And she was a brilliant cook. Suddenly hungry, Serina applied herself to an entrée of grilled mussels with bacon and almonds.

'It's one of my favourites,' Alex said, 'and I noticed you enjoyed seafood at the dinner for the wedding party, so I assumed you'd like this.'

After one mouthful she said enthusiastically, 'It's delicious. Is it a New Zealand favourite?'

'I don't know where Caroline found the recipe, or if she made it up. Ask her when she comes back. One of these days I'm probably going to lose her to a restaurant, but in the meantime she seems content enough to stay here while her children are young. Her husband is the livestock manager on the station.'

'The station?' she enquired.

'In New Zealand and Australia a large farm is called a station.'

Grateful for the neutral subject, Serina asked questions diligently while they ate, enjoying the sound of his voice, the sight of his lean, tanned hands across the table, the warmth from the flames in the fireplace, the silence of the darkening countryside…

She learned that Haruru had been his father's inheritance, that his mother had been the link through which Alex was related to Gerd and his brother Kelt—they shared the same New Zealand great-grandfather. And she deduced that, while Alex called the station home, the corporation he ran kept him too busy to spend much time there.

She learned that Haruru in Maori meant rumbling.

'There's a waterfall in the hills that can be heard rumbling through the ground for some distance,' Alex told her.

'How?'

'It's volcanic land, and it's probably a trick of acoustics.'

Above all, she learned that the delicious irritant of her attraction to him had deepened, turning into something darker and more dangerous—something that might teach her the meaning of heartbreak…

CHAPTER SIX

THAT night Serina slept well and the next morning Alex showed her around his garden, but for the first time ever she couldn't fully concentrate on the beauty and harmony of flowers and foliage and form. Her attention was fixed on the man beside her.

She wondered dismally if this—*whatever*—she felt for Alex was going to destroy her pleasure in gardens.

Not that it could be love. The mere thought of that shocked her.

She couldn't afford to love him. He'd made his attitude brutally clear; the unfulfilled desire that pulsated between them indicated a relationship, nothing more.

It was a relief to get into the Land Rover for a quick overview of the station. The track wound up to an airstrip along a ridge, providing a magnificent view over green hills and bush-clad gullies and the Pacific Ocean, a wide stretch of brilliant blue under the bright winter sky.

'Tomorrow we'll go down to the nearest beach,' he told her on their way back to the homestead. 'I hope you have some warm clothes with you?'

'Of course I have,' she returned crisply. 'But you don't need to entertain me, you know. Tomorrow I'll see about hiring a car so I can visit some of the gardens in the guidebook you found for me.'

He gave her a narrow glance. 'Have you ever driven on the left?'

'Oh, yes,' she said absently, trying not to look down the hill. Although the track was well-maintained, the ground fell away sharply on her side without any barrier and she refused to let him see how nervous she was. Heights intimidated her.

But he must have sensed it because he slowed the Land Rover down. 'When? And how much?'

Warmed by his unspoken consideration, she said, 'I used to visit Doran at his school in England. Also, when our nanny was ill I drove down to Somerset quite frequently to visit her.'

And on other occasions when she'd been checking out gardens and interviewing their owners.

He said, 'So you're experienced on both sides of the road.'

'And I'm a careful driver.' Scrupulously, she added, 'I did once set off from an intersection and head straight towards the wrong side. I was lucky—there was no other traffic, but it scared me and I've been super-cautious ever since.'

'If there had been other traffic you'd probably have kept to the left,' Alex said. He glanced at her. 'You don't need to hire a car; I'll drive you around.'

'I can't ask you to do that,' she protested, hiding her quick flare of pleasure.

'You didn't,' he said, reacting instantly when a bird

sunning itself in the gravel flew up suddenly in front of the Land Rover.

Serina's sharp intake of breath wasn't necessary. Without stamping on the brake, Alex slowed the vehicle but held it to the line.

'Never try to avoid a bird or an animal,' he said calmly. 'Probably more people have been killed taking abrupt evasive action than actually hitting something. Always stay on the road, and on your side if it's a public road.'

'Surely it's human instinct to try not to hurt anything?' she protested, feeling her tense muscles relax.

'Control it. You're good at control.'

Serina flushed. Except when he touched her...

He added, 'Unless you're faced with hitting another person and, even then, you need to weigh the consequences.'

Soberly, she said, 'I hope I never have to.' She returned to the original subject. 'But you don't need to drive me—you must have plenty of things to do without that. I'll buy a good map and I'm capable of finding my way around.'

'I can spare the time.'

When she began to object again, he said, 'Serina, I know lots more people—and gardens—than whoever wrote that guidebook, and most of them aren't open to the public.'

Serina was torn. She had to make this visit worthwhile, which meant seeing as many gardens as she could fit in. The more material she gathered, the better.

For *worthwhile* read profitable, she thought as the track they were on joined another wider and more travelled one.

But the real reason for her reluctance to have Alex for a chauffeur was the intensity of her response to him.

Thoughtfully, she said, 'There are occasions when you sound like my father in his most aristocratic mood.'

His tone matching hers, he responded, 'I do not feel in the least like your father.' After a taut few seconds he added dryly, 'Or your brother.'

She glanced sideways, her heart thumping erratically as she took in his autocratic profile. He might not work on the station, but his hands on the wheel were strong and competent. Some wicked part of her mind flashed up an image of them stroking slowly across her pale skin. Heat flamed deep within her, and she had to stare stonily ahead and concentrate on a flock of sheep in the field.

'One of them is cast,' Alex said, and brought the Land Rover to a stop.

Serina opened her door and scrambled down too, eyes on the sheep lying in the grass, its legs sticking out pathetically. 'What's the matter with it?' she asked as Alex swung lithely over the wire fence.

He set off towards the animal. 'It's heavy with wool and couldn't get up, and now its balance has gone. It will die if it's left like that. Stay there—I can deal with it.'

But Serina climbed the fence too, making sure she kept close to the post as he had done. The wires hurt her hands a little; she rubbed them down her jeans as she joined him. The rest of the flock scattered at their approach, but they stopped a safe distance away and turned to eye the two intruders curiously as Alex strode over to the struggling sheep.

It didn't seem likely that he'd need help but, just in case, Serina followed him across the short grass.

The sheep registered its dislike of being approached by bleating weakly and struggling. Serina watched as

Alex bent and, without seeming to exert much effort, turned the animal so that it stood. It panted and hung its head, but seemed stable enough until he stepped back.

'Damn,' he muttered as it staggered. He grabbed it and held it steady.

Serina said, 'If we both hold it for a while until it gets its balance, would that help?'

'Probably, but you'd get dirty.' His voice held a sardonic note.

'So?' Irritated, she positioned herself beside the panting animal and pressed her knee against it. Greasy wool, warm from the winter sun, clung to the denim of her jeans.

'It smells,' he said, adding, 'and the wool will leave unfiltered, dirty lanolin on your hands and clothes. Those extremely well-cut jeans may never be the same again.'

'I've smelt a lot worse than this,' she said, meeting his eyes.

'In that case, thanks for helping,' he said coolly. 'They're due to be shorn today, so if we can get it steady it will be all right.'

It was oddly intimate, standing there with the animal panting between them. Serina concealed a wry smile, wondering how many of the women who'd stayed at that beautiful homestead had got this close to a sheep.

And what would his business rivals and allies think if they could see him now? Clad in a plaid shirt with sleeves rolled up to reveal strongly muscular arms, and a pair of trousers in some hard-wearing fabric that showed off narrow hips and strongly muscled thighs, he stood with booted feet braced, taller than her by some inches.

Accustomed to looking most men in the eyes, Serina felt overshadowed, yet oddly protected.

The silence was weighted too heavily with awareness, and she found herself saying, 'I somehow got the impression that most farmers in New Zealand travel with packs of eager dogs.'

'Usually only one or two,' he told her.

A note in his deep, amused voice sent a thrill of excitement through her. Serina nodded and looked away, trying to concentrate on the sunny day, the sounds of birds she'd never heard before, the earthy smell of the sheep—*anything* to take her mind off Alex's nearness.

Nothing worked.

He said, 'And I'm not a farmer. I'm a businessman. I don't have a dog because I'm away a lot and dogs—like spouses—need companionship to be happy.'

'Is that why you haven't married?'

The moment the words emerged she wished she could unsay them. Tensely, she waited for a well-deserved snub.

But he replied coolly, 'No. When—if—I marry I'll organise my life differently. Why are you still obstinately single?'

'I've got plenty of time,' she said lamely, and risked a glance upwards.

She met crystalline steel-blue eyes that heated instantly. 'Indeed you have,' he said lazily. And smiled, the sort of disturbing smile that should have sent her fleeing.

Instead, it further stimulated her rioting senses. This attraction was mutual, and she'd already decided to let things happen, so why wasn't she flirting with him, letting him know in a subtle way that she was—

Well, what *was* she?

Ready sounded over-eager and, anyway, she didn't know that she was ready.

With a pang, she realised she wanted something more solid and lasting than flirtation. She wanted to be wooed.

Like some Victorian maiden with a head stuffed full of unrealistic dreams, she scoffed. It didn't happen in her world, where people responded to strong attraction by embarking on an affair. Sometimes they married, but once the glamour became tarnished they called everything off, often to repeat the whole process with someone else.

Love was a temporary aberration, and marriage an alliance made for other, infinitely more practical reasons.

Except for rare, fortunate exceptions like Rosie and Gerd, of course. And, although she wished them every good thing in their life together, she couldn't help wondering how long Rosie's incandescent joy would last.

She looked up. Alex was watching her, and something about his waiting silence made her heart flip madly so that when she spoke her voice was husky and soft.

'What is it? Do I have lanolin on my face?'

Colour tinged her skin when he inspected her even more closely, but she held her gaze steady when he drawled, 'Not a speck on that exquisite skin. I was just admiring the way the sun strikes blue sparks off your hair. But I'll give you a hat when we get home—the sun can burn even in winter here.'

She swallowed. 'Thank you.'

'And it would be a crime to singe that exquisite skin.' Taking her by surprise, he bent his head and kissed the tip of her nose.

Eyes enormous in her face, Serina held her breath and froze. The sun suddenly seemed brighter, the colours more vivid, the unseen birds more piercingly musical. A wave of heat broke over her.

Until he straightened and said, 'We'll see if this old girl can stand up by herself now. Let her go and step slowly away.'

Fighting a fierce, foolish disappointment, Serina obeyed. The ewe lurched, but as Alex moved back she stood more firmly. After a few seconds she dropped her head and, ignoring them, began to crop the grass eagerly.

'She should be all right,' Alex said.

Serina didn't dare speak until they were well away, then she said, 'What will happen if she falls again?'

'I'll tell Caroline's husband and he'll make sure someone keeps an eye on this mob.'

He reached out and took her hand. Serina almost stumbled, heart pounding as they finished the walk back to the Land Rover.

The fence negotiated, Alex leant past her to open the door but, before she could get in, he slid an arm around her and held her loosely, his eyes intent.

Serina's breath locked in her throat. Mutely, wondering how on earth other women signalled that they'd decided they were ready for an affair, she followed the instinct that prompted a sigh, then turned her head into the strong tanned column of his throat, unconsciously letting her lips linger on his skin.

Alex's big frame hardened, sending fierce little shivers through her, but he made no attempt to tighten his embrace. In a voice that alerted every nerve, he said, 'Sure, Serina?'

'Absolutely.' The word sounded faint and faraway, so to make sure there could be no doubt she lifted her head, her lips curving in a smile that hinted at a sultry promise when her smoky gaze met the narrowed, glittering intensity of Alex's. 'Are you always going to ask me if I'm sure?'

'Until I'm sure of *you*.'

Her stomach dropped several inches, but it was too late for any second thoughts. He bent his head and kissed her.

The kiss was everything she'd been secretly craving, a passionate seal on their almost wordless pact. Her tumbling thoughts vanished under the barely leashed sensuality of his mouth as he showed her just what his kiss could do.

The arm across her back slid downwards, catching her hips and pulling them against him. His fierce response to the erotic pressure made her gasp, and he immediately took advantage, claiming more than her lips, his deep, deep kisses carrying her into some unknown world of the senses where all she could feel was the rising urgency of her own needs and a fierce, unbelievable hunger.

Abandoning herself to desire, she pressed against him, some unknown part of her relishing the unchained compulsion to lose herself entirely in this dazzling, sensuous world.

It came as a shock when he lifted his head and said in a voice that rasped with a blend of passion and frustration, 'Someone's coming.'

Sure enough, when he let her go Serina registered the sound of an engine. Another vehicle was heading towards them along the track.

Alex held her for a moment as she struggled for balance—just like the ewe, she thought half-hysterically. He frowned as he looked above her head and let his hands drop. 'Lindy.'

Taking what tiny comfort she could from the narrow

frown between his brows, Serina realised she wasn't surprised. With the intuition of a woman in an equivo-cal situation, she'd realised that Lindy wanted Alex. They might have been brought up as brother and sister, but that wasn't how Lindy saw him.

Serina tried to feel sorry for her, but she couldn't prevent a cold prickle of foreboding when she met the other woman's flat stare as she drew up beside them in a sleek, only slightly dusty ute.

'What on earth are you two up to?' Lindy asked through the window.

Alex nodded towards the sheep, all watching them. 'One of them was cast,' he said. 'We got her on her feet, but she's still shaky.'

'Oh, poor Serina,' Lindy said with a glittery smile. 'What an introduction to the place! Smelly old sheep aren't in the least romantic, are they? Never mind—get Alex to take you out to dinner.'

She waved an airy hand and shot off, scattering stones.

Alex said, 'Would you like to go out to dinner?'

Not at Lindy's behest she wouldn't!

'I don't think that would be a good idea,' Serina hedged. 'Although I slept like a top last night, I'm feeling a bit washed out right now.'

The glint in his eyes told her he was amused, but he said soberly, 'Then we'll have a quiet meal at home tonight and see how you feel tomorrow.'

But the other woman's arrival had somehow cast a cloud over the afternoon.

Back at the homestead, Serina thanked him, then said, 'I'd like to try my camera out in your garden, if that's all right with you?'

'I don't want you writing about my garden,' he said crisply.

'I know, and I won't, but I'll want to take photographs when I visit other gardens, and the light here, especially during the middle of the day, is very clear and stark. I'd like to work out what settings are best.'

He held her eyes a second longer than necessary, then nodded. 'Have you always taken your own photographs?'

'Not at the beginning, but I do now,' she said a little aloofly, still chilled by his initial distrust. 'When I was working for Rassel I became interested in photography, so I soaked up as much knowledge about the way professional photographers do it as I could. I was lucky—one in particular used to critique my shots.' She gave a slight smile. 'He was cruel, but I learned an awful lot from him.'

His mouth thinned, then relaxed. 'I have a few calls to answer,' he said, 'so I'll be busy for an hour or so. Enjoy the garden.'

Still on edge, Serina collected her camera and went out into the garden again. The flowers in a wide border glowed as she relived Alex's kisses and their explosive effect on her.

He'd kissed her like a lover, she thought dreamily.

She walked beneath a huge tree and closed her eyes for a moment.

Of course she wasn't his lover. If it existed, true love had to mean you knew the person you loved, trusted them deeply and intimately and were completely convinced they'd never let you down.

Like Rosie and Gerd. They'd known each other since they were children. Whereas she'd only met Alex a few times before she'd embarked on this crazy trip across the world with him.

Yes, she'd felt an instant attraction, and been strangely elated to realise he felt it too. And she'd trusted him enough to come to New Zealand with him, she reminded herself and bit her lip—then muttered, 'Ouch!' when her teeth grazed the tender skin there.

When Alex kissed a woman she certainly knew she'd been kissed, she thought, trying to find some humour to lighten her mood.

But his reaction when she'd suggested she take photographs of his garden showed her how little he trusted her. Tension wound her tight, set her pacing restlessly out into the sunlight, still warm but now thickening into a gold that edged close to amber as the sun sank towards the hills to the west.

It was stupid to feel hurt. Alex certainly wasn't in love with her, so why did she expect him to trust her?

Because what she felt for him—all she could allow herself to feel—was a mad, wild, unreasonable desire. Just *thinking* of him made her body spring into instant life, as though charged with electricity, and when she was with him she teetered on the most deliciously terrifying tenterhooks, so aware of his every movement that it was almost a relief to walk away.

Lust, she told herself sternly. Not love…

'Forget about him,' she told herself, startling a small bird with a tail like a fan into darting upwards. It landed on a tall stem a few feet away and surveyed her with black button eyes, scolding her with high-pitched chirps as it flirted its tail at her.

Smiling, she lifted her camera and got a shot of it,

using it to get some pointers on how to deal with the bright, clear light.

But, try as she did to concentrate on photographic techniques, her obstinate mind kept replaying the way Alex had held her hand as they'd walked back to the Land Rover.

Somehow, that most casual of caresses meant more—just *more*, she thought in confusion.

Not more than his kisses, which had rocked her world, yet in a strange way that casual linking of hands satisfied something she didn't recognise in herself, a kind of yearning…

For what?

She shook her head. Romance?

Giving up, she went inside and inspected her shots, relieved when several showed up really well—so well, she emailed a couple to her editor as a sample of what was in store for her.

Then she surveyed her clothes, finally choosing a little black dress. Discretion itself, she thought satirically. Ladylike and quite forgettable, although it did nice things for her skin and eyes.

And it was useless to wish now she'd brought something more daring, something that would subtly signal the change in her. Pulling a face at her reflection, she combed back her hair and caught it behind her head with a neat, unobtrusive clip. It didn't seem likely that for a quiet dinner for two at home Alex would dress too formally, but she had no idea what New Zealanders wore for such occasions.

Or even if it mattered. Last night she'd changed into a pair of tailored silk trousers and a simple soft blouse, relieved when Alex had been equally casually attired. And it was foolish to think anything had altered just because he'd kissed her again, and she'd somehow—she hoped—managed to convey how much she wanted him.

Butterflies swirled through her stomach when she left her room, setting up a frenzied internal tornado when Alex came through a door a few metres along the wide hallway. To her relief, he was clad informally in a well-tailored linen shirt and narrow-cut trousers that set off the powerful body beneath.

Without trying to hide the gleam of appreciation in his eyes, he said, 'Tell me, is it training or do you somehow just know the perfect way to look for any occasion?'

Colour heated her skin, but she managed to say demurely, 'What a lovely compliment.'

He laughed and opened a door into a room that looked more like a library than a study. Standing back to let her go in first, he said, 'That is no answer.'

'Because your question was unanswerable. I choose what I hope will be appropriate for the occasion and leave it at that.'

He surveyed her through his lashes. 'And an elegant, very chic *that* it is tonight.'

His response washed a deeper tinge of colour through her translucent skin. For a moment the violet eyes were clouded by an emotion Alex couldn't define.

They cleared almost instantly and she said, 'I wonder why I have the feeling you're testing me in some subtle way I don't understand?'

He already knew she wasn't the stock princess he'd first thought, but he was surprised she'd dropped her usual reserve for such a forthright statement. Ignoring a sharp rush of adrenalin, he said, 'You have an overactive imagination. I like to see you blush—it's a charming reaction.'

How many other men had summoned that swift, rapidly fading heat? The photographer who'd been cruel but helpful? That thought brought with it a fierce, baseless anger that startled him.

He asked, 'What would you like to drink?'

After a cool glance she said, 'Wine would be great, thank you.'

To her surprise, he opened a bottle of champagne-style wine. Pouring it for her, he said, 'This is from the Hawkes Bay, a big wine-growing region. Like Aura and Flint, most Northland vineyards tend to concentrate on growing for red wines. Some vintners buy in grapes to make their white wines. In the far north there are several vineyards, some of them with magnificent grounds. I've included them in a list of places you might find interesting. You can look at it after dinner, and tomorrow I'll contact any you'd like to see.'

She took a sip of the liquid. Alex watched the curve of her artfully coloured mouth as it kissed the glass, and felt his gut tighten. Cynically he thought that for someone who'd never put a foot wrong, never figured in any scandal, she certainly knew all the tricks.

And she kissed like a houri. She'd learned that from someone. Or several someones. So his Princess was nothing if not discreet.

For no reason—because she *wasn't* his Princess—the thought burned like acid.

Serina set her champagne flute down and met his eyes, her gaze level. 'You're being very helpful,' she said, 'but I'd feel better if I contacted them.'

'People here know who I am,' he said matter-of-factly. 'Like it or not, it does make a difference.'

sumptuous.' She looked at him. 'I've just realised I have a confession to make—I took photographs of your garden and sent them to my editor as an indication of what gardens are like here. I'm sorry, I'll get her to delete them.'

Irritated, he said shortly, 'Just make sure she doesn't publish them.'

'She knows they're not for publication.'

She took another sip of her wine and this time he watched deliberately, noting the way she tasted—as though she was an expert.

Perfectly trained, he thought, and wondered why, when he wanted so urgently to kiss the wine from her lips, to feel the soft meltdown of her body against his, all he could do was search for flaws. Just looking at her was enough to scramble his brain, and he couldn't afford to allow this unusual desire to overwhelm his common sense.

Only an hour ago he'd spoken to Gerd on the secure line and discovered that, although Doran seemed more than happy to explore the delights of Vanuatu wrecks and reefs, his band of gaming companions had turned up in one of the coastal towns in the border region of Carathia and Montevel.

Ostensibly on holiday.

Had Princess Serina made the somewhat surprising decision to come to New Zealand in order to throw any suspicious person off the scent? He had every reason to believe her brother had gone to Vanuatu for just that reason. That afternoon Gerd had told Alex that the security man he'd sent to infiltrate the group had been overeager and raised suspicion. Alex had ordered the plant's immediate withdrawal, but from now on they'd have to work on the assumption that the group knew they'd been infiltrated.

How deeply in their confidence was Serina? She'd used her email that afternoon to send photographs. Had she contacted Doran, or the plotters?

He glanced down at her face, as serene as her name, beautiful and remote and desirably tempting.

Her explanation of her brother's activities had been almost believable, but she hadn't been persuasive enough to quite convince him. According to his man, there was an excellent chance she was fully aware of what was going on.

With the spy gone, he and Gerd had no other way of finding out anything more but, from what they'd learned, the plotters were getting ready to make a move.

Perhaps it was time to find out whether Serina was ready to sacrifice her body to the cause.

He forced back an instinctive distaste. Lives would be lost if the group were allowed to proceed and, although he had no sympathy for those who believed the end justified the means, he suspected this was one of the times when it really did.

Besides, although Serina was extremely aware of him, she was no fluttering ingénue, hoping that an affair would lead to marriage. Her father, a notorious libertine, would have taught her that such things were transitory.

And he wouldn't be faking. From the moment he'd met her, he'd found the aloof Princess Serina very alluring and he was enjoying crossing swords with her.

Plenty of very satisfactory relationships, he thought cynically, had been built on much more shaky grounds than that.

CHAPTER SEVEN

MADE wary and somewhat confused by Alex's silence, Serina took another sip of wine.

He said calmly, 'So it's agreed then that I'll make the first contact, and I'll come with you.'

Why was she hesitating? His suggestion made sense, yet some recalcitrant part of her urged her to be cautious, to cling to her independence. And long periods spent with Alex in the close confines of a car would dangerously weaken her resistance.

What resistance?

In his arms she'd completely surrendered, offering him anything he wanted. What would have happened if Lindy hadn't come along?

Nothing, she thought sturdily. Alex was super-sophisticated; she couldn't imagine him making love in a Land Rover, or on the grass in full view of a mob of sheep...

The thought should have made her smile. Instead, heat curled up through her, seductive and taunting. Imposing rigid constraint on her treacherous thoughts, she said, 'Yes. Thank you very much for being so helpful.'

Something moved in the depths of his eyes and his

smile held a touch of mockery, as though he understood her reluctance and found it amusing. However, his tone was almost formal. 'It will be my pleasure. How are you enjoying that wine?'

'It's delicious.'

'Someone taught you how to evaluate it.'

She set the glass down. 'My father was a true connoisseur and did his best to make sure Doran and I were too.'

Her father's cellar and her mother's jewels had helped pay off his debts after her parents had been killed. Selling the villa, with its magnificent gardens, hadn't been enough. The only things she'd been able to salvage were her mother's tiara—paste, she'd discovered to her shock—and her father's telescope.

'So I've heard,' Alex said.

A note in his voice made Serina wonder what else he'd heard about her father. That he was also a great connoisseur of women?

Ignoring the cynical thought, she said lightly, 'And of course anyone who likes wine knows that New Zealand produces really interesting, fresh vintages that have won some top competitions.'

She relaxed when they moved on to more general topics. Alex's keen mind fascinated her, and she quickly learned to respect his breadth of knowledge.

Yet his every word, each disturbing look from those ice-blue eyes, was enriched by an undercurrent of muted, potent sensuality. Focused on her, hot and intense, it sharpened her senses into an unbearably exciting awareness of everything about him—from the deep timbre of his voice to the lithe masculine grace of his movements.

During the superb meal and coffee in the library afterwards, Serina was not only aware of a smouldering arousal, but was shocked to find herself unconsciously sending subtly flirtatious glances his way.

Enough, she commanded after a pause that had gone on too long. Much more of this, and you'll be asking him to kiss you again.

Or take you to bed...

But it took a huge effort of will to uncoil herself from an elderly and extremely comfortable leather sofa in front of the fireplace and say huskily, 'I suspect I haven't entirely got over jet lag. I know I should try to stay awake, but I'm going to drop off to sleep right here if I don't go.'

He got to his feet. The renewed impact of his height and the fluid power of his body stirred a heady stimulation more potent than the champagne she'd drunk before dinner.

Terrified that he'd recognise her chaotic mixture of need and longing, she kept her gaze fixed on the arrogant jut of his jaw and dredged up enough composure to say almost steadily, 'Thank you for a delicious meal and a very pleasant evening.'

But, when she turned to go, a hand on her shoulder froze her into stillness. Heart juddering into overdrive, she opened her mouth to object, then closed it again and allowed herself to be eased around to face him.

Their eyes duelled—his narrowed in an intent, direct challenge so forceful she shivered.

'Tell me what you want,' he said, each word harsh and distinct.

She swallowed and nodded, stunned at her trust in

this man she barely knew. 'You already know,' she said in a tone she'd never used before.

His chest rose and fell. Mindlessly, she swayed into his arms as they closed around her.

'Look at me,' he commanded, his voice low and raw.

Serina obeyed, and abandoned the final remnants of caution when she saw his gaze heat with a blaze of desire.

It was far too soon to surrender, she thought vaguely, but when his mouth claimed hers her mind closed down, yielding to the pure carnal rapture of sensation, releasing the barriers of her will to let her body enjoy what it craved—had craved so desperately since their first kiss.

No, even before that, although she'd rarely let herself admit it. Their first meeting a year ago had sparked a hunger that the long months apart had only increased.

His lips opened on hers, coaxing and persuasive. Shivering deliciously at the silent invitation, she accepted it. His tongue plunged, and she wriggled against him, her body insistently demanding a satisfaction she'd never yet experienced.

Alex's arms tightened, bringing her into intimate, explosive contact with the hardness of his loins. Rivulets of fire ran through her, turning into ashes all the convictions that had kept her a virgin.

He lifted his head. Serina sighed, turned her face into his neck and sank her teeth lightly into his skin.

'Serina.'

The way he said her name—in a voice raw with passion—sounded more wonderful to her than the most exquisite music. She kissed the tanned, subtly flavoured skin she'd bitten, inhaling the faint sensuous scent that was his alone. A shudder flexed his lean body and she felt the latent power there, the male strength she both desired and feared.

'Alex,' she said softly and, in her own language, the language of her ancestors, she murmured, 'Your kiss has stolen my soul…'

'What are you saying?'

Realisation iced through her. How could she have been so swept away as to come out with that? Shocked, she overcame her reckless need sufficiently to say tonelessly, 'It's something from an old Montevellan folk song. My first nurse used to sing it to me…'

The words faltered in her mouth and she could have bitten her tongue out. If this was what lust did to you— unlocked the bars of your mind so that all the secrets came spilling out—it was terrifying.

And love had to be even worse—a total revelation. How could anyone bear it? Closing her eyes, she turned her head away.

'Translate it for me,' Alex said.

Ever since she'd been old enough to realise the depths of passion in the simple words, she'd refused to believe anyone could feel so desperately lost to desire. Now she'd known that same reckless capitulation, she understood, and the knowledge locked her lips.

A lean finger turned her head, tilted it. She forced her eyelids up, braced herself to meet and repel the leashed authority of his gaze.

'Serina?'

And, when she couldn't move, he said, 'All right, you don't want to tell me, but you can come out of hiding.'

Shrugging, she tried for a smile. It wobbled precariously, but she managed to say in a reasonably level voice, 'It's nothing, really. Take the music away and it turns into the usual treacly sentiments you find in every pop song. And I'm not going to sing it to you!'

She felt his chest lift, and his quiet laughter reverberated against her. 'It seems only poets can do true justice to our deepest emotions. Whatever was said in your old song, it's entirely mutual.'

Swift and sure, he kissed her. His previous kisses had taken her to an unknown place where the rules she'd lived her life by were shattered. This one was so frankly carnal it set her head reeling. Her mouth softened under his, opened again.

A prisoner of dangerous need, she melted into him, taking reckless delight in the harsh intake of his breath. Whatever he felt, she thought with her last remnant of logic, he couldn't hide his hunger.

When he lifted his head she tensed, thinking he was going to stop, but he transferred his attention to her throat, and after he'd found the vulnerable hollow at the base he trailed kisses across the silken skin to reach the acutely sensitive spot at the junction of her neck and shoulder.

Her knees buckled at the sensation—urgent and savagely consuming—that drowned her in molten pleasure, singing through her body with a primal magnetic summons.

His teeth grazed her skin, repeating the erotic little caress she'd given him. Sensation stormed through her. In her innermost heart Serina realised that she had been born for his touch.

Born for this man...

Panic clogged her throat.

Alex raised his head. Half-closed gaze holding her still, he shifted one hand to cup a pleading, sensitised breast.

Anticipation, wild and feverishly sweet, clamoured through Serina. Unable to bear the intensity of it, stunned by the discovery she'd just made, she let her lashes droop to hide her eyes.

But he commanded, 'Look at me.'

Barely able to articulate, she whispered, 'It's too much…'

'It's not enough,' he rasped.

'Alex,' she muttered, unable to say anything more, clinging to his name as a life-raft in this turbulent sea of emotional discovery.

He lowered his head again and took her mouth.

The kiss was urgent and compelling. Inside, she became hot and slick, her body preparing her for the ultimate embrace. For a fleeting moment she stiffened but, when his other hand found her hips and eased her even closer, she knew that if she didn't follow where her heart led she'd always regret it. No matter what happened, what lay ahead, she wanted this—wanted *Alex*—with a desperation that made rejection unthinkable.

Her breath stopped in her lungs as his thumb moved slowly, lightly across the nub of her breast, sending jagged white-hot darts of excitement through her.

She needed…something else; without volition, her back arched, pressing the curve of her breast into his palm.

His smile taut and humourless, Alex repeated the small movement. Its impact went right down to her toes, sizzling from nerve to nerve and melting her spine. A soft, erotic little sound in her throat startled her.

He had to be able to hear—and feel—the thunder of

her heart as her breasts lifted and fell more and more rapidly, in time with the tormenting glide of his thumb over the acutely sensitive centre.

Waves of pleasure swelled through her in intolerable yearning. Buttressing them was an emotion even stronger and more durable than this shimmering, incandescent desire.

Somehow, without realising it, she'd fallen in love with Alex.

Knowing full well that it wasn't returned…

Dimly, Serina knew she should be afraid, shocked, bewildered—should feel *anything* other than this sensuous delight that gave her the courage to raise her lashes when the kiss had finished.

Alex's eyes gleamed like midnight sapphires in the bronzed, autocratic angles of his face. Her pulse rocketed when she saw the evidence of her fierce response to his kisses on his mouth—both the thinner top lip and the sensuous curve of the bottom were fuller than normal.

Her hands had somehow worked themselves across his back. She let them quest further down, her body tightening in exquisite supplication when she felt his response beneath her palms. Emboldened, she went further, only to freeze when the powerful thigh muscles stirred against her.

His eyes blazed a question.

Colour burned across her skin. With a lingering kiss to his throat, she signalled her wordless agreement but he demanded, 'You're sure?'

'Very sure.' Could that be her voice, vibrant with languorous promise?

But should she tell him that this was very new to her?

It seemed only fair, although a cloud darkened the surface of her excitement. After nervously wetting her lips, she muttered, 'I haven't…haven't actually…'

'You're not protected?' He held her away from him, his expression difficult to read. 'Don't worry about that,' he said swiftly and hugged her. 'I can deal with it.'

Her eager anticipation dimmed a little more. Of course he would have protection. No doubt his other lovers had spent time with him in this house—although they, she thought on a pang of sharp jealousy, had probably slept in the big bed she'd glimpsed in his room.

Alex said, 'But not here, I think. Would you like time to get ready?'

No, she would not; it might give her time to rethink this. And if she did that she'd always regret it.

She looked at him with something like challenge. 'Like a Victorian bride?' she said, then wondered what trick from her unconscious had brought that to mind.

Because *bridal* was exactly how she felt—a little afraid, more than a little self-conscious, and yet eager, longing for what was going to happen.

And she still hadn't let him know that she was totally inexperienced.

She opened her mouth again to do so, but he stopped the tumbling words with a kiss, and under that passionate onslaught she forgot what she'd been going to say, forgot everything but the elemental need to make love to him.

When he lifted his head she leaned into him to kiss

his throat again. Daringly, she licked the place she'd just kissed, savouring the essence of him.

'Hardly a Victorian bride,' he said unevenly. 'Your bedroom, I think.'

Her acquiescence turned into a squeak when he swung her up into his arms.

'I'm too heavy,' she protested.

'You're tall, but far from heavy.'

His smile revealed a flash of sheer male pleasure in his strength and, held against his heart, Serina felt more secure than she'd ever been in her life.

Outside her room, he slid her down his body and held her for a moment before turning the door handle. Inside, the room was warmed by the glow from the lamp on the bedside table.

Serina went in ahead and turned, holding the door wide. 'Welcome,' she said in a smoky little voice, and immediately felt foolish.

This was his house, after all.

But he said, 'Thank you,' as though he understood the obscure impulse that had summoned the words. And then he said with a wry twist of his lips, 'I'll leave you here for a few seconds.'

Of course. Protection…

Why hadn't he chosen his bedroom to make love to her? Serina closed the door behind him and stared sightlessly around the beautifully furnished room. Perhaps he liked his privacy, she thought with a hint of hysteria.

She had no idea how to behave, probably for the first time since childhood—and now there was no mother, no governess to school her.

This was just her and the man she loved, the man she

wanted with all her heart and with every importunate cell in her body.

A tap on the door made her start. She swung around and after a cowardly second opened it.

Awkwardness overwhelmed her. Fixing her eyes on the middle of Alex's chest, she searched desperately for something to say, finally coming out with, 'When I was a child my nurse always left the light on so I never went into a dark room.'

'Because of the nightmares?'

She nodded. 'I'm afraid I still make sure of it, even though I know I shouldn't waste power.'

'Your peace of mind is as important as saving electricity,' he said quietly. 'Why are you looking so intently at my button?'

The question jerked her head up, as perhaps he'd hoped it would, and her knees buckled under the heat of his gaze.

'It's a very nice button,' she said idiotically.

He took her hand and placed it squarely over the button so that the heavy, fast thud of his heartbeat reverberated into her palm.

'Perhaps you'd like to undo it,' he suggested, a hint of laughter in his tone surprising her, and somehow relieving a little of her shyness.

She accepted the challenge, then with great daring slid her hand into the opening she'd made. Excitement flared within her at the immediate increase in his pulse rate.

'See what you do to me?' he asked roughly.

His skin was hot and taut, a fine scroll of hair giving it texture above a firm contrasting layer of muscle.

Serina luxuriated in the novelty of exploring him, and bravely undid the button above the first. When he made no objection, she freed the one above that too.

'You might as well finish the job,' he said when she hesitated.

Head bent, she did just that, then pushed the shirt back from his shoulders and drew in a long uneven breath at what her fingers revealed.

The only word her dazed mind could come up with was *magnificent*. The lamplight gleamed richly on supple, sleek skin, lovingly burnishing the clean, strong lines of him. Next to him, she felt small, delicate, even fragile. She couldn't speak, couldn't think and her hands shook as they fell to her sides.

Almost immediately, he reached for her and said into her hair, 'My sweet girl, don't be afraid.'

'I'm not,' she blurted. 'I'm—I'm overwhelmed.'

She kissed his shoulder, then remembered the caress he'd given her—only a few minutes ago, yet she felt she'd come so far since then—and raised her hand to flick her thumb across one tight male nipple.

His sharply indrawn breath filled her with delight. He tilted her face so that he could see her, and she met his narrowed blazing eyes with something like a challenge in her own.

'I'm glad,' he said smoothly. 'And now it's my turn to be overwhelmed.'

He unzipped the back of her dress and unhooked her bra with an ease that showed how familiar he was with a woman's clothes—with a woman's body. Ignoring the pang that thought gave her, she took refuge in silence when the dress fell free of her shoulders, revealing the black silk bra and briefs that hugged a narrow waist and slender hips.

'You are…utterly, dangerously beautiful,' he said, each word raw, as though torn from him.

Colour burned up from her breasts and heated her cheekbones.

Scanning legs clad in sheer black and the high-heeled courts she'd packed because of their versatility, he said, 'You might be more comfortable if you take off the shoes.'

It was easy enough to kick them off, but she gasped when he dropped to his knees and eased the stockings from her legs. His hands stroked up again from her calf to her thighs, lingering a few seconds on the satin skin there. Pierced by uncontrollable bliss, Serina shivered.

Alex looked up, his hard-hewn face tense. The smile that curved his mouth was just short of savage, and she shivered again.

He got to his feet with less than his usual litheness, towering over her for a charged moment until he turned away abruptly.

Hot anticipation pooled in the pit of Serina's stomach. Still unable to speak, she watched the muscles in his wide shoulders coil as he hauled back the covers of the bed. Uncertain, yet aware that she'd arrived at a place she'd never known she wanted to be, she stood tall, meeting his eyes with something close to anxiety when he straightened up.

It seemed he understood her shyness because he drew her into his arms, shielding her from his gaze with his own body. He bent his head, but this time his lips found the soft swell of her breast.

Ardent anticipation drummed through her. Enthralled,

she dragged in a gasping impeded breath. He flicked the bra free and when she automatically tried to cover herself with her forearms he said, 'That's a crime, Serina.'

She gaped at him, and he smiled. 'A crime,' he repeated, his voice rough, and added as he reached for her, 'like covering the Venus de Milo with sackcloth…'

He forestalled her instinctive step backwards by picking her up and carrying her across to deposit her carefully on the bed. Serina had to stop herself from huddling the sheet over her almost nude body when he looked down at her, heat kindling in the dark depths of his eyes.

Yet, in spite of her embarrassment, the roving survey of his gaze warmed her, stirred her excitement to fever-pitch. Desire clamoured up through her, but she managed a smile that held more than a hint of challenge. 'I'm beginning to suspect you're shy.'

Laughing, and without obvious haste or embarrassment, Alex shucked off the rest of his clothes.

Serina fought back the shock that almost saw her close her eyes. She wanted—*needed*—to see him without sophisticated tailoring and superb fabrics.

Naked, he was a warrior, she thought hazily. Big body poised and intent, something in his eyes, in his stark, stripped features, in the primal power of his body made her think of a more primitive age.

In a thin voice, she broke the charged silence. 'I feel like plunder.'

He said abruptly, 'I'm no pirate, Serina.'

'I know that.' She held out her hands, fingers slipping lightly over his heated skin, a smile trembling on her lips. 'You don't have to keep reassuring me.'

Serina had thought she knew quite a lot about making

love; after all, she'd read about it, seen it acted out in movies and on television.

But nothing had—nothing could *ever* have—prepared her for Alex's caresses, his absorbed expression when he bent his head to her breasts, or the searing, surging flames that ignited every cell in her body as his mouth closed around the rosy aureole.

A groan was torn from her. Obeying an impulse as old as time, her body arched instinctively into him, taut as a bow, while he wrapped his arms around her. Closing her eyes against the unbearable enchantment of his lovemaking, she surrendered completely.

He took her on a wildfire journey of the senses—touch, taste, the faint erotic scent from their entwined bodies, the sight of his tanned hand against her white skin, the sound of his breathing when she mimicked his caresses and discovered the flexible line of his spine, the lean, potent strength so miraculously curbed in deference to her.

Sensation built and built inside, slowly at first, then with such ferocity that her breathing began to match his. Every muscle, every sinew tense with expectation, she craved an unknown satisfaction. When he found the little hollow of her navel with his tongue, she gave a gasping cry. Her body clenched, pushed upwards into him.

'Ah, you like that,' he said, and slid a hand down past her hips to cup the mound that ached for him.

Once again, her reaction was mindless—she jerked, thrusting herself against his delicately probing fingers, mutely demanding something…anything…

'Is this what you want?' he asked, guiding a lean finger inside her, his thumb performing magic on her.

Serina gasped, gripped by a roiling ecstasy, and her body took over, such rapture engulfing her that she had no idea she was almost sobbing as waves of unbearable pleasure forced her into fulfilment and then receded, leaving her replete and utterly relaxed.

Alex's arms around her were all she needed to feel utterly safe. He held her while she came down, and only then swung off the bed. Stunned, Serina opened her eyes to a slit, closing them again when she realised he was getting something from his trouser pocket.

She shivered. If he gave her nothing more than that, she thought, she'd still be grateful. But she was greedy now— she wanted more, to fully experience his possession, to take him into her and give him all she had, all she was.

The mattress sank slightly under his weight beside her and she turned into his arms with a confidence that banished all fear. One hand curved around the hard line of his jaw as he began to kiss her—gently at first, then with more passion when she responded with languor-ous ardour.

That new confidence persuaded her to make her own discoveries, trailing her hand down his chest and across the flat plane of his stomach.

But when she got too close he said thickly, 'Not now, Serina—not unless you're content with what you've already had. I'm not superhuman.'

She snatched her hand away, but he caught it and held it against his chest. 'Next time you can do what you like with me, but right now it would mean the end.'

'We wouldn't want that.' Her voice, throaty and se-ductive, startled her.

Alex moved over her. 'No,' he growled. Holding her

gaze with his own, he lowered himself and in one steady thrust pushed into her.

Serina's body stiffened at the intrusion. His brows contracted and she realised he was going to pull away.

'No,' she said, clutching his shoulders. Consciously, desperately, she relaxed internal muscles she hadn't known existed.

To her incandescent joy, sensation returned in a rush, filling her with fire. This time he eased into her, and when he met no resistance he drove deeper, and then even more deeply, each movement of his body a claim she couldn't resist, a bold statement that forced her further and further up a slope towards ecstasy.

When it came she sobbed again, only this time the rapture was so vehement, so overwhelming she was completely lost in it.

Only then did Alex give way to his own desire; awed and delighted all over again, she watched as he flung his head back. That control she thought so inborn a quality was etched into his face until he too surrendered and she saw it vanish under the same unbearable pleasure that still racked her.

And then it was over, and he went to ease himself off her.

'No,' she said, barely able to get the word out but determined not to let him go.

'I'm too big.'

'No,' she repeated, her arms constricting around him.

He looked down at her, the fierce flames dying in his eyes, and then yielded, letting her bear his comforting weight.

Happier than she had ever been in her life, yet

acutely aware that her happiness was fragile and fleeting, Serina luxuriated in his care until she felt herself slipping into sleep.

She barely recognised the moment when he lifted himself from her; a murmured protest died away when he turned on his side and gathered her into his arms.

'Sleep now,' he said.

Her head on one strong shoulder, Serina allowed herself one last glance at his face, one last sensation of sated delight before she turned her face into his shoulder and allowed exhaustion to overtake her.

CHAPTER EIGHT

SERINA woke and stretched, startled by the pleasant pull of muscles never previously used. She wasn't surprised to discover she was alone; somehow she must have registered Alex's departure in her sleep. A glance around the room told her it was light outside, and she could hear birds singing lustily in the gardens outside.

The dawn chorus, she thought dreamily, remembering his words.

In a way she was glad Alex had left. She needed time and solitude to sort out her emotions.

But, although she tried hard to concentrate, her thoughts kept drifting into memories, and after a while she gave up and just let herself float in their sensuous warmth. She'd had no idea that making love could be so...so *ultimate*.

Alex had been by turns tender and fierce, always passionate. She'd wondered what he would be like if he ever slipped the bonds of that control...

Now she knew.

Yet even at that climactic moment she hadn't felt wary or constrained, and he certainly hadn't treated her as an object, a mere vehicle to sate his desire.

As for a wildness to match her own complete surrender—well, Alex's self-possession was an integral part of him. It was as inborn as the polar blue of his eyes, the angles of that tough jaw, the timbre of his deep voice.

And the way he walked, the gentleness of his hands on her skin, the subtle male scent that set her senses whirling…

He wasn't ever going to let loose that control.

Enjoy his lovemaking without asking for more, she advised herself, calling on some common sense to banish the unsettling hunger that ached through her. Enjoy *him* while you can, because it isn't going to last.

She loved him, but he'd never even mentioned the word, never asked for her love—and why should he? He assumed she was sophisticated, mature, sensible—and experienced.

Lying in his house, sprawled between sheets still crumpled from their lovemaking, she saw the future as clearly as if she were clairvoyant. They would remain lovers for…oh, for six months or so, possibly even a year or two, then slowly he'd become tired of her or meet someone else he wanted more. He'd expect a civilised ending to their affair; they'd agree it was over and they'd remain friends.

Pain shafted through her, so acute she froze and hardly dared to breathe.

It would kill her. She flung an arm up to shield her eyes, but caught sight of the time on the bedside clock.

'Nine o'clock!' she gasped, and leapt out of bed.

Fifteen busy minutes later, she was walking out of her room. The wild-haired woman she'd seen in the mirror was replaced by a carefully coiffed, sleekly made-up,

A steely note in her voice, she answered, 'I realise that, and of course I'm grateful for the offer, but I'm not accustomed to being sponsored.'

Alex had researched her work, concentrating on places he'd visited himself, and been surprised to discover she had a rare skill for evoking the soul of a garden. For a reason he wasn't going to inspect too deeply, her refusal to accept his help sparked his temper.

'With respect,' he said sardonically, 'I suggest you stop cutting off your nose to spite your face. This is New Zealand, and although I'm sure the magazine you write for has some readers here, it's probably not enough to make you famous.'

'I didn't—'

He overrode her protest. 'It will be much easier for you if I do stand sponsor to you—and at least the owners will know you won't be casing their properties for a future robbery.'

Her head came up proudly. 'As if that's likely to happen,' she retorted scornfully, her eyes sparkling with outrage.

Alex shrugged. 'New Zealand has a low level of crime, but we're not free of it. You can't blame people if they are a little suspicious of an unknown person who not only asks if she can come and check out their properties, but brings a camera with her.'

She frowned, and before she could speak he went on levelly, 'In your world, Princess, you're very well known. Here, you're not. I am.'

He waited while she absorbed that, watching her frown smooth out and her thoughtful nod.

Slowly, she said, 'Of course. I didn't mean to be prement of their rapturous time together would be—well, *comforting*.

Serina thought she'd be unable to eat anything, but once in the sunny breakfast room she discovered an appetite. Coffee helped too.

And so did the news that Alex had contacted a couple of gardeners who were happy to let her look over their domains. 'Although,' he added, 'they wanted a month or so to prepare them.'

She had to laugh. 'And when we go to their gardens they'll tell us it looked superb a week ago, or will look magnificent in another week, but unfortunately it's not quite perfect right now.'

'I see you know the breed,' he said dryly. 'I suggested we go tomorrow. You said you'd need at least three hours in each garden and then you'd want to do an interview afterwards, so I've organised a morning appointment and an afternoon one, and in between we can have lunch. I know a good restaurant not too far from the first garden.'

A certain glint in his eyes warmed her. 'That sounds very pleasant,' she said demurely.

Building high romantic hopes and castles in the air would be foolish, a sure recipe for a broken heart. She couldn't afford to expect more from this liaison than he'd offered.

Love hadn't been a part of their unspoken agreement. Alex had made it obvious he wanted her, and for her own reasons—delicious, dangerous, but irresistible—she'd decided he should be the man to initiate her into the delights of sex.

Good instincts—she'd made an excellent choice, she

told herself stoutly. Inspired, even; Alex was everything a first lover should be.

She hoped he hadn't found her wanting in any way...

Too late to worry about that now.

And, to fill in the silence between them, she embarked on the sort of inconsequential chat she knew so well.

Alex's raised brows showed her that he knew what she was doing—possibly even why—but he responded. Slowly her tension evaporated and somehow, without being aware of how it happened, she found herself talking about her brother.

'He was my father's favourite,' she said without rancour. 'For years Papa was sure he'd be able to return to Montevel, and I'm afraid Doran was brought up to believe it was a possibility. Then, when Doran was about fourteen, Papa finally accepted it was not, and for some reason he more or less ignored Doran after that.'

Alex looked surprised. 'Why?'

Carefully keeping a futile anger from her words, she said, 'I think he could only see Doran as a prospective king. Once he finally accepted there was no longer a throne—and never would be—to inherit, Papa lost interest in him.'

'You're describing a rather grotesquely self-centred man,' Alex said austerely.

'I know. I'm afraid Papa was.' It still hurt to remember how Doran had tried to win his father's attention in any way he could, and his despair and anger when he realised it was no use.

Aware of Alex's scrutiny, she said quietly, 'It's almost as though Papa felt that our family's only value was to produce rulers of Montevel. So when he accepted that

Doran was never going to be King, it meant we were worthless.'

Alex frowned. 'How did your father treat you?'

'The same way he treated all women,' she said lightly. 'With compliments—whether earned or not—on my beauty and an expectation that I would forgive him anything because of who he was.'

Startled, she stopped. Confiding her family's dynamics was not a conversational topic she'd ever indulged in before—and to Alex, of all people!

Hardly sophisticated behaviour on her part. She said dismissively, 'He was an excellent father in many ways, and it's too late to wish he'd treated Doran differently.'

Alex let her steer the conversation towards New Zealand's native plants—about which he was very knowledgeable. Serina allowed herself to think it gave them something else in common.

Something apart from wild passion, she thought, her skin heating as a stray memory barged into her brain.

'That is a very fetching blush,' Alex said softly.

Their gazes met, lingered, and he reached across the table and carried her hand to his lips. Little rills of excitement zinged through her at the touch of his mouth on her palm, and her breath came quickly.

'I have a bach,' he said and smiled at her incomprehension. 'That's what North Islanders call small beach houses.'

'Do you have dialects?' she asked in astonishment.

'No, just the occasional different word. South Islanders use the word crib to describe the same thing. The Maori language has dialects, although it's mutually intelligible right through the country—and through the parts of the

Pacific colonised by Polynesians. My bach is beside one of the prettiest beaches on the station. Would you like to spend some time with me there?'

When she hesitated, he added, 'It's not far away, so we can go out each day to check up on gardens.'

And they'd be private—no chance of Lindy Harcourt interrupting. Uncertainly, Serina asked, 'Can you afford the time?'

'I'll be in contact if I need to be. The bach is set up for communications.'

So she'd be able to keep in touch with Doran—not, she thought wryly, that he was missing her at all. She looked across the table, thrilled at the impact of cool blue eyes, and made up her mind. 'Yes, thank you, it sounds lovely.'

'I don't think lovely,' she said wryly when they arrived at the bach, 'was exactly the right word.'

Alex looked at her. 'So what is the right word?'

'If I were writing about this I'd use breathtaking,' she told him, her stunned glance travelling along a beach of amber sand, curved like a slice of melon between headlands made sombre by the huge silver-edged domes of trees she knew were called pohutukawas.

'And as you're not writing about it?' he said coolly, unloading the Land Rover.

She stiffened, then shrugged, some of her delight in the cove evaporating. 'Breathtaking still does it for me,' she said lightly, reaching for a refrigerated box.

'That's too heavy for you,' Alex said, handing her a bag of groceries. 'Take this.'

Packing the contents away would take her mind off

his casual strength as he hefted her case and the box of food out of the Land Rover.

The bach was larger than she'd imagined and extremely comfortable, furnished in a style that breathed a sophisticated beachside ambience. It certainly didn't lack amenities.

As she looked up from a swift inspection of the kitchen he asked, 'Can you cook?'

Her brows shot up. 'Of course. Can you?'

'Several dishes extremely well, scrambled eggs being my forte. And I can do labouring stuff like peeling potatoes. Where did you learn?'

'I took lessons.'

'While you were at finishing school?' His voice was satiric.

'No,' she said quietly. 'After my parents died. When Doran came home during the holidays I realised I'd have to do better than the few meals and techniques I'd mastered, so I learnt how. My godmother paid for the course.'

He said, 'Losing your parents must have been tough.'

'Yes.' She added, 'But you lost your mother early so you know what it's like. At least I had mine for longer.'

To her astonishment, he came and pulled her into his arms. She stiffened, but he held her close and because there was nothing sexual in his embrace she relaxed, taking comfort from the solid thump of his heart and the warmth of his body.

He said quietly, 'There are several bedrooms here. Do you want a room to yourself?'

Stunned, Serina kept her head down. How to deal with this? With courage, she told herself.

She looked up into narrowed gleaming eyes. 'No,' she said, heart thumping erratically. 'I don't need a room to myself.'

Four days later Serina woke early, her head pillowed on Alex's shoulder, and faced the stark fact that she'd made the wrong decision. Coming to the bach with Alex had been more than a mistake—it had been stupid. It would have been far safer to stay at the homestead, where the housekeeper was a sort of chaperone, someone to make sure emotions didn't run riot.

Alone here with him, Serina had fallen deeper and deeper in love, become happier than she'd ever been in her life.

Lax after a strenuous night's loving, completely adjusted to the sleek strength of his body against hers, she had never felt so secure.

The past days had been...

She searched for the right word to describe them, but for once her mind failed her. Her life before Alex seemed faded and dim, like an old photograph left in the sun too long. With him, everything was more vivid, her emotions infinitely more intense, her physical reactions richer, so that the colours of the world around her almost hurt her eyes.

Even food tasted better, she thought, amused by the thought.

But then that could be because Alex's scrambled eggs were superb.

And he was certainly appreciative of the simple French country cuisine she knew so well. He enjoyed helping, too. A smile curled her lips as she recalled his expertise with a potato peeler.

Carefully still, she lay soaking up the quiet delight of these moments. The muted hush of wavelets on the glowing sand made a serene background to the quiet sound of his breathing.

She glanced up at his sleeping face, her eyes caressing the uncompromising sweep of cheekbones, the blade of his nose, the compelling forcefulness of the features that would keep him a handsome man all his life.

Her heart contracted and she fought back the desire to reach out and touch him, reassure herself that she was truly with him. Loving Alex had added a different dimension to her life.

For as long as it lasted.

Wincing, she urged her thoughts in a less painful direction. These past days he'd taken her to small gardens and large ones, gardens overlooking the sea and gardens high in the hills that ran up the central spine of Northland's narrow peninsula.

Some of the houses had been intensely luxurious, their owners clearly wealthy folk who employed gardeners to take care of extensive grounds; other owners lived in comfortable farmhouses and did all their own work. A couple of cottages had been almost spartan in their simplicity, but without fail every owner had been hospitable and pleasant, eager to show off their hard work and the driving inspiration that had led to their superb gardens.

Because of Alex. They all knew him, admired him and responded in their various ways to his inbuilt authority.

The previous morning they'd visited a particularly

idiosyncratic garden overlooking a long white beach. Native shrubs had clothed the hills around, and in their shelter a middle-aged woman with an eye for amazing colour combinations had made herself a stunning garden, assisted by a husband wryly resigned to ever more of his farm being co-opted as she dreamed up new schemes. A passionate follower of growing organically, their hostess produced her own vegetables and tended an orchard filled with fruits Serina had never seen before.

It had been fascinating and fun; the couple knew Alex well, and the warmth of their welcome was genuine and open.

As well, they had an enchanting granddaughter, a solemn little girl of about six called Nora, who shyly showed Serina her favourite places in the garden and, when she realised Serina could speak a different language, begged to be taught a French song. They'd spent a laughing ten minutes while she learned a simple nursery rhyme under the indulgent eyes of Alex and her grandparents.

After that Nora had stuck close to Serina, watching as she took photographs and having to be coaxed to go with her grandfather and Alex to see some new calves when Serina had settled down in the sun to interview the owner.

That too went off extremely well and their hostess insisted on them staying for lunch, a superb spread she'd cooked herself.

As they drank coffee afterwards, Nora edged up to Serina and said, 'Grandma said you're a princess. Why aren't you wearing your crown?'

'Nora!' her grandmother said swiftly. 'Darling, that's not very polite.'

Serina said, 'It's all right. I expect Nora's seen a lot of pictures of princesses with crowns. But princesses only look like princesses when they're wearing their crowns. Once they take them off, they're just ordinary people.'

Nora frowned. 'In my fav'rite book Princess Polly wears her crown even when she's riding her pony.'

'Ah, but that's in a book,' Serina said. 'And I'm not really a princess because you have to belong to a country to be a true princess, and I don't.'

Nora considered that, then said, 'You could belong to us.'

Touched, Serina said, 'Even if I did, I wouldn't wear a crown very much. They only come out for special occasions—like balls and big parties. They're like high-heeled shoes—you don't wear them when you go to visit friends, or lovely gardens like your grandma's.' She leaned forward and lowered her voice. 'Actually, they're quite heavy.'

Nora's eyes widened and a thought struck her. 'Well, if you married Uncle Alex you could be *our* princess and then you could wear your crown when you came here, couldn't you?'

Colour burned a trail along Serina's cheekbones. What on earth could she say to that—certainly not that it was something she didn't dare hope for!

Alex said, 'Serina lives on the other side of the world, Nora. She might be wanting to marry someone there.'

Serina managed a laugh. 'Not right at this moment,' she said and smiled down at Nora, whose face had fallen. 'Before we go, why don't you write out your name and address on a piece of paper and give it to me? When I get home I'll send you a postcard of the place I live. It's very beautiful, but quite different from here.'

Nora's face brightened but she said seriously, 'You could come and see us a lot if you married Uncle Alex.'

Alex interposed smoothly, 'How would it be if Princess Serina sent you a photo of herself wearing her crown?'

After a moment's hesitation and a glance at her grandmother, Nora clearly recalled her manners. 'Yes, thank you,' she said unconvincingly.

Recalling the conversation now, Serina's skin burned again. Until the little girl's artless suggestion, she hadn't even considered marriage—and she wasn't going to consider it now, she told herself sternly.

Because it was never going to happen.

But, in spite of her resolution, she allowed herself a moment or two of imagining herself walking down the aisle on Doran's arm towards Alex…picturing happy domesticity with perhaps a little girl like Nora one day.

He'd been good with the child, and Nora clearly loved him.

Stupid, she scolded and ruthlessly banished the fantasy, ignoring the bleak ache in her heart and concentrated on how nice the New Zealanders she'd met had been…

From outside a seagull called, its harsh screech over-riding the muted hush of the waves only a few steps from the bach. Alex's breathing altered and the arm about her tightened, but after a moment he relaxed and the regular rhythm of his breaths resumed.

Serina relaxed too, setting her mind to assess whatever it was about him that had made her fall so far and so headlong into love.

Nice was the last word she'd use for him—it was far too pallid a description of his keen mind and charged energy, a word totally unable to convey the authority with which he harnessed both attributes to an iron-clad will.

As for the particular sexual charisma that made him stand out in any crowd…

She gave a voluptuous little wriggle. Without opening his eyes, Alex said, 'No.'

'No what?' she asked cautiously.

'No to anything.' He lifted lashes that were unfairly long for a man and skewered her with a long considering stare. 'I'm exhausted.'

Serina pretended belief. 'In that case, I suppose we'd better get up.'

'Mmm,' he murmured and clamped her more closely to his side. 'How many more gardeners did I misguidedly contact for you?'

'Seven,' she returned promptly. 'Why misguidedly? That was the whole purpose of my visit, remember.'

In one swift movement that took her by surprise, Alex turned and pinned her underneath him. He certainly didn't *feel* exhausted, she decided, her body responding with unrestrained eagerness.

'Because, if it weren't for all those phone calls, we could be spending the day in bed together,' he said calmly and kissed her.

When she melted beneath him, already hot and yielding, he lifted his head so his breath fanned across the tender curves of her lips in a way that made her wriggle again.

Breaking the kiss, he murmured, 'So I suppose we'd better get up and sally forth.'

'You dare,' she breathed, linking her hands across his back and narrowing her eyes.

He laughed, challenge glinting blue and brilliant in his eyes. 'How are you going to stop me?' he said, and startled her by turning onto his side, and then onto his back so he could gaze up at the ceiling.

Serina absorbed the arrogant lines of his profile against the sunlight outside. 'I'm not going to,' she said demurely. 'If you're exhausted you'd be no use to me anyway.'

'Of no use to you?' he said in a tone that made her instinctively try to sit up.

He forestalled her by stretching a languid arm across her waist—languid until she tried a little harder, when it turned to steel and pinioned her to the bed.

'Let's see, shall we?' he said thoughtfully, and turned to face her again.

Her breath blocked her throat and she surrendered to the slow glide of a hand from her throat, across her breasts and onwards, inching by painfully exciting increments to that certain spot between her thighs where he knew a welcome awaited him.

Held a willing prisoner, she sneaked a seething glance from half-closed eyes. His expression a mixture of amusement and lust, he was clearly enjoying his sensuous exploration, his fingers brushing at the satin skin, tracing an old scar.

'What was this?'

'Appendix,' she said vaguely as those tormenting, tantalising fingers drifted closer…closer…closer…

Heat burned through her and her wilful body arced off the sheet.

Alex looked down at her with a wicked gleam.

'Useless?' he enquired, and let his hand drift back up to her breasts. 'It's unusual for anyone to have their appendix out nowadays.'

'It wasn't nowadays.'

'How old were you?'

'Six. My father believed that a grumbling appendix should always be removed—his grandmother had died from appendicitis.' Serina's voice sounded vague and fluttery, the words jumping out unevenly as her breath came in swift pants.

Alex bent his head. Her breasts had already peaked, the small aureoles standing proud and expectant, eager for the warm stimulation of his mouth.

But, to her astonishment and intense frustration, he kissed the scar.

'What—?' she muttered.

The imperative summons of a cellphone jerked her out of the sensuous haze he'd summoned so swiftly.

Alex said something under his breath and got out of bed to pick it up. Gaze fixed on her face, he barked, 'Yes?'

Serina lay still, intent on the way the morning sun glowed on his bronze skin, turning it gold, picking out the swell of each muscle, the long powerful lines of his torso and legs.

An alteration in his tone whipped her attention back to his face. It had set like stone and the heat had vanished from his eyes, leaving them hard and cold.

'When?' he demanded, turning abruptly and striding out of the room.

Serina hauled the sheet over her and listened to his voice in the next room, crisp and decisive, clearly giving orders. A swift fear chilled her.

CHAPTER NINE

SERINA wondered uneasily if she should get up. Judging by the icily formidable tone of Alex's voice, something had gone seriously wrong. But, before she had a chance to move, he came back in and said, grim-faced, 'Your brother has left Vanuatu.'

She sat upright. 'What?'

'You don't know?' He scrutinised her face with a flat, lethal gaze.

She shook her head to clear it, then went to fling back the sheet. 'I'll check my email.'

'In a moment,' Alex said curtly. 'You told me he was having a great time there.'

It sounded too close to an accusation for her to be comfortable.

Spiritedly, she said, 'He is—was. But he's always been impulsive—and I've been surprised his passion for diving has lasted so long. I think I told you that. He probably got tired of the heat, or there weren't enough pretty girls there to flirt with…'

Her voice trailed away under Alex's cold, uncompromising survey. This was a man she didn't know— but one whose existence she'd always suspected. No longer a lover, he was the ruthless warrior she'd sensed beneath the cool sophistication.

He said sternly, 'Serina, if you value your brother's life and safety, tell me everything—*anything*—you know about this so-called game he's been involved with.'

Bewildered, she said, 'I've already told you.'

'Not enough.'

Panic kicked beneath her ribs and she demanded urgently, 'What is going on? Why should you be so concerned about Doran leaving Vanuatu, and what *is* it about that stupid computer game?'

'Because he's heading for the border region between Carathia and Montevel, and the game you've been so blithely unconcerned about is no video fake; it's for real.'

Serina stared at him, reacting with a pang of fear to the uncompromising conviction in his expression. 'Don't be silly,' she said, but half-heartedly. 'What do you mean—for real?'

'This is no joke. Face it. You've been fed a fairy tale—a very clever fairy tale—to keep you quiet while Doran, his friends and several others finalised their plans to foment a popular uprising in Montevel in the hope that they'll eventually be able to take over the country.'

Stomach clenching as though to ward off a blow, she blurted, 'That's ridiculous! It sounds as though someone's been feeding *you*—or Gerd—a fairy tale.'

'No,' he said inflexibly.

Only one word, but it was delivered in a voice that delivered absolute conviction.

Trying to convince herself now as much as him, she said, 'Doran and his friends aren't stupid—why would they think they have any chance of *taking over* Montevel?

They don't have any money—exiled aristocrats don't do terribly well once they have to earn their living, it seems. And none of them have any tactical or military knowledge, or contacts in Montevel or…or anything.' She firmed her voice and said more strongly, 'If that call was from Gerd, he's overreacting. He must be.'

Lethally, Alex said, 'He's not. Your brother and his merry little band of romantic idiots plan to use Carathia's Adriatic coast as a safe haven and jumping-off point. As for money and military knowledge—they have a backer who is providing both.'

Fear forcing adrenalin through her, Serina scrambled out of bed. She glanced down, realised she was naked and yanked the sheet from the bed, winding it around herself. Alex's gaze didn't waver and she realised that, whatever was going on, he believed Gerd's version—if it was Gerd who'd contacted him. She dragged in a breath and tried to persuade her whirling brain to reason logically.

It was too far-fetched—it had to be.

She risked another glance at Alex's stony face and into the turmoil of her fears about her brother there infiltrated a sad little thought that he'd probably invited her out here—perhaps even seduced her—hoping she'd…

Stop it, she told herself. Doran was too important to let her own barely-born, unacknowledged hopes and longings get in the way of his welfare.

Alex was a formidable magnate, used to the ruthless cut and thrust of the business world, and Gerd was another powerful, intelligent man, a ruler who'd fought and won a civil war in the mountains of Carathia.

Neither they—nor their security organisations—

were likely to suffer delusions. They must really believe that Doran planned to use Carathia as a base for some forlorn hope concerning Montevel. And, if that was so, then her brother had deliberately and systematically lied to her. Worse—much worse—than that; he was in terrible danger.

The cold pool beneath her ribs expanded right through her. Numbly, she said, 'Alex, are you sure?'

Relentless eyes rebuffed her pleading gaze. 'Completely sure.'

She didn't need the assurance; her own words had already told her that she accepted what he'd said.

She could feel the colour drain from her face. 'I have to go,' she said starkly. 'See if I can talk sense into them.'

'You can't.' Alex's statement sounded unmistakably like a man in charge.

Shivering, she pulled the sheet tighter around her and walked out of the bedroom, coming to a stop by the wall of glass that looked out onto the cove. Although she concentrated fiercely on the view, she could see nothing but blurred colours and shapes.

'So how much do you know about this supposed game?' Alex asked her from behind, his question hammering at her. 'Has he discussed any of the manoeuvres, the twists and turns, the basic plot lines?'

'No.' She squared her shoulders. 'Apart from the vampires,' she added, her voice cracking on the final word. Doran's little joke, obviously. She blinked hard and asked, 'Who is backing them—and why?'

'The less you know, the better.'

Angry, Serina turned to meet his eyes—implacable, so arctic she felt as though they pierced through to her innermost being. There would be no negotiation. She'd been kept in ignorance by him too.

'I don't know anything.' She added bitterly, 'And, as his sister, I don't have enough influence with Doran to persuade him to stop.'

'I didn't imagine you would,' he agreed. 'I wasn't going to suggest it.'

'What are you going to do?'

He said briefly, 'I don't have any official standing at all, so Gerd will deal with it.'

Her lips trembled. 'And he's on his honeymoon. Poor Rosie.'

The knot of panic in her stomach stopped any further words. If anyone could extricate Doran from this, she'd trust Gerd to do it.

But after a moment she said, 'I—I'm just finding it impossible to accept that they thought there was any chance they'd be able to start a revolution. It's—just so *crazy*.'

'They were fed a line,' Alex said curtly. 'By someone unscrupulous enough to use their youth and their innocence against them. Any sort of revolution is damned difficult to get off the ground and, although the current regime there isn't exactly a benign one, it's a lot better than the dictator who booted your grandparents out. And infinitely better than the civil war they endured to get rid of him. Most of the citizens seem happy enough with their present situation.'

He waited and when she said nothing he added harshly, 'If Doran and his cohorts go ahead with this hare-brained plot, people will die.'

Serina clutched at the sheet, huddling into it to stop herself shivering. 'I've been trying to reject the whole idea because I don't *want* to believe it.' She met his formidable blue gaze squarely, knowing she wasn't going to get the reassurance she craved. 'You're sure—utterly and completely sure—that this is not just some student prank that will evaporate into thin air as soon as the practicalities become too much for them to cope with?'

'I'm sure,' he said levelly and not without sympathy. 'As far as I can gather, they're hyped on a mixture of romantic Ruritanian fantasy and a cast-iron conviction that the people of Montevel will welcome them with open arms.'

'Why should they believe that?' she asked despairingly, not expecting an answer.

Cuttingly, Alex said, 'Because they want to, and because they've been told that by someone they trust.'

'Does this—*someone*—have anything to do with the organisation that tried to take over the carathite mines in Carathia a while ago?'

Anxiously, she waited for his answer. A rare and valuable mineral found on the border of Carathia and Montevel, carathite was used in electronics. The crown of Carathia owned the mines and Gerd had been forced to battle his own civil war, one fomented by an unscrupulous firm with its eyes on the mines.

'No. That firm no longer exists, and the men who started that uprising are either dead or in jail. Between us, Gerd and Kelt and I made sure they got their just deserts.'

His ruthless tone lifted the hairs on the back of Serina's neck. Before she could ask another question, he went on, 'I'll tell you this much—if they're who we think they might be, the instigators aren't in the least interested in Gerd or any possibility of carathite being found in Montevel.' He paused, giving weight to his next words. 'They're possibly using your brother's rebellion as a diversion.'

Horrified, she stared at him. Although her lips formed the word *Why?*, no sound emerged.

Alex read her correctly. 'Right now, the reason doesn't matter. I just wanted to make sure you knew how serious this is.'

'You're trying to frighten me,' she said numbly.

He didn't soften. 'I hope I'm succeeding.'

'Oh, you are,' she said bleakly. 'What…do you know what Doran is planning to do?'

'I suspect the plan is to sail to Montevel in a hired yacht and slip ashore once they've made landfall.'

She swallowed. 'I see.' She shivered again, but said fiercely, 'I want to go home.'

'No.'

She said curtly, 'Alex, I can't stay here without trying to do something.'

'You can,' he said with calm authority. 'Because there is nothing you can do, and you're safe here.'

'I might be able to convince Doran—'

'You said yourself you have no influence on him,' he reminded her implacably. 'How are you going to get back?'

'I'll fly, of course—' She stopped abruptly because she didn't have the money to get her halfway round the world.

One glance at his saturnine face told her she wasn't going to persuade him to provide her with the jet he shared with his cousins.

Never mind; her credit card would get her there, and somehow she'd pay it off.

'Alex, he's my *brother*. I have to do what I can.'

Alex could see that the words were wrung from her. She knew how unlikely it was that she'd be able to do anything to stop this mad scheme of Doran's, but she wanted to be as close to her brother as she could be.

He didn't blame her. What she didn't know was that if Doran was killed, she could well be next on the list. She was the last member of the royal family there, and while alive she would be a constant focus for any dissatisfaction.

But, even if he told her that, he suspected she'd go anyway.

So he said bluntly, 'It's not a good idea.'

She met his eyes with a level, determined look that warned him she refused to be intimidated. 'Perhaps not, but I'm going just the same. I'll ring the airline.'

'Princess, you're not going anywhere.'

Mouth drying, she stared at him, her heart thumping with heavy emphasis. 'You can't stop me,' she challenged starkly. 'You might be lord of all you survey here, but you have no power over me.'

'I can prevent you from leaving New Zealand,' he said coolly, 'and I plan to do just that.'

'How? I hope you don't think that your prowess in bed is enough to dazzle me into submission?'

He showed his teeth in a smile that pulled every tiny hair on her body upright. 'That has nothing to do with this.'

'Then you'll have to be a jailer,' she flung at him furiously.

'Serina, you're not going anywhere near this mess.

You'll stay out of danger if I have to chain you to the bed to keep you here.'

The ruthless note in his voice made her shiver. She stared mutely at him, wrenched by anger and terror for her brother. She wanted nothing more than to have Alex take her in his arms and tell her that everything would be all right, that Doran was safe and that the whole thing had been an elaborate hoax, a joke...

In a slightly more gentle voice, Alex said, 'I suggest you get dressed and see if Doran has left any message for you.'

Serina started. 'Oh—yes. I'll do it right now. If you'll excuse me, I'll put some clothes on,' she said evenly.

He paused, his gaze speculative, then nodded. Stomach churning, Serina dashed into the bedroom and hauled her laptop from its case. While it fired up, she pulled on her wrap and pushed her tangled hair back from her face, urging the computer to hurry up, still gripped by a cold, sick panic.

Doran had sent her two lines.

Don't worry, everything's going to be fine. I'll see you soon.

Hastily, she fired off a message in return. *Don't do anything*, she wrote, fingers shaking so much she had to stop and clench her hands for a moment before she could tell him their plans had been discovered.

She jumped, quivering with shock when a hand reached over her and deleted her words. Unable to bear the fear scything through her, she froze as Alex closed down her computer.

'I can't let you send it,' he said tersely. 'The only safety he has is that we have some idea of what's going to happen. If they realise they've been rumbled, God knows what they might do.'

She asked dully, 'How do you know their plans?'

'They set the whole scheme up like a video game,' he told her. 'My men have managed to hack into one computer.'

Hope whispered through her. 'Then how do you know it's not just a game?'

'One of my men infiltrated the group. Stop grasping at straws, Serina. It's not a game. It's deadly serious.'

Stumbling, she got to her feet and Alex turned her into his arms and held her, enveloping her in the heat of his body.

She said fiercely, 'I could kill him, the idiot.' Then caught her breath, horrified by the tumbling words.

'It's all right,' Alex said quietly.

But she shook her head. 'Where is he?'

'He's still in flight.'

'Where to?'

'He's landing in Rome,' he told her.

Stiffly, aching as though she'd been beaten, she pulled away from the unexpected comfort of his arms. 'I need a shower.'

'I'll make breakfast.' And, when she opened her mouth to say she couldn't swallow anything, he said bluntly, 'Starving yourself is not going to help either Doran or you.'

Serina gathered her clothes and walked into the bathroom. She was already under the water when she thought savagely that he clearly didn't expect her to climb out of a window and flee.

No doubt because he knew very well she had no

way of working out how to travel cross-country back to the homestead. And, as she had no idea where he kept the keys to the Land Rover, she couldn't steal that and drive out.

But she had to get back...

Her passport and credit card were in her bag.

Leaving the shower on, she scrambled out, grabbing a towel to blot off some water as she headed towards the door.

Scrabbling in her bag revealed that neither passport nor credit card were there any longer. Her terror gave way to outrage when she realised Alex had also taken her cellphone. Furious, she stormed through to the kitchen and confronted him.

'Give them back to me!' she commanded. 'Right now, or I'll—I'll...'

With intensely infuriating control, he said, 'You'll get everything back when you leave New Zealand.'

Serina stared at him, her anger almost boiling over, and realised he hadn't responded in any way to her semi-nakedness.

With stark pain, she accepted that he'd got her here, lured her into his arms, into his bed, made love to her with heart-stopping passion, brought her to the bach—all to coax what information he could from her.

She'd never felt so helpless, so utterly without resources. So completely at someone else's mercy. So blazingly angry.

So wrenchingly unhappy...

It took every last ounce of fortitude she possessed to say grittily, 'I despise you.'

Without waiting for any answer, she turned and

stumbled blindly back into the bathroom. Frustration and grief churning through her, she lifted her face to the showerhead, trying to wash away her fear for her brother, her anger with Alex and a frozen, bitter anguish because he'd used her.

A knock on the door made her start and turn off the water.

Through the door, Alex asked, 'Are you all right?'

'Yes,' she called, a little warmed by his thoughtfulness. Surely…surely it hadn't just been a cold-blooded seduction?

She stepped out of the shower, slicking her wet hair back from her face and started to dry herself. Face facts, Serina, she thought starkly.

Alex and Gerd must have decided to get her and Doran out of the way in the hope that this would stop the group from going ahead with their plans. Which meant that, however thoughtful he was, however great a lover, Alex's seduction had been a deliberate ploy, a subterfuge to keep her out of the way while he and Gerd tried to find out what Doran's group were plotting.

Shattered by just how much that thought hurt, she hastily got into her clothes and combed her hair straight back from her face, lecturing herself all the time.

Love was transient; she knew that. People had their hearts broken on a regular basis; they wept, they suffered, they told the tabloids all about it and then, six months later, they were happily in love with someone else.

She'd get over it.

Another tap on the bathroom door had her whirling around. No, she thought in panic, she wasn't ready…

Uncannily echoing her thoughts, Alex said, 'Breakfast's ready.'

She hadn't blow-dried her hair or applied any cosmetics. She stared at her reflection, then gave a quick shrug. It no longer mattered. If he couldn't cope with the real Serina she didn't care.

But deep down—so deep she could almost bury it—lurked a painful understanding that Alex was the only man she would ever love like this, the only one able to hold her heart in his keeping.

Even though he didn't want it.

Five minutes later, a bleak smile curved her mouth when she realised he had scrambled eggs for them both, grilled tomatoes and made toast.

He examined her face. 'You look pale,' he said abruptly.

'It's not every day I'm told I'm a prisoner. I dare say I'll get used to it.'

He gave her a hard, sardonic smile. 'You manage to look ravishing in spite of it,' he told her, bringing a wash of colour to her skin as he surveyed her. 'And coffee will probably give you some colour.'

He set a plate in front of her and, in spite of her anger and her fear for Doran, her stomach growled. 'Thank you,' she said stiffly and picked up her utensils.

The food put new heart into her; although she couldn't eat everything he'd piled on the plate, she made good inroads into it. Pride kept her shoulders straight, her eyes level, her voice cool and uninflected.

And coffee helped. After pouring herself a large mug, she said, 'What do you think Doran will do once he reaches Rome?'

'I suspect he'll be picked up by someone from the conspiracy and taken by boat to a safe place inside Carathia—a port town. From there, they'll probably island-hop to somewhere on Montevel's coast in a yacht.'

She set her mug down with a small crash. 'They're mad! How on earth do they think they're going to topple the rulers there—a group of university kids with more brains than sense?'

'They're expecting the populace to rise up with them once they've been given a leader.'

'Doran,' she said numbly.

'Yes—and it just might work. To people who've had a pretty rough time for the past fifty years, the idea of the King returning and bringing good times with him could be potent enough to start an uprising.'

'But the rulers control the military,' she said, her voice dragging.

He nodded. 'Exactly—although even the forces have been restive lately. Their pay has been cut and a very popular general was court-martialled and shot by firing squad for mutiny.'

Serina picked up the coffee cup, noting with an odd detachment that her hand was trembling. She finally managed to drink the rest of the liquid down before asking a question that had been bothering her.

'Why is Gerd so concerned about this? It's really nothing to do with him—and, anyway, I'd have thought he'd be happy with a less repressive regime on his doorstep.'

'The last time Montevel suffered a revolt Carathia had to deal with about fifty thousand refugees,' Alex told her bluntly.

'I see,' she said, startled by the number. 'I hadn't even thought about that.'

'And unrest along the borders makes every ruler uneasy.' He glanced at his watch. 'Right, are you ready to go?'

His words made no sense. She stared at him and he elaborated, 'We're looking at gardens, Serina.'

'I couldn't,' she said involuntarily, stunned that he should expect her to carry on as though nothing had happened.

He shrugged. 'I'd have thought it a much better way to deal with the situation than sitting here anguishing over it.'

At that moment she hated him. 'This is my *brother* we're talking about,' she said between her teeth.

'So you're going to sit here and worry without being able to do a thing to affect the outcome?' he returned, coolly challenging.

She glared at him. 'I thought I was a prisoner here.'

'A prisoner, yes, if you want to think of yourself like that,' he agreed calmly. 'Not necessarily confined to one place, though.'

Serina got to her feet. Which didn't make much of a difference to the intimidation factor—he still towered over her. Tonelessly, she said, 'All right, I'll go.'

It was a strange day. She managed to behave normally—smiling, making polite conversation to both garden owners, conducting the interviews with something of her usual concentration. Stony professional pride drove her to compose her photographs with as much care as usual.

But she felt as though she'd been sliced in two; no,

she thought on the way home, in three. One part was the magazine columnist, the other the sister anguishing over her brother, and the final part the lover coping with betrayal.

When at last they drove up to the bach, she barely waited for the Land Rover to stop before bolting out.

Alex watched her run into the bach and followed her. She'd done well, but for the whole day he'd felt the barriers firmly in place.

As though she blamed him for this whole situation, even though it had been caused by her brother. Damn the kid—if he weren't heading straight towards death, Alex would have carpeted him, amongst other things pointing out just how much his actions upset his sister.

And some part of him was angry with Serina for being so intransigent. He'd expected her to want to go to Carathia; what he hadn't expected was his exasperation and anger at her flinty resistance to him.

Once inside, he said, 'I'll make you some tea while you write up your notes.'

She swallowed and flashed him a stunned glance, then seemed to shrink. 'Thank you,' she said quietly.

Writing up her notes by hand took up the rest of the afternoon. After a meal she didn't taste, she said, 'I'd like to watch the news on television.'

He switched on the set and joined her on the sofa. Tension tore at her—not the exciting, sensuous tension of the previous days, but a feeling that was rooted in pain.

Gradually—so gradually she hadn't really realised what was happening—she'd learned to trust Alex. That cautious, hard-won faith lay in shards around her now.

Without taking much in, she watched the parade across the screen of statesmen and politicians, celebrities and unfortunates whose lives had somehow become camera fodder.

Nothing about Montevel...

When it was over, Alex said, 'Is there anything else you want to watch?'

'No, thanks.'

'In that case, I suggest you go to bed.'

She glanced at her watch. 'It's barely eight o'clock.'

'Neither of us got much sleep last night.'

She flinched, memories flooding back of the previous night's passion. Scrambling to her feet, she said stiffly, 'I'll make up a bed in the other bedroom.'

'No.'

Her head came up and she eyed him with frozen composure. If she had to spend the night in his bed something inside her would die, she thought fiercely. 'I am not sleeping with you.'

He got to his feet, lithe and big and completely determined. 'I can't force you to sleep, of course, but you're spending the night in my bed.'

His cool insistence goaded her into saying, 'I give you my word I won't try to run away.'

'Good, but that doesn't change anything,' he said, his tone telling her there was no option. 'I won't expect sex, if that's what's worrying you.'

White-lipped, she said, 'You can't—*won't*—force me to sleep with you, surely.'

His eyes narrowed as he said softly, 'Of course I wouldn't, Princess.'

Her composure cracked. Hands clenched by her

sides, she snapped, 'Don't call me that! How would you feel if I called you Businessman all the time?'

'Irritated,' he conceded, a glimmer of amusement in the blue ice of his eyes shattering what was left of her precarious poise.

'You might think it's funny, but I find it demeaning and insulting and completely infuriating, and I'm sick and tired of it and I want you to stop.' She stopped, biting back the even more intemperate words that jostled for freedom in her brain.

'Very well, I won't do it again. Now, get ready for bed.'

They measured gazes like duellers. Then she said savagely, 'At least you can't force me to enjoy sleeping with you.'

'I could,' he said with cool, threatening insolence, 'but I'm not going to.'

Serina whirled and stormed into the bedroom, hauling off her clothes with a carelessness that should have shocked her. She crawled into the bed, turned on her side and lay still and fuming, waiting for him to come.

CHAPTER TEN

TRY as she did, Serina couldn't fall sleep before Alex came in. Frantic thoughts jostled in her brain, drowning out the voice of reason that told her she was transferring her anguish and anger to Alex because she couldn't vent it on Doran.

And it was less painful to be furious with Doran than lie there terrified he might be killed.

Eyes clamped shut, she heard Alex come in and the small sounds that indicated he was undressing. Her already rigid body stiffened even further when he slid into the bed beside her.

He didn't touch her. Humiliatingly, her anger dissipated in a flood of bitter, aching regret for the pleasure they'd taken from each other, the joy of discovering how desire enriched her life...

Except that the hours spent in his arms had almost certainly been a means to an end.

And it didn't help that she almost understood his motivation. She would do anything for her brother; it was entirely understandable that Alex should do what he could to help Gerd and Rosie...

Every muscle strained and taut, she fought the urge

to turn over. She could hear Alex breathing—steady, relaxed—and decided she hated him. Hot tears squeezed through her lashes; she refused to humiliate herself by giving in to them.

'Go to sleep, Serina,' Alex said lazily.

She couldn't trust her voice enough to give an answer. Eventually, she did sleep, only to wake in the grip of the nightmare. Only this time she was held firmly against Alex and he was saying, 'It's all right, sweetheart. Go back to sleep now.'

But when she woke in the morning she was alone in the bed. It had been a dream, she thought in confusion—a deceiving, treacherous dream, especially the part where he'd held her close to his solid warmth and strength and called her *sweetheart*…

Did he regret their affair, deciding he'd wasted time making love to her when she knew nothing—had been totally taken in by the video game fabrication Doran and his friends had fed her?

Limbs heavy and weighted, she climbed out of the bed and showered, getting into jeans and a T-shirt. It took all of her will to get herself through the bedroom door, but the need to know if Alex had learned anything more about Doran's movements drove her out.

Alex didn't look as though he'd spent a difficult night. He was standing outside in the crisp winter sunlight, talking into a mobile phone, his brows drawn together, but he swung around as soon as she came out.

'All right, then,' he said concisely, snapped the telephone shut and examined her critically. 'All right?'

'Fine, thank you,' she said automatically.

'Doran has managed to evade surveillance,' he said

succinctly. 'He hasn't been seen since he left the airport at Rome, but I imagine he's already sailing across the Adriatic towards Carathia. Gerd's got his coastguard on full alert.'

Alex's voice was neutral, but she turned away from his intent scrutiny. 'So we just have to wait.' And pray, she thought bleakly.

'I'm afraid so.' The leashed impatience she detected in his tone indicated he wasn't accustomed to waiting.

She knew the feeling well, she thought bleakly. Impetuously, she demanded, 'Why won't you tell me who is backing them? Doran hasn't got the money to fly all around the world.'

'Because we still don't know exactly who is producing this show. It could be one of two organisations.' He glanced at his watch. 'Breakfast,' he said curtly. 'And then we'll get on the road.'

She bit back her protest. Staying here, or going back to the homestead to worry the day away wasn't sensible.

That day and the following one were repetitions of the first. Almost sick with worry, Serina plodded doggedly on with her schedule, reluctantly grateful to Alex, who supported her unobtrusively.

Jailer he might be, but he was always there.

Even in bed, she thought on the third morning after Doran's bombshell. She'd woken thinking she was once more in his arms, only to find it was another dream…

Once more he'd left her alone; she got up and dragged herself through her morning routine.

Her heart stopped when she heard Alex call. Still in her pyjamas, she raced through the door, almost colliding with him.

'What?' she gasped, staring up into his face. 'What news?'

'Gerd's security men picked up Doran and several others off the coast of Carathia.'

So relieved she couldn't speak, she felt tears start to her eyes. His arm came around her shoulders. Steadfastly resisting the temptation to sink against him, use his strength to bolster her own, Serina pulled away and finally managed to breathe, 'Thank God.'

'Indeed,' Alex agreed dryly, stepping back.

'He's all right?'

'He's fine, although he's refusing to believe just how close he came to killing not only himself, but all his friends and probably thousands of others too.'

'Is there a way of contacting him?'

'Once Gerd's security men have finished with him, he'll be free to go home, where you can try to make him aware of how dangerously he's been playing.'

She firmed her trembling lips, so awash with conflicting emotions she found it difficult to think. 'Then I'll go home too,' she said swiftly.

He said calmly, 'All right.'

'I'm not asking permission,' she flashed.

His brows lifted, but he said mildly enough, 'I wasn't granting it. I know how you feel—you want to lash out at Doran. It would be a lot more sensible to hurl your feelings at me.'

But she'd regained control of her temper. 'I don't blame you for anything,' she said as calmly as she could.

Only for stealing my heart…

And that was over-dramatising. Hearts stayed firmly lodged in their owners' chests. They might crack or break, but they mended. This pain, the dragging anguish, would ease.

It had to, because she couldn't bear much more of it.

Alex said, 'Doran is going to be acutely defensive; if I can give you some advice, treat him as an adult who's made a mistake and has learned from it. Although I'd point out the inadvisability of lying to those who love him.'

Of course he hadn't meant that to hurt. He didn't know she loved him. Quietly, she said, 'I just hope that he realises once and for all that he has no hope of going back to Montevel.'

'So does everyone,' Alex said austerely. 'He's caused enough trouble—and I'm sure Gerd has made that more than clear to him. If he's got any sense, he'll apply himself to his final year at university and find a career that will keep him busy.'

She asked tentatively, 'Are you going to hold him to working off his plane flights?'

'I am,' Alex said uncompromisingly.

And, during the long journey back to France, she hugged that promise to her heart. It was foolish, of course, but it offered her some comfort at a time when she needed it. If Alex kept in touch, they might…

No, she thought, inserting the key into the lock of her apartment. Don't even think of it. It's not going to happen. This time next year you'll have difficulty remembering Alex's face, and the only mementoes you'll have of the whole episode will be the columns and your photographs.

Because Kelt and his family were using the private jet, Alex had organised a flight for her on commercial airlines, which had left her exhausted. The noise and heat of a Mediterranean summer in the city beat around her and she was already missing New Zealand, green and crisp and lush.

Doran was home. He came to meet her with a carefully blank face, an expression that turned to alarm and shock when she dropped her luggage and began to weep silently at the sight of him.

'Oh—don't,' he choked and came and took her in his arms, holding her carefully, as if afraid she'd shatter. Awkwardly, he patted her back. 'It's all right, Serina, it's all right. Don't cry—please don't cry. I'm fine, and I'm sorry—I'm sorry I lied to you.'

She gulped back her tears, unable to tell him that they were only partly for him. 'I should hope so,' she said, but her voice wavered. 'I've been sick with worry.'

'I know.' He set her away from him. 'Alex Matthews told me.'

Something in his voice told her that the talk had not been a pleasant one. She remembered Alex's advice—*treat him like an adult.*

'When?'

'He flew into Carathia yesterday, just before I came home.' He pulled a face and said lugubriously, 'We had a long talk, he and I.'

Serina digested this, wondering why Alex hadn't come at least part of the way with her.

No, not *wondering*, she thought bleakly. She knew why. It was his way of showing her that everything was over.

'A long talk?' She tried to conceal her avid interest. 'About what?'

Doran shrugged. 'Oh, everything really. Want something to eat, or coffee?'

'Coffee, thanks. I'm going to have to stay awake until nightfall if I possibly can.'

Chatting of nothing, he made her a drink and, when she'd sat down and picked up her coffee cup, he said, 'It wasn't a pleasant conversation. To put it bluntly, Alex tore strips off me.'

'Did he?' she said neutrally.

He shrugged, looking embarrassed. 'I suppose he had every right to be furious. I hadn't thought of the fallout for Carathia if we actually made it, and Gerd Crysander-Gillan is his cousin.' He frowned. 'Not to mention that his half-sister is Gerd's wife now.'

'I have to admit I didn't think of the possible refugee problem until Alex mentioned it,' Serina said, cautiously feeling her way with Alex's advice very much in mind.

Doran flashed her a relieved look. 'Yes, well, neither had I. And when he told me that the whole scheme had been engineered by the opposition in Montevel—it made me feel *sick*.'

'The opposition in Montevel?' Stunned, Serina stared at him. 'I didn't know there was one.'

'Well, to gain any sort of aid they need an opposition—it's tolerated, but not encouraged.' He leaned forward, face earnest. 'A group of—well, they call themselves freedom fighters and I suppose they are—from the opposition knew they didn't have a chance of gaining power any legitimate way, so some bright spark came up with this idea. They *used* us.'

The coffee bitter in her mouth, she swallowed and said thinly, 'Go on.'

'Apparently, the idea was that we'd stir up a lot of trouble on the border—enough to keep the regime leaders occupied so the freedom fighters could grab power for themselves. They didn't care a bit what happened to us—in fact, Alex didn't say so but, from comments he and Gerd made, I think they were hoping we'd all be killed so they wouldn't have to concern themselves about anybody ever claiming the throne again.' He shrugged. 'I suppose they realised you weren't likely to try, but when I heard that I was very glad you'd stayed in New Zealand.'

Was that why Alex had been so adamant it wasn't safe for her to go back?

'I hope you've realised now that the return of the monarchy in Montevel is not going to happen,' she said, but mildly.

Apparently, she'd struck the right note. Even more seriously, Doran told her, 'Something Alex said made me realise that the people should choose their leaders, not have them imposed on them by—well, by any means. If the Montevellans want a return of the monarchy, then they'll have to get rid of the regime they've got now and ask me if I'll take it on.'

He paused and finished on a wry smile, 'That's if they want me, of course. And I'd want a referendum before I'd accept.'

Thank you, Alex, Serina thought, so grateful she had to put the cup down and take a couple of deep breaths before asking mildly, 'Is there any reason to be concerned about your safety?'

He looked startled. 'Why should there be? We were picked up well before we got anywhere near Montevel, and no one else knows about us.'

'Only those so-called freedom fighters,' she said

dryly, 'whose hides might be nailed to the wall if anyone in power in Montevel finds out what they've been up to.'

He gave a short unamused laugh. 'I could almost say it would serve them right. Alex didn't think that would happen. The man they used as our contact—another student at college—has just been told we decided not to go ahead with it.'

'How did he take that?'

He shrugged. 'Oh, called us cowards and so on.'

It was obvious the accusation still stung, but he went on, 'Which was pretty rich, because he stayed safely in Paris while we went off in that yacht. After talking to Gerd and Alex, we all decided we'd been led up the garden path, so we weren't impressed by his ranting. I'm the only one who knows who was actually running the show, and they don't know I know. They'll be certain we can't give them away. As far as anyone is concerned, we've been creating a game.'

Serina said quietly, 'That's a relief. I've been so worried.'

He hesitated, then asked, 'Forgive me for lying to you?'

'Yes.' She looked him straight in the eye. 'Just don't ever do it again.'

'Promise.' He cheered up. 'And, talking about a video game, guess what? One of the big gaming firms wants to have a look at the idea. Alex thinks we should go into discussion with them; he's given us the name of a very good negotiator and says he'll back us!'

Serina swallowed and said brightly, 'That's wonderful.'

He laughed. 'Well, actually, we now have to come up with a proposition,' he said, 'but that's OK. We always viewed it as a game anyway, so it won't take us long to get something together.'

Serina viewed him with wry relief. It was typical of him to put the bad things behind him and move easily onto the next part of his life.

She'd do that too—although, she thought wearily, Alex had been such a magnificent lover she suspected she'd compare any other man with him in the future.

A wave of revulsion at that thought made her get up and start unpacking. It would take her time to get over him.

She could do it.

That night Serina penned what she intended to be a brief thank you letter to Alex. By the time she'd finished it had turned into several paragraphs. She addressed it and sealed it. Tomorrow she'd post it, and that would be an end to everything.

Serina sat down and opened the magazine. Her first column on New Zealand…

How long ago those weeks seemed now. And how foolish she'd been then, how incredibly naïve. A couple of months after she'd got home, she still longed for Alex. She'd somehow assumed she could be like her father, moving from lover to lover without pain.

Instead, she'd been forced to accept that she was her mother all over again—a one-man woman, unable to cut the bonds of her love and move on. She still dreamed of Alex, still opened her email every morning hoping to see something from him, shuffled through the post each day, still devoured the financial pages eagerly, because every so often there was something about him…

Of course he hadn't contacted her. He was a busy

magnate, head of a huge empire, and he probably had another lover now, someone much less inhibited than she was, someone who knew the rules and wouldn't fall in love with him.

She picked up the magazine and flicked through the pages, her brows shooting up when she caught a feature on Rassel, who appeared to have taken his latest inspiration from space travel. If he thought women were going to wear clothes that made them look fat and ungainly, he was sadly wrong…

Pulling a face, she found her page and settled down to check the photographs and read the copy. Halfway through it, she suddenly realised she was staring at the garden at Haruru.

'No,' she breathed, horrified. Perhaps it was an illusion—like her dreams. If she blinked, it might go away.

But it didn't.

She swallowed and read on. 'Oh, God,' she groaned. Alex's name was there.

Wincing, she recalled taking the photograph—the night they'd made love…

She'd emailed the shots to her editor to make sure they'd reproduce well enough for the magazine, stressing they were not to be used.

How had it happened?

Leaping to her feet, she called the editor. Ten minutes of profuse apologies later, she lowered herself into the chair again and looked once more at the photographs.

'All right,' she said aloud. She was tired of longing uselessly, weary of her own futility. This gave her the chance to contact Alex.

She glanced at her watch, did a mental calculation and relaxed. He'd still be awake—if he was at the homestead.

Cold with apprehension, she dialled the number, only to feel a huge let-down when the housekeeper answered and told her Alex was overseas on a business trip.

'I'm afraid I don't know when he'll be back. Can I get him to ring you when he returns?' she asked politely.

'Thank you,' Serina said, equally politely.

That night she woke in darkness into terror. Hand held over her thudding heart, she couldn't stop shaking. Thick silence enveloped her, pressed down on her chilled skin, froze her.

Slowly, slowly, she turned to face the thing that had hunted her for so long. At first she couldn't see in the darkness around her, but slowly a form coalesced out of it, tall and solid, standing still and watching her.

'Alex,' she breathed in aching supplication.

He said nothing.

She called to him then, frantically trying to break through the cocoon of silence and rejection, and after long moments of silence his lips moved as he said her name.

She heard it in every cell of her body.

He turned away and walked into the darkness. Serina collapsed, sobbing, to her knees, rocking herself back and forward in paroxysms of grief.

Now she understood just what she'd been running from all her life. Herself. The strictures she'd grown up with, the need to be always in control…

Her sexuality.

But, most of all, she'd been fleeing from love.

The shock jolted her fully awake. She was alone in

her own bedroom and she was shivering feverishly, tears burning her eyes.

She should have heeded that dream and avoided love. It hurt so much, so much more than she'd ever imagined it could. At last she understood how her mother had felt with each infidelity, each betrayal of her love for her husband.

Serina pressed her hands to her eyes, wishing she could go back, reclaim her heart, go on with her cool, unemotional life...

And knew she was lying to herself. Whatever the cost, loving Alex was worth it. With him, she'd discovered her own blossoming sexuality, a vividness to life that would fade, but that she'd remember.

She woke the next morning with a headache and during the morning found herself flinching at the noise that poured in from the street. Memories flooded through her of Haruru, fresh and green and fragrant with flower scents, the faint tang of the sea, the clear light...

She felt a longing that was physical, an ache in her heart for the place and the man...

After lunch she'd have a nap, she promised herself as she tidied and cleaned the apartment. Surely that would banish the lingering miasma of the dream.

The doorbell rang. Biting back a sigh, she walked across to the door and opened it.

And there was Alex, tall and dominating and very controlled—except for eyes as cold as a polar winter.

'Oh, dear God,' Serina said, stark fear stopping any logical thought.

'Surely you expected me?' he enquired, all smooth menace. 'Invite me in, Serina.'

She wasn't afraid of him—she was *not*! Stepping back, she held the door open. And she wasn't ashamed of her apartment, either. It was all she could afford, and she'd made it as pleasant as she could.

He didn't even look around. That lethal gaze was fixed on her, sending a shiver scudding the length of her spine.

'No, I didn't expect you,' she told him, aching with love for him. 'I've only just seen the magazine. I'm sorry. It was a mistake.'

'It certainly was.' He paused, then added softly, 'Your mistake.'

It was then that Serina knew she was never going to stop loving this man. *Never.* She'd go to her grave loving him.

And, judging by the look on his face, that could happen sooner rather than later. In spite of his cold anger, the dull heaviness of the past few months lightened, miraculously lifting her spirits. She had to stop herself from devouring his face with loving eyes.

Instead, she asked spiritedly, 'Have you contacted the editor?'

'Of course. She apologised. For about half an hour in a mixture of French and English.' His tone told her he didn't believe in the sincerity of the apology.

'As I do.' She added, 'Alex, it was my fault for sending those first photographs to her. I have no idea how they got into the magazine—and she doesn't seem to know either—but, believe me, neither of us deliberately organised it.'

'You promised me that they wouldn't be used.' He paused, then added, 'And my name is there too.'

'I know,' she said wretchedly. 'I'm so sorry.'

Eyes narrowed, he said abruptly, 'Have you missed me?'

Serina felt her jaw drop. 'What?' she asked so faintly she could barely hear her own voice.

'You heard,' he said determinedly and came towards her, his face dark and set.

Breath blocked in her throat, eyes widening, she couldn't move. He stopped a few inches away from her and looked down with blazing, steel-sheen eyes. 'Because I've missed you,' he said quietly. 'Every day, every minute, every second—as though an essential part of me has been torn away. Damn it, Serina, I've waited over a year for you—and when at last you came to me, it was—sheer joy. Like nothing I've ever experienced. But then you did this.'

Consumed by incredulous joy alloyed by bewilderment, she fixed on the one thing she could process. 'I did not,' she blazed, careless of the fact that she, who never lost control, had finally and completely lost it. 'I don't lie—and if you can't accept my word on this, then—then—'

She stopped as the import of what he'd actually said sank in. 'What do you mean—you've waited a year for me?'

Savagely, he said, 'Waited for you to see me, of course—not as a substitute for Gerd, not as a temporary lover, but the man who—'

He stopped. Serina froze, unable to speak, unable to even mentally articulate a thought. Her whole future depended on the next few moments, she thought dazedly, yet she couldn't speak.

Roughly, his hands clenched at his sides, he said, 'Well, *say* something.'

'What?' she finally managed to choke out.

He seemed to relax. The frozen fire of his eyes warmed and a set smile tugged at the corners of his mouth. 'You could try saying that you missed me.'

She nodded.

Then he laughed and caught her in his arms and kissed her, and suddenly…it was all right.

No, she thought, every fear and inhibition evaporating as his mouth came down on hers, it wasn't just all right; it was marvellously, wonderfully, exhilaratingly *perfect*.

Opening her mouth to his ravenous demand, she melted into Alex's kiss, so completely happy in that moment that she didn't hear the door open behind them, or see Doran stand there, dumbfounded.

However, through the roaring of her impetuous heart in her ears, she did hear her brother say, 'Ah—OK, I think I'd better go out and come in again.'

Alex broke the kiss and said something she was glad she didn't understand. Above her head, he said curtly, 'You have extremely bad timing, Doran. Get the hell out of here.'

Her brother laughed. 'I think I'd better stay and ask you what your intentions are.'

'Doran!' Serina managed in a horrified croak.

'I'm planning to marry her and make her extremely happy. Any objections?'

'Hell, no,' Doran told him cheerfully. 'Right, I'll leave you to it, then. Serina, I'll be back some time tonight.'

Serina tried to tear herself free from Alex's arms, only to find them tightening around her. She looked up into his face and said in a low, furious voice, 'You'd better ask *me* for an answer, not my brother.'

He looked down at her, his eyes gleaming, and said, 'I know what your answer is going to be. You're going to tell me to go to hell, and then you're going to marry me and have my children and love me for the rest of your life—but not as much as I love you.'

Her anger fled, leaving her shaking with such a wild mixture of emotions she had no idea of what to say or how to feel. Dimly, she heard the door close behind Doran.

She looked up and saw something in Alex's eyes she'd never seen there before—a fierce tenderness. Her heart stopped, then started again jerkily and, to her shock and dismay, she felt hot tears start to her own eyes.

'Don't,' he said in an anguished voice. 'My dearest girl, my darling, don't—please, don't cry.'

But she wept until finally she calmed enough to say, 'Why did you wait so long?'

'At first—' He kissed the top of her head and then her forehead. In a voice roughened by emotion he said, 'I waited for a year after Gerd's coronation because I didn't know how you felt about him. If you'd loved him—or even banked on being his wife—'

'I didn't,' she interrupted swiftly. 'Not either of them—in fact, about a month before Rosie erupted into his life, I told him that, although I liked him enormously, I didn't really feel it was a good idea for us to get too closely linked because it wasn't going anywhere!' She lifted her head and scowled at him. 'You could have asked Gerd.'

He said, 'I did. Gerd wouldn't discuss his relationship with you but he did say you'd indicated that you weren't interested in him.'

'So why—'

Alex shrugged. 'I wondered if you'd realised he didn't feel for you what he should, and were driven by pride to call it off. So I decided to give you a year.'

Serina made a small sound of exasperation. 'As for *seeing* you—I did that right from the start. Believe me, Gerd wasn't the only one to fall in love at his coronation ball.'

'You could have given me some indication,' he said tersely.

'Would you have believed me?'

Unusually, he hesitated before admitting with a wry smile, 'I suppose I'm not accustomed to people I love staying around for long; my mother died, my father was rarely there, I really didn't get to know Rosie until I grew up. Some time when I was quite young I must have decided that love meant pain. When it hit me I was—afraid…'

Serina hugged him fiercely. 'I know. That's how I felt too—that terror that loving someone meant being hurt by them. But it made no difference—I loved you from the very first.' She stopped, then said starkly, 'I'll love you until I die.'

His arms tightened around her. 'My dearest Serina.' And kissed her—not with the intense passion of a few minutes previously, but with such gentle tenderness that her heart filled with hope.

Against her brow he said, 'I wish I hadn't waited before coming. I think—I suspect it was the fear that your warmth and charm and love would dissipate with distance and time. When I saw that photograph—and my name—I grabbed at anger, because anger is much safer. I didn't want to come to you as a supplicant. But that's what I am.'

'And you came,' she said, shaken to the core.

'I couldn't stay away.' He said it harshly, as though owning to a weakness, and then again, but this time simply, with a kind of awe. 'I feel—stripped,' he said unevenly. 'Filled with such intense happiness because you love me, yet exposed, as though everything I've based my life on until now has been taken from me, and all I have to offer you is myself.' He gave a sudden mirthless laugh. 'And I feel that's not enough.'

'It's everything,' she told him, her voice trembling, unable to smile in spite of the fierce joy that shone through her, washing away the past weeks of pain and grief and longing in a torrent of delight and peace. 'Alex, I love you so much—it's been misery.'

He held her out a little. 'Would you have come to me?'

She said, 'I was going to ring you tonight to apologise for your garden being used in my column.' This time she managed a smile, one that glimmered with mischief and love and such intensity that Alex felt his heart contract. 'I was going to suggest that somehow we should get together to discuss the situation…'

They were married on the beach outside the bach, with only their family and best friends around them. Alex had managed to fend off the insistent clamour of the media, his influence making sure that none of the helicopters in the country were hired to take photographs of the wedding.

As she dressed in the homestead under Rosie's supervision, Serina felt such joy well in her that she had difficulty holding back the tears.

'Hey, that's enough of that—apart from wrecking your eye make-up, it's friends and family who cry at weddings, not the bride,' Rosie told her briskly and hugged her, careful not to disturb her short, exquisite wedding dress and veil.

She stood back and surveyed her with a slight frown. 'You look—radiant,' she said on a sigh. 'And I'm glad you decided to wear your tiara. Little Nora is going to be ecstatic. It was a lovely thought on your part to ask her to be your flower girl.'

'Alex insisted on replacing the stones with real diamonds,' Serina said.

'Of course he did,' Rosie said practically, and beamed at her. 'It's great to see you both so happy. Alex is going to take one look at you and know he's the luckiest man in the world today. Welcome to the family, Serina.'

It was a radiant day too—a soft winter day with a blue, blue sky and the sea hushing quietly a few feet away. Doran, outrageously handsome in his wedding gear, gave Serina away and together she and Alex stood side by side and pledged their troth.

And later, when everyone had gone, they made love in the bach and then lay in each other's arms and talked quietly.

'Why did you want to have the first night of our honeymoon here?' he asked quietly into her hair.

'Because this is where I found you, and myself too.'

She sighed and hid a tiny yawn against his bare shoulder. 'I'm going to love spending the rest of our honeymoon in your house in Tahiti, but tonight is perfect...'

She no longer cynically supposed that this transcendent joy would fade after a couple of years; she knew now that other emotions—deeper, stronger, more intense as the years went by—would join it, adding to a happiness that seemed almost too great to bear.

With Alex she was completely safe—as safe as he was with her. Together, she thought dreamily, there was nothing they couldn't face down and win.

Smiling, she whispered his name and slid into sleep, secure in the protection of their love.

BEAUTY AND THE BILLIONAIRE

BY
BARBARA DUNLOP

Barbara Dunlop writes romantic stories while curled up in a log cabin in Canada's far north, where bears outnumber people and it snows six months of the year. Fortunately she has a brawny husband and two teenage children to haul firewood and clear the driveway while she sips cocoa and muses about her upcoming chapters. Barbara loves to hear from readers. You can contact her through her website at www.barbaradunlop.com.

Prologue

A one-night stand only lasted one night. Sinclair Mahoney might be far from an expert, but she could guess that much.

So, while Hunter Osland's bare chest rose and fell in his king-size bed, and a door slammed somewhere in the far reaches of the mansion, she pushed her feet into her low-heeled black pumps and shrugged into her pinstriped blazer. She was only guessing at the protocol here, but she suspected it wasn't a lingering goodbye in the cold light of day.

Peacefully asleep in the gleaming four-poster, Hunter had obviously done this before. There were three brand-new toothbrushes in his en suite, along with half a dozen fresh towels and an assortment of mini toiletries in a basket on the marble counter. He had everything a woman needed if she wanted to make a simple, independent exit—which was exactly what Sinclair had in mind.

Last night had been good.

Okay, last night had been incredible. But last night was also over, and there was something pathetic about hanging around this morning hoping to see respect in his eyes.

So, she'd washed her face, brushed her teeth, and pulled her auburn hair into a simple ponytail, glancing one last time at the opulent cherry furnishings, the storm-tossed seascape that hung above his bed, and two potted palms that bracketed a huge bay window. It was nearly 8:00 a.m. She had just enough time to find her twin sister in the maze of the rambling Osland mansion. She'd say a quick goodbye before hopping a taxi to the Manchester, Vermont, airport and her flight to JFK.

She had a planning meeting at noon, then a conference call with the Cosmetics Manager at Bergdorf's. There were also two focus-group reports on Luscious Lavender beauty products tucked in her briefcase.

Last night was last night. It was time to return to her regular life. She squared her shoulders and reached for her purse, her gaze catching Hunter's tanned, toned leg. It had worked its way free from the tangled ivory sheets, and she followed its length to where the sheet was wrapped snugly around his hips.

She cringed at the telltale tightening beneath her ribs. His broad shoulders were also uncovered, along with the muscular arms that had held her tight into the wee hours of the morning. At five foot seven and a hundred and fifteen pounds, she wasn't used to feeling small and delicate in a man's arms. But she had in Hunter's.

In fact, she'd felt a lot of things she hadn't expected for a one-night stand.

Her friends had talked about them. But Sinclair had only imagined them. She always assumed they'd be stilted and awkward, each party self-conscious and trying to impress the

One

Hunter was here.

Six weeks later, Sinclair's stomach clenched around nothing as he strode into the Lush Beauty Products boardroom like he owned the place.

"—in a friendly takeover bid," Sinclair's boss, company president Roger Rawlings, was saying. "Osland International has purchased fifty-one percent of the Lush Beauty Products voting shares."

Sinclair reflexively straightened in her chair. Good grief, he *did* own the place.

Could this be a joke?

She glanced from side to side.

Would cameramen jump out any second and shove a microphone in her face? Were they filming even now to record her reaction?

She waited. But Hunter didn't even look her way, and nobody started laughing.

"As many of you are aware," said Roger, "among their other business interests, Osland International owns the Sierra Sanchez line of women's clothing stores across North America, with several outlets in Europe and Australia."

While Roger spoke, and the Lush Beauty managers absorbed the surprising news, Hunter's gaze moved methodically around the big, oval table. His gaze paused on Ethan from product development, then Colleen from marketing. He nodded at Sandra from accounting, and looked to Mary-Anne from distribution.

As her turn grew near, Sinclair composed her expression. In her role as public relations manager, she was used to behaving professionally under trying circumstances. And she'd do that now. If he could handle this, so could she. They were both adults, obviously. And she could behave as professionally as he could. Still, she had to wonder why he hadn't given her a heads-up.

The Hunter she'd met in Manchester had struck her as honorable. She would have thought he'd at least drop her an e-mail. Or had she totally misjudged him? Was he nothing more than a slick, polished player who forgot women the second they were out of his sight?

Maybe he didn't e-mail because he didn't care. Or, worse yet, maybe he didn't even remember.

In the wash of her uncertainty, Roger's voice droned on. "Sierra Sanchez will offer Lush Beauty Products a built-in, high-end retail outlet from which to launch the new Luscious Lavender line. We'll continue seeking other sales outlets, of course. But that is only one of the many ways this partnership will be productive for both parties."

Hunter's gaze hit Sinclair.

He froze for a split second. Then his nostrils flared, and his eyebrows shot up. She could swear a current cracked audibly between them. It blanketed her skin, shimmied down her nervous system, then pooled to a steady hum in the pit of her stomach.

Hunter's jaw tightened around his own obvious shock.

Okay. So maybe there was a reason he hadn't given her a heads-up.

There were days when Hunter Osland hated his grandfather's warped sense of humor. And today ranked right up there.

In the instant he saw Sinclair, the last six weeks suddenly made sense—Cleveland's insistence they buy Lush Beauty Products, his demand that Hunter take over as CEO, and his rush to get Hunter in front of the company managers. Cleveland had known she worked here, and he'd somehow figured out Hunter had slept with her.

Hunter's grandfather was, quite literally, forcing him to face the consequences of his actions.

"So please join me in welcoming Mr. Osland to Lush Beauty Products," Roger finished to a polite round of applause. The managers seemed wary, as anyone would be when the corporate leadership suddenly shifted above them.

It was Hunter's job to reassure them. And he now had the additional duty of explaining himself to Sinclair. God only knew what she was thinking. But, talking to her would have to wait. He refocused his gaze on the room in general and moved to the head of the table.

"Thank you very much," he began, smoothly taking control of the meeting, like he'd done at a thousand meetings before. "First, you should all feel free to call me Hunter. Second, I'd like to assure you up front that Osland International has no plans to make staffing changes, nor to change the current direction of Lush Beauty Products."

He'd mentally rehearsed this next part, although he now knew it was a lie. "My grandfather made the decision to invest in this company because he was excited about your product redevelopment—such as the Luscious Lavender line—and about your plans to expand the company's target demographic."

Hunter now doubted Cleveland had even heard of Lush Beauty Products before meeting Sinclair. And Cleveland would be a lot less excited about the product redevelopment than he was about yanking Hunter's chain.

"Osland International has analyzed your success within the North American midprice market," Hunter told the group. "And we believe there are a number of opportunities to go upscale and international. We're open to your ideas. And, although Roger will continue to manage day-to-day operations, I'll be hands-on with strategic direction. So I want to invite each of you to stop by and see me. I expect to be on site several days a month, and I believe I'll have an office on the twentieth floor?"

He looked to Roger for confirmation.

"Yes," said Roger. "But if any of you have questions or concerns, you should feel free to use me as a sounding board."

The words surprised Hunter. Was Roger telling them not to go directly to Hunter?

"We'll try to make this transition as smooth as possible," Roger continued in a silky voice that set Hunter's teeth on edge. "But we understand some of you may feel challenged and unsettled."

Oh, great little pep talk. Thanks for that, Roger.

"There's no need for anyone to feel unsettled," Hunter cut

in. "As far as I'm concerned, it's business as usual. And my door is always open." Then he looked directly at Sinclair. "Come and see me."

An hour later, Sinclair took Hunter up on his invitation. On the twentieth floor, she propped herself against the doorjamb of his airy corner office. "This," she said, taking in the big desk, the credenza piled with books and the meeting table that sat eight, "I have *got* to hear."

He straightened in his high-backed chair and glanced up from his laptop, a flash of guilt in his eyes.

Ignoring the way her heart lifted at his reaction, she took two steps inside and closed the door behind her. He cared that he'd blindsided her. At least that was something.

Not that she cared about him in any fundamental way. She couldn't. They were a brief flash of history, and nothing more.

"It was Gramps," answered Hunter. "He bought the company and sent me here to run it."

"And you didn't know about me?" she guessed.

"I didn't know," he confirmed.

"So, you're not stalking me?"

He hit a key on his computer. "Right. Like any reasonable stalker, I bought your company to get close to you."

She shrugged. "Could happen."

"Well, it didn't. This is Gramps' idea of a joke. I think he knows I slept with you," said Hunter.

"Then there's something wrong with that man." And there was something frightening about a person with enough economic power to buy a four-hundred-person company as a joke. There was something even more frightening about a person who took the trouble to actually do it.

"I think he's losing it in his old age." Then Hunter paused

for a moment to consider. "On the other hand, he was always crotchety and controlling."

"Kristy likes him," said Sinclair. Not that she was coming down on Cleveland Osland's side. If Hunter was right, the man was seriously nuts.

"That's because he's batty over your sister."

Sinclair supposed that was probably true. It was Cleveland Osland who had helped Kristy get started in the fashion business last month. And now her career was soaring.

A soaring career was what Sinclair wanted for herself. And what she really wanted was for Hunter not to be a complication in that. She had a huge opportunity here with the planned company expansion and with the development of the new Luscious Lavender line.

She advanced on his wide desk to make her point, forcing herself to ignore the persistent sexual tug that had settled in her abdomen. Whatever they'd had for that brief moment had ended. He was her past, now her boss.

Even if he might be willing to rekindle. And she had no reason to assume he was willing. She was not.

She dropped into one of his guest chairs, keeping her tone light and unconcerned. "So what do we do now?"

A wolfish grin grew on his face.

All right, so maybe there was a reason to assume he was willing.

"No," she said, in a stern voice.

"I didn't say a word."

"You thought it. And the answer is no."

"You're a cold woman."

"I'm an intelligent woman. I'm not about to sleep my way to the top."

"There's a lot to be said for being at the top."

"I guess you would know."

He leaned back in his chair, expression turning mischievous. "Yeah. I guess I would."

She ignored the little-boy charm and leaned forward to prop her elbows on his desk. "Okay, let's talk about how this works."

"I thought we'd pretty much demonstrated how it worked last month."

She wished he'd stop flirting. It was ridiculously tempting to engage. Their verbal foreplay that night had been almost as exciting as the physical stuff.

"Nobody here knows about us," she began, keeping her tone even.

"I know about us," he pointed out.

"But you're going to forget it."

"Not likely," he scoffed.

She leaned farther forward, getting up into his face. "Listen carefully, Hunter. For the purposes of our professional relationship, you are going to forget that you've seen me naked."

"You know, you're very cute when you're angry."

"That's the lamest line I've ever heard."

"No, it's not."

"Can you be serious for a second?"

"What makes you think I'm not serious?"

"Hunter."

"Lighten up, Sinclair."

Lighten up? That was his answer?

But she drew back to think about it. Could it be that simple? "Am I making too much of this?"

He shrugged. "I'm not about to announce anything in the company newsletter. So, unless you spread the word around the water cooler, I think we're good."

She eyed him up. "That's it? Business as usual?"

"Gramps may have bought Lush Beauty Products for his own bizarre reasons. But I'm here to run it, nothing more, nothing less. And you have a job to do."

She came to her feet and gave a sharp nod, telling herself she was relieved, not disappointed, that it would be easy for him to ignore their past.

"See you around the water cooler, I guess," she said in parting.

"Sure," Hunter responded. "Whatever."

Despite the casual goodbye, Hunter knew it would be hell trying to dismiss what they'd shared. As the office door closed behind her, he squeezed his eyes shut and raked a hand through his hair. Their past might have been short, but it was about as memorable as a past could get.

For the thousandth time, he saw Sinclair in the Manchester mansion. She was curled in a leather armchair, beneath the Christmas tree, next to the crackling fireplace. He remembered thinking in that moment that she was about as beautiful as a woman could get. He'd always had a thing for redheads.

When he was sixteen years old, some insane old gypsy had predicted he'd marry a redhead. Hunter wasn't sure if it was the power of suggestion or a lucky guess, but redheads were definitely his dates of choice.

The flames from the fire had reflected around Sinclair, highlighting her rosy cheeks and her bright blue eyes. Her shoulder-length hair flowed in soft waves, teasing and tantalizing him. He'd already discovered she was smart and classy, with a sharp wit that made him want to spar with her for hours on end.

So he'd bided his time. Waiting for the rest of the family to head for bed, hoping against hope that she'd stay up late.

She had.

And then they were alone. And he had been about to make a move. She was his cousin's new sister-in-law, and he knew their paths might cross again at some point. But he couldn't bring himself to worry about the future. There was something intense brewing, and he owed it to both of them to find out what it was.

He came to his feet, watching her closely as he crossed the great room. Her blue eyes went from laughing sapphires to an intense ocean storm and, before he even reached her chair, he knew she was with him.

He stopped in front of her, bracing a hand on either arm of the chair, leaning over to trap her in place. She didn't flinch but watched him with open interest.

He liked that.

Hell, he loved that.

"Hey," he rasped, a wealth of meaning in his tone and posture.

"Hey," she responded, voice husky, pupils dilated.

He touched his index finger to her chin, tipping it up ever so slightly.

She didn't pull away, so he bent his head, forcing himself to go slow, giving her plenty of time to shut him down. He could smell her skin, feel the heat of her breath, taste the sweet explosion of her lips under his.

His free hand curled to a fist as he steeled himself to keep the kiss gentle. He fought an almost overwhelming urge to open wide, to meet her tongue, to let the passion roar to life between them.

Instead, he drew back, though he was almost shaking with the effort.

"Stop?" he rasped, needing a definite answer, and needing it *right now.*

"Go," she replied, and his world pitched sideways.

self-reliant princess whose only betraying feature was a mouth slightly more full than it had been yesterday.

She hoped the mask hid the turmoil inside her. Making love with Alex had been heart-shakingly wonderful, so why on earth was she nervous at the thought of seeing him again?

Her pulse jumped wildly when a door down the corridor opened and he strode out. His frown dissipated a little when he saw her, but she sensed that wall of inherent reserve implacably back in place.

Her mouth dried. He looked no different. A cynical voice inside her head asked, *Why would he? He's not in love*.

'You should have woken me,' she said, colouring when she realised the implications of her words. Rapidly, she added, 'I didn't intend to sleep in.'

Although he smiled, his eyes were watchful. 'You needed it.' He dropped a swift, almost impersonal kiss on her cheek.

Serina had to stop herself from reaching up to him.

When he straightened his eyes were narrowed and intent and he said softly, 'Another morning I'll enjoy waking you, but this time I thought it best to let you sleep. Now you're up, come and have some breakfast.'

Fighting back a niggling disappointment, Serina went with him. What had she expected him to do? Sweep her into his arms and kiss her passionately there in the corridor, where the housekeeper might walk past at any minute?

Not Alex's style, she thought with a secret grimace, and not hers either.

But some slightly more significant acknowledge-

"Right," he agreed from between clenched teeth.

"I have something I'd like to discuss with you."

At the moment, he had something he wished he could discuss with her, too.

"Fire way," he said instead.

She took up the guest chair again and crossed her legs. Her makeup was minimal, but she didn't need it. She had a healthy peaches-and-cream glow, accented by the brightest blue eyes he'd ever seen. Sunlight from the floor-to-ceiling bay window sparkled on her hair. It reminded him of the firelight, and he curled his hands into new fists.

"I have this idea."

He ordered himself to leave that opening alone.

"Roger's been reluctant to support it," she continued.

She wanted Hunter to intervene?

Sure. Easy. No problem.

"Let's hear it," he said.

"It's about the ball."

Hunter had just read about the Lush Beauty Products' Valentine's Ball. They were going to use it to launch the Luscious Lavender line. It was a decent idea as publicity went. Women loved Valentine's Day, and the Luscious Lavender line was all about glamming up and looking your best.

"Shoot," he told her.

"I've taken the lead in planning the ball," she explained, wriggling forward, drawing his attention to the pale tank top. "And I've been thinking we should go with something bigger."

"A bigger ball?" He dragged his attention back to her face. They'd rented the ballroom at the Roosevelt Hotel. It didn't get much bigger than that.

Sinclair shook her head. "Not a bigger ball. A bigger product launch. Something more than a ball. The ball is fine.

It's great. But it's not…" Her lips compressed and her eyes squinted down. "Enough."

"Tell me what you had in mind," he prompted, curious about how she conducted business. He'd been struck by her intelligence in Manchester. It would be interesting to deal with her in a new forum.

"What I was thinking…" She paused as if gathering her thoughts. "Is to launch Luscious Lavender at a luxury spa. In addition to the ball." Her voice sped up with her enthusiasm. "We're going after the high-end market. And where do rich women get their hair done? Where do they get their facials? Their body wraps? Their waxing?"

"At the spa?" asked Hunter, trying very, very hard not to think about Sinclair and waxing.

She sat back, pointed a finger in his direction, a flush of excitement on her face. "Exactly."

"That's not bad," he admitted. It was a very good idea. He liked that it was unique, and it would probably prove effective. "What's Roger's objection?"

"He didn't tell me his objection. He just said no."

"Really?" Hunter didn't care for autocracy and secrecy as managerial styles. "What would you like me to do?"

Whatever it was, he'd do it in a heartbeat. And not because of their history. He'd do it because it was a good idea, and he appreciated her intelligence and creativity. Roger better have a damn good reason for turning her down.

"If you can clear it with Roger—"

"Oh, I can clear it with Roger."

Her teeth came down on her bottom lip, and a hesitation flashed through her eyes. "You agreed awfully fast."

"I'm agile and decisive. Got a problem with that?"

"As long as…" Guilt flashed in her eyes.

"I'm reacting to your idea, Sinclair. Not to your body."

"You sure?"

"Of course, I'm sure." He was. Definitely.

"I was going to approach New York Millennium." She named a popular spa in the heart of Manhattan.

"That sounds like a good bet. You need anything else?"

She shook her head, rising to her feet. "Roger was my only roadblock."

Two

"Obviously," Roger said to Sinclair, with exaggerated patience. "I can't turn down the CEO."

She nodded where she sat in a guest chair in his office, squelching the lingering guilt that she might have used her relationship with Hunter as leverage. She admitted she'd been counting on Roger having to say yes to Hunter.

But she consoled herself in being absolutely positive the spa launch was a worthwhile idea. Also, Roger had been strangely contrary lately, shooting down her recommendations left and right. It was all but impossible to do her job the way he'd been micromanaging her. Going to Hunter had been her option of last resort.

Besides, Hunter had invited all the employees to run ideas past him. She wasn't taking any special privilege.

"I'm not holding out a lot of hope of you securing the Millennium," warned Roger.

Sinclair was more optimistic. "It would be good for them, too. They'd have the advantage of all our advance publicity."

Roger came to his feet. "I'd like you to take Chantal with you."

Sinclair blinked as she stood. "What?"

"I'd appreciate her perspective."

"On…" Sinclair searched for the logic in the request.

Chantal was a junior marketing assistant. In her two years with the company, she'd mostly been involved in administrative work such as ad placement and monitoring the free-sample program.

"She has a good eye," said Roger, walking Sinclair toward the door.

A good eye for what?

"And I'd like her to broaden her experience," he finished.

It was on the tip of Sinclair's tongue to argue, but she had her yes, so it was time for a strategic retreat. She'd figure out the Chantal angle on her own.

Her first thought was that Roger might be grooming the woman for a public relations position. Sinclair had been lobbying to get an additional PR officer in her department for months now, but she had her own assistant, Amber, in mind for the promotion, and Keely in reception in mind for Amber's job.

"Keep me informed," insisted Roger.

"Sure," said Sinclair, leaving his office to cross the executive lobby. First she'd set up a meeting at the Millennium, then she'd sleuth around about Chantal.

Three days later, Sinclair lost the Millennium Spa as a possibility. The President liked Lush's new samples, but he claimed using them over the launch weekend would put him in a conflict with his regular beauty products supplier.

She'd been hoping the spa would switch to Luscious

Lavender items on a permanent basis following the launch. But when she mentioned that to the spa President, he laughed and all but patted her on the head over her naiveté. Supply contracts, he told her, didn't work that way.

Chantal had shot Sinclair a smug look and joined in the laughter, earning a benevolent smile from the man along with Sinclair's irritation.

Then the next day, at a pre-Valentine's event at Bergdorf's on Fifth Avenue, Chantal earned Sinclair's irritation all over again.

It was twelve days before Valentine's Day and the main ball and product launch. Sinclair had worked for months preparing for both events.

For Bergdorf's, she'd secured special space in the cosmetics department, hired top-line professional beauticians, and had placed ads in *Cosmopolitan, Elle* and *Glamour.* She'd even talked Roger into an electronic billboard in Times Square promoting the event. Her spa plan might have fallen flat, but she knew if they could get the right clientele into Bergdorf's today for free samples and makeovers, word of mouth would begin to spread in advance of the ball.

The event should have come off without a hitch.

But at the last minute Roger had inserted Chantal into the mix, displacing one of the beauticians and making the lineups unnecessarily long. Amber, who had already heard about Chantal's appearance at the spa meeting, was obviously upset by this latest turn of events. Sinclair didn't need her loyal employee feeling uncertain about her future.

The result had been a long day. And as the clock wound toward closing time, Sinclair was losing energy. She did her hourly inventory of the seven makeover stations, noting any dwindling supplies on her clipboard. Then she handed the list to Amber, who had the key to the stockroom and was in charge of replenishing.

She reminded the caterers to do another pass along the lineup, offering complimentary champagne and canapés to those customers who were still waiting. The cash register lineup concerned her, so she called the store manager on her cell, asking about opening another till.

The mirrors on stations three and six needed a polish, so she signaled a cleaner. In the meantime, she learned they were almost out of number five brushes and made a quick call to Amber in the back.

"How's it going?" Hunter's voice rumbled from behind her.

She couldn't help but smile at the sound, even as she reflexively tamped down a little rush of pleasure. They hadn't spoken in a few days and, whether she wanted to or not, she'd missed him. She twisted to face him, meeting his eyes and feeling her energy return.

"Controlled chaos," she mouthed.

"At least it's controlled." He moved in beside her.

"How are things up on the executive floor?" she asked.

"Interesting. Ethan gave me a tour of the factory." Hunter made a show of sniffing the back of his hand. "I think I still smell like a girl."

"Lavender's a lovely scent," said Sinclair, wrinkling her nose in his direction. She didn't detect lavender, just Hunter, and it was strangely familiar.

"I prefer spice or musk."

"Is your masculinity at stake?"

"I may have to pump some iron later just to even things up."

"Are you a body builder?"

Even under a suit, Hunter was clearly fit.

"A few free weights," he answered. "You?"

"Uh, no. I'm more of a yoga girl."

"Yoga's good."

"Keeps me limber."

"Okay, not touching that one."

"You're incorrigible."

"My grandfather would agree with you on that point."

A new cashier arrived, opening up the other till, and the lineup split into two. Sinclair breathed a sigh of relief. One problem handled.

Then she heard Chantal's laughter above the din and glanced at the tall blonde, who wore a cotton-candy-pink poof-skirted minidress and a pair of four-inch gold heels. She was laughing with some of the customers, her bright lips and impossibly thick eyelashes giving her the air of a glamorous movie star.

With Hunter here, Sinclair felt an unexpected pang of self-consciousness at the contrast between her and Chantal. Quickly, though, she reminded herself that her two-piece taupe suit and matching pumps were appropriate and professional. She also reminded herself that she'd never aspired to be a squealing, air-kissing bombshell.

She tucked her straight, sensibly cut hair behind her ears.

"So what happened at the spa?" asked Hunter.

"Unfortunately, it was a no go."

"Really?" He frowned with concern. "What was the problem?"

"Some kind of conflict with their supplier."

"Did you—"

"Sorry. Can you hang on?" she asked him, noticing a disagreement brewing between the new cashier and a customer. She quickly left Hunter and moved to step in.

It turned out the customer had been quoted a wrong price

by her beautician. Sinclair quickly honored the quote and threw in an extra tube of lipstick.

When she looked back, Chantal had crossed the floor. She was laughing with Hunter, a long-fingered, sparkly-tipped hand lightly touching his shoulder for emphasis about something.

He didn't seem the least bit disturbed by the touch, and an unwelcome spike of annoyance hit Sinclair. It wasn't jealousy, she quickly assured herself. It was the fact that Chantal was ignoring the customers to flirt with the CEO.

Sinclair made her way along the counter.

"Chantal," she greeted, putting a note of censure in her voice and her expression.

"I was just talking to Hunter about the new mousse," Chantal trilled. Then she fluffed her hair. "It works miracles."

Sinclair compressed her lips.

In response, Chantal's gaze took in Sinclair's plain hairstyle. "You should…" She frowned. "Uh…have you *tried* it?"

Hunter inclined his head toward Sinclair. He seemed to be waiting for her answer.

"No," Sinclair admitted. She hadn't tired the new mousse. Like she had time for the Luscious Lavender treatment every morning. She started work at seven-thirty after a streamlined regime that rarely included a hairdryer.

"Oh." Chantal pouted prettily.

Sinclair nodded to a pair of customers lingering around Chantal's sample station. "I believe those two ladies need some help."

Chantal giggled and moved away.

"Nice," said Hunter after she left.

"That better have been sarcasm."

All men considered Chantal beautiful, but Sinclair would

have been disappointed in Hunter if he hadn't been able to see past her looks.

"Of course it was sarcasm." But his eyes lingered on the woman.

Sinclair elbowed him in the ribs.

"What?"

"I can tell what you're thinking."

"No, you can't."

"Yes, I can."

"What am I thinking?"

"That her breasts are large, her skirt is short, and her legs go all the way to the ground."

Hunter coughed out a laugh.

"See?" blurted Sinclair in triumph.

"You're out of your mind."

"The doors are closing," murmured Sinclair, more to herself than to Hunter, as she noticed the security guards stop incoming customers and open the doors for those who were exiting.

"You got a few minutes to talk?" he asked.

"Sure." Hunter was the CEO. She was ready to talk business at his convenience.

She nodded to two empty chairs across the room.

They moved to the quiet corner of the department, and Sinclair climbed into one of the high leather swivel chairs. She parked her clipboard on the glass counter.

Hunter eased up beside her. "So what's the plan now?"

She glanced around the big room. "The cleaning staff will be here at six. Amber will make sure the leftover samples are returned to the warehouse. And I'll write a report in the morning." Later tonight, she was going to start painting her new apartment, but she didn't think Hunter needed that kind of information.

His gray eyes sparkled with merriment. "I meant your plan about the spa."

"Oh, that." She waved a hand. "It's dead. We couldn't make a deal with the Millennium."

Her gaze unexpectedly caught Chantal. The woman was eyeing them up from across the room, tossing her glittering mane over one shoulder and licking her red lips.

Under the guise of more easily conversing, Sinclair scooted a little closer to Hunter. Let miss Barbie-doll chew on that.

Hunter slanted a look toward Chantal, then shot Sinclair a knowing grin.

"Shut up," she warned in an undertone.

"I never said a word."

"You were thinking it."

"Yeah. And I was right, too."

Yeah, he was. "It's something Pavlovian," she offered.

His grin widened.

"I didn't want her to think Luscious Lavender mousse trumps brains, that's all."

"It doesn't."

"I don't even use mousse. It's nothing against Luscious Lavender. It's a personal choice."

"Okay," said Hunter.

"Kristy has always been the glitter and glam twin. I'm—"

"Don't you dare say plain Jane."

"I was going to say professional Jane."

He snorted. "You don't need a label. And you shouldn't use Kristy as a frame of reference."

"What? You don't compare yourself to Jack?"

"I don't." But his expression revealed a sense of discomfort.

"What?" she prompted.

"Gramps does."

Sinclair could well imagine. "And who comes out on top?"

Hunter raised an eyebrow. "Who do you think?"

"I don't know," she replied honestly. Jack seemed like a great guy. But then so did Hunter. They were both smart, handsome, capable and hard-working.

"Jack's dependable," said Hunter. "He's patient and methodical. He doesn't make mistakes."

Sinclair found herself leaning even closer, the noise of the store dimming around them as the last of the customers made their way out the door. "And you are?"

"Reckless and impulsive."

"Why do I hear Cleveland's voice when you say that?"

Hunter chuckled. "It's usually accompanied by a cuff upside the head."

In the silence that followed, Sinclair resisted an urge to take his hand. "That's sad," she told him.

"That's Gramps. He's a hard-ass from way back." Then Hunter did a double take of her staring. "Don't look at me like that."

She swallowed. "I'm sorry."

"It makes me want to kiss you," he muttered.

"Don't you—"

"I'm not going to kiss you." He glanced back to Chantal. "*That* would definitely make the company newsletter." He focused on Sinclair again. "But you can't stop me from wanting to."

And she couldn't stop herself from wanting to kiss him back. And it didn't seem to matter what she did to try and get rid of the urge, it just grew worse.

"What can we do about this?" She was honestly looking for help. If the feelings didn't disappear, they were going to trip up sooner or later.

Hunter rose to his feet.

"For now, I'm walking out the door. Chantal is already wondering what we're talking about."

Sinclair shook herself and rose with him. "Check." If they weren't together, they couldn't give in to anything.

"But later, I need to talk to you."

She opened her mouth to protest. Later didn't sound like a smart move to her at all.

"About the spa," he clarified. "Business. I promise. What are you doing tonight?"

"Painting my apartment."

"Really?" He drew back. "That's what you do on Saturday night?"

Yeah, that was what she did on Saturday night. She rattled on, trying not to seem pathetic. "I just bought the place. A great little loft in Soho. But the colors are dark and the floor needs stripping, and the mortgage is so high I can't afford to pay someone to do it for me."

"You want a raise?"

"I want a guy with sandpaper and a paint roller."

"You got it."

"Hunter—"

"Give me your address. We can talk while we paint."

Her and Hunter alone in her apartment? "I don't think—"

"I'll be wearing a smock and a paper cap. Trust me, you'll be able to keep your hands off."

"Nothing wrong with your ego."

He grunted. "I know you can't resist me under normal circumstances."

"Ha!" The gauntlet thrown down, she'd resist him or die trying.

Now that she thought about it, maybe painting together

wasn't such a bad idea. Hunter's family had bought the company. He was a permanent part of Lush Beauty Products, and the sooner they got over this inconvenient hump, the better. In fact, it was probably easier if they smoothed out the rough spots away from Chantal's and other people's prying eyes.

"Seventy-seven Mercy Street," she told him with a nod. "Suite 702."

"I'll be there."

On his way to Sinclair's house, Hunter stopped in at the office. He was pretty sure Ethan Sloan would still be around. By all accounts, Ethan was a workaholic and a genius. He'd been with Lush Beauty Products for fifteen years, practically since the doors opened with a staff of twenty and a single store.

He had developed perfumes, hair products, skin products and makeup. The man had a knack for anticipating trends, moving from floral to fruit to organic. In his late thirties now, he'd wisely set his sights on fine quality, recognizing a growing segment of the population with a high disposable income and a penchant for self-indulgence.

Hunter was also willing to bet Ethan had a knack for management and the underlying politics of the company. And Hunter had some questions about that.

He found Ethan in his office, on the phone, but the man quickly motioned to Hunter to sit down.

"By Thursday?" Ethan was saying as Hunter took a seat and slipped open the button on his suit jacket.

Ethan was neatly trimmed. Hunter had noticed that he generally wore his shirtsleeves rolled up, although he'd wear a jacket on the executive floor. Smart man.

"Great," said Ethan, nodding. "Sign 'em up. Talk to you then."

He hung up the phone. "New supplier for lavender," he explained to Hunter. "Out of British Columbia."

"We're running short?"

"Critically. And it's our key ingredient." He rubbed his hands together. "But it's solved now. What can I do for you?"

Hunter settled back in his chair. "Not to put you on the spot. And way off the record."

Ethan smiled. He brought his palms down on the desktop, standing to walk around its end and close the office door. "Gotta say." He returned, taking the second guest chair instead of sitting behind his desk. "I love conversations that start out like this."

Hunter smiled in return. "Tell me if I'm out of line."

"We're off the record," said Ethan. "You can get out of line."

"What do you think of Chantal Charbonnet?"

Ethan sat back. "Sly, but not brilliant. Gorgeous, of course. Roger seems to have noticed her."

"She was at the Bergdorf's promotion this afternoon."

"Yeah?" asked Ethan. "That's a stretch for her job description."

"It got me wondering," confided Hunter. "Why was she there?"

"Eye candy?"

"Women were the target demographic." Hunter had been thinking about this all the way over.

"Maybe she asked Roger really, really nicely?"

Hunter had considered that, too. But he didn't have evidence to support favoritism. He was coming at this from another angle. "Could she have been a role model for the consumers?"

Ethan considered the idea. "There's no denying she knows how to wear our products."

"Lays it on a bit thick, wouldn't you say?"

Ethan grinned. "My kind of consumer. We want them all to apply it like Chantal."

Ethan's words validated the worry that was niggling at Hunter's brain. Chantal was dead center on the new target demographic. Hunter was worried that Roger had seen that in her, and it wasn't something he'd seen in Sinclair. Sinclair was a lot of things—a lot of very fabulous, fun, exciting things—but she wasn't a poster child for Lush Beauty Products.

He filed away the information and switched gears. "Did Sinclair mention her spa plan to you?"

Ethan nodded. "Had lots of potential. But I hear it went south with Millennium."

"I'm going to try to revive it."

"I hope you can. If you secure the outlet, we can provide the product."

"Including lavender."

"Got it covered."

"Do you have any thoughts on a spa release overall?"

Ethan stretched out his legs, obviously speculating how frank he could be with Hunter.

Hunter waited. He wanted frank, but there was no way to insist on it.

"If it was me," said Ethan. "I wouldn't target a single spa, I'd go for the whole chain. And I'd try for the Crystal. The Millennium is nice, but the Crystal has the best overseas locations."

Hunter didn't disagree with Ethan's assessment. The Crystal Spa chain was as top of the line as they came.

"You get into Rome and Paris," said Ethan. "At that level. You'll really have some momentum."

"Tall order."

Ethan brought his hands down on his thighs. "Osland International usually shy away from a challenge?"

"Nope," said Hunter. When he was involved, Osland International always stepped up to the plate.

He could already feel his competitive instincts kick in. Although he'd come into the job reluctantly, making Lush Beauty a runaway success had inched its way to the top of his priority list.

He also knew he wanted Sinclair as a partner in this. He liked the way she thought. He liked her energy and her outside-the-box thinking. And, well, okay, and he just plain liked her. But there was nothing wrong with that. Liking your business associates was important.

All his best business relationships were based on mutual respect. Sure, maybe he didn't want to sleep with his other business associates. But the principle was the same.

Sinclair hit the buzzer, letting Hunter into the building.

She didn't know whether she'd been brilliant or stupid to take him up on his offer to paint, but there was no turning back now.

She'd dressed in a pair of old torn blue jeans and a grainy gray T-shirt with "Stolen From the New York City Police Department" emblazoned across the front. Her hair was braided tight against her head, and she'd popped a white painter's cap on her head. She had no worries that the tone of the evening would be sexy in any way.

The bell rang, echoing through the high-ceilinged, empty room. Her living room furniture was in storage for another week. But she'd already finished the small bedroom, so it was back together.

She opened the front door and the hinges groaned loudly in the cavernous space as Hunter walked in.

"Nice," he said, looking around at the tarp-draped counters and breakfast bar, the plastic on the floors, and the dangling pieces of masking tape around the bay window.

"It has a lot of potential," she told him, closing and locking the oak door. There was no doubt it was smaller than he'd be used to, but she was excited about living here.

"I wasn't being sarcastic, honest." He held up a bottle of wine. "Housewarming."

"That might be a bit premature." She still had a lot of work to get done.

He glanced around the room for somewhere to set the bottle down. "In a cupboard?" he asked, heading for the alcove kitchen.

"Beside the fridge," she called.

He got rid of the wine and shrugged out of his windbreaker. Then he returned to the main room in a pair of khakis and a white T-shirt that were obviously brand-new.

She tried not to smile at the outfit.

It really was nice of him to come and help. Still, she wasn't about to pass up an opportunity to tease him.

"You don't do home maintenance often, do you?"

He glanced around the tarp-draped room. "I've seen it done on TV."

"It's not as easy as it looks," she warned.

He shot her an expression of mock disbelief. "I have an MBA from Harvard."

"And they covered house painting in graduate school?"

"They covered macroeconomics and global capitalism."

She fought a grin. "Oh sure, go ahead and get snooty on me."

"Dip the brush and stroke it on the wall. Am I close?"

"I guess you might as well give it a try."

"Give it a *try?*"

Her grin broadened at his insulted tone.

He bent over and pried open a paint can. "You might want to shift your attitude. I'm free labor, baby."

"Am I getting what I paid for?"

"Sassy," he said, and her heart tripped a beat.

"You need to shake it," she told him, battling the sensual memory. He'd called her sassy in Manchester. In a way that said he wanted her bad.

"Shake it?" he interrupted her thoughts.

She swallowed. "You need to shake the paint before you open the can."

He raised his brow as he crouched to tap the lid back down. "You're enjoying this, aren't you?"

"You bet. Nothing like keeping the billionaire humble."

"Don't stereotype. I'm always humble."

"Yeah. I noticed that right off, Mr. Macroeconomics and Global Capitalism."

"Well, what did you take in college?"

She hesitated for a second then admitted it. "MBA. Yale."

"So, *you* took macroeconomics and global capitalism?"

"Magna cum laude," she said with a hoity toss of her head.

"Yet you can still paint. Imagine that."

She glanced at him for a moment, trying to figure out why he hadn't escalated the joke by teasing her about the designation. Then it hit her. "You got summa, at least, didn't you?"

He didn't answer.

"Geek," she said.

He grinned as he shook the paint. Then he poured it into the tray.

She broke out the brushes, and he quickly caught on to

using the long-handled roller. Sinclair cut in the corners, and together they worked their way down the longest wall.

"What do you think of the Crystal Spa chain?" he asked as his roller swished up and down in long strokes.

"I've never been there," said Sinclair from the top of the step ladder. This close to the ceiling lights, she was starting to sweat. She finally gave in and peeled off her cap.

Wisps of strands had come loose from her braid. Probably she'd end up with cream-colored specks in her hair. Whatever. They were painting her walls, not dancing in a ballroom.

"You want to try it?"

She paused at the end of her stroke, glancing down at him. Was he talking about the Crystal Spa? "Try what?"

"I was thinking, we shouldn't let the Millennium's refusal stop us. We should consider other spas."

Was he serious? More importantly, why hadn't she thought of that?

She felt a shimmer of excitement. Maybe her spa idea wasn't dead, after all. And the New York-based Crystal Spa chain would be an even better choice than the Millennium.

She'd learned from the Millennium experience. She'd make sure she was even better prepared for a pitch to the Crystal.

"Can I try out the Crystal on my expense account?" she asked with a teasing lilt.

"Of course."

Scoffing her dismissal, she went back to painting. "Like Roger would ever go for that."

Besides, she didn't have to test out the Crystal Spa to know it was fantastic. Everyone always raved.

"Forget Roger, will you?" urged Hunter. "Here."

She glanced back down.

With the roller hooked under one arm, he pulled out his wallet. Then he tossed a credit card onto her tarp-covered breakfast bar. "Consider this your expense account."

She nearly fell off the ladder. "You can't—"

"I just did."

"But—"

"Shut up." He went back to the paint tray. "I know the spa idea's great. You know the spa idea's great. Let's streamline the research and make it happen."

"You can't pay for my spa treatments."

"Osland International can pay for them. It's my corporate card, and I consider it a perfectly legitimate R & D expense."

Sinclair didn't know what to say to that. Trying out the spa would be great research, but still…

He rolled the next section. "It's not like I can go in there and check out the wax room myself."

She cringed, involuntarily flinching. "Wax room?"

He chuckled at her expression. "Buck up, Sinclair. Take one for the team."

"You take one for the team."

"I've done my part. It's my credit card."

"They're my legs."

"Who said anything about legs?"

She stared at him. He didn't. He wouldn't.

"We were this close!" She made a tiny space with her thumb and index finger. "*This* close to having a totally professional conversation."

"I'm weak," he admitted.

"You're hopeless."

"Yeah. Well. Irrespective of what you get waxed, and whether or not you show me, it's still a good idea."

It was a good idea. And her gaze strayed to his platinum

card sitting on the canvas tarp. Even if he couldn't keep his mind on business, this was not an opportunity she was about to give up. "I'm thinking a facial."

"Whatever you want. I need to know if they can deliver the kind of opportunity we're looking for."

"What if they're locked into a supplier contract like the Millennium?"

Hunter shrugged. "Every business is different. We'll deal with that when and if it happens. Tomorrow good for you?"

She nodded.

With only twelve days until Valentine's Day. There was no time to lose.

Three

The next day, lying on her back in uptown Manhattan's Crystal Spa, a loose silky robe covering her naked body, Sinclair was feeling very relaxed after her facial massage. A smooth, cool mask was drying on her face. Damp pads protected her eyes, and she found herself nearly falling asleep.

"Sinclair?"

She was dreaming of Hunter's voice. That was fine. Dreaming never hurt anybody.

"Sinclair?" the voice came again.

No.

No way.

Hunter was *not* in this room.

Warm hands closed up the wide V of her robe. "No sense playing with fire," he said.

With a groan of surrender, he dropped to one knee, clamping a hand behind her neck, firmly pulling her forward for a real kiss.

There was no hesitation this time. Their tongues met in a clash. She shifted in the chair to mold against him, her breasts plastered against his chest while desire raced like wildfire along his limbs.

Her hair was soft, her breath softer, and her body was pure heaven in his arms.

"I want you," he'd muttered.

"No kidding," she came back.

His chuckle rumbled against her lips. "Sassy."

"You know it," she whispered in the instant before he kissed her all over again.

The kiss went harder and deeper, until he finally had to gasp for air. "Can I take that as a yes?"

"Can I take that as an offer?" she countered.

"You can take it as a promise," he said, and scooped her into his arms.

She placed her hands on his shoulders and burrowed into the crook at his neck. Then her teeth came down gently on his earlobe. Lust shot through him, and he cursed the fact that his bedroom was in a far corner on the third floor.

A knock on his office door snapped him back to reality.

"Yeah?" he barked.

The door cracked open.

It was Sinclair again.

She slipped inside, still stunningly beautiful in that sleek ivory skirt and the matching blazer. Her pale-pink tank top molded to her breasts, and her shapely legs made him long to trail his fingertips up past her hemline.

"Since it's business as usual," she began, perkily, crossing the room, oblivious to his state of discomfort.

"What are you doing here?"

"I need permission to cancel your appointments for this afternoon."

She tried to form words, but they jumbled in her brain and turned into incomprehensive sputters.

"We need to fly to L.A.," Hunter told her matter-of-factly.

"This is a dream, right? You're not really here."

"Oh, I'm really here. But, hold on, are you saying you dream about me?"

"Nightmares. Trust me."

He chuckled. "The only appointment I could get with the president of Crystal Spas was in their head office in L.A. at three today. We have to get going."

She blinked. Why did they need to talk to the president?

"I want to pitch the idea of debuting the whole chain."

Sinclair gave her head a little shake. "Seriously?"

"Yes, seriously."

They were going to debut Luscious Lavender in the entire Crystal chain? That would be a phenomenal feat.

"I could kiss you," she breathed.

"Bad idea. For the obvious reasons." Then he looked her up and down. "Plus, you're kind of…goopy."

She just grinned.

"It's not a done deal yet," he warned.

"But we are going to try."

"We are going to try. Can I cancel your appointments?"

"You got a cell phone?"

He pulled it out of his suit pocket.

She dialed Amber's number.

The whole chain. She could barely believe it. The whole damn chain.

* * *

Hunter was sorry now that he'd even told Sinclair about Crystal Spas. The meeting hadn't gone well, and she was clearly disappointed as she climbed into the jet for the return trip to New York.

"We knew it was a long shot," she said bravely, buckling up across from him.

"I'm sorry."

"It's not your fault. Some people can't make quick decisions."

The whole thing had frustrated the hell out of Hunter.

"At his level, the man had better learn to make quick decisions. He had a chance to get in on the ground floor in this."

"His loss," said Sinclair with conviction.

"They're superior products," replied Hunter.

"Of *course* they're superior products," she agreed.

Hunter did up his own seat belt. "We say emphatically as two people who've never tried them."

She smiled at his joke.

"We should try them," he said.

"I'm not trying the wax."

He chuckled. "I'll try the wax."

"Yeah, right."

"Right here." He pointed to his chest. "I'll be a man about it. You can rip my hair out by the roots if I can massage your neck with the lavender oil."

She stared into his eyes as the jet engines whined to life. "You don't think we'd end up naked within five minutes?"

"I don't think your ripping the hair from my chest would make me want to get naked."

She obviously fought a grin. "Waxing your chest is probably the worst idea I've ever heard."

"But it cheered you up."

She sighed, and some of the humor went out of her eyes. "Crystal Spas would have been perfect."

He reached for her hand. "I know."

The jet jerked to rolling, and he experienced a strong sense of déjà vu. It took him a second to realize it was Kristy, Kristy and Jack on this same airplane. During their emergency landing in Vegas, Jack had held Kristy's hand to comfort her.

Right now, Sinclair's hand felt small in Hunter's, soft and smooth. The kind of hand a man wanted all over his body.

"You want to go see your sister?" he asked.

Sinclair looked startled. "What?"

"She's in Manchester. It's on the way."

"We'd be too late."

She had a point.

"Maybe not," he argued. A visit with Kristy might cheer Sinclair up.

"Thanks for the thought."

Hunter wished he had more to offer than just a thought. But then she smiled her gratitude. Hunter realized that was what mattered.

Business deals would come and go. He'd simply find another way to make Sinclair happy. Even as the thought formed in his mind, he realized it was dangerous. But he ignored the warning flash.

"You don't need to worry about me," she told him. "I'm a big girl. And I still have the ball to plan."

"The ball's going to be fantastic," he enthused. "It'll be the best Valentine's ball anybody ever put on anywhere."

"I hate it when people humor me."

"Then why are you still smiling?"

"Because sometimes you can be very sweet."

"Hold that thought," he teased, and he brought her hand to his lips.

"I'm not going to sleep with you." She retrieved her hand, but the smile grew wider. "But, maybe, if you're very, very good, I might dance with you at the Valentine's ball."

"And maybe if you're very, very good, I might bring you flowers and candy."

"Something to look forward to."

"Isn't it?"

They both stopped talking, and a soft silence settled around the hum of the engines as they taxied toward the runway.

"It's just that we've worked day and night on this product launch," she said, half to herself.

"I can imagine," he responded with a nod.

"All of us," she added. "The Luscious Lavender products are strong. The sales force is ready. And marketing showed me a fantastic television commercial last week. I really want to make sure I do my part."

"You are doing your part." He had no doubt of that. "There's still the ball."

She gave a shrug and tucked her hair behind her ears. "The ball's pretty much ready to go. I know it'll be fine. But I wanted that something extra, that something special from the PR department." Then she sighed. "Maybe it's just ego."

"Contributing to the team is not ego. Taking all the glory is ego."

"Wanting recognition is a form of ego," she countered.

"Wanting recognition for a job well done is human."

Her voice went soft. "Then I guess I don't want to be human."

He watched her for a silent minute, trying to gauge how

deep that admission went. For all her bravado, he sensed an underlying insecurity. What Sinclair presented and who she really was were two different things. She was far more sensitive than she showed.

In the privacy and intimacy of the plane, he voiced a question that had been nagging at him for a while. "Why did you sleep with me?"

She startled and retrieved her hand. Then her shell went back into place. "Why did *you* sleep with me?"

"Because you were funny and smart and beautiful," he said. Then he waited.

"And, because I said yes?" she asked.

He didn't respond to her irreverence. "And because when I held you in my arms, it was where you belonged."

She stayed silent, and he could almost see the war going on inside her head.

"You going to tell me?" he asked.

"It was Christmas," she finally began. "And you were fun, and sexy. And Kristy had just married Jack. And life at your amazing mansion is really very surreal."

She'd buried the truth. He was sure of it.

Kristy had married Jack, and for that brief moment in time, Sinclair had felt abandoned. And there had been Hunter. And she'd clung to him. And that's what it was. He was glad he knew.

Even though he shouldn't, he switched seats so he was beside her. He wanted to be the one she clung to.

She stiffened, watching him warily.

"The steward's only a few feet away," he assured her. "Nothing can happen."

His reassurance seemed to work.

She relaxed, and he took her hand once again.

The cabin lights dimmed, the engines wound out, and the plane accelerated along the runway, pushing them back against their seats. Hunter turned his head to watch her profile, rubbed his thumb against her soft palm and inhaled her perfume, as he captured and held a moment in time.

The next morning, for the first time in her life, Sinclair came late to the office.

Amber jumped up from her desk, looking worried. "What happened?"

"I got home really late," she said as she passed by.

"Roger was down here. He wanted your files on the Valentine's ball."

Sinclair crossed the threshold to her office, dropping her briefcase and purse on her credenza, and picked up a stack of mail on the way to her desk. "Why?"

"So *Chantal* could review them."

"What?" She stared at Amber. "Why would she do that?"

"Because she's queen of the freakin' universe? Is there something I should know, Sinclair? Something pertaining to PR?"

"No." Sinclair set down the mail. "There's nothing for you to worry about." She moved to the door. "Wait here."

"I'm not going anywhere."

"I assume you gave him the files?" Sinclair called over her shoulder.

"I didn't have a choice."

No. She didn't.

When the president asked for the files, you gave up the files. But there was nothing saying you didn't go get them back again. Roger's micromanaging was getting out of hand. So was Chantal's apparent carte blanche in the PR department. Sinclair took a tight breath, pressed the button, and waited as the elevator ascended.

This inserting of Chantal into Sinclair's projects had to stop. You didn't add a new voice ten days before the ball. And you sure didn't empower a neophyte like Chantal on a project of this size and importance.

What was the matter with Roger? Was he trying to sabotage Sinclair's efforts?

Maybe it was due to her frustration over the failure of the spa plan, but Sinclair was feeling exceedingly protective of the ball. It was her one chance for the PR department to shine, and she was determined to do it or die trying.

The doors slid open on twenty, revealing burgundy carpet, soft lighting and cherrywood paneling. Myra, Roger's secretary, looked surprised to see her.

"Did you have an appointment?"

"I need two minutes with Roger."

Myra glanced at Roger's door. "I'm afraid he's—"

The office door opened.

Chantal Charbonnet stepped out, a stack of files tucked under her arm. She was wearing a leather skirt today, with a glittering gold blouse. Her heels were high, her neckline low. She gave Sinclair a disdainful look and passed by with a sniff of her narrow pert nose

"Looks like he's free," said Sinclair.

Myra picked up the phone. "Let me just—"

"I'll only take a second." Sinclair didn't give the woman a chance to stop her.

Before Roger's door could swing shut, she blocked it. "Excuse me, Roger?"

He glanced up, lips compressing, and a furrow forming in the middle of his brow.

"I don't recall a meeting," he said.

"I believe you have my files?"

"Chantal's taking a look at them."

Sinclair struggled hard to keep her voice even. "May I ask why?"

"I've asked her to provide her opinion."

"On?"

"On the Valentine's ball preparation. She's taking a bigger role in the new product launch. I think we all recognize Chantal's talents."

Well, Sinclair sure didn't recognize Chantal's talents. And the ball preparations were all but done. She just needed to babysit it for the next week and a half. She sure didn't need somebody messing with the plans at this late date.

Roger took in her expression, and his tone suddenly turned syrupy. "I appreciate how hard you've been working, Sinclair. And I know you're busy. This will take some of the burden off your shoulders."

"There's no—"

"You'll get your files back in a couple of days. Thanks for stopping by."

Thanks for stopping by?

He'd pulled the most interesting and important project of her career out from under her, and *that's* all she got?

Short of a raid on Chantal's office, Sinclair didn't know what to do. If the woman started messing with things, the ball could be completely destroyed. What if she called Claude at the Roosevelt? The head chef was temperamental at the best of times, and Chantal might push him right over the edge.

The conductor also needed hand-holding. The music was cued to coincide with speeches and product giveaways. Entrances and exits of VIPs were specifically timed, and the media appointments had to come off like clockwork.

But Sinclair couldn't outright defy Roger.

She headed for the elevator, desperately cataloguing potential problems and possible solutions. By the time she punched the button, she realized there were too many variables. With a rising sense of panic, she knew she couldn't possibly save the ball from Chantal. That left her with Roger. How could she possibly make Roger understand the danger of Chantal?

She entered the elevator, then froze with her finger on the button.

Wait a minute. She had this all wrong. She shouldn't be fighting them. What better way to demonstrate the error in their thinking than to go along with it? Ms. Chantal wanted to take over the ball? She could bloody well take over the ball. It would take less than twenty-four hours for her to get into a mess. Sinclair wouldn't argue with the president. She'd graciously step aside. She'd take the day off and leave Chantal with just enough rope to hang herself.

When Sinclair came back tomorrow, hopefully they'd be ready to listen to reason. As the elevator dropped, Sinclair drew a deep, bracing breath.

It was all but suicidal. But it would be worth it.

Ha!

Roger wanted to give Chantal a chance to shine? Sinclair would graciously step aside. When she came back tomorrow, hopefully they'd be ready to listen to reason.

As the elevator dropped, Sinclair warmed to the idea. When she got back to her office, she informed Amber they'd have the files back in a couple of days, and that she was going home to paint.

* * *

A few hours later, with U2 blaring in the background, Sinclair's frustration had translated itself into a second coat on most of one wall. She was busy at one corner of the ceiling when there was a banging on the door.

She climbed down the ladder and set her brush on the edge of the paint tray.

The banging came again.

"I'm coming," she called. She wiped off her hands, then pulled open the door.

It was Hunter, and he was carrying a large shopping bag.

"I've been buzzing you downstairs for ten minutes." He marched across the room and turned down the music. "Thank goodness for the lady on the first floor walking her dog."

"I was busy," said Sinclair.

Hunter dropped the bag onto the plastic-covered floor. "What happened?"

"I decided I should spend the day painting my living room."

"I talked to Amber."

Sinclair shrugged, picking up her paintbrush, and mounting the ladder. "What did she tell you?"

"That you were painting your living room instead of working."

"See that?" she gestured to the brushes, paint cans and tarps. "All evidence points to exactly the same thing. I am, in fact, painting my living room."

"She also told me you haven't taken a day off in eight years."

Sinclair dipped the brush in the can on the ladder and stroked along the top of the wall. "Meaning I'm due."

"Meaning you're upset."

"A girl can't get upset?"

He crossed his arms over his chest. "What happened?"

"Nothing much." The important thing now was to get the painting done, then go in tomorrow and see if her plan had worked.

"Do I have to come up there and get you?"

She laughed, dabbing the brush hard against the masking tape in the corner. "Now that would be interesting."

"Quit messing around, Sinclair."

She sighed in defeat. Being micromanaged was embarrassing. "You want to know?" she asked.

"Yes," said Hunter. "I want to know."

"Roger gave Chantal my Valentine's Day ball files. She needed to review them because, apparently, we've *all* recognized her *talents*."

"We have?"

Sinclair dipped the brush again. "Therefore, she's ready to be the PR assistant. No. Wait. I think she's ready to be the PR manager."

"What exactly did Roger say?"

"Not much. He just gave her the files. He seems hell-bent on involving her in every aspect of my job."

"Oh."

There was something in Hunter's tone.

Sinclair stopped painting and looked down. "What?"

He took a breath then paused.

"What?" she repeated.

"There's something we should discuss."

"You know what's going on?"

"Maybe."

Sinclair took a step down the ladder. "Hunter?"

He dropped his arms to his sides. "I have a theory. It's only a theory."

She climbed the rest of the way down. "What is it?"

Hunter took the brush from her hand, setting it on the paint tray just before it dripped on the floor. "Chantal asked if you used the mousse."

He lifted the shopping bag. "I think that might be what Roger's picking up on. Chantal's, well, pizzazz."

A sick feeling slid into Sinclair's stomach.

Roger thought Chantal knew better than Sinclair?

Hunter thought Chantal knew better than Sinclair?

"You have to admit," Hunter continued. "She's the demographic Luscious Lavender is targeting."

"You sure you want to keep on talking?"

"We both know she's not you. We both know you're smart and talented and hard-working."

"Well, thank you for that."

He opened the bag to reveal the full gamut of Luscious Lavender products. "I think you should try these out. See what you think, maybe—"

"Right. Because all my problems will be solved by a good shampoo and mousse." Her problem wasn't a bad hair day. It was the fact that Roger, and maybe Hunter, too, preferred beauty over brains.

Hunter attempted a grin. "Don't forget waxing."

She reached down for the paintbrush. "I'm forgetting all of it."

"Will you at least hear me out?"

"No." Without thinking she waved the brush for emphasis, and paint splattered on the front of his suit.

Her eyes went wide in horror. "Oh, I'm so sorry," she quickly blurted out.

"Forget it."

"But I ruined your suit." She could only imagine how much it had cost.

"I said to forget it."

How was she supposed to hang on to her moral outrage when he was being a gentleman?

"It's more than just a good shampoo," he said. "It's about relating to your customers. Having your customers relate to you."

She started up the ladder.

"They relate to Chantal in a particular way," he said. "They see her look as an idealized version of themselves. These are people that put great stock in the value of beauty products to their lives, and they want to know that you put great stock in them, as well."

"You're suggesting I could replace an MBA and eight years of experience with a good makeover?"

What kind of a man would think that?

"Yes," he said.

She stopped. She couldn't believe he'd actually said it out loud.

"But," he continued. "I'm also suggesting you'll blow the competition out of the water when you have both."

"You think Chantal is my competition?"

"I think *Roger* thinks she's your competition. I think you could do a makeover with your eyes closed. And I think she's only a threat to you if you let her be a threat to you."

"So *I'm* choosing to have this happen?"

All she'd ever done was her job. She'd shown up early every day for eight years. She'd written speeches and press releases, planned events, supported her coworkers, solved problems and taken the message of Lush Beauty far and wide. If her performance evaluations were anything to go by, she'd been more than successful in her role as PR manager.

"You're choosing not to fight it," said Hunter.

"I shouldn't have to fight it." When had hard work and success stopped being enough?

"Too bad. So sad. Are you going to let her win?" He paused. "Do you *want* your career path to end?"

"Don't be ridiculous." She loved her job.

"I'm the one being ridiculous? Chantal's nipping at your heels, and *I'm* the one being ridiculous?"

"Why do you care?"

There were a few seconds of silence. "Why do you think I care?"

Sinclair didn't have an answer for that, so she finished climbing the ladder.

"I'm not saying it's right," he spoke below her. "I'm saying that's the business you're in. And you're the PR manager. And, yes, I'm sorry, but it matters. And, as for why I care."

He stopped talking, and she held her breath.

"I like you? I slept with you? You're an asset to Lush Beauty? You're family? Take your pick. But I'm about done fighting, Sinclair. If you don't want my help, I'm out of here."

She dipped her paintbrush, feeling hollow and exhausted. Hunter's words pulsed in her ears, while paint dribbles dried on her hands. She pretended to focus on the painting while she waited for the door to slam behind him.

Emotion stung her eyes.

She didn't mean to fight with him.

It wasn't his fault that Chantal was prancing around the city like a poster child for Luscious Lavender. It wasn't his fault that Roger was interfering in her management of the PR department. And what did Sinclair want from Hunter, anyway? For him to intervene with Roger?

Not.

She could take care of her own professional life.

Sort of. Maybe.

Because a tiny, little voice inside her told her some of what Hunter said made sense.

She focused on the paint, stroking it into the corner, listening for his footfalls, for the door slamming, for him walking out of her life.

"I'm sorry," his unexpected words came from behind and below her. "I should have approached that differently."

She stopped midstroke. Shocked, relieved and embarrassed all at the same time. She set down the brush.

"No," she spoke to the wall. "I'm the one who's sorry."

Silence.

"Will you come down then?"

She gave a shaky nod. She couldn't bring herself to look at him as she started down the ladder. Maybe all of what he said made sense. Maybe she'd been hasty in dismissing a makeover. After all, what could it hurt to try?

What exactly was the principle she was standing on? She'd always wanted the world to take her seriously. She hadn't wanted a free ride because of looks and glamour. But did she want to put herself at a disadvatange?

"I suppose," she said as her foot touched the floor and she turned toward him. "It wouldn't kill me to try the shampoo."

"That a girl." His voice was full of approval.

"It's just that I never wanted to cheat," she tried to explain. "I never wanted to wonder if a promotion or a pay raise, or even people's reactions to me were because of my looks."

"You're not cheating. You're leveling the playing field. Besides, being beautiful has nothing to do with makeup and mousse." He shrugged out of the ruined jacket and tossed it on the floor. He whipped off his tie. "You're beautiful, Sinclair. And there's not a damn thing you can do about it."

Her heartbeat thickened in her chest, wondering what would come off next.

But he rolled up his sleeves. "Okay, let's get to work."

That threw her. "We're going to the office?"

"We're painting your walls."

"You want to spend the afternoon here?"

"You bet."

By late afternoon, Sinclair's arms were about to fall off. Her shoulders ached, and she was getting a headache from the paint fumes. Her latest can was empty, so she climbed down the ladder to replace it.

Hunter appeared, taking the can from her hands.

"You're done," he said.

"There's another whole wall."

He pointed across the room. "See that bag over there? Full of bath oil, shampoo and gel?"

"Uh-huh."

"I want you to take it into the bathroom and run a very hot, very deep bath. In fact—" he set down the paint can and propped up his roller "—I'll do it for you."

Before she could protest, he picked up the shopping bag and marched into the bathroom.

She heard the fan go on and the water gush from the faucet. She knew any self-respecting woman would fight against his high-handed behavior. But, honestly, she was just too tired.

After a few minutes, he returned to the living room. He didn't talk, just unplugged her CD player and gathered up the two compact speakers. He popped out U2 and replaced it with Norah Jones.

Then he was back to the bathroom.

Curiosity finally got the better of her, and she wandered in to find her tub full of steaming, foamy water, and three cinnamon-scented candles flickering at the base of the tub. They'd been a Christmas gift from somebody at the office. But she'd never used them.

"I never have baths," she admitted.

"Why not?"

"Showers are more efficient."

"But baths are more fun."

"You have baths, do you?" she couldn't help but tease.

He faced her in the tiny room. "Guys don't take baths. They want girls to take them. It makes them all soft and warm, and in the mood to get beautiful."

She gave a mock sigh. "It's time-consuming being all girly."

He grinned. "Piece of cake being a guy."

"Double standard."

"You know it."

"Still." She glanced down at the steaming water. "It does look inviting."

"That's because it is." He reached across her shoulder and flicked off the light.

"Time to take off your clothes," he rumbled.

A sensual shiver ran through her, and she reflexively reached for the hem of her T-shirt.

But his large hands closed over hers to stop them. "I mean after I leave."

"You're leaving?"

He kissed her forehead. "I didn't come here to seduce you, Sinclair."

Suddenly, she wished he had.

"Don't look at me like that. I'm going to paint for a while, or we'll never finish."

"I can paint later."

His finger brushed over her lips to silence her. "The price of being a guy. Your mission is to get all glammed up and frou frou. My mission is to give you the time to do that."

Then he winked, and left the room, clicking the door shut behind him. And Sinclair shifted her attention to the deep, claw-footed tub.

It looked decadently wonderful. He'd set out the shampoo, bath gel and lotion. And he'd obviously poured some of the Luscious Lavender foaming oil into the water. She'd spent the last six months thinking about the artsy labels, the expensive magazine ads, the stuffed sample gift baskets for the ball, and the retail locations that needed some extra attention promotions-wise. Funny, that she'd never thought much about the products themselves.

The water steamed, and the lavender scent filled the room, and the anticipation of that luxurious heat on her aching shoulders was more than tempting.

She peeled off her T-shirt, unzipped her jeans, then slipped out of her underwear. She eased, toe-first, into the scorching bathwater, dipping in her foot, her calf, her knee. Then she slowly brought in her other foot, bracing her hands on the edges of the tub to lower her body into the hot water.

After her skin grew accustomed to the temperature, and her shoulders and neck began to sigh in pleasure, her thoughts made their way to Hunter. He was on the other side of that thin wall. And she was naked. And he knew she was naked.

She pictured him opening the door, wearing nothing but a smile, a glass of wine in each hand. He'd cross the black and white tiles, bend to kiss her, maybe on the neck, maybe on the lips. He'd set down their glasses. Then he'd draw her to her feet, dripping wet, the scented oil slick on her skin. His hands would roam over her stomach, her breasts, her buttocks, pulling her tight against his body, lifting her—

Something banged outside and Hunter swore in frustration. Clearly, he wasn't out there stripping off his clothes and popping the wine cork. She was naked, not twenty feet away, and he was dutifully painting.

She sucked in a breath and ducked her head under the water.

Four

By the time Sinclair emerged from her bathroom, wrapped in a thick, terry robe, her face glowing, her wet hair combed back from her face, Hunter had cleaned up the paint and ordered a pizza. The smell of tomatoes and cheese wafted up from the cardboard box on the breakfast bar while he popped the cork from his housewarming bottle of wine.

"How did you know sausage and mushroom is my favorite?" she asked as she padded across the paint splattered tarps.

"I'm psychic." He retrieved two stools from beneath the tarp, then opened the top of the pizza box.

"How'd it go in there?" he asked her, watching her climb up on one stool.

She arranged the robe so that it covered her from head to toe, and he tried not to think about what was under there.

She smiled in a way that did his heart good. "I'm a whole new woman."

"Not completely new, I hope," he teased as he took the stool facing her. The covered breakfast bar was at their elbows.

She grinned. "Don't worry. I saved the best parts."

"Oh, good." He poured them each a glass of the pinot. "So, are you ready to move on to makeup?"

She reached for a slice of pizza. "You planning to help me with that, too?"

He took in her straggled hair, squeaky clean face and oversized robe. If he had his way, he'd keep her exactly as she was. But this wasn't about him.

"I don't think you want to arm me with a mascara wand."

"But you've done such a good job so far." She blinked her thick lashes ingenuously.

"We could call one of the Bergdorf ladies."

She waved a dismissive hand. "I'll be fine."

"You sure?"

She hit him with an impatient stare. "It's not that I *can't* put on a lot of makeup. It's that I *don't* put on a lot of makeup."

"Oh."

She chewed on her slice of pizza, and he followed suit. After a while, she slipped her bare feet off the stool's crossbar and swung them in the air while they ate in companionable silence.

"What about clothes?" he asked.

"I'll call Kristy and get some suggestions."

He nodded his agreement. Having a sister in the fashion design business had to help. "Sounds like you've got everything handled," he observed.

She shifted on the stool, flexing her neck back and forth, wincing. "It's not going to be that big of a deal. I'm a pretty efficient project manager. The only difference is, this time the project is me."

Hunter wasn't convinced project management was the right approach. There was something in the art and spirit of beauty she seemed to be missing. But he was happy to have got her this far, and he wasn't about to mess with his success.

She lifted her wineglass and the small motion caused her to flinch in obvious pain.

He motioned for her to turn around.

She glanced behind her. "What?"

"Go ahead. Turn." He motioned again, and this time she complied.

"You painted too long," he told her as he loosened her robe on her neck and pressed his thumbs into the stiff muscles on her shoulders.

"I wanted to finish."

"You're going to be sore in the morning." He found a knot and began to work it.

"I'll live. Mmmmm."

"That's the spot?"

"Oh, yeah."

He'd promised himself he'd stick to business, and he would. But his body had reacted the instant he'd touched her. Her skin was warm from the bath, slick from the bath oil, and fragrant from the water and the candles. But he scooted his stool closer, persisting in the massage, determined to keep this all about her.

To distract himself, he glanced around at the freshly painted room. It was small, but the windows were large, and he could see that it had potential to be cozy and inviting. In fact, he preferred it to the big, Osland family house on Long Island.

He stayed there whenever he was in town, but with just him and a couple of staff members, it always seemed to echo with emptiness. Right now, he wished he could invite Sinclair over to fill it up with laughter. "Have you always lived in New York?" he asked her instead.

She nodded. "Kristy and I went to school in Brooklyn. You?"

"Mostly in California."

"Private school, I bet."

"You're right."

"Uniforms and everything?"

"Yes."

She tipped her head to glance up at him. "You must have looked cute in your little short pants and tie."

"I'm sure I was adorable." He dug his thumb into a stubborn knot in her shoulder.

"Ouch. Was that for calling you cute?"

"That was to make you feel better in the morning."

She flexed her shoulder under his hands. "Did you by any chance play football in high school?"

"Soccer and basketball. You?"

"I edited the school newspaper."

"Nerdy."

"Exciting. I once covered a murder."

He paused. "There was a murder at your high school?"

She gave a long, sad sigh of remembrance. "Mrs. Mitchell's goldfish. Its poor, lifeless body was found on the science table. Someone had cruelly removed it from its tank after hours. We suspected the janitor."

Hunter could picture an earnest, young Sinclair hot on the trail of a murder suspect, all serious and no-nonsense, methodically reviewing the evidence.

"Did he do it?" Hunter asked.

"We couldn't prove it. But it was the best headline we ever had. Broke the record for copy sales." She sounded extremely proud of the accomplishment.

"You were definitely a nerd," he said.

"I prefer the term intellectual."

"I bet you ran in the school election."

"True."

"There you go." He'd made his point.

"Billy Jones beat me out for class president in ninth grade." She put a small catch in her voice. "I was crushed. I never ran again."

"I'd have voted for you," said Hunter.

"No. Like everyone else, you'd have fallen for Billy's chocolate coconut snowballs—"

"His *what?*"

"Chocolate and coconut on the outside, marshmallow cream on the inside. He brought five boxes to school and handed them out during his speech. I didn't have a chance."

"Marshmallow cream, you say?"

Sinclair elbowed him in the chest. "Quit salivating back there."

"I'd still have voted for you."

"Liar."

He chuckled at her outrage and eased her back against his body. "Oh, I'd have eaten the snowball. But it's a secret ballot, right?"

"Traitor." But her muscles relaxed under his hands, and her body grew more pliant.

Finally, he stopped massaging and wrapped his arms around her waist. "I bet you were a cute little nerd."

She rested her head against his chest. He didn't dare move. He barely dared breathe. All it would take was one kiss, and he'd be dragging her off to the bedroom.

She tipped her head to look up at him, all sweetness and vulnerability.

"Hunter?" she breathed, lips dark and parted, eyes filled with passion and desire.

He closed his, fighting like hell to keep from kissing her lips. "I don't want to be that guy," he told her, discovering how true that was. Because he didn't want to screw up their budding friendship.

"That guy?"

"That guy with the bath and the candles and the shoulder massage."

"I liked that part."

He opened his eyes again. "It's Seduction 101 for losers."

"Are you calling yourself a loser?"

"I'm saying if I make love with you, I'll feel like I cheated."

"There's a way to cheat?"

He reflexively squeezed her tight. "I cheated, and you never had a chance."

"As in, I don't know my own mind?"

"Is there an answer for that that won't get me in trouble?"

"Not really."

He ruthlessly ignored the feel of her in his arms. He wasn't willing to risk that she might regret it in the morning.

"You're tired. You're vulnerable. And we haven't thought this through. We turn that corner," he continued, "we can't turn back."

"I know," she acknowledged in a soft voice.

He leaned around her, placing a lingering kiss on her temple. "I'll see you at the office?"

"Sure."

He forced himself to let go of her. Then, using every ounce of his strength and determination, he stood up and walked away.

* * *

By 7:00 a.m., Sinclair was in her office.

After Hunter left last night, she'd lain awake, remembering his soft voice, his easy conversation, and the massage that had all but melted her muscles. She would have willingly made love with him. But, he was right. They hadn't thought it through. It was hard enough ignoring what had happened six weeks ago, never mind rekindling all those memories.

Hunter was a thoughtful man. He was also an intelligent man, and she'd spent some time going over his professional advice. He saw Chantal as her competition. And he saw Roger in Chantal's corner. Sinclair realized she had to do this, and she had to do it right. It was time to stop fooling around.

So, she'd arrived this morning with a plan to do just that. She submitted an electronic leave form, rescheduled her meetings, plastered her active files with Post-its for Amber, and left out-of-office messages on both her voice mail and e-mail.

She was working her way through the mail in her in-basket when Roger walked in.

"What's this?" he asked, dropping the leave form printout on her desk.

"I'm going on vacation," she answered cheerfully, tossing another piece of junk mail in the wastepaper basket.

"Why? Where?"

"Because I haven't taken a vacation in eight years. Because I'm entitled to vacation time just like everybody else. And because I'm not currently needed on the Valentine's Day ball file."

"Of *course* you're needed on the file."

"To do what?"

Roger waved his arms. "To make plans. To order things."

"Plans are made. Things are ordered." She rose from her

chair and smiled at him. "You'll be fine, Roger. You've got Chantal on the case. She can oversee things."

"But, where are you going?"

"Chapter Three, Section Twelve of the employee manual. Employees shall not be required to disclose nor justify their vacation plans. All efforts will be made to ensure employees are able to take leave during the time period of their choosing. And leave shall not be unreasonably withheld."

"She's right," came Hunter's voice from the doorway.

Roger looked from Hunter to Sinclair and back again. "You knew about this?"

"Hadn't a clue." Hunter looked to Sinclair. "Taking a vacation?"

"I am."

"Good for you. A refreshed employee is a productive employee."

"I plan to be refreshed," she said.

Hunter smirked. "I'm looking forward to that."

"I've left notes for Amber," Sinclair said to Roger. "The meetings with the Roosevelt Hotel have been rescheduled. Unless Chantal wants to take them. You could ask her. The florist order is nailed down. The music…Well, there's a little problem with the band, but I'm sure Chantal or Amber can handle it."

She dropped the last piece of mail in the waste basket and glanced around the room. "I think that about covers it."

"This is unexpected," said Roger through clenched teeth.

"Can I talk to you for a minute?" asked Hunter.

"My office?" Roger responded.

"I meant Sinclair," said Hunter, stepping aside from the open door.

Roger frowned.

Sinclair should have cared about his annoyance, and she should have been bothered by the fact that the CEO had just dismissed the president in order to talk to her. But she truly didn't care. She had things to do, places to go, beauticians to meet.

Roger stalked out of the office, and Hunter closed the door behind him.

"Career-wise," said Sinclair. "And by that, I mean *my* career. I'm not sure that was the best move."

"You're taking some time for the makeover?" asked Hunter.

She straightened a stack of reports and lifted them from her desktop. "You're right that Lush Beauty Products is going through a huge transition. And you're right I should thwart Roger by getting a makeover. And, honestly, I believe Roger and Chantal need some time alone to get to know one another."

Hunter grinned, obviously understanding her Machiavellian motives.

"I'm a goal-oriented woman, Hunter. Give me a week, and I can accomplish this."

"I'm sure you can. Any interest in accomplishing it in Paris?"

She squinted. She didn't understand the question.

"I had an idea," he said. He paused, obviously for effect. "The Castlebay Spa chain. It's a very exclusive, European boutique spa chain, headquartered in Paris."

She got his point and excitement shimmered through her. "We're going to try again?"

"Oslands don't quit."

Enthusiasm gathered in her chest at the thought of another shot at a spa. She squared her shoulders. "Neither do Mahoneys."

"Good to hear. Because that platinum card I gave you works in Paris."

"Oh, no." She shook her head. "You don't need me to do

the spa deal, and I don't need to go to Paris. I've got things to do in New York."

He took her hand. "I want you in on the spa deal. And Paris is the makeover capital of the world."

"Paris is definitely overkill." She didn't need to cross an ocean to get a haircut and buy dresses. Plus, in Paris, she'd be with Hunter. And there was the ever present danger of sleeping together. Since they'd so logically decided against it last night, it seemed rather cavalier to take off to Paris together.

"Do I need reinforcements? I could call your sister. She'll back me up."

"Don't you dare call Kristy." Kristy would be over the moon at the thought of a Paris makeover for her sister. And Sinclair would have two people to argue with.

He pulled out his cell phone and waggled it in the air. "She's on speed dial."

"That's cheating."

"I've got nothing against cheating."

His words from last night came back to her, but she didn't mention it.

"I need you in Paris," he said.

She didn't believe that for a second. "No, you don't."

"I need your expertise on the Castlebay deal."

She rolled her eyes. "Like my track record on spa deals is any good."

"You know the Lush Beauty company and the products, and you can describe them a lot better than I can."

"There's a flaw in this plan," she told him. But deep down inside, she knew Hunter was winning. If she wanted to beat Chantal at her own game, a Paris makeover would give her the chance she needed.

"Only flaw I can think of," he said, shifting closer, "is that I desperately want to kiss you right now."

"That's a pretty big flaw," she whispered.

"We're handling it so far." But he moved closer still, and his gaze dropped to her lips.

"How long would we be in Paris?"

"A few days."

Her lips began to tingle in reaction to his look. "Separate rooms?"

"Of course."

"Lots of time in public places."

He returned his gaze to her eyes. "Chicken."

"I'm only trying to save you from yourself."

"Noble of you."

She couldn't help but smile. "If we do this—"

"The jet's waiting at the airport."

"Did I miss the part where I said yes?"

He reached for her hand. "I'm generally one step ahead of you, Sinclair."

She shook her head, but she also grabbed her purse. Because she realized he was right. He had an uncanny knack for anticipating her actions, along with her desires.

Five

They slept on the plane, and arrived in Paris a week before Valentine's Day. Then a limousine took them to the Ciel D'Or Hotel. And Hunter insisted they get right to the makeover.

So, before Sinclair could even get her bearings, they were gazing up at the arched facade of *La Petite Fleur*—a famous boutique in downtown Paris. A uniformed doorman opened the gold-gilded glass door.

"Monsieur Osland," he said and tipped his hat.

Sinclair slid Hunter a smirking gaze. "Just how many makeovers do you do around here?"

"At least a dozen a year," said Hunter as their footfalls clicked on the polished marble floor.

"And here I thought I was special." They passed between two ornate pillars and onto plush, burgundy carpeting.

"You are special."

"Then how come the doorman knew you by sight? And don't try to tell me you've been shopping for Kristy."

"Like good ol' cousin Jack wouldn't kill me if I did that. They don't know me by sight. They know me because I called ahead and asked them to stay open late."

Sinclair glanced around, realizing the place was empty. "They stayed open late? Don't you think you're getting carried away here?" She'd agreed to a makeover, not to star in some remake of Pygmalion.

He chuckled. "You ain't seen nothing yet."

"*Hunter.*"

"Shhh."

A smartly dressed woman appeared in the wide aisle and glided toward them.

"Monsieur Osland, Mademoiselle," she smiled. "*Bienvenue.*"

"*Bienvenue,*" Hunter returned. "Thank you so much for staying open for us."

The woman waved a dismissive hand. "You are most welcome, of course. We are pleased to have you."

"*Je vous présente Sinclair Manhoney,*" said Hunter with what sounded like a perfect accent.

Sinclair held out her hand, trying very hard not to feel as if she'd dropped through the looking glass. "A pleasure to meet you."

"And you," the woman returned. "I am Jeanette. Would you care to browse? Or shall I bring out a few things?"

"We're looking for something glamorous, sophisticated but young," Hunter put in.

Jeanette nodded. "Please, this way."

She led them along an aisle, skirting a six-story atrium, to a group of peach and gold armchairs. The furniture sat on a large dais, outside a semicircle of mirrored changing rooms.

"Would either of you care for a drink?" asked Jeanette. "Some champagne?"

"Champagne would be very nice," said Hunter. "Merci."

Jeanette turned to walk away, and Hunter gestured to one of the chairs.

Sinclair dropped into it. "Overkill. Did I mention this is overkill?"

"Come on, get into the spirit of things."

"This place is…" She gestured to the furnishings, the paintings, the clothing and the atrium. "Out of my league."

"It's exactly in your league."

"You should have warned me."

"Warned you about what? That we're getting clothes? That we're getting jewelry? What part of makeover didn't you understand?"

"The part where you go bankrupt."

"You couldn't bankrupt me if you tried."

"I'm not going to try."

"Oh, please. It would be so much more fun if you did."

Jeanette reappeared, and Sinclair's attention shifted to the half a dozen assistants who followed her, carrying a colorful array of clothes.

"Those are pink," whispered Sinclair, her stomach falling. "And fuzzy. And shiny." Okay, there was makeover, and then there was comic relief.

"Time for you to go to work," said Hunter.

"Pink," she hissed at him.

Hunter just smiled.

Jeanette hung two of the outfits inside a large, well-lit changing room. It had a chair, a small padded bench, a dozen hooks and a three-way mirror.

In the changing room, Sinclair stripped out of the gray skirt suit she'd worn on the plane, and realized her underwear was looking a bit shabby. The lace on her bra had faded to ivory from the bright white it was when she'd bought it. The elastic had stretched in the straps, and one of the underwires had a small bend.

She slipped into the first dress. It was a pale pink sheath of a thing. It clung all the way to her ankles, leaving absolutely nothing to the imagination. Making matters worse, it had an elaborate beading running over the cap sleeves and all the way down the sides. And it came with a ridiculous ivory lace hood thing that made her look like some kind of android bride.

There was a small rap at the door. "Mademoiselle?"

"Yes?"

"Is there anything you need?"

Cyanide? "Would you happen to have a phone?" Or maybe an escape hatch out the back? She could catch a plane to New York and start over again.

"*Oui. Of course. Un moment.*"

Sinclair stared at the dress, having some very serious second thoughts. Maybe other women could pull this off, taller, thinner, crazier women. But it sure wasn't working for her.

Another knock.

"Yes?" If that was Hunter, she wasn't going out there. Not like this. Not with a gun to her head.

"Your phone," said Jeanette.

Sinclair pulled off the hood, cracked the door and accepted the wireless telephone.

She dialed her sister Kristy, the fashion expert.

Kristy answered after three rings. "Hello?"

"Hey, it's me."

"Hey, you," came Kristy's voice above some background

noise of music and voices. "What's going on? Everything all right?"

"It's fine. Well, not fine exactly. I'm having a few problems at work."

"Really? That's not like you. What kind of problems?"

"It's a long story. But, I'm in Paris right now, and we're trying to fix it."

"Hang on," said Kristy. "I'm at the Manchester Hospital Foundation lunch. I need to get out of the ballroom." The background noise disappeared. "Okay. There. Did you say you were in Paris?"

Sinclair's glance went to the three-way mirror. "Yes. I'm doing a makeover, but I think I many have taken a wrong turn here, and I need some advice."

"Happy to help. What kind of advice?"

"What do I ask for? Is there something that's stylish but not weird?"

"Define weird."

"At the moment, these crazy people are trying to dress me like an android bride, porn queen."

There was laughter in Kristy's tone. "Crazy people? What did you do to upset the French?"

"It's not the French. It's Hunter."

"Hunter's in Paris?"

"Yes."

Kristy was silent for a moment. "Are you sleeping with him again?"

"No."

More silence. "You sure?"

"Yes I'm sure. What? You think I wouldn't notice? We're shopping for clothes."

"I know things about Hunter that you don't."

"We're not having sex, we're shopping for clothes. And I'm all for that. Just not these clothes." Sinclair glanced in the mirror again and shuddered.

"Where are you shopping?"

"La Petite Fleur."

"Well, they're good. Is somebody assisting you?"

"Yes. A nice lady named Jeanette, who appears to have horrible taste in dresses."

"Put her on."

"Just a minute."

Sinclair cracked the door again. "Jeanette?"

"Oui?" The woman instantly appeared.

Sinclair held out the phone. "My sister wants to talk to you."

If Jeanette was surprised by the request, she didn't show it. She was gracious and classy as she took the phone, and Sinclair was grateful.

"Allô?" said Jeanette.

Sinclair closed the door. She didn't want to risk Hunter calling her to come out there.

She stripped out of the dress and tried the other. It was made of black netting, with shoulder-length matching gloves. A puffy neckline of feathers nearly made Sinclair sneeze, while rows of horizontal feather stripes camouflaged strategic parts of her body. The netting base was see-through, so underwear would be out of the question beneath it.

Another knock.

"Yes?"

"You going to show me something?" asked Hunter.

"Not a chance."

"Why? What's wrong?"

She took in her own image. Maybe she just didn't have the

body for high fashion. Other women looked good. Kristy always looked good.

"I really don't want to go into it," she said to Hunter.

"Keep an open mind. It can't be that bad."

"Trust me. It's that bad."

"Perhaps you'd care to try a different designer?" came Jeanette's voice.

"Is Kristy still on the phone?"

"She will ring you back. But she made some suggestions."

Sinclair flipped open the door latch. "No peeking," she warned Hunter.

Then his cell phone beeped and she heard him answer it. Good. Hopefully he'd be busy for a while.

She opened the door wide enough to take the new dresses from Jeanette. They were in blues and golds, and these ones didn't appear to be pornographic.

She closed the door, took a breath, and tried on another one. It was much better, and she felt a surge of hope.

It clung to her body, but not in an indecent way, and the fabric was thick enough that she could wear underwear beneath it. The netting on this dress was brown, and it was only used for a stripe across the top as well as a flirty ruffle from midcalf to the floor. In between was a glittering puzzle pattern of gold, brown, purple and green material.

Sinclair turned. She liked the way the ruffle flowed around her ankles, and the dress molded nicely to her rear end and her thighs.

There was another rap on the door. "How are you, madame?" called Jeanette.

Sinclair opened the door.

Jeanette cocked her head to one side. "Not bad," she said

of the outfit. "You'll need some shoes with a little jazz to compete. And maybe a little more support in your bra."

Was Sinclair offended by that last remark? No way. She was starting to like her new image.

"One moment," said Jeanette.

She returned promptly with a bra, matching panties, a pair of stockings, and some spike-heeled, precarious-looking, rhinestone-studded sandals.

When Sinclair walked out of the change room, she nearly took Hunter's breath away. The dress was a dream. Well, mostly her body beneath it was a dream. She looked glamorous and stylish, and it only added to her innate class.

"Can you hang on a minute?" he asked Richard Franklin, one of the Osland International lawyers.

"Sure," Richard responded.

Hunter covered the phone. "Perfect," he stated to Sinclair.

She smiled and, as usual, it lifted his mood. He found himself thinking about the evening ahead, and tomorrow, and the next few days. What could he show her in Paris? How could he keep her smiling?

He forced himself to switch his attention to Jeanette. "Can you do two or three more like that? And a couple of ball gowns, and some daywear?"

"*Absolument.*"

"You look fantastic," he said to Sinclair.

It was a rocky start. But then she reflexively glanced in the mirror beside her, and he could tell by the shine in her eyes that she liked the outfit, too.

"Try to have fun," he told her.

"I'm getting there."

He gave her a thumbs-up.

They'd need some jewelry to go with it, of course. But that could be tomorrow's mission.

It occurred to Hunter that he was probably having a little too much fun at this himself. But he shrugged it off. Dressing a beautiful woman ought to be fun. And if a man couldn't have fun spending his money, what was the point in making any of it?

Jeanette herded Sinclair back into the change room, and Hunter returned to his phone call.

"Thanks for waiting," he said to Richard.

"Do you have a contact name?" asked Richard.

"Seth Vanderkemp. The Castlebay Spa headquarters is on Rue de Seline. Do we have a contract lawyer on standby?"

"We do. In fact, I can get someone there overnight. When will you know?"

"Tomorrow. If it looks like we can get a contract, I'll give you a call." Hunter knew this was their last chance to get Luscious Lavender into a spa chain in time for the Valentine's launch. If Castlebay was open to making a deal, he didn't want to lose a single minute.

He ended the call.

Immediately, his phone rang again.

"Hunter Osland."

"What the hell?" came his cousin Jack's voice.

"What the hell what?" asked Hunter, reflexively cataloguing his actions over the past couple of weeks to see what could have upset his cousin.

"One, you've got Sinclair in Paris? Two, there's trouble with her job. Three, you're dressing her like an android hooker. And four, you're probably sleeping with her? Take your pick."

"Oh, that," said Hunter.

"*That's* your answer?"

"What do you want me to say?" Hunter could tell his cousin to shut up and mind his own business. It was hardly a crime to go shopping. And he was behaving responsibly, particularly considering the attraction that still simmered between them.

"That you're not sleeping with my sister-in-law."

"I stopped."

"Good. Stay stopped. She works for us. And you're you."

"What the hell is that supposed to mean?"

"You know what it means."

Hunter sighed in exasperation. His reputation as a womanizer was not deserved.

"Tell Kristy I am not having a fling with her sister. Sinclair's job is not in jeopardy. And she doesn't look the least bit like a hooker."

"And you're not going to break her heart?"

Hunter pulled the phone away from his ear and frowned at it for a second. Then he put it back.

"Obviously, that was Kristy's question," Jack went on.

"What exactly have you told her about me?"

"Anything she asks. Plus, Gramps gave her the lowdown on some of your previous relationships. And you and Sinclair did start out with a one-night stand."

"Thanks for the support there, cousin."

Hunter hadn't had that many relationships. All right, some of them may have been short-lived. But they simply hadn't worked out. It wasn't as if he went around breaking hearts on purpose.

"Personally," said Jack, with more than a trace of amusement in his tone. "I'm more concerned about you. She's got red hair."

Hunter didn't bothering answering. He hit the end button and shoved the phone back in his pocket.

His cousin's joke was lame.

When Hunter was sixteen years old, he'd accidentally burned down the tent of an old gypsy fortune-teller. The woman had predicted Jack would marry a woman he didn't trust. They'd lose the family fortune. They'd buy a golf course. And Hunter would marry a redhead and have twins.

So far, the only thing that had come close to happening was Jack marrying Kristy before he trusted her. But it was enough to get Jack fixated on redheads and the possibility of twins.

The door to the changing room opened again.

Sinclair emerged in a strapless, jewel-blue, satin evening gown that revealed creamy cleavage on top and silver-strapped, sexy ankles on the bottom. She'd pinned her hair up in an ad hoc knot. As she moved gracefully toward him, the fabric rustled over her smooth calves, while her deep, coral lips curved into a satisfied smile.

Hunter's body reacted with a lurch, but then his stomach went hollow when he realized he couldn't touch her.

Kristy had absolutely nothing to worry about. If anybody was getting their heart broken around here, it sure wasn't going to be Sinclair.

Sinclair knew she'd be disappointed if Castlebay didn't work out. There was her job, her future, Hunter's reputation at the company, the success of the Luscious Lavender product line all to consider. And she'd reminded herself, she'd lived through two letdowns already. Still, walking up the stone steps to the Castlebay Spas head office, she was determined to fight the butterflies in her stomach.

"What should I focus on first?" she asked Hunter, anxious to get her part right.

She was wearing a mini, tweed coat dress, with pushed up sleeves, large black buttons, black stockings and high-heeled ankle boots. She'd pulled her hair into a simple, tight bob, as Jeanette had advised, and put on a little extra makeup, especially around the eyes.

"Leave the financial details to me. Give out product information only. If I brush your hand, stop talking. And, mostly importantly, walk, talk and act like a winner."

She gave him a swift nod.

"Oh. And mention that you've tried the mousse."

She shot him a disgusted stare.

"That was just to lighten you up." He pulled open the heavy brass and glass door. "Relax."

She took a breath. "Right."

They didn't talk in the elevator. And while they crossed the marble floor of the Castlebay lobby, Sinclair concentrated on her new shoes. She did not want to stumble.

"We have an appointment with Seth Vanderkemp," Hunter said to the receptionist.

Sinclair caught the woman's admiring look at her outfit, and she couldn't help but smile. Wouldn't the woman be surprised to find out she was staring at plain, old Sinclair Mahoney from Soho?

"Mr. Vanderkemp is expecting you," said the woman. "Right this way."

She stood and led them down a long hallway to an opulent meeting room. It had round beech-wood table, with a geometric, inlaid cherry pattern. There were four high-backed, burgundy leather chairs surrounding it. And the bank of windows overlooked the Seine.

"Good morning, Mr. Osland. Sorry to keep you waiting."

"Not at all," said Hunter. "We just got here. And, please, call me Hunter." He turned to Sinclair. "This is my associate, Sinclair Mahoney."

"Seth," said the man, holding out his hand to Sinclair. "Pleasure to meet you."

Sinclair shook. "Sinclair," she confirmed.

Seth gestured to the round table. "Shall we sit down?"

Hunter pulled out a chair for Sinclair, then the men sat.

"Osland International's latest acquisition," Hunter began, getting right to the point, "is a boutique beauty-products company out of New York called Lush Beauty."

"I've heard of Lush," said Seth with a nod.

Sinclair thought that fact boded well for the discussions, but Hunter's expression remained neutral.

"We're in Paris for a few days," explained Hunter, "looking for partners in the upcoming launch of a promising new line called Luscious Lavender."

Sinclair mentally prepared herself to talk about the products. She'd start with skin care, move to cosmetics, then introduce some of the specialty personal care items.

"With Osland International's involvement," Hunter continued, "we're in a position to launch simultaneously in North America and Europe. A spa would naturally be an ideal outlet for us, and we believe Castlebay's clientele are dead center for our target market."

Seth continued nodding, which Sinclair took to be a great sign.

"Under normal circumstances," he said, "I would agree with you. And I've no doubt that Luscious Lavender would serve our client market well. But, there's a complication."

Sinclair's stomach sank.

Hunter waited.

"There's an offer on the table to purchase Castlebay Spas in its entirety."

"What kind of an offer?" asked Hunter.

"I'm sure you realize I'm not in a position to discuss the particulars."

Hunter sat back in his chair. "Let me put it another way."

This time Seth waited.

So did Sinclair.

"What would it take to get the offer off the table?"

Seth looked puzzled. "In terms of…"

"In terms of another offer to purchase."

Seth's eyes narrowed. "Are you empowered—"

"I'm empowered."

Seth stood up, crossing to a telephone on a side table, and picked it up.

Sinclair stared at Hunter.

Seth asked, "Do you mind if the head of my legal department joins us?"

"Not at all," replied Hunter. "I assume you have a prospectus and some financials I could review?"

"It's all in order. Plus a full set of appraisals."

"Thank you," said Hunter.

Then he turned to Sinclair, he penned a few words on a business card he'd pulled from his pocket and handed it to her. "Could you call Richard Franklin? Have him set up a meeting at our hotel this afternoon. I'll meet you there."

Sinclair palmed the card and quietly left the room.

On the way across the lobby, heart pounding, mouth dry, she flipped over the card. On the back was Richard's name, his number and the phrase NO ONE ELSE.

Six

When Hunter reached the ground floor of the office building that housed Castlebay Spas, Sinclair was waiting on a bench near the exit.

She jumped to her feet as he neared. "I couldn't wait," she said.

"Apparently."

"If you came down with anyone else, I was going to hide."

Hunter couldn't help but grin.

"What happened?"

"Looks like we may be buying ourselves some spas."

Richard would have to review the contract, but Hunter was satisfied with the price. And, the combination of Lush Beauty and Castlebay Spas was going to be dynamite. His grandfather insisted Hunter run Lush Beauty Products? He was damn well going to run Lush Beauty Products.

"Just like that?" asked Sinclair, with a snap of her fingers.

"Just like that," echoed Hunter.

"I can't believe it." She skipped a step to keep pace with him. "So we can use Luscious Lavender in the spas?"

"That would be the point."

"How much—" She stopped. "Never mind." She shook her head. "None of my business."

"Lots," said Hunter. He'd drained the available cash in the Osland investment account, and put up a manufacturing plant as collateral to secure low ratio interest.

"How many spas?" she asked.

"Twelve. I have a list if you want it."

They started down the steps.

"You bet." Her face nearly burst with a grin. "So, what do we do now?"

"Who is Richard sending to the hotel?"

"Miles something…"

"We drop the papers off with Miles something for review. Then we carry on with your makeover."

"Do we celebrate?"

"As soon as the deal is approved," Hunter answered as they turned onto the sidewalk. "The financing has to be put in place first. And we need to get the signatures on the contracts."

She nodded eagerly.

"And, until then, we carry on as normal." He hesitated over the wording of the next part. "And we don't tell anyone about it."

She squinted up at him. "Anyone being?"

"Anyone. Including Kristy and Jack."

"But, why—"

"Convention." Hunter shrugged with feigned unconcern. "We investigate things like this all the time. No point in cluttering up everyone's desk over it until there's something concrete."

It wasn't exactly a lie, but it wasn't the whole truth, either. The deal was somewhat larger than Hunter would normally undertake on his own. And he hadn't yet figured out exactly how to tell Jack and his grandfather. He knew they'd be worried, and they'd definitely come at him with accusations that he was being reckless and impulsive. But he didn't have time for his grandfather's plodding approach to due diligence, which had taken weeks, even when he'd "rushed" the Lush deal.

Still, Hunter was fully confident in his decision. And he was fully confident time would prove it to be an excellent investment. But, for the short term, he needed a few days to work up to an explanation.

In the meantime, all the reasons for Sinclair's makeover remained.

"Jewelry store?" he asked her.

She laughed and unexpectedly captured his hand. "You *are* in a spending mood."

"I am," he agreed, kissing her knuckles and pointing to a five-story, stone-arched jewelry store across the street.

They dashed across the traffic and entered to discover the building decorated for Valentine's Day. Golden hearts, red ribbons and bows hung from the ceiling. Massive bouquets of red roses covered every surface. And tiny, heart-shaped boxes of truffles were being handed out to the ladies as they exited.

Hunter scanned the glass cases and the stairway leading to the second floor. Then he looked down at their clasped hands.

"You with me on this?" he asked.

She nodded.

He rubbed a finger across her nose. "No complaints now."

She took in the festive scene. "I'm not complaining."

"I may buy you something expensive."

"Just so long as you take it back when we're finished."

He frowned. "Take it back?"

"Save the box," she said. "Or you can give it to a girlfriend in the future."

Hunter had no intention of taking anything back, or giving it to some future girlfriend. But he didn't see any point in sharing that with Sinclair.

"Sure," he agreed.

Sinclair smiled and turned her attention to the display cases.

Convinced she was buying for some other mythical girlfriend—who Hunter could not remotely picture at the moment—Sinclair plunged right into the game.

She selected a sapphire-and-diamond choker, a pair of emerald-and-gold hooped earrings, teardrop diamonds, delicate sapphire studs, a ruby pendant that Hunter was positive she thought was an imitation stone, and a whimsical little bracelet with one ruby- and one diamond-encrusted goldfish dangling from the platinum chain.

Hunter bought them all, clipping the bracelet on her wrist so she could wear it back to the hotel.

Then they walked to a nice restaurant, taking seats overlooking the river. The maître d' brought them a bottle of merlot and some warm French rolls.

Sinclair jangled her bracelet. "You're very good at this."

"I have a mom and a sister."

"Nice answer," she nodded approvingly, lifting her long-stemmed glass. "Never buy for girlfriends?"

"Why do you keep setting me up?" He didn't want to talk to Sinclair about his former girlfriends. "Tossing out questions I can't answer without being a jerk?"

"I know you've had girlfriends."

"But I don't want to tell you about them."

"Why not? Wouldn't I like them?"

"You're really going to push this?"

"No reason not to."

"Is that what you're telling yourself?" He didn't know what was going on between them, but he sure as hell didn't want to hear about any of her old boyfriends.

Then again, maybe her feelings were different than his. There was one way to find out.

"Melissa," he said, watching Sinclair's expression carefully, "was a weather girl in Los Angeles. We dated for three months, played a lot of squash and beach volleyball. She was a vegetarian and a social activist. She wouldn't let me buy anything from a very long list of countries with human or animal rights infractions."

Sinclair's expression remained impassive.

Hunter tore one of the rolls in two. "Sandra worked in a health club. She also played squash. We dated maybe two months. Deanne taught parasailing. We did a lot of mountain climbing, and some swimming, and she loved dancing at the clubs. But I introduced her to one too many movie stars, and she was gone."

Sinclair's expression faltered. "Did she break your heart?"

Hunter scoffed out a laugh. "It was at the six-month mark, normally my limit. Now, Jacqueline—"

"Is this going to take the entire dinner?"

"You did ask."

"I've had two boyfriends," she offered.

"I *didn't* ask," Hunter reminded her.

"Roberto decided his mother was right after all, and Zeke drove off on his Harley."

They left her? Now, that surprised Hunter.

"They break your heart?" he found himself asking, genuinely wanting to know.

"I thought so at the time. But, you know, neither of them even took me to Paris."

Hunter grunted. "It's a sad day when a man won't even take his girlfriend to Paris."

"Now that I've seen Paris—" Sinclair spread her hands palms up "—that's going to be the baseline."

"Smart girl."

"Thank you."

"You might want to add diamonds to that list."

"You think?"

Hunter nodded and pretended to give it serious thought. "Private jet, too."

Sinclair picked up the other half of his roll. "How else does one get to Paris?" She took a bite.

"A woman needs to be smart about these things."

"Thank you so much for the advice."

To his surprise, Hunter wasn't jealous of Roberto and Zeke. The men were morons.

He signaled the waiter for menus, and sat back to enjoy the company.

Sinclair awoke with a smile on her face in the river-view room at the Ciel D'or Hotel in downtown Paris. She felt different. The clothes Hunter had bought her were hanging in the closet and the jewelry package was sitting on the nightstand. Someone was tapping gently on her door.

She flipped back the comforter and slipped into the plush, white hotel robe, tying the sash around her waist. The fish bracelet dangled at her wrist. She knew it was silly, but she hadn't wanted to take it off.

Through the peephole, she could see a black-tuniced waiter carrying a silver tray. Coffee. Her entire body sighed in anticipation.

She opened the door, and the man set the tray down on a small table beside the window. She realized she didn't have any money for a tip, but he assured her it was taken care of.

Before she had a chance to pour a cup of coffee or tear into one of the buttery croissants, the phone on the bedside table began to ring.

"Hello?" She perched on the edge of the unmade bed.

"You awake?" came Hunter's voice.

"Barely."

"Did the coffee arrive?"

"It did."

His breath hissed in. "Call me when you're dressed."

Her gaze darted to their connecting door. "I'm covered from head to toe."

"You sure?"

She glanced down. "Well, maybe not my toes. But everything else. Come and have coffee."

"Toes are sexy," he said in a rumbling voice.

"My nails need trimming, and I haven't had a pedicure in months."

"In that case, I'll be right over."

She grinned as she hung up the phone and opened her panel of the connecting door. Then she settled into one of the richly upholstered chairs and poured a cup of extremely fragrant coffee and gazed at the sparkling blue sky against the winter skyline.

The door on Hunter's side opened. "Did I mention the Castlebay Spa offers pedicures?"

"Are you offended by my toes?"

He took the seat across from her, pouring his own coffee.

"I'm not even going to look at your toes. If you lied about their condition, they'll probably haunt my dreams."

She tore a croissant in two. "You got a fetish?"

"Only for gorgeous women." His gaze caught her bracelet. Their eyes met, and there was something excruciatingly intimate in his look.

And then it hit Sinclair. They were having an affair. They were having an affair in every possible way except sleeping together. The awareness brought a warm glow to her stomach. She deliberately moved her hand so the bracelet would tap against her wrist. The sensation sent a shot of desire through her body.

Hunter cleared his throat. "So, do you want to continue the makeover in Paris, or perhaps we should switch our base of operations to London…or Venice?"

"Is there a better place than Paris for a brand-new hairdo?" She had absolutely no desire to leave.

"Not that I know of."

"Then I vote we stay here."

She sipped her coffee from the fine china cup and bit into the most tender croissant she'd had in her life.

Hunter selected an apple pastry sprinkled in powered sugar, and Sinclair decided she'd try that one next.

"Are you at all worried I'll get spoiled and refuse to go home?" she asked, taking another bite.

He grinned. "Go ahead."

"You're not serious."

He paused for a moment, gazing at her in the streaming sunlight. "Actually, I am. But you're not."

Sinclair didn't believe it for a second. Although it was nice of him to say so. As fantasies went, Hunter sure knew how to put on a good one.

"Have you called for a special opening of a hair salon?"

He shook his head. "I don't know anything about hair salons in Paris. But I do know people who know people."

"And they'll do you favors."

"They will."

"Why is that?"

"Because I'm a nice guy."

"That you are."

Sinclair sat back, gazing around the room, at the ornate moldings, the carved ceiling, the marble bathroom, and the four-poster bed. "But the money must be frustrating. I mean, how can you tell if people like you or not?"

He shrugged. "How does anybody tell? They're friendly. They don't jeer at me. They laugh at my jokes."

"But how can you tell it's you and not the money?"

"You can tell."

"I bet you can't."

"Most people are terrible liars."

Sinclair pushed her hair behind her ears. "Not me. I'm a great liar." She and Kristy had pulled the wool over her parents' eyes on numerous occasions.

"Yeah?" asked Hunter, his disbelief showing.

"Yeah," she affirmed with a decisive nod.

He put down the pastry and dusted the sugar off his hands with a nearby linen napkin. "Okay. Go ahead. Tell me a good lie."

Like she'd fall for that. "You'd already know it's a lie."

"Then tell me something that may or may not be a lie, and I'll tell you if it's the truth."

"Oh…kay." Sinclair thought about it. After a minute, she sat forward, warming to the game. "That morning at the Manchester mansion, I stole something from your room."

Hunter sat back in apparent surprise. "What did you steal?"

"Is it a lie or not?"

He peered at her expression. "You're telling me you're a liar and a thief?"

She shook her head. "I'm either a liar *or* a thief. If I'm lying about being a thief, then I'm only a liar. But if I'm telling the truth about being a thief, I'm only a thief."

His eyes squinted down.

"Come on," she coaxed. "Which is it?"

"You're a liar," he said. "You didn't steal anything from my bedroom."

"You sure?"

"I'm positive."

"You got me," she admitted.

"Okay. Now it's my turn." He folded the napkin and set it aside. "I once wrestled an alligator."

"A real alligator?"

He nodded.

She was intrigued. Who wouldn't be? But she wasn't sold, yet. "Where?"

"A little town in Louisiana."

"Was it a trained alligator? Like in a zoo or something?"

"Nope. Out there in the bayou."

"It must have been pretty small."

"I didn't measure it or anything, but Jack guessed it was about six feet long."

"Jack was there, too?"

Hunter nodded.

Sinclair held out her hand. "Your phone."

"What?"

"I'm calling Jack."

"Oh, no, you're not."

"Oh, yes, I am." She wiggled her fingers.

Hunter shrugged and handed her the phone.

"You're *so* lying," she said. "Which speed dial?"

He grinned. "Four. And I'm not lying."

Sinclair hit number four, and waited while it rang. "You are busted," she said to Hunter.

"Jack Osland," came a sleepy voice. Too late, she remembered the time-zone difference.

"Hi, Jack," she offered guiltily. "It's Sinclair."

There was a pause. Jack's voice turned grave. "What did he do?"

She watched Hunter while she spoke. "He claims he wrestled a six-foot alligator in a Louisiana swamp."

"He told you that?"

"He did."

"Well, it's true."

Sinclair blinked. "Really?"

"Saved my life."

"Really?"

"Anything else?" asked Jack.

"Uh, no. Sorry. Bye." She shut off the phone. "You saved *his life*."

Hunter shrugged. "He exaggerates."

Sinclair whooshed back in the chair. "I'd have bet money you were lying."

Hunter took a sip of his coffee. "I was."

She stilled. "What?"

He nodded "I was lying. I didn't wrestle a six-foot alligator. Are you kidding? I'd have been killed."

She looked down at the phone. "But…Jack…"

"Was lying, too."

"You couldn't possibly have set that up."

"We didn't have to." He lifted the phone from her hand. "You started the conversation by saying 'Hunter told me he wrestled an alligator.' Jack's my cousin; of course he's going to back me up."

"Tag-team lying?"

"It's the very best kind. Your turn."

"I'm not going to be able to top that."

"Give it a try."

Sinclair racked her brain. What could she possibly say that might throw him? Something believable, yet surprising.

Aha!

"I'm pregnant."

Hunter's face went white. "What?" he rasped.

Oh, no. No. She'd gone too far. "I'm lying, Hunter."

He worked his jaw, but no words came out.

"Hunter, seriously. I'm *lying*."

"You're not pregnant?"

"I am not pregnant."

"If you were, would you tell me?"

"I'm not."

"Because we'd get married."

"Hunter. It's a game."

"Will you take a pregnancy test?"

"*No.*"

"I let you phone Jack."

She stood up and rounded the table to him, bending over and putting all the sincerity she could muster into her eyes. "I'm sorry I said I was pregnant. I'm not."

He searched her expression. "You scared me half to death."

She smiled at that, reaching out to pat his cheek. "Not ready to be a daddy?"

He snagged her wrist and pulled her down into his lap. "Not ready for you to keep that big of a secret."

She shook her head. "I wouldn't. I'd tell you."

"Promise?"

"I promise."

He kissed the inside of her wrist. And then his gaze dipped down to her stomach.

She followed it and realized her movements had opened the robe. Her cleavage was showing, and the length of one thigh was visible nearly to her hip.

But Hunter wasn't looking at her thigh. His gaze was fixed on her stomach. His big, warm hand moved to press against the robe. It stayed there, and electricity vibrated between them. Then he slipped his hand beneath the robe to cup her soft stomach.

Arousal bloomed within her, radiating out to tingle her limbs. Her lips softened. Her eyelids went heavy. And she molded against his body.

He drew her head down, kissing her softly on the lips, trailing across her cheek, to the crook of her neck, to the tops of her breasts, burrowing down and inhaling deeply.

"I can't fight it anymore," he rasped, tipping to look up at her. "I can't."

"Then don't." She shook her head as she stared into the molten steel of his eyes. "Because it's killing us."

He bracketed her hips with his hands, lifting and turning her, so her legs went around his waist.

She ruffled her hands through his hair, kissing his hairline, his forehead, the tip of his nose.

He tugged the sash, and her robe fell away.

Then he smoothed his hands along her waist, wrapping around, splaying on her bare back, pulling her close over the rough fabric of his slacks. She bent her head and kissed his lips, slanting her mouth over his.

He met her tongue with his own, and she savored his taste,

content to let it last forever. But his hands slipped down, ratcheting up her arousal.

She whimpered.

"I know," he breathed, kissing her harder and deeper, letting his hands roam free, along her thighs, over her breasts, between her legs.

Her breathing turned labored, and she fought a war within herself. Part of her wanted him, right here, right now. Another part wanted to wait, to make it last. He felt good. He felt right.

She arched her back, pressing herself against his slacks.

He braced his forearms beneath her bottom, and came to his feet. She clung to his neck, anchoring her legs around his waist.

A few short steps, and they were there. The high four-poster. He set her down, then laid her back, pushing away the robe until she was completely naked.

She watched his hot gaze linger on her, not even considering adjusting her spread-legged pose. He traced a line between her breasts, down her belly, over her curls, into her center.

She closed her eyes, held on to the image of the unbridled arousal on his face.

She heard him stand.

Heard the rustle of his clothes.

The slide of his zipper.

The creak of his shoes.

"Sinclair?" he whispered, and she opened her eyes to see him standing naked above her.

She stretched out her hands, and he came down beside her, covering her with the weight of one thigh, smoothing her hair back from her face, kissing her gently on her cheek and on the tip of her shoulder.

"You are astonishingly, outrageously beautiful." His tone was reverent.

His words made her shiver.

He was beautiful, too. But more than that, he was Hunter. He was tender and funny, smart and determined—everything she could possibly dream of in a man.

"I want you so bad," he confessed.

Her throat closed up. She was beyond words, but she managed a nod of agreement.

"Do you remember?" he asked.

She nodded again, finding her voice. "Everything," she rasped. *"Everything."*

He inched a hand up her ribcage, finding the soft underside of her breast. He smoothed his thumb over the peak, drawing a lazy circle, pulling her nipple to a pebble. "I remember it, too."

Then he proved his knowledge, finding secrets and hollows, making her purr and moan.

She reached for him in return, running her fingertips over his chest and abdomen. He sucked in a breath as she brushed his erection. He let her test the length and texture, before trapping her wrist and calling a halt.

He pushed her arms over her head, where they had to behave. Then he kissed her mouth, and her neck, and her breasts. He released her hands, as his lips roamed free, testing and suckling. She tangled his hair, moaning his name, everything inside her tightening and heightening.

But he kissed his way back. And merged with her mouth. He moved atop her, linking his fingertips with hers, pressing them down against the softness of the comforter. Her knees moved apart, and their bodies met, slick and hot and impossibly sweet.

He eased inside her, slower than she could bear. She thrashed her head and squeezed his hands, her kisses growing deeper and more frantic. Then she instinctively flexed her hips, and he pushed the final inch to paradise.

He set a rhythm, speeding up and slowing down. She felt the fire of passion build within her. Her eyes squeezed shut, and her focus contracted to the spot where their bodies met.

The world turned to heat, and sensation and scent. She felt his muscles clench, and his desire take over. He sped up and stayed there, his thrusts intent and solid. A moan started low in her throat. It grew louder and more frantic, until she cried out his name, and the world fell apart, and his body pulsed within her.

They breathed in sync for long minutes after.

"You okay?" His voice seemed to come from a long way off. His body was a delicious weight on top of her, and she couldn't move a muscle, including her eyelids.

"Sinclair?" he pressed, sounding worried.

"I think we've cured the tension," she mumbled.

There was a chuckle low in his throat, and he eased his weight to the side, gathering her in his arms. "I do believe you're right."

Seven

Sinclair caught sight of her new haircut in the mirror at Club Seventy-Five. She'd second-guessed herself about getting it so short, but she had to admit, she loved it. Textured to spiky wisps around her ears and neck, it was light on top, and her new bangs swooped across her forehead, while the foil, blond highlights brought out the color in her cheeks.

Of course, the color could have come from the tote bag full of Luscious Lavender cosmetics that she'd had applied this afternoon. The beautician had painstakingly shown Sinclair how to apply the makeup herself, but she wasn't so sure she'd be successful—at least not without a lot of practice.

But, for tonight, she felt gorgeous.

She was wearing one of the jazzier dresses they'd bought at La Petite Fleur. A Diana Kamshak, it was a mint-green satin party dress. The short, full skirt sported blue horizontal stripes, and it was accented by a blue and silver border at the mid-thigh hem.

Above the wide silver belt, the top was tight and strapless, with a princess neckline that drew attention to her breasts. She wouldn't normally be comfortable in something so revealing. But every time she looked into Hunter's eyes, she felt beautiful.

She'd had dozens of covetous looks at her sapphire-and-diamond choker. Or perhaps it was because she was also wearing the Diana Kamshak dress. Or perhaps it was because she was with Hunter.

She'd decided on the teardrop diamond earrings, and she liked the way their weight bounced on her ears. She still hadn't taken off the goldfish bracelet, and it made a kicky addition to the outfit. She liked it. She liked it all.

The lights and the music pounded lifeblood through her bones. Or maybe it was Hunter that pounded through her bones. They were out on the floor, amidst the crowd, alternating between touching, smiling, and just moving independently to the beat.

He slipped an arm around her waist, tugging her close, spinning her to the rhythm of the house band. Sinclair smiled, then laughed out loud, she couldn't help it. The musicians launched into another lively and compelling tune.

"You thirsty?" he called in her ear as the song finished with a metallic flourish.

She nodded.

He put at hand at the small of her back, guiding her off the dance floor. "Water? Wine? Champagne?"

Sinclair did a little shimmy next to their table. "Champagne."

He gave her a kiss on the cheek. "My kind of girl."

Then he helped her into the high bar chair and disappeared into the crowd.

Sinclair liked being Hunter's kind of girl.

She liked the fashions. She liked the limos. She loved the sex. And she loved the way they arrived at a club and got escorted immediately through the side entrance. No waiting around on the curb for Hunter Osland.

But putting all that aside, what she liked most of all was Hunter—the person. Period.

Okay, the one thing she didn't like was the high shoes. She supposed she'd get used to them at some point, but right now, they just made one of her baby toes burn and both calves ache.

She slipped the heels off under the table.

Hunter returned with the drinks as the band announced a break. She sipped at the bubbles and grinned.

"Good?" asked Hunter, picking up his own glass.

"Great," said Sinclair.

Two men slid into the other chairs at the table. "Hey, Osland," one greeted.

"Bobby," said Hunter. "Nice to see you." Then he nodded to the other man. "Scooter."

Scooter nodded back.

Then both men smiled appreciatively at Sinclair.

"Sinclair Mahoney," Hunter introduced. "This is Bobby Bonnista and Scooter Hinze from Blast On Black."

"Sorry," said Sinclair, leaning into Hunter's shoulder. "I should have recognized you right away but I guess I was focused on Hunter."

Hunter's chest puffed out, and he put an arm around her. "What can I say?"

Both men guffawed at his posturing, but smiled at Sinclair and held out their hands.

She shook. "Loved the music."

"Thanks," Bobby nodded. "We're trying out some new stuff tonight. It's always a challenge."

"Well, it's great," she said sincerely.

"Got time for a drink?" asked Hunter.

Bobby shook his head. "We're on in ten minutes."

A server stopped at the table and topped up Sinclair's glass of champagne.

The two musicians rose from their chairs. "Coming to the party?" asked Bobby. "Suite 1202 at the Ivy."

"Not sure," said Hunter.

The men glanced at Sinclair with a sly, knowing grin. But, surprisingly, Sinclair found she didn't mind.

"Sorry about that," said Hunter after they'd left.

She shrugged. "Were they wrong?"

He leaned very close to her ear. "That," he rumbled, "is entirely up to you."

Blast On Black took the stage once more.

Sinclair wriggled her feet back into the strappy sandals. "Want to dance?"

Sinclair's shoes dangled from her fingertips as they made their way down the hotel hallway.

"Tired?" asked Hunter, slipping the key card into her room lock.

"A little tipsy," she admitted, crossing the threshold and tossing her shoes in the corner. The bed had been turned down and the adjoining door left open.

"Champagne in France will do that to you."

"It was delicious." She took a deep breath and blinked away the buzzing in her head.

Hunter locked the door, then reached into his pocket to retrieve his cell phone. He pressed the on button and sighed.

"Messages?" she asked, digging into her purse to check her own phone.

"Thirty-five," he said, hitting the scroll button with his thumb.

"I have six," she frowned. "Boy, do I feel unpopular." Two of them were from Kristy, the rest from the office. She'd been keeping in touch with Amber via e-mail, making sure the ball plans were under control, despite Chantal's meddling.

"Enjoy it," he advised. Then he pressed a couple of keys, putting the phone to his ear.

"Hey, Richard," he said.

Then he waited in silence.

Sinclair struggled to reach the zipper on her dress.

"They did?" said Hunter.

She gave up and crossed the room to Hunter, turning her back. She automatically reached to pull her hair out of the way, but it wasn't there. She touched the top of her head, raking her fingers through her new short hair, enjoying the light feel while Hunter tugged down her zipper.

She wandered into the bathroom to find fresh towels and robes. Stepping out of her dress, she shrugged into a robe. She scrubbed off her makeup and carried the dress to the closet. She'd have to send it for cleaning tomorrow, but she didn't have the heart to toss it on a chair overnight. It was a fabulous dress.

"Thanks, Richard," Hunter was saying. "That's great news." The tone of his voice caught Sinclair's attention.

Hunter snapped his phone shut. "It's done."

"What's done?"

"You are looking at the new owner of Castlebay Spas. Everything should clear escrow tomorrow."

A huge grin burst out on Sinclair's face. "That's fantastic!" She skipped across the room to give him a hug.

He nodded against her shoulder, squeezing her tight.

"Sweetheart, the two of us are going to launch Lush Beauty to the stars."

"As long as I can keep up the glam charade so Roger is happy."

"I'll fire Chantal tomorrow if that's what it takes."

Sinclair sobered. "You wouldn't do that, would you?"

"I won't have to."

"But, even if you did. You'd never do that. I mean, I couldn't live with myself if I built a career based on your intervention."

He took both her hands in his and squeezed. "It'll never happen. Seriously. Stop borrowing trouble. We just had some amazingly good news, and we need to celebrate. And we need to plan a tour of the spas. Rome, London…"

She felt better. The makeover was moving along as planned, and the spa launch was more than she'd ever dreamed.

He loosened the knot in his tie. "I'm going next door to shower."

"Okay."

"While I'm gone, you get happy again. Okay?"

"I will."

"Good." He winked at her, stripping off the tie as he strode through the adjoining door.

Sinclair curled up in an armchair. She mentally did the math on time zones and realized she could safely return Kristy's calls.

"Hello," came Kristy's voice.

"Hey, it's me."

"*You.* Finally! What the heck's going on?"

"I'm still in Paris."

"Wonderful, dear sister. But tell me how you ended up in Paris in the first place?"

"We took the jet. That's one very cool jet, by the way."

"Funny. What on earth happened at work?"

"You remember my boss, Roger?"

"Short guy, big nose."

"That's him. Well, he's got this new protégée, Chantal, who's off the charts avante garde, giggly and girly and squealy. And he's decided she's the face Lush Beauty needs for PR."

"They fired you?"

"No. Nobody fired me. But I can easily see her at the podium and me in a dingy back file room if things keep going like this."

"You know Hunter's the CEO now, right?" asked Kristy.

"And, so?"

"Well, you are my sister...."

Sinclair was slightly insulted. "You're suggesting nepotism?" That was as bad as sleeping her way to the top.

"You don't need nepotism. But if Roger and this Chantal are out to lunch—"

"Actually, Hunter agrees with them."

Silence.

"He thinks my image could use some updating."

Kristy's voice took on an incredulous quality. "And you're okay with that? That doesn't sound like you."

Sinclair had to agree that it didn't sound like her. And she'd been avoiding delving too closely into her motivations for going along with him.

"True. But the new wardrobe is nice."

Concern grew in Kristy's voice. "Sinclair, you're not—"

"I'm not."

"—falling for Hunter. Because I've been talking to Jack, and to his grandfather, and he's not a good long-term prospect."

"You're getting ahead of yourself," said Sinclair, embarrassed that Kristy would have discussed the situation with the Osland family.

"You remember how you were after Zeke."

"I got over Zeke just fine." It hadn't taken that long, maybe a few weeks. "And I have Hunter completely in context."

"You sure?"

"I'm sure." Well, kind of sure. "It's all business," Sinclair insisted. "In fact, we're about to launch Lush Beauty in the biggest way." She thought about the spa deal and the time spent with Hunter. "Do you ever find your new life with Jack surreal?"

Kristy laughed. "All the time."

"Hunter and I went to a club tonight. First class all the way. The band even stopped by. And the weird thing? It seemed pretty normal."

"It does take some getting used to," Kristy agreed.

"Yeah, for the launch of the new Luscious Lavender line across Europe, Hunter bought a chain of spas!" She heard him moving around next door. "Sounds like he's out of the shower."

"Hunter is in your *shower?* What the—"

"He's next door. We have adjoining rooms." Then Sinclair realized she probably didn't want to have a detailed conversation on that, particularly when Hunter was about to waltz back into her room. "Better go."

"Wait—"

"Bye." Sinclair quickly disconnected.

"Hey, babe," said Hunter, padding inside in one of the white robes. "You're not going to shower?"

She stifled a yawn, dropping her phone on the little desk beside the armchair. "Tomorrow."

He crossed toward her. "Works for me." He smiled as he leaned down to kiss her. "Ready for bed?"

"Just let me find something to change into."

He burrowed into her neck, planting kisses along the way. "You're not going to need a nightgown."

She chuckled at his gravelly voice and the way his rough skin tickled hers.

His hands slipped beneath her robe. "What's this?"

"It's called underwear."

"You trying to slow me down?"

"Not worth the work, am I?"

"Always." He drew her to her feet.

Then his cell phone rang.

He swore, but picked it up and checked the number. "Richard."

"You need to take that?"

"Tomorrow," he said. "Tomorrow, we need to strategize."

"Over the spas?"

He nodded.

Sinclair squinted. "I thought the deal was done?"

"It is." His lips compressed. "Tomorrow I figure out how to explain to my family I spent several hundred million."

Everything inside Sinclair went still. "How do you mean?"

"I mean, I'm going to hear words like *reckless* and *impulsive*. They'll be ticked, so I need to figure out how to present this just right so Gramps doesn't go ballistic."

Her stomach turned to a lead weight. "But I thought…"

He waited.

"I thought you were ready to tell them."

He coughed out a cold laugh. "Not hardly." He tossed the phone down and moved toward her. "But it can wait until tomorrow; you're what's important tonight."

"I have to use the bathroom," Sinclair blurted.

"Sure," he said, obviously puzzled as to why she was

making a big deal about it. "You should go ahead and do that."

Hesitating only a second, she grabbed her phone.

He glanced at her hand. "Expecting a call?"

"Maybe. I don't know." She headed for the door. "Time zones, you know." Then she quickly shut herself in.

Her hands were shaking as she dialed Kristy.

"Come on. Come on," she muttered as the connection rang hollow. "Pick up."

She got her sister's voice mail and jiggled her foot as she waited for the beep.

"Kristy? It's me. I *really* need to talk to you. I'll try again in a few minutes. Make sure you pick up."

What to do now? She needed Hunter out of the way. She needed Hunter…asleep.

Okay, this was going to be tricky. He didn't seem like he was in the mood for anything remotely quick.

She exited the bathroom, and was pulled immediately into his arms, engulfed in a major hug, peppered with kisses that under any other circumstances would have been erotic and totally arousing.

"Uh, Hunter?"

"Yeah?"

"I'm…not…"

He pulled back. "Something wrong?"

"I'm still woozy from the drinks," she lied.

His eyes glowed pewter as he waggled his eyebrows. "You maybe need to lie down?"

She shook her head. "No. I mean yes. I mean." She hit him with the most contrite expression she could muster. "Can we wait until morning?"

His gaze grew concerned. "That bad?"

She nodded. It was worse, only not in the way he was imagining.

"Come on, then." He led her to the bed, pushing aside the comforter and tucking her in.

He slipped under the covers beside her and spooned their bodies together. He kissed the back of her neck, smoothing her hair. "Sleep," he muttered.

She nodded miserably, and pretended to do just that.

Half an hour later, his breathing was deep and even. Engulfed in his warmth, she was struggling to stay awake herself. She didn't dare wait any longer.

She cautiously slipped from the bed, snagged her phone, and tiptoed into the bathroom.

She tried Kristy again, still coming up with voice mail.

"Kristy?" she whispered harshly. "You have to call me. I'm sleeping with my phone on vibrate. Wake me up!"

Then she clicked it off, forced herself to swallow her panic, took a drink of water to combat her dry throat, and headed back to bed.

"You okay?" Hunter mumbled as she climbed back in.

"Thirsty," she responded guiltily as he drew her against him.

"You'll be better in the morning," he assured her with a kiss.

She'd be better when Kristy called and was sworn to temporary secrecy. That's when she'd be better.

Sinclair awoke to Hunter's broad hand on her breast. His lips were kissing her neck, and his hardened body was pressed against her backside.

"Morning, sweetheart," he murmured in her ear.

She smiled. "Morning."

He caressed her nipple, sending sparks of desire to her

brain. His free hand trailed along her belly. She gasped, the warmth of arousal swirling and gathering within her.

"I've been waiting," he rumbled. "You slept too long."

"Sorry."

"Make it up to me." His hand slipped to the moisture between her legs.

He flipped her onto her back.

"Right now," he growled.

In answer, she kissed him hard.

A pounding sounded on the door, and someone shouted his name.

Hunter jerked back. "What the—?"

It took her a second to realize the person was pounding outside Hunter's room.

"Don't move," he commanded, staring into her eyes. Then he jackknifed out of bed and stuffed his arms into the robe. He pushed the adjoining door shut behind him. Sinclair sat up, shaking out the cobwebs.

She felt a lump under her thigh, and realized it was her phone. Flipping it open, she quickly checked for a return call from Kristy.

Nothing.

The voices rose in the room next door, drawing Sinclair's attention.

"—be so freaking reckless and impulsive!"

It was Jack's voice, and Sinclair was afraid she might throw up.

"We have talked and *talked* about this," came another gravelly voice. It had to be Cleveland.

The family knew. They were here. And they were angry. And it was all her fault. Sinclair wrapped her arms around her stomach and scrunched her eyes shut tight.

* * *

At first, Hunter was too shocked to react.

He'd gone from Sinclair, soft and pliant in his arms, to his grandfather's harsh wrath in the space of thirty seconds. His brain and his hormones needed time to catch up.

"I can give you the prospectus," he told them. "The financials and the appraisals."

"You can bet your ass you'll be giving us the prospectus, the financials and the appraisals," shouted Gramps.

Then it was Jack's turn. "You can't make unilateral decisions!"

"I can. And so can you and Gramps."

"Not like this."

"Yes, like this. There's no advantage in three guys spending time on what one can do alone." Hunter was warming up now. He just wished he was wearing something other than a bathrobe. "This is a good deal. It's a *great* deal!"

"That's not the point," Jack said.

"The point being that you and Gramps are control freaks?"

"The point being you need to play with the team."

Hunter turned on his grandfather. "You thought it was funny to send me to Lush Beauty. You thought it was funny to send me to Sinclair. Well, guess what? You send me to run a company, I run the damn company."

"I have half a mind to take away your signing authority," Cleveland threatened.

"Because that wouldn't be an overreaction," Hunter countered, folding his arms across his chest.

"You, young man, spent hundreds of millions without so much as an e-mail."

"It's amortized over twenty years. The property values alone—"

"If it wasn't for Sinclair telling Kristy—"

"*What?*" Hunter roared, unable to believe what he'd heard.

Jack and Cleveland stopped dead.

Hunter stared hard at them. "You got information from your wife because my…Sinclair talked?"

"And thank God she did," said Cleveland.

But Hunter was past listening to Jack and his grandfather.

"We're done," he said to them, moving to open the door. "Richard has the details. You take a look at the deal. If you don't like it, I'll sell my Osland International stock and go it on my own."

Jack squinted. "Hunter?"

Hunter swung open the hotel room door. "Talk to you later."

"It wasn't Sinclair's—"

"*Talk* to you later."

Jack moved in front of him. "I can't let you—"

"What?" Hunter barked. "What do you think I'm going to do to her?"

"I don't know."

"Give me a break," he scoffed. He wasn't going to hurt Sinclair. He wouldn't let anybody hurt Sinclair. But the woman had one hell of a lot of explaining to do.

Eight

Hearing the latch click on the adjoining door, Sinclair broke out in a cold sweat. Her fingertips dug into the arms of the chair as she stared straight at the dove-gray painted panel.

The hinges glided silently and Hunter filled the doorway, his eyes simmering obsidian. But his voice was cool with control. "I thought we were a team."

She wished he'd shout at her, wished he'd rant. She could take his anger a lot more easily than his disappointment.

She'd let him down. She wanted to explain. She wanted to apologize. But her vocal cords were temporarily paralyzed.

"I trusted you," he continued. "I trusted your confidentiality. I trusted your discretion."

She fought to say something, to gather her thoughts. "I didn't know," she finally blurted out.

"Didn't know what? Was there something ambiguous about 'don't tell anyone, including Kristy and Jack'?"

"But that was before the deal went through."

"The deal went through at 3:00 a.m. this morning. Are you telling me in the five minutes I was in the shower—" He snapped his jaw. "You called Kristy." He gave a cold laugh. "You were so anxious to share gossip about my business dealings that you couldn't even wait until morning?"

"It wasn't gossip."

"Do you have any idea what you've done?"

She slowly shook her head. She could only imagine the implications of her behavior now that she had all the facts.

"Well, that makes two of us," he said. "Because I just offered to sell out of Osland International."

The contents of her stomach turned to a concrete mass.

She opened her mouth, but he waved a dismissive hand. "Much as I'd like to sit around and debate this with you, I've got a few problems to solve this morning. I'll have to talk to you later."

Then he turned back to his own room, shutting the door firmly behind him.

Sinclair's cell phone chimed.

She glanced reflexively down to see Kristy's number on the readout. She couldn't talk to her sister now. She didn't think she could talk to anyone.

There was every possibility she'd ruined Hunter's life. The worry that she might not get plum assignments or choice promotions at Lush Beauty faded to nothing in the face of that reality.

She stared at nothing for nearly an hour, then shoved herself into a standing position. She crossed to the closet and took out the clothes she'd been wearing when she arrived in Paris. They looked pale and boring compared to the new outfits, but she didn't have the heart to wear any of them.

She combed her hair, brushed her teeth, left the cosmetics on the counter and gathered up the suitcase with her old clothes inside. It seemed like a long walk to the elevator, longer still across the marble-floored atrium in the hotel lobby.

She figured Hunter would check out for her, so she wound her way past smiling tourists, bustling bellboys and intense businessmen. The men reminded her of Hunter and made her sadder by the moment.

Finally, she was out on the sidewalk, glancing up and down for a taxi. A hotel bellhop asked her a question in French. She tried to remember how to ask for a taxi, but it had slipped her mind.

In the sidewalk café next to her, propane heaters chugged out the only warmth in her world. People were eating breakfast, enjoying the sights of the busy street, their lives still intact.

The bellhop asked the question again.

She remembered. "Cabine de taxi?"

"Going somewhere?" came Hunter's voice from behind her.

"The airport," she answered without turning.

"I thought Mahoneys didn't run away."

"I'm not running away."

"You mad at me?"

The question surprised a cold laugh from her.

"Because I'm pretty mad at you," he said.

"No kidding."

A taxi pulled up, but Hunter let someone else take it. "So, what's your plan?"

She sighed. "Why'd you do that?"

"We're not finished talking."

"I thought you had problems to solve."

He snorted. "And how. But I want to know your plans first."

Sinclair looked pointedly down at her suitcase.

"You left the rest of your clothes in the closet," he said.

"Those are your clothes."

"So, you're going to pout? That's your plan?"

"I'm not pouting." She was making a strategic exit from an untenable situation before he had a chance to ask her to go himself.

Another taxi came to a stop, and Hunter sent it away.

"Do you think we could sit down?" he asked with a frustrated sigh, gesturing to the café.

Sinclair shrugged. If he wanted to ream her out some more, she supposed she owed him that much.

He picked up her suitcase, and she moved to one of the rattan chairs. She folded her hands on the round glass table and looked him straight in the eyes.

"Go ahead," she said, steeling herself.

"You think I'm here to yell at you?"

She didn't answer.

"Good grief, you're as bad as Jack." Hunter signaled the waitress for coffee, and Sinclair decided it might be a very long lecture.

"It seems to me…" said Hunter, as the uniformed woman filled their cups. He shook out a packet of sugar, tore off the corner and dumped it into the mug.

Sinclair just stared at the rising steam.

"You have two choices," Hunter continued. "You can slink back to New York with your makeover half done and take your chances with Roger. Or you can buck up and stay here a few more days to finish it."

"It seems to me," she offered, forcing him to get to the heart of the matter. "Those are your choices, not mine."

"How so?"

"Why would you want me to stay? Why would you want to help me? I ruined your life."

"We don't know that yet."

"Well, I might have."

"Possibly. Did you do it on purpose?"

"Of course not."

"So you weren't dishonest, you simply lacked certain details and a little good judgment."

She tightened her jaw. She normally had great judgment. "Right," she said.

A small glimmer flickered in his eyes. "You want to fight me, don't you?"

She wrapped her hands around the warm stoneware mug. "I'm in the wrong. I can take it."

"Very magnanimous of you."

"Are we done? Can I go now?"

"Do you want to go now?"

She didn't answer.

"Seriously, Sinclair. Do you want to walk out on Paris, the makeover and me just because things went off the rails?"

Things had done a lot more than go off the rails. She forced herself to ask him, "What do you want?"

"I want to turn the clock back a couple of hours to when you were sleeping in my arms."

"I want to turn it back nine."

He nodded, and they sat in silence for a few moments while dishes clattered and voices rose and fell at nearby tables. A gust of cool wind blew through, while the propane heaters chugged gamely on.

Hunter took a sip of his coffee. "Let me tell you why Jack and Gramps were so upset."

"Because you spent hundreds of millions of dollars without

telling them?" As soon as the flip answer was out, she regretted it. "Sorry."

But Hunter actually smiled. "Good guess. It's because they wanted me to call them first. They wanted to jump in and assess the deal before I made a decision. They wanted to research and analyze and contemplate. Do you have any idea how long Jack and Cleveland's brand of due diligence takes?"

Sinclair shook her head.

"The deal would have been lost before they even lined up the legal team."

"Did you explain that to them?"

He shot her a look. "That was my plan. Until you stepped in."

"Sorry," she said again, knowing it would never be enough.

"I know you are." But he didn't sound angry. He sounded resigned.

Cars whizzed by on the narrow street, while a contingent of Japanese businessmen amassed on the sidewalk nearby.

"What will you do now?" Sinclair asked.

"That's entirely up to you."

"You're seriously willing to keep this up?"

He nodded. "I am. There may be a lot of yelling from Jack and Gramps over the next few days, but I want to finish what we started."

"I can handle yelling."

"Good. You know anything about ballroom dancing?"

"Not much."

"Then that's next on our list." His expression softened. "You are going to take their breath away."

A knot let go in Sinclair's stomach.

"Flower for the pretty lady?" came an old woman's gravelly voice. She held a white rose toward Hunter, her bangles and hoop earrings sparkling against colorful clothing and a bright silk headscarf. "I will tell her fortune."

Hunter accepted the flower and nodded.

The old woman clasped Sinclair's hands, her jet-black eyes searching Sinclair's face. Then she smiled. "Ahhh. Fertility."

"I'm going to be a farmer?"

The woman revealed a snaggle-toothed smile, her gaze going to Sinclair's stomach.

Sinclair sure didn't like the implication of that.

"Trust your heart," said the old woman.

"I'm not pregnant," Sinclair pointed out.

The old woman released Sinclair's hands and touched her chin. "I see wealth and beauty."

"That's a whole lot better than fertility," Sinclair muttered.

Hunter laughed and reached for his wallet.

Sinclair caught the numbers on the bills he passed to the woman. Both hers and the old woman's eyes went wide.

The woman quickly hustled away.

"Did you know her or something?" Sinclair asked.

"I once knew somebody like her." Hunter tucked his wallet into his pocket and handed Sinclair the rose.

She held it to her nose and inhaled the sweet fragrance. Hunter wanted her to stay. The relief nearly brought tears to her eyes.

"Somebody like her?" she asked Hunter, inhaling one more time. "I once burned down a gypsy's tent." Then he smiled gently at Sinclair.

He swiveled his coffee mug so the handle was facing him. "When I was a teenager, a gypsy at the local circus told my fortune. She said I'd fall for a redheaded girl and have twins."

Sinclair reflexively touched her hair.

"The thought of twins freaked me out, too. I wanted to be a rock star."

"So, you burned down her tent?"

"She also said Jack would marry a woman he didn't trust, and we'd buy a golf course."

"But, you burned down her tent?" Sinclair repeated.

"It was an accident."

"You sure?"

He rocked back. "Hey, is there anything about me that strikes you as vindictive?"

"I guess not," she admitted, a small smile forming on her lips. Heck, he wasn't even kicking her out for ruining his life.

"It was an accident. And Gramps compensated her fairly. But, I guess I've always felt a little guilty."

"Have you been giving money to random gypsies ever since?"

"It's not like I come across a lot of them. Alhough…" He pretended to ponder. "I suppose a charitable foundation wouldn't be out of order."

"I'm sure they appreciate it."

Sinclair's cell phone chimed.

She opened her purse to check the lighted number. "Kristy." It chimed again under her hand.

"Better answer it," Hunter advised. "She's probably worried."

"So was I," Sinclair said over the sound.

His hand covered hers for a brief second. "We'll talk more."

Sinclair pressed a button and raised the phone to her ear. "Hey, Kristy."

"You okay?"

"Yeah. I'm fine."

"And Hunter?"

Sinclair looked at him. "He's had better mornings."

"What was he *thinking?*" There was a clear rebuke in

Kristy's tone. "Going out on his own. Jack says that Hunter was being dangerously cavalier with the family fortune."

Some protective instinct leapt to life within Sinclair. "He was thinking it was a good deal."

Hunter shook his head, mouthing the word, "Don't."

Sinclair ignored him. "And they might want to look closely at it before they decide it's a bad risk."

Hunter stood to lean over the table, but Sinclair turned away, protecting the phone. The least she could do was come down on his side.

"Are you *defending* him? Did he try to make this your fault? It wasn't your fault, you know. You were being honest. He was being underhanded."

"He was being smart."

There was a shocked silence on the line.

"Are you sleeping with him again?" Kristy demanded.

"None of your business."

"That's it. I'm coming to Paris."

Hunter lunged forward and grabbed the phone from Sinclair's hands.

"Goodbye," she quickly called as he snapped it shut.

"Have you lost your mind?" asked Hunter.

"She said you were being underhanded."

"You can't fight with your sister over me."

Sinclair folded her arms over her chest and blew out a breath. "Sure, I can."

Hunter handed back the phone. "No. You can't. She's your sister. Keep your eye on the long game."

Meaning Hunter was the short game?

"And she loves you," he said.

"She's coming to Paris."

"You want to go to London?"

Sinclair grinned. "We couldn't."

Hunter sighed. "You're right. We couldn't."

She caught a figure in her peripheral vision, turning to see Jack pulling up a chair at their table.

"You okay?" he asked Sinclair.

"You're as bad as Kristy," Sinclair responded. "What exactly do you think he'd do to me?"

"What *did* he do?"

"He invited me to go ballroom dancing. We're getting ready for the Valentine's Day ball on Thursday."

Jack shot his gaze to Hunter. "That true?"

"What if it is?"

"I just had a call from Kristy," said Jack.

"She's coming to Paris," announced Sinclair.

Jack nodded. "That's what she said." He was still eyeing up Hunter suspiciously. "You'd better sign us up, too."

After the day they'd had, Hunter wanted nothing more than to curl up in bed and hold Sinclair tight in his arms. He'd discovered he hated fighting with her. And he hated that her family and his had decided to protect her from him. Even now, across the floor in the Versailles Ballroom, Kristy was scoping them out, staring daggers at him.

A private jet had whisked her across the Atlantic in time for dinner.

Part of him wanted to thumb his nose at the lot and haul Sinclair away so they could be alone. Another part of him recognized they had legitimate concerns. His efforts to help her had gotten all mixed up with his desire for her.

He didn't want to hurt her, but he might in the end. The Lush Valentine's Day ball was only a few days away. He'd make sure she was a smash hit there, but then what?

She'd still work for him. Could they possibly keep sleeping together? Could they keep it a secret? And what did that say about them if they did?

As he guided her through a simple waltz, he considered the possibility that Kristy was right. After all, who would have Sinclair's best interests at heart more than her twin sister? A twin sister whose thinking wasn't clouded by passion?

God knew his was clouded by something.

Sinclair had dressed for the evening in a brilliant-red strapless satin gown. When he glanced at her creamy shoulders, the hint of cleavage, and her long, smooth neck, his thoughts were definitely on his own best interest. And that best interest was in peeling the gown off inch by glorious inch to reveal whatever it was she had, or didn't have, on underneath.

The bodice molded gently over her breasts, it nipped in at her waist, then molded over her bottom, while the full skirt whispered around her gorgeous legs.

"How am I doing?" she asked as the music's tempo changed.

"Fine," he told her, forcing his thoughts back to his job as dance instructor. "Ready to try something more?"

She nodded, blue eyes shining up at him, making him wish all over again that he could whisk her away.

He led her into a turn. She stumbled, but he held her up, tightening his hand in the small of her back, filing the sensation away in his brain.

"Sorry," she told him.

"No problem. Just pay attention to my hand," he reminded her, demonstrating the touches. "This means left. This means right. Back, and forward."

He tried the turn again.

She stumbled.

He tried one more time, and this time she succeeded.

But, while she grinned, she fumbled the next step.

He tried not to smile at her efforts. "I can see this is going to take practice."

"You're too sudden with your signals. And why do you get to call all the moves?"

"Because I'm the man."

"That's lame."

"And because I know how to dance."

"Okay, that's better."

Someone tapped Hunter on the shoulder. He turned to see Jack, looking to switch partners. Before he knew it, Kristy was in his arms.

"Hello, Hunter." She smiled, but he could see the glitter of determination behind her eyes.

"Hello, Kristy."

"I see you've spirited my sister away to Paris."

"I'm helping her out."

"That's one way to put it."

"What's another?" he challenged, keeping half an eye on Jack and Sinclair.

"Why don't you tell me what your intentions are?"

To have sex with Sinclair—the most amazing woman I've ever met—until we can't see straight. "I don't know what you mean?" he stalled.

"You know exactly what I mean."

He did. And that was the problem. His interests and Sinclair's did not coincide.

"I have no intention of hurting her," he told Kristy honestly.

"You think Jack intended to hurt me?"

"I think Jack was insane to marry you."

Kristy's eyes flashed.

"You know what I mean. He went into it for all the wrong reasons."

"Unlike you and Sinclair?" She didn't give him a chance to respond. "She's going to fall for you, Hunter. You're wining her and dining her and she's thinking she's become a fairy princess. How could she help but fall for you?"

"Point taken." Hunter tried a turn with Kristy, and she easily followed his lead. But it wasn't the same as dancing with Sinclair. It was nothing at all like dancing with Sinclair.

"So, what are you going to do?"

"For tonight—" Hunter took a deep breath and made up his mind "—I'm going to switch rooms with you and Jack."

Kristy and Jack were on a different floor of the hotel. And Hunter knew deep down in his heart that the adjoining door with Sinclair would prove too much of a temptation.

"You're a good man, Hunter," said Kristy, her eyes softening.

"Can I have that in writing? It might sway your husband."

"I'm talking about your moral code, not your business savvy."

"Nice."

"But that's none of my business."

"The push and pull has been going on a long time," said Hunter. "Jack, Gramps, the investors gripe and complain, but they take the dividends all the same."

"Your investments make dividends?"

"And capital gains, each and every one of them."

Kristy shook her head in obvious confusion. "Then why—"

"Because they think the odds are catching up with me, and they're sure I'm taking the entire flagship down one day."

"Will you?"

"Not planning on it." He danced her toward Jack and Sinclair. He might not be able to hold Sinclair in his bed tonight, but he could at least hold her on the dance floor until the clock struck midnight.

Nine

When Hunter had squeezed her hand in front of Kristy and Jack, down in the lobby and said, "See you in the morning," Sinclair knew it was all for show. So she brushed her hair, put on fresh perfume, and changed into the purple negligee from La Petite Fleur. She'd even touched up her face with a few of the Luscious Lavender cosmetics.

So, when the knock came from the adjoining hotel room, she was ready. Pulse pounding, skin tingling, anticipation humming along her nervous system, she opened the door.

"Hey, sis," sang Kristy. Then she tossed a command over her shoulder, "Avert your eyes, Jack."

Sinclair's jaw dropped open.

"I brought a nice Chardonnay." Kristy waved an open bottle in the air. "You got some glasses?"

Kristy breezed past her, and Sinclair met Jack's eyes.

"Jack," Kristy warned.

"Sorry," he called, lowering his gaze.

Sinclair turned to her sister. "What on earth—"

"You might want to shut the door," said Kristy.

"Where's Hunter?"

"We traded rooms."

Sinclair swung the door shut, battling her shock. "I can't believe you would—"

"It was his idea. He asked me to do it."

Why would Hunter ask to trade rooms? "Did you threaten him?" Sinclair asked suspiciously.

Kristy poured two glasses of wine. "Yeah. I did, so he backed off. Does that sound like Hunter?"

"No," Sinclair admitted. Hunter refused to back down from Jack and his grandfather. He sure wasn't going to back down from Kristy.

Kristy rounded the small coffee table and flopped down on one of the armchairs. "He traded rooms, because he doesn't want to hurt you. I admire that."

"He's not going to hurt me." Hurting was the furthest thing from what would happen between Hunter and Sinclair tonight.

Kristy took in Sinclair's outfit. "Well, he'd sure be doing something with you dressed like that."

Sinclair glanced down. "What? So we bought a few things at La Petite Fleur."

Dressed in a snazzy workout suit, Kristy curled her legs beneath her.

"And where do you see this thing going?"

"I haven't thought about it," Sinclair lied. She'd pictured everything from an "hasta la vista, baby" to a tear-stained goodbye, to a white dress and a cathedral.

"You work for him."

"I know. Don't you think I know?"

"Reality check," said Kristy. "Hunter's not a one-woman man."

"Reality check," Sinclair countered. "I'm not a one-man woman."

"Not before now."

"Do you honestly think I've fallen in love with him?" She hadn't.

"Not yet," said Kristy. "But you're taking an awfully big risk. You'll have to work with him afterward no matter what. With all the money he's invested in Castlebay, he's going to have to spend one heck of a lot of time at Lush Beauty. He *needs* this to work. And if your past becomes a problem, guess who's going to be gone?"

"You think Hunter would fire me?" Talk about extrapolating facts to the worst-case scenario.

"I think he might have to make a choice."

Sinclair took a long swallow of her wine, hating the fact that the scenario was possible.

She spun the stem of her glass around her fingertips. "What does Jack think?"

"Jack thinks Hunter's playing with fire. He's been reckless and impulsive before."

Sinclair tipped up the glass for another swallow. Reckless and impulsive, everybody seemed to agree on that, including Hunter.

"And it was his idea to switch rooms with you?" Sinclair confirmed.

Kristy nodded.

Sinclair played around with that little fact. Switching rooms meant Hunter thought it wouldn't last. Chivalrous of him to back off, really. Telling, but chivalrous.

"Did you get my message from last night?"

"I did."

Sinclair couldn't keep the hurt from her voice. "Why didn't you call me?" At least then she would have known to give Hunter a heads-up.

"I'd already told Jack what you said."

Sinclair watched her sister closely. "And Jack told you not to call me."

Kristy hesitated, then she gave a nod. It was her turn to drain her glass.

"Men coming between us," said Sinclair. "Who'd have thought?"

"He's my husband. And Hunter's his cousin. And this was family business."

"And I'm not family."

"Not the Osland family."

Sinclair nodded. "Not the Osland family."

Kristy tucked her blond hair behind her ears. "You sure you're not in love with him?"

She wasn't. Of all the things going on here, that, at least, wasn't an issue. "We've known each other a week. We've slept together exactly twice."

"I fell for Jack in a weekend."

"Are you *trying* to talk me into loving Hunter?"

"I'm wondering if you should come back to New York with me tomorrow."

"My makeover's not done yet."

She wouldn't run away. But she could keep it professional. They'd finish the dance lessons, take the planned tours of Castlebay locations, then she'd return to the U.S. and normal life. Her career would get back on track, and Hunter would go out and make more millions.

No big deal. No huge goodbye. They'd settle into their respective lives, and he'd forget all about her.

* * *

The next morning, as arranged, Sinclair entered the hotel dining room for a goodbye breakfast with Kristy. The maître d' recognized her and escorted her through the maze of diners, around the corner to a huge balcony overlooking the atrium.

There, the entire contingent of Oslands sat at a round table, heads bent together, talking rapidly and earnestly, frustration clear on Jack's and Cleveland's faces.

When Jack spotted Sinclair, he touched Cleveland's arm. The man looked up and stopped talking. Hunter and Kristy caught on, and all four shifted back. Forced smiles appeared on their faces.

She'd never felt so much like an outsider in her life.

Kristy stood. "Morning, sis." She came forward for a quick hug, gesturing to a chair between her and Cleveland.

Sinclair pointed to the way she'd come in. "I can…"

"Don't be silly," said Kristy. She shot a glance to the men.

They all came to their feet, talking overtop of one another as they insisted she stay.

She looked at Hunter, but his gaze was guarded. The intimacy was gone, and she couldn't find a clue as to whether she should be here or go.

Hunter moved around Cleveland to pull out her chair.

Sinclair sat down.

"Where were we?" asked Kristy. "Oh, yes. We were talking about the cruise."

Jack smoothly picked up on his wife's cue. "Can you be ready tomorrow afternoon?" he asked. "The captain could wait in port until Tuesday morning, but it's best if we keep the ship on schedule."

Cleveland sat in sullen silence.

"Do you think I should pick up a few sundresses before we go?" Kristy chirped. "Or maybe do a little—"

"This is ridiculous," said Sinclair.

Everyone looked at her.

She started to rise. "I'm going back to my—"

Reaching behind Cleveland, Hunter grabbed her arm. "You're not going anywhere."

She stared at him, then included everybody. "You have things to talk about. And it's not Kristy's sundresses."

Jack spoke up. "I happen to have a passionate interest in Kristy's sundresses. More so in her bikinis."

"Sinclair's right," barked Cleveland.

"Thank you," said Sinclair.

He swiveled in his chair to face her. "But she doesn't have to leave."

Sinclair didn't know what to say to that. The hollow buzz of voices from the atrium washed over her while his piercing eyes held her in place.

"I understand you were involved in the Castlebay acquisition."

"Gramps," warned Hunter.

"Well?" Cleveland pressed. "Were you or were you not?"

Sinclair struggled not to squirm under his probe, excruciatingly aware that this man held controlling interest in Osland International, which held controlling interest in Lush Beauty Products, and he could end her career with the snap of his fingers.

"Yes," she answered. "It was my idea."

"It was *my* idea," said Hunter.

"But—"

"Sinclair may have mentioned something about a single spa in New York. But I approached Castlebay. I did the research. I agreed to the price. And I signed the check. So, back off on Sinclair."

Cleveland turned to Hunter. "I'm interested in how much influence she has over you."

"None," said Hunter. "It was a business decision, and it was a good one. You read the reports."

Sinclair tried not to react to that statement. Of course it was a business decision. And she never assumed she had any influence over Hunter. But, somehow, his words hurt all the same.

Cleveland nodded. "I read the reports. The problem is cash flow."

"I just told you, borrow against the Paraguay mines."

"With currency fluctuations and the political instability? Do you want Osland International to fall down like a house of cards, boy?"

"Jack could give up the cruise ships he's just acquired," said Hunter.

"Jack cleared the cruise ship with the Board of Directors," Jack drawled.

Sinclair was afraid to move. She wanted to speak up, to explain. But couldn't summon the words.

Kristy leaned over and whispered in her ear. "Relax."

"We have options," Hunter spat.

"Are you kidding?" Sinclair hissed to her sister.

"They do this all the time," said Kristy.

"Castlebay is going to turn Lush Beauty into a gold mine," said Hunter with grim determination. "And *that's* what you sent me to do there."

"I sent you there to apologize to Sinclair."

Sinclair couldn't hold back. "He doesn't need—"

"You don't want a piece of this," Hunter warned her. Then

he set his sights back on his grandfather. "Next time you have a problem with my behavior, talk to me."

"Why? You never listen."

"And where the hell do you think I might have inherited that trait?"

"Insolent young pup," Cleveland muttered.

"Wait for it," Kristy whispered.

Cleveland squared his shoulders. "Don't you forget who built this company from an empty warehouse and a corner store."

"And you took exactly the same risks as me back then," Hunter practically shouted. "You didn't check with the Board of Directors, and you didn't convene a thirty-person legal panel with six months' lead time. You flew by the seat of your pants. *That's* how you built this company."

"Times have changed," said Cleveland.

"Maybe," Hunter allowed.

"And our current cash position is appalling."

"I'm not returning the cruise ships," said Jack, his arm going around his wife. "Kristy's buying a sundress."

"You're not returning the cruise ships," Cleveland agreed. "Hunter's going to fix this."

Hunter stared stonily at his coffee mug.

"I think we can join one of the ships in Fiji by the day after tomorrow," said Kristy in a perky voice that was completely at odds with the conversation.

Jack stroked her hair. "You'll look great on the beach," he cheerfully told her, clearly picking up on her lead.

Kristy elbowed Sinclair.

"Uh… What color bikini?" Sinclair tried, unable to take her eyes off Hunter.

"Purple," said Kristy. "And maybe a matching hat."

"Did you put any hats in the spring collection?" asked Cleveland. "I think we should start a new trend."

Hunter drew a deep breath. "Hats were up across the board at Sierra Sanchez last fall. Gramps may have a point."

Jack took a drink of his coffee and signaled for the waiter to bring refills, while Cleveland picked up his menu.

Sinclair glanced from person to person in complete astonishment. That was it? The blowup was over, and they were all having breakfast?

Hunter's family was insane.

Hunter could handle his family.

What he couldn't handle was his growing desire to be with Sinclair. When Gramps left and Jack and Kristy checked out of the Ciel D'Or Hotel yesterday, Hunter gave up the room adjoining Sinclair's, keeping the one on the top floor instead.

It didn't help.

Or maybe it did.

He still wanted to hold her, talk to her and laugh with her all night long. But being ten floors away made it harder for him to act on those impulses.

Before she left, Kristy had given him a lecture. Telling him in no uncertain terms to put Sinclair's interests first. Office affairs never ended well, and it was Sinclair who stood to get hurt. So, if Hunter cared for her at all, even just a little bit, he'd back off and let her get her career under control.

Then, just in case the lecture didn't take, Kristy had pointed out that things generally went bad for men whose cousins-in-law were gunning for them, as well. While Hunter was willing to take his chances with Cleveland and Jack's wrath, he didn't want to cross Kristy.

Plus, he cared for Sinclair. He cared for her more than just a little bit. Although he'd never admit it, she had influenced him in the Castlebay deal. Every time his instincts had twitched, or when Richard had pointed out a potential weakness in the deal, Hunter had seen Sinclair's smiling face, and he'd imagined the rush of telling her they owned the spas.

Castlebay wasn't a bad deal. But it wasn't a "pull out all the stops and get the papers signed in forty-eight hours" deal, either.

Yes, he cared about Sinclair. And he wanted her happy. And sleeping with her wasn't going to make her happy in the long run—even though it would make him ecstatic, short term.

Right now, he heard her heels tap on the hardwood floor. He glanced over to see her cross the dance studio in strappy black sandals and a bright, gauzy blue dress that flowed in points around her tanned calves. The skirt sections separated to give him glimpses of her thighs as she walked.

The dance instructor cued up the music, and Hunter braced himself.

"Ready?" Sinclair asked, her eyes sparkling sapphires that matched the brilliance of the dress.

He took a breath and held out his arms.

"You need to remember," he told her, watching them together in the big mirror. "From the minute you walk into the ball to the minute you leave, you're on stage. Roger will be watching what you do and how you do it."

"You're making me nervous again," she complained. But she glanced into the nearest mirror, then pulled back her shoulders and straightened her spine.

Hunter splayed his palm flat against her back. "Don't be nervous. Look into my eyes. Pay attention to my hand. We're in this together."

She met his gaze, and longing catapulted within him. Other

than a chaste peck on the cheek, he'd kept to himself since Kristy's lecture. But now Sinclair was fully in his arms. The back of her dress dipped to a low V, and his thumb brushed her bare skin.

He felt her shiver at the touch, and her reaction ratcheted up his own desire. Damn. He had to get his mind on the dancing.

Hunter led her through the opening steps.

"Go back, Sinclair," the instructor said. "Now left foot. Shoulders parallel. That's good. Get ready for the turn."

Hunter turned her, and Sinclair didn't stumble. Hunter smiled at her achievement.

"Promenade," said the instructor, and Hunter slipped his arm around Sinclair's waist, settling his hand above her hipbone.

"Good start," said the instructor. "Now, take it away, Hunter. Let's see what we've got to work with."

"Watch out," Hunter smiled at Sinclair, pulling her with his fingers, then pushing with the heel of his hand. She moved to the right, then the left, then backward, then into a turn. And she stumbled.

"Again," said the instructor, and Hunter started over.

She got it right. Then nailed it again.

After four times through the pattern, Hunter altered the ending and caught her by surprise.

"Hey," she protested.

"Stick with me. It's boring if we never do anything new."

"We never do anything at all, anymore," she muttered under her breath.

He didn't think he could have heard her right. "Excuse me?"

"Nothing."

He switched her to a cuddle position. He leaned down, intending to murmur in her ear. She wanted to flirt? He was there.

"Head high," the instructor called.

Hunter corrected his posture and caught her smirk.

He went back to the basic pattern, then changed it up, then whirled her through an underarm turn, her skirts flaring around her knees.

"You are absolutely gorgeous," he whispered.

"Thank you," she said on a sigh. "But I'm tired of being gorgeous."

The song faded to an end.

"What do you mean?" he asked.

She fingercombed her hair. "Restaurants and dances and fancy clothes are all well and good. But I want to kick back. Maybe hop into sweats, watch a sappy movie and cook something for myself." She pouted prettily. "I miss cooking."

"I don't miss cooking."

"That's because you're spoiled."

"I'm not spoiled."

She looked pointedly around the big, mirrored room. "We're having a private dance lesson."

The music started, and he took her into his arms once again, not fighting his feelings so much anymore.

"That," he said as he squared his shoulders and checked their lines, "is because *I'm* spoiling *you*."

She seemed to contemplate his words as the notes ascended. "That is also true."

Hours later, Sinclair glanced around at the huge arched windows, the kitchenette and the overstuffed leather furniture. "All this time you've had a kitchen?" she asked Hunter.

Hunter set two grocery bags down on the marble counter in the small kitchen alcove while Sinclair checked out the other rooms.

"Jack likes nice things for Kristy," Hunter called.

"Kristy doesn't need a four-person whirlpool," Sinclair called back. "I've been camping with that woman."

"The whirlpool's nice," said Hunter, meeting Sinclair in the main room.

She trailed her fingertips along the leather-accented bar. "So, you basically traded me in on a whirlpool and a veranda?"

She'd missed him.

She'd lain awake at night wishing he was there beside her. It would be nice to make love, sure. But she also wanted to feel his warmth, hear his breathing, even read the morning paper side by side.

"Don't forget the microwave," he said, and picked up one of the hotel phones, punching in a number.

"Well, then. No wonder. I can hardly compete with a microwave." She kicked off her high-heeled sandals and eased up onto a bar stool, arranging the gauzy skirt around her legs. She'd had fun dancing tonight. It seemed as if it was finally coming together. She was reading Hunter's signals, and she found herself looking forward to meeting him on the dance floor at the ball.

Of course, she'd have to dance with other people. But she'd savor the moments with Hunter, even though it would signal the end of their personal relationship. She couldn't see them spending much time together once they were back in New York.

She tried not to feel sad about that. Instead, she gazed at him across the room, taking a mental snapshot of his relaxed posture and smiling face.

He spoke into the telephone receiver. "I'm looking for some ladies' sportswear."

Sinclair turned her attention to the gilded mirror and the assortment of liquors behind the bar. In the meantime, she knew how to make a great mushroom sauce for their chicken breasts, if they had...there it was. Calvados brandy.

She slipped down and padded around the end of the bar. She doubted she could compete with the chefs who must cook for Hunter, but she'd give it her best try.

"Ladies' sweatpants," said Hunter. "Gray."

Sinclair grinned to herself, snagging the bottle of brandy. As he'd done so many times, he was giving her exactly what she'd asked for.

"Maybe a tank top?" He looked at her, and she nodded her agreement.

"Size small," he said while she headed for the kitchenette, scoping out the few cupboards for dishes. They were going to have a relaxing evening. Just the two of them. She hadn't felt this relaxed in weeks.

"Great," he said into the phone. "No, that should do it."

"A baking dish," Sinclair called, finding plates, silverware and glasses.

Hunter relayed the message.

"Oh, and a pot," she said. "With a lid."

"One pot and one lid," Hunter said into the phone. Then he looked to Sinclair. "That everything?"

She nodded, closing the cupboards and removing the groceries from the sacks.

"Thank you," Hunter said into the phone. Then he hit the off button.

"Wine?" he asked Sinclair.

"You bet." She'd worked hard today. In fact, she'd worked hard all week. Glamming up was no easy business.

"Red or white?"

"You pick."

"Mouton Rothschild," he decided, retrieving a bottle from the wine rack and snagging the corkscrew from the bar top.

"What's the occasion?"

"You," he said, slicing off the foil cover. "In gray sweat-pants." Then he twisted the corkscrew.

"If that doesn't cry out for a fine beverage, I don't know what does."

"Me, neither." He popped the cork and poured the dark liquid into two wide-mouthed wineglasses. Then he carried them to the counter where she was working.

"Know how to make a salad?" she asked, setting out lettuce, tomatoes, peppers and cucumber.

"Nope," he answered, sipping the wine.

"Know how to eat a salad?"

"Of course."

She opened a drawer, pulled out a chopping knife and set it on the counter. "Then wing it."

"Hey, you were the one bent on giving up luxury."

"And you get to help."

"I bought the sweatpants," he grumbled.

"Don't forget to wash everything."

Hunter stared blankly at the assortment of vegetables. "Maybe I should call the chef."

"And how would that be a home-cooked meal?"

"He'd be in our home while he cooked it."

Sinclair pulled in her chin, peering at him through the tops of her eyes. "Shut up and start chopping."

"Okay," he agreed with a tortured sigh. "It's your funeral."

She removed the butcher's paper from the chicken breasts. "You can't kill me with a salad."

"I have never, I mean never, cooked anything in my life."

She stared at him in disbelief. "Don't you ever get hungry, like late at night?"

"Sure."

"And?"

"And I call the kitchen." He looked doubtful as he unwrapped a yellow pepper.

"You seriously need a reality check."

"I seriously need a chef."

"Peel off the label, then wash the pepper, cut it vertically and take out the seeds."

Hunter blinked at her.

She rattled into one of the bags, looking for spices. "That's not going to work."

"What's not going to work?"

"That, oh-so-pathetic, lost-little-boy expression."

He gave up and peeled off the label, then turned to the sink. "It's tried and true on about a dozen nannies."

"You must have been incorrigible."

"I was delightful."

"I'm sure."

She spiced the chicken breasts, then chopped up the mushrooms, while Hunter butchered a number of innocent vegetables beyond recognition.

"Did you get cream?" she asked, peering into the bottom of the sack.

"Over here." He reached around her, and her face came up against his chest. His clean scent overwhelmed her, while her breasts brushed his stomach. Everything inside her contracted with desire.

"Here you go." He set the carton of cream on the counter in front of her. If he'd noticed the breast brush, he didn't let on. She, on the other hand, was still tingling from the contact.

She turned away and set the oven temperature. It was too early to make the sauce, so she put the cream in the half-sized fridge and moved to put some distance between her and Hunter.

"Can we get a movie?" she asked.

"There's a DVD library behind the couch. Or pay-per-view if you want something current."

"A classic?" she asked, skirting the couch.

"It's your night," he responded. "If it was mine, the fantasy would include waiters."

It was on the tip of her tongue to ask for details about his fantasy night, but she quickly realized that would take them down a dangerous road.

A knock sounded.

"The sweatpants," said Hunter from where he was running the cucumber under cold water.

Sinclair left the DVD library to go for the door.

She took the sweatpants and tank top into Hunter's bedroom, stripping off her dancing dress and hanging it in the closet. The V back of the dress hadn't allowed for a bra, so she wasn't wearing one. The sweats were loose and rode low on her hips. While the pale-purple-and-gray-striped tank top left a strip of bare skin on her abdomen. But the cotton fabric was soft and cool, and she felt more relaxed than she had in days.

"You should take off your tie," she said to Hunter as she reemerged into the living room.

He glanced up, and his gaze stopped on her outfit for a few seconds.

"Good idea." He dried his hands then worked open the knot. He unbuttoned his cuffs and rolled up the sleeves.

She crouched in front of the DVD rack. *"Notting Hill?"* she asked. "Or *While You Were Sleeping? Sweet Home Alabama?*"

"Is that the chick-flick shelf?"

"How about *Die Hard?*"

"Now *that's* a movie."

"Fine, but nobody ever got lucky watching *Die Hard.*"

"Am I getting lucky?"

She ignored him. "Here we go. *The Last of the Mohicans.*"

He nodded. "Good compromise."

She pulled it from the shelf. "Action, adventure, emotion and romance."

"Sounds like a winner to me."

"It's not very funny."

"Apparently, we can't have everything." He stepped back from the counter. "However, we have achieved salad."

She walked over to check it out. The lettuce pieces were too large, the peppers were practically pureed, and there was a puddle of water forming at the bottom of the bowl.

"Good job."

"Thank you. But I'm pretty sure it's going to be a once-in-a-lifetime experience."

She snagged a crooked slice of cucumber and popped it in her mouth. "Then I'll be sure to savor it."

He looked down into her eyes. "Excellent idea," he said, and her breath caught at the tone of his voice. "Savoring those experiences that are rare."

Ten

Dinner over, Hunter and Sinclair each found a comfortable spot on the leather couch. They had a box of chocolate truffles between them, and another bottle of Château Rothschild on the coffee table. He would have liked to draw her into his arms, or into his lap, or at least over beside him. But until she sent a signal, he didn't intend to make a move.

She curled up, her legs beneath her, and her pert breasts rounded out against the tight tank top. He could make out the outline of her nipples in the dim light, and he stared at them with a fatalistic longing. Her shoulders were tanned and smooth, her bare waist and cute belly button were nipped in above the low cut pants. And he could see the barest hint of her satin panties along the line of her hip.

She reached for a chocolate. "Did you try the Grande Marnier?" Her lips wrapped halfway around the dark globe, and she bit down with an appreciate groan.

He wasn't going to make it through the movie.

There was absolutely no way he was going to make it through the movie.

"Here." She held out the other half of the chocolate.

He leaned forward, and she popped it into his mouth. Then she licked the remaining chocolate cream from her fingertips.

"Good?" she asked.

He nodded, unable to form an actual word.

The American frontier bloomed up on the wide screen.

Sinclair reached for her wine. "Here we go."

He didn't even glance at the colorful screen. Instead, he stared at her profile, remembering what it felt like to kiss her lips, to taste the smooth skin of her shoulders and breasts, to stroke his fingers along the most intimate parts of her body.

She sipped her wine, and he watched her swallow. She smiled, then frowned, her eyes squinting down in reaction to the story.

"You done?" he asked, moving the chocolate box to the coffee table, clearing his path. If he had an opportunity to move closer, he'd take it in a split second.

She glanced at the box. Then she nodded.

Using the excuse of replacing the lid, he eased toward the middle of the couch, then he settled back to bide his time while the story unfolded.

As the heroine's party made their way through the bush and the music signaled the tension and danger, Sinclair pushed herself to the back of the couch.

Hunter moved a little closer, stretching his arm across the back. "You okay?" he asked.

She nodded, gaze not leaving the screen.

The first attack came, and she jerked in reaction. Hunter

covered her shoulder in comfort, and her hand came up to squeeze his. Her skin was soft and warm against his palm, and her fingers were delicate where they entwined with his own.

The story moved on until the hero and heroine were pinned down in the woods. They joined forces, and Sinclair sighed. Hunter had to admit this was a much better date movie than *Die Hard*.

He shifted closer still, so that their thighs brushed together. When, under gunfire, the hero and heroine finally came together to make love, Sinclair leaned her head on Hunter's shoulder.

Unable to resist, he kissed the top of her head, and wrapped an arm tight around her.

By the time the action got bloody, she was burying her face in his chest. And, at the resolution, she relaxed, molding against his body while she tipped her chin up to look him in the eyes.

"Hey," he said gruffly.

"Inspiring story," she returned.

Neither moved away, and they stared at each other in silence, her eyes reflecting the longing in his blood.

"Your sister's right," he finally offered in a last ditch attempt to be a gentleman.

Sinclair didn't answer, instead her hand crept up along his chest, finding the bare skin of his neck, and caressing it in a way that made him groan.

"My sister's sleeping with your cousin," she said.

Hunter didn't understand the point, but he couldn't formulate the right question.

Sinclair stretched up to kiss the corner of his mouth. "That means she can afford to be right." She gave him a swift kiss on the center of his lips.

He automatically puckered in response.

"I, on the other hand, am in the mood to be very, very wrong."

"So am I," he breathed, scooping his hand beneath her bottom and easing her into a reclining position beside him.

His lips came down on hers with all the purpose in the world.

Then he stripped off her tank top, wrapping his arms around her bare back and pulling her breasts flush against his body.

"I want you so bad," he rasped, kissing her collarbone, her breasts, the tight pebble of her nipple that he'd been watching for two long, painful hours.

"I've missed you," she confessed. "I don't care that we have to go back. I don't care that it has to end."

He slipped a hand beneath her sweatpants, beneath her satin panties, to her bare buttocks. "Nothing's going to end tonight. Not for a very, very long time."

She smiled up at him, her blue eyes turning to midnight sky as her fingers tugged his shirt from his waistband. "I want to touch every inch of your body."

"Good."

"I want you inside me for hours."

"Better."

"I want to make love so long and so hard…."

Hunter kissed her mouth, over and over, completely speechless with desire.

"What should I do?" she breathed.

"You're already doing it."

His hot gaze took in her bare breasts. He stripped off the sweat pants and stared at the satin panties he'd glimpsed earlier. He ran his hand down her thigh, along her calf, over the arch of her foot.

She managed to slip off his shirt.

Her hands went to his chest, stroking upward, pausing on his nipples. "I don't think we'll be waxing," she said, and he chuckled at her joke.

He ran his hand up her calf again. "Somebody's been waxing."

"It doesn't hurt that much."

"Glad you're tough." He ran the hand back down. "Really glad you're tough."

"Smooth, huh?"

"Smooth as silk." He trickled his fingers up her thigh, slipping them beneath her panties, teasing the smooth skin near the top.

Sinclair gasped at the sensation, arching her back, plastering her body against his, feeling the rough texture of his slacks against her thighs.

"You are amazing," he gasped.

"You are… You are…" She didn't even have words for it.

"Impatient," he supplied, pushing his way out of his slacks.

"Thank goodness." She smiled.

But he stopped, their naked bodies flush against each other. He rubbed a thumb across her sensitive lips, kissed them thoroughly, then rubbed it once more. "You sure you're ready?"

She nodded. Her entire body tingled in anticipation. Hunter. She was getting Hunter again. Finally.

He stroked her thighs, parting them, then slowly pushed his way inside.

A powerful, unfamiliar feeling surged through her body. She tunneled her fingers into his hair, she clutched his back, arching against him, delving into their kiss until the rest of the world disappeared.

"Damn," he muttered, pulling back ever so slightly, blinking his eyes. He glanced down to where their bodies met. "This has to last."

"Make it last," she whispered. Forever and ever and ever.

She kissed his forehead, his eyelids, his cheeks. Then she got serious again on his mouth.

His fingers moved to the small of her back. Then his hands cupped her bottom and he rocked her pelvis as his hard length moved in and out. The low buzz in her body ratcheted up to a roar. Shots of sparkling heat radiated out from her center. Her breath came in small gasps against his lips.

Her hands fisted on his back. Her thighs tightened, her eyes fluttered closed, and she rocked herself hard into his rhythm.

"I…can't…" she panted. "Oh…please…"

He lifted her ever so slightly, changing the angle, making her eyes pop open in wonder.

They both stilled, faces mere inches apart, staring at each other, gasping the same air. And then he moved, and she groaned, and her universe contracted to the place where their bodies were joined.

She wrapped her arms around his neck and held on tight, inhaling his scent as deep as she could manage, tasting the salt of his skin, feeling his taught muscles surround her and block out the world.

They both made it last, refusing to give in to the ultimate pleasure as the minutes ticked by and slick sweat gathered between their bodies.

Hunter's name began pounding in her brain. An exquisite pulse started low, becoming more insistent, forcing a moan from her lips and making her hips buck uncontrollably.

He whispered her name, and she was lost.

He followed her, her name on his lips over and over and over again.

* * *

They switched to the bed and made love again. Sinclair clung to him with all her might, wishing she could hold off the morning.

But when they finally separated, gasping and exhausted, the sun was an orange glow on the horizon.

"Now *that* was reckless and impulsive," said Hunter.

"Your family should really stop trying to beat those impulses out of you."

"You want to tell them that?"

"I do. Hand me your cell phone."

He did.

She pressed Jack's speed-dial button before Hunter whisked it out of her hand.

"I thought you were bluffing," he said.

She grinned. "And I thought you could wrestle a six-foot alligator."

"Okay," he groaned, dropping the phone on the bedside table. "All kidding aside. We've got trouble."

"We certainly do."

He propped himself up on his elbow and traced a line from her shoulder to her wrist. "Question is," he drawled softly, "what do we do about it?"

"You're still my boss," she said.

"I am."

"We still can't have an office fling."

"Agreed."

"Of course, we're not in the office now."

"I like the way you're thinking."

She popped up on her elbow, facing him, matching his posture. "We could keep it up until we get home."

Hunter watched her for a few minutes, concern flitting across his expression. "Kristy's afraid you'll fall for me."

"I know she is."

He took a breath as if he was steeling himself. "You gonna fall for me, Sinclair?"

"Don't flatter yourself," she quickly put in. "You're too reckless and impulsive to be a long-term bet."

"Plus, I lie."

"Plus," she agreed with a nod, "you lie."

He reached out to stroke her cheek with the pad of his thumb, brushing back her hair.

"I don't want to hurt you," he said.

She squelched her softer feelings. It was a fling or nothing, and that was the hard, cold truth of the matter. And she didn't want nothing, so she was taking the fling.

"What if I hurt you?" she suggested in return, just to keep things fair.

"I don't think Kristy cares so much about that." He paused. "We've got three whole days until the Valentine's ball."

"And two whole nights to go with them."

He kissed her nose. "So we're decided then?"

She nodded against him. "I think our only hope is to get it out of our system."

"Agreed."

Sinclair pushed to a sitting position. "We're going to see the spas today, right?"

"Paris, London and Brussels."

"Then we should get going."

Hunter groaned, tugging her back into place and pulling the covers over them. "First, we sleep."

"The sooner we get going, the sooner we get back."

He paused and opened one eye. "To this big, lovely bed."

"In this big, lovely suite."

"Can we get room service this time?"

"Poor baby," she cooed, drawing his fingertips to her lips and kissing them one by one. "Did you cut yourself chopping?"

"It's a time-saving ploy," he explained. "I have my sights set on the whirlpool."

Sinclair hopped up. "I'm in."

They laughed their way through the shower and into their clothes. Hunter had Simon pour on the power across the Channel and then back through Belgium. Sinclair gave the spa managers an orientation to the Luscious Lavender products, put them in touch with Ethan, and with Mary-Anne from distribution, then they hightailed it back to the heart of Paris.

By early evening, they were in the whirlpool.

Hunter pulled Sinclair back into the cradle of his thighs, handing her a flute of champagne and kissing her damp neck. She sighed in contentment, sipping the sweet, bubbly liquid while he lazily scrubbed a foamy loofah sponge over her back.

With his other hand, he touched the jeweled fish on her bracelet.

Sinclair had forgotten she still had it on. She jangled it in front of her eyes. "I think it's my favorite."

He drew her wrist forward to kiss the tender, inside skin. "*This* is my favorite."

"Really?" She pointed to her elbow. "I thought this was your favorite."

He kissed her there. "That, too."

"And this?" she pointed to her shoulder.

"Of course."

"This?" Her neck.

"All of it."

She laughed.

He sat back and his sponge strokes grew longer along her spine.

"Did you get a hold of Roger?" he asked.

"I did. He wasn't thrilled about me delaying my return even longer."

"You mean Chantal's not the wunderkind we all imagined?"

"He didn't complain about her. He said I was setting a bad example."

"By taking your holidays?"

"I guess."

"Want me to talk to him?"

"Oh, yeah. Great idea. Why don't you call him up?"

Sinclair's cell phone chimed.

"If that's Roger," said Hunter. "Tell him I say 'hey.'"

She elbowed Hunter in the ribs, drying one hand before reaching for her phone. "Hello?"

"Hey, you."

Sinclair guiltily pushed Hunter's sponge hand away. "Hi, Kristy."

He continued to rub her back.

"What's up?" asked Kristy.

"Not much. Where are you?"

"Off the coast of New Zealand. We just got cell service back."

"Great."

"So, what are you doing?"

Hunter's hand slipped around to her stomach. "Went to the spa in Brussels today, and the one in London. Met with the managers. Got them all set up for Friday's launch."

"Good for you." Kristy paused. "Hunter still in Paris?"

"He's here. But he was a little standoffish after you left."

Hunter choked back a laugh.

"I guess he came to his senses," said Kristy.

"I guess he did," Sinclair agreed, as the sponge meandered toward her breast. She clutched it to her stomach to stop his progress.

"So, when are you coming home?"

"By the fourteenth, for sure. I need to be there for the ball."

Hunter wrenched his hand free.

Sinclair bit down on her lip to keep from gasping as the sponge brushed between her legs. "I better go," she blurted, grappling for Hunter's meandering hands.

"Anything wrong?"

"Uh, something's boiling on the stove."

"The *stove?*"

"I moved to a suite. Talk to you in a few days." She disconnected.

She turned on him. "Are you crazy?"

"No." He kissed her mouth.

"Do you know what would happen—"

He kissed her again.

"If they—"

He kissed her a third time.

She gave in and wrapped her arms around his neck, turning to press her body into his, the water slick and hot between them.

Hunter's phone rang.

"For the love of—"

"Give me the sponge," she said, holding out her hand.

"Forget it."

She snapped her fingers, then wiggled them in a *give it* motion. "Fair's fair."

He dried his hand, then lifted his phone, at the same time tossing the sponge to her.

She eased back on her heels and snagged it with both hands.

"Hunter Osland," he greeted.

There was a pause. "Hey, Jack." And he grinned at Sinclair, spreading his arms, giving her a wide-open target.

She couldn't decide whether to go for it or not.

Then Hunter's attention clearly shifted to the phone call. "I'd still use the mine as collateral."

He paused.

"Maybe in the short term, sure." He slicked his wet hair back from his forehead.

"Of course he'll be ticked off. Everything ticks him off."

Hunter absently smoothed the droplets of water down Sinclair's arm. She gave up goofing around and curled against him, leaning her head on his shoulder.

"Get in and out before the Paraguay election, and you won't have a problem." Hunter's hand worked its way across her stomach.

She glanced up to see if he was teasing her again, but he seemed absorbed in the call. He wasn't messing with her, just unconsciously caressing her body. She sighed and relaxed against him.

Hunter chuckled, jiggling his chest. "We'll check it out sometime." A pause. "I mean me, of course. *I'll* check it out sometime. None of your business." Hunter's hand squeezed Sinclair. "I'm going now," he said to Jack. "A nap, that's what. Time zone change. Okay by me. I'm turning off my phone. Uh-huh. Goodbye."

He hit the off button with his thumb and held it down until it chimed. Then he dropped it on the shelf beside them and hauled Sinclair up for a kiss.

"You are *so* distracting," he muttered.

"I was being good."

"You were being damn good."

She giggled as his mouth came down, hot and moist and demanding against her own.

The water splashed around the whirlpool in waves as they rediscovered each other's bodies.

Eleven

They were back in the U.S. by midmorning on the fourteenth, and Sinclair couldn't resist checking in at Lush Beauty in one of her new outfits.

Her hair and makeup perfect, she strolled into the office in a slim peacock-blue coat dress, with three-quarter sleeves, leather details on the collar, appliqué pockets, large contrasting silver buttons and high-heeled leather ankle boots. She carried a tiny purse, holding nothing but her cell phone, keys and a credit card.

Amber's jaw literally dropped open as Sinclair crossed through the outer office.

"I was going to check messages," Sinclair called over her shoulder. "You coming to the ball tonight?"

She pushed open her office door and stopped dead.

Chantal sat at her desk, computer open to e-mail, file folders scattered in front of her, and Sinclair's phone to her ear.

Neither woman spoke for a moment.

"Can I call you back?" Chantal said into the phone.

"You're at my desk," said Sinclair.

"You're back early," said Chantal.

Amber apparently recovered her wits and rushed into the office. "Roger asked—"

"I'll be needing it now," Sinclair informed Chantal. "Right now."

Chantal hit a few keys on the computer. "If you'll just give me a few minutes."

"I don't think so," Sinclair stated, walking around the desk. "Those the Valentine's ball files?"

"The Castlebay files," Chantal admitted.

"Oh, good. Just what I wanted." Sinclair dropped her small purse on the desk. She was vindictive enough to put it label up so that Chantal could see it was a Vermachinni.

She inched in closer, crowding the woman until Chantal finally stood up and clicked the close button on her e-mail program. Chantal started to pick up the files.

"You can leave them here," Sinclair told her. "I'll call you if I need anything."

Chantal glared at her.

"Did Roger mention the private party at the Castlebay Spa Manhattan tonight?"

Chantal didn't answer.

Sinclair pursed her lips, knowing full well Roger himself didn't even know about the after party yet.

The woman's eyes glittered black. "Amber said she e-mailed you the catering contracts yesterday?"

"She did. And we've substituted duck for the pheasant. We got rid of the peanut oil because of possible allergies. And the gift bags are now recycled paper, which will stave off any media grab by Earthlife."

Chantal scooped up her briefcase and stomped out of the office.

"Uh," Amber stammered in the wake of Chantal's departure. "Is there anything…you, uh, need?"

Sinclair turned. "Hi," she said to her assistant.

"Coffee?" asked Amber, quickly straightening a pile of magazines on the credenza. "Tea?"

"It's *me*," Sinclair pointed out.

Amber nodded. "Mineral water, maybe?"

"Amber."

"You look…"

Sinclair waved a dismissive hand. "I know. Did you see the ads for the Chastlebay locations? They're having special midnight openings tonight to coincide with the ball over here."

"Sinclair?" came Ethan's voice.

Amber quickly ducked out of the office.

"Good for you," Ethan said to Sinclair.

She assumed he was talking about her appearance and smiled.

"Somebody needs to stand up to Roger."

She realized Ethan was referring to her absence. "All I did was take a vacation."

"On the eve of the product launch."

"True."

"It took a lot of guts."

"I wasn't trying to make a statement." She was merely trying to keep her career path alive.

"I thought you were trying to prove we couldn't live without you."

Sinclair paused. "Can you?"

"It's tough. Not that Roger would ever admit it. Amber really stepped up to the plate."

"Good for her. What about Chantal?"

Ethan cocked his head. "I think she has a future as eye candy."

"That's it?"

"That's it."

Sinclair nodded, glad of Ethan's assessment.

"I really just wanted to give you a high five on the spa deal," said Ethan.

Sinclair grinned and held up her hand.

Ethan smacked his palm against hers. "Hunter's a smart man," he said.

Sinclair nodded her agreement.

"He told me the idea originated with you. So, you know, you probably have a supporter in that corner."

"That's good to know," said Sinclair, trying to keep the secretive glow out of her eyes. Earlier this morning, as the jet taxied to the terminal building at JFK, Hunter had kissed her goodbye and pledged admiration for her business savvy and his support for tonight.

Ethan made for the door. "See you tonight?"

"You will."

As Ethan left, Amber peeked through the doorway. "I hope you don't mind." She took in Sinclair's outfit one more time. "I gave your name and cell phone as an after-hours contact for the caterer tonight."

"Of course I don't mind." That was standard operating procedure.

"Oh, good." Amber disappeared.

Sinclair straightened the Castlebay files, hoping her makeover went a whole lot better tonight than it went today.

Ethan hadn't noticed, Amber was afraid of her, and who knows what Roger had thought? She'd hardly wowed them here on the home front.

* * *

Freshly shaved, in his dress shirt and tuxedo slacks, Hunter looped a silk bow tie around his neck. Sinclair would be wearing her most elegant dress tonight, and he wanted them to go well together. Although they were trying to keep their relationship under wraps—okay, their former relationship under wraps—he seriously wanted her to shine. And he was planning on at least a couple of dances.

He stepped in front of the hallway mirror in the Oslands' New York apartment and leveled the two ends of the tie.

Then his cell phone rang.

He retrieved it from the entry-room table and flipped it open. "This is Hunter."

"Two things," said Jack.

"Go," Hunter replied, squinting at a strand of lint on the crisp white shirt. He brushed it off.

"The incumbent president of Paraguay just dropped dead from a heart attack."

"No kidding?"

"No kidding."

Hunter sat down on the entryway bench. "Did you use the mine as collateral?"

"I did."

"Damn." That was a setback.

"And two," Jack continued. "Frontier Cruise Lines is filing for Chapter Eleven tomorrow morning. There are three ships up for sale in the next twelve hours."

"And our cash position sucks."

"It sucks."

Hunter paused. "You really want to get into the cruise-ship business?"

"Kristy loved it."

Hunter could relate. Sinclair loved the spa business.

Wait.

He shook the comparison out of his mind. He had to get used to thinking of himself and Sinclair as separate entities, not as the same thing.

"Where are you?" he asked Jack.

"Sydney."

Hunter glanced at his watch. "Banks open in London in four hours. You serious about this?"

"What does your gut say?" asked Jack. "You're the quick thinker."

"There's no denying the quality of Frontier ships. And it's an expanding market. We could dovetail Castlebay marketing with a new cruise-line marketing strategy, maybe even put Castlebays on each of the ships." Hunter clicked through a dozen other details in his mind. "You have a sense of the Frontier prices versus market?"

"Fire sale."

"We might be able to do something with the Lithuania electronics plant. Restructure the debt…."

"Gramps will kill us."

"Welcome to my world."

There was silence on the line.

"You know," said Jack. "I think I'm understanding the appeal of this. It's like Vegas."

"Higher stakes," Hunter quipped.

"No kidding," said Jack.

Hunter glanced at his watch. "I'd have to go to London." The Lithuania banking was done through Barclays, and they needed the time-zone jump start to pull it together.

"That a problem?" asked Jack.

Hunter's mind flashed to Sinclair. She'd be all right at

the ball. Truth was, he was merely window dressing tonight.
She was *so* ready for this. And, anyway, he could make it
up to her later.

"I need to make a couple calls," he said.

"You get the financing in place, and I'll nail down the contracts with Richard."

"Where is he?" asked Hunter.

"L.A."

"Too bad."

"Should I send him to New York?"

"It'd be better if you could get him to London." Hunter
paused. "No. Wait. New York will work. Tell him I'll call him
around 4:00 a.m."

"Perfect." It was Jack's turn to pause. "And, Hunter?"

"Yeah?"

"Thanks."

"All part of the game, cousin." Hunter disconnected.

He dragged off the bow tie and released the buttons to his
shirt.

On the way to the bedroom, he dialed Simon and asked him
to have the jet ready. Then he changed into a business suit,
put another one into a garment bag and called down to his
driver to let him know they'd be heading for the airport.

Sinclair stood in the lobby of the Roosevelt Hotel. She
hadn't expected Hunter to pick her up and escort her every
movement. It wasn't as if they were on a date. Still, she would
have felt a little less self-conscious with somebody at her side.

Tuxedoed men accompanied glittering women dressed in
traditional black or brilliant-red evening gowns. The couples
were smiling and laughing as they made their way past the
sweeping staircase and a central glass sculpture. Plush arm-

chairs dotted the multi-story rotunda, while marble pillars supported sconce lights and settees along a lattice-decorated walkway to the main ballroom.

Flashbulbs popped and cameras rolled as the media vied for footage of the A-list event. The PR person in Sinclair was thrilled with the hoopla, the woman in her was disappointed to be there alone. She squelched the silly, emotional reaction and answered a few questions from a reporter for a popular magazine. But then the reporter spotted someone more exciting and quickly wrapped it up.

"Sinclair," came Sammy Simon's voice.

She turned to see one of the Lush Beauty Lavender suppliers decked out in a black tux and tie.

He took both of her hands in his. "Lovely," he drawled appreciatively, taking in her strapless white satin dress. It had a sweetheart neckline and tiny red hearts scattered over the bodice. The hearts gathered into a vertical, then cascaded down one side of the full skirt.

Sammy kissed her on the cheek. "I had no idea you were a fan of haute couture."

She gave him a laugh. "A little something I picked up in Paris."

He squeezed her hands. "Find me later for a dance." And he joined the throng headed for the party.

"Sinclair," came another voice, and an arm went around her shoulders.

"Mr. Davidson." She greeted the owner of a chain of specialty shops that had featured Lush Beauty Products for years.

"This is my wife, Cynthia."

Sinclair smiled and leaned forward to shake the woman's hand. As she did, Wes Davidson's hand dropped to an uncomfortable level near her hip.

"And one of my store managers, Reginald Pie."

"Nice to meet you, Mr. Pie." Sinclair shook the man's hand.

Wes Davidson spoke up. "It's such a pleasure to see you, Sinclair. I've been meaning to arrange a meeting to talk about the new product lines."

"Absolutely," she agreed.

"I'll call you," he said. "Great to see you looking… so…great."

Mrs. Davidson reddened.

Sinclair gently pulled away. "Oh, look. There's Ethan. I need to say hello. So good to see you Mr. Davidson. Mrs. Davidson."

Sinclair slipped away.

She made a beeline for Ethan. He was talking to two of their distributors.

"But if the price breaks don't work for the small retailers," one of the men was saying, "you're going to compromise your core business."

"Hello, Ethan," Sinclair broke in, grateful to find a safe conversation.

The men stopped talking and turned to stare at her.

"You remember Sinclair," said Ethan.

What a strange thing to say. Of course they remembered her.

"Sinclair," said Ron. "You look incredible."

"Fabulous to see you again," said David.

Then the conversation stopped dead.

Sinclair glanced from one man to the other. "You were talking about price breaks?" she prompted.

David chuckled. "Oh, not tonight," he said. "You look incredible," he repeated Ron's sentiment.

"Thank you." But that didn't mean her brain had stopped working.

There was another strained silence.

"I'll see you all inside?" Sinclair offered.

The men seemed to relax.

"Yes," said David.

"Looking forward to it," said Ron.

Ethan winked.

Sinclair walked away and immediately spotted Chantal.

She was surrounded by admirers, and she didn't seem to mind they were focused on her looks and not on her business savvy. She was a glittering jewel in low-cut bright red, and she seemed to revel in the role.

Sinclair, on the other hand, was having serious reservations about her makeover. Men used to take her seriously. She couldn't remember the last time she felt so awkward in a business conversation.

Her cell phone rang in her evening purse, and she welcomed the distraction. She picked up the call.

"Can you hang on?" she asked, not expecting to be able to hear the answer.

She sought out an alcove behind the concierge desk, next to a bank of phone booths.

"Hello?"

"It's Hunter," came a welcome and familiar voice.

"Hey, you," she responded, her voice softening, and the tension inside her dissipating to nothing. "Are you out front?" She glanced at the foyer, straining to see him coming through the main doors.

"I've had a complication."

"Oh?"

He was going to be late. Sinclair tried to take the news in stride. She really had no expectations of him. At least, she had no right to have any expectations of him. But in that split second, she realized she'd been counting the minutes until he'd arrive.

"I'm on my way to London."

"Now?" she couldn't help but ask.

"There's a couple of cruise ships, and a bankruptcy, and a complication in the Paraguay election."

"I understand," she quickly put in.

"I'm sorry—"

"No need. It's business." She'd been warned he'd hurt her. Hadn't she been warned?

She heard him draw a breath. Traffic sounds came through his end of the phone.

"We only have twelve hours," he told her.

She forced a laugh. "Another quick deal?"

"Jack's on board this time."

"That's good."

"We can get a really great price."

"Of course." She tried to ignore the crushing disappointment pressing down on her chest. She had no right to feel this way. He'd done so much for her already.

"You're great," he told her. "You'll do fine on your own."

"I know," she nodded, realizing how very much she'd been counting on their last dance tonight. There was something about their relationship that cried out for closure—a closure she hadn't yet experienced.

"I wouldn't do it, except—"

"Hunter, stop."

"What?"

"I knew this going in," she pointed out, proud of her even tone.

"Knew what?"

"You. You're reckless and impulsive. You have to fly to London. You have to buy ships. And you have to do it in less than twelve hours. That's you. That what I lo…like about you. Have a great time."

He was silent on the other end.

"You sure?" he finally asked.

"Do I sound sure?"

"Well, yeah."

Her lying skills had obviously improved. "There you go. I'll see you at the office. I gotta go now."

"But—"

"See you." Sinclair clicked off the phone.

She rounded the corner, taking in what now looked like a daunting mix of finely dressed people. And at the same time, she was beginning to fear her colleagues wouldn't take her seriously. While Chantal seemed to be managing the glam persona with aplomb. And now Hunter wasn't even going to show up.

Damn.

She had to stop caring about that.

Had she expected to be Cinderella tonight?

Had she expected he'd sweep the new her onto the dance floor, realize he'd fallen madly in love, and carry her off to happily ever after?

It was a ridiculous fantasy, and Sinclair was horrified to realize it was hers.

Her fingers went to the ruby-and-diamond goldfish bracelet—the one she hadn't taken off in a week.

She'd thought about him every moment while she'd primped tonight. She'd worn a white, whale-boned bustier. It gave body to the dress, but it was also shamelessly sexy. She told herself no one would see it. But, secretly, deep down inside her soul, she'd hoped he would. She'd hoped they'd find an excuse to make love one more time, or maybe a hundred more times.

Truth was, Kristy's fear had proven true. Sinclair had fallen hopelessly in love with Hunter. Hunter, on the other hand, skipped the ball to make a new business deal.

Her eyes burned while a knot of shame formed in her belly. Suddenly the designer clothes felt like zero protection for her broken heart.

She should have stuck with her regular wardrobe. Beneath her skirts and blazers and sensible blouses, she was in control of her world. People saw what she wanted them to see, and they respected what she represented. She was a fool to think she could beat Chantal at her own game. And she was a fool to think she could hold on to Hunter.

Reckless and impulsive. She'd heard those words so many times. There was nothing Sinclair could offer him that would compare to a high-risk, hundred-million-dollar deal in London at midnight.

She stepped away from the alcove, determined to get this horrible evening over with as soon as possible.

Twelve

The jets taking off from JFK squealed above Hunter's head as his driver circled his way through the terminals. He had his PDA set to calculator, running the numbers he knew he needed banking software to properly compute.

But the mini screen kept blurring in front of his eyes. He was seeing Sinclair in her white and red dress. The piping along the neckline. The teardrop diamonds. The ruby necklace. Her expression when she'd realized the massive ruby was real.

He chuckled at that, particularly the part where he realized she still liked the goldfish bracelet better.

He wondered if she'd worn it tonight.

He wondered if she'd got her makeup just right.

Had her hair behaved?

Were her feet getting tired?

She'd gamely practiced for hours in those high shoes, but he knew she didn't like them.

He wondered who she was dancing with right now, and quickly acknowledged that he cared. Something pulled tight inside him at the image of someone else holding her, their broad hand splayed across her back, another man's jacket nearly brushing her breasts, the jerk's lips whispering secrets into her ear.

If he was in the room, he'd probably rip her from the guy's arms.

His cell phone beeped.

"Hunter Osland," he greeted.

"Hey, Hunter."

"Sinclair?" His heart lifted.

"It's Kristy."

"Oh."

"Were you expecting Sinclair?"

"No."

"Because I think she's at that ball tonight."

"She is." He shifted in the backseat of the car. All alone at the ball.

"I just talked to Jack," said Kristy.

Sinclair was all alone, because Hunter had let her down.

"Jack's cell was running low on battery power," Kristy continued.

It wasn't like he'd had a choice. Osland International needed him, and his grandfather was always after him to be more dependable. That's what he was doing by helping Jack.

"Jack wants you to call Richard for him."

This was being dependable—and patient and methodical. Those were the other things his grandfather wanted.

Kristy's words rambled together on the other end of the

phone without making a whole lot of sense. "He said you'd know why."

Though he'd also been patient and methodical when he convinced Sinclair to get a makeover, then when he took her to Europe, then when he bought her clothes, then when he taught her to dance. He also made sure she was completely ready to face Roger and the rest of Lush Beauty.

"Hunter?" prompted Kristy.

And…then he'd abandoned her for the first exciting project that came along.

Oh no.

He pictured her in his mind, stunningly gorgeous and all alone, other men circling like wolves.

Was he out of his mind?

"No!"

"What?" came Kristy's worried voice.

The Sinclair project wasn't over. There were things left to do for her. A whole lot of things left to for her, patient and methodical things left to do for her, some of them involving the rest of their natural lives.

"Hunter? What's going on."

"Tell Jack I'm sorry."

"Huh?"

"Tell him I can't call Richard. I can't go to London. If he can't work it out himself, well, tell him there'll be other cruise ships."

"Other cruise ships?" Kristy parroted in confusion.

"For once in my life I'm not going to be reckless and impulsive. I'm going to be dependable." Why hadn't he thought about that before? He was such a fool.

"What are you talking about?" Kristy was obviously trying to be patient.

"I have to go see Sinclair."

"How'd Sinclair get into this?"

"Because," Hunter hesitated. Part of him didn't want to say it out loud, and part of him wanted to shout it from the rooftops. "I'm in love with your sister," he admitted to Kristy. "I'll have to call you back."

Then he disconnected and caught the driver's amused gaze in the rearview mirror.

"The Roosevelt Hotel," he hollered.

The driver's face broke into a full fledged grin.

"No, wait," said Hunter. "Make it the apartment. I have to change."

If he was going to do this, he was going to do it right.

It was Sinclair's job to stay for the entire ball, not to mention the after party at the Castlebay Spa. While the orchestra played on, she looked longingly at her watch, then over to the exit. Maybe she could lay low in the lobby for a while. At least then she wouldn't have to dance with men she'd rather be talking promotions and P and L statements with.

What was it about a pretty dress and bit of makeup that turned men into babbling idiots? And why didn't Chantal care? Her life must be exhausting.

Mind made up, Sinclair headed for the lobby exit. At the very least, she deserved a break.

"Going somewhere, Sinclair?"

She whirled toward the familiar voice, sure her mind must be playing tricks.

He was dressed in a classic black tux, with a black bow tie and a matching cummerbund. His hair was perfect, his face freshly shaven, and his smile was the most wonderful thing she'd seen all day.

"I thought you'd be on the jet," she blurted out.

"I changed my mind."

"About going to London?"

"About a lot of things." He held out his arm. "Dance?"

Her spirit lifted, but her heart ached. Still, there was no way she'd turn him down.

"You look stunning, by the way," he mumbled as they moved toward the dance floor. "Zeppetti should pay you to wear his dresses."

"You're good for me," she said.

"No, you're good for me."

They attracted a small amount of attention as they moved through the crowd, probably more Hunter than her. People recognized him, and knew his position in the company.

When they reached the other dancers, he drew her into his arms. It felt like the most natural thing in the world, and she had to caution herself against reading anything into his actions. He was probably off to London tomorrow morning. When you had your own plane, you could do things like that. And Hunter enjoyed every facet of his freewheeling, billionaire lifestyle.

But, for now, she couldn't seem to stop herself from melting into his arms and pretending, just for a moment, that things could be different. They were still drawing glances from the other dancers. She could only hope her expression wouldn't make her the office gossip topic tomorrow.

Hunter drew her tight against his chest.

She wasn't sure, but she thought she felt a kiss on the top of her head.

Risky move in this crowd.

"You leaving after the ball?" she asked, hoping to keep some semblance of professionalism between them.

"Here's the thing," Hunter muttered, leaning very close to her ear. "I've gotten rather used to seeing you naked."

She coughed out a startled laugh. Then she tipped her head back to play along. "Why, you sweet talker."

He smiled down at her. "I've also gotten used to waking up with you wrapped in my arms."

Sinclair sobered. That was the part she thought she'd miss most—Hunter first thing in the morning, unshaven, unguarded, and always ready for romance.

"An office affair still isn't going to work," he went on.

She nodded and sighed. "I know." They'd talked about all the reasons why. And they were right about them.

"It would make us crazy to keep the secret. Plus, we'd eventually get caught."

Sinclair followed the steps as Hunter led her through the dance. He wasn't telling her anything she didn't already know.

"So, I was thinking," he said. "We should get married."

Sinclair stopped dead.

He leaned down. "Sinclair?"

She didn't answer. Was that her fevered imagination, or did he just…

"Better start dancing," he advised. "People are beginning to stare."

She forced her feet to move. "Did you just…"

"Propose?"

She nodded.

"Yes," he growled low. "I'm proposing that you and I get married, so we can spend every minute together, and nobody in the office will be able to say a damn thing about it."

Her brain still hadn't made sense of what he was saying. "Is this one of those reckless, impulsive things of yours?"

He shook his head. "Absolutely not. I've been considering this for at least an hour."

Despite the serious conversation, his tone made her chuckle.

"Okay, probably twenty-four hours," he said. "Ever since leaving you became a reality."

Sinclair blinked back tears of emotion.

"Or maybe it's been ten days, ever since I walked into that boardroom. Or," he paused. "Maybe since the first second I laid eyes on you." He wrapped her in a hug that didn't resemble any of the waltz moves she'd learned.

"It feels like I've loved you forever," he said.

"I love you, too." Her voice was muffled against his chest.

He drew back. "Is that a yes?"

"If you're sure."

"I am one-hundred-percent positive. I blew off the London deal for this."

"You're not going to London later?"

"Actually, I'm never leaving you again." He kissed her mouth, and she caught Roger's astonished expression as he danced by.

"Uh oh," she said.

"Well, we can separate occasionally. You know, during the day. But not overnight. I'm not—"

"Roger just saw you kiss me."

"Who cares?"

"He thinks I'm your floozy now."

"Don't worry about Roger. I caught him kissing Chantal behind the pillar when I walked in."

Sinclair was shocked. "Roger and Chantal?"

Hunter nodded.

It actually made sense. It explained a whole lot of things. But, strangely, Sinclair didn't care.

She shrugged.

Hunter sobered, looking deeply into her eyes. "You, me,

us, your job. You know none of it has anything to do with the other, right?"

Sinclair glanced at Roger a few dance couples away, straining his neck for a view of her and Hunter. "Roger doesn't."

In response Hunter kissed her again, longer this time.

Roger's eyes nearly popped out of his head.

"Wait till he gets a look at the rock on your finger."

"You have a rock?"

"Actually, no. I have nothing at the moment."

"Reckless and impulsive."

"Not at all. This is good planning." He took her hand in his, rubbing the knuckle of her ring finger. "We can glam this up as much as you want. But I was thinking something custom-made, to match you bracelet."

Sinclair held up her wrist. "I do seem to have developed a fondness for the fish."

Hunter fingered the delicate gold and jewels. "I always assumed I was the diamond one, and you were the ruby."

"I never thought about it," said Sinclair.

"Liar."

"Takes one to know one."

"Well, whatever we do, it better be fast."

"Good idea. Since that last kiss totally trashed my reputation with my coworkers."

Hunter glanced Roger's way. "He looks at you like that one more time, I'm making him president of the Osland button factory in Siberia."

"You don't have a button factory in Siberia."

"I'll buy one. It'll be worth it."

Sinclair's phone buzzed in her little purse.

"That'll be Kristy," said Hunter, nodding toward the faint sound.

"How do you know that?"

"Because she knows I'm here. I bet it's killed her to wait this long."

"You told her…"

"That I loved you? Yeah. I'll be telling everybody soon."

Sinclair snapped the clasp on her purse and retrieved the phone, putting it to her ear.

"Is he there?" Kristy stage-whispered.

"Who?" asked Sinclair innocently.

"You know who. What's going on? Tell me everything?"

"We're dancing."

"And?"

"And, I think we're getting married."

"You *know* we're getting married," Hunter called into the phone.

Kristy squealed so loud Sinclair had to pull it away from her ear.

"When? Where?" asked Kristy.

"Hunter seems to be in a hurry. Could you maybe give us the name of that place you and Jack used in Las Vegas?"

Hunter scooped the phone. "Negative on Vegas," he told Kristy. "I've reformed my impulsive ways. We're doing some methodical planning on this one." He glanced softly down at Sinclair. "I want it to be perfect."

Then he handed the phone back.

"I'm designing the dress," said Kristy.

"You bet you are," Sinclair agreed, watching the heat build in Hunter's eyes. "I better go now."

"Okay. But I'm flying out there as soon as possible."

"Just as long as you don't come tonight," said Sinclair, hanging up the phone over Kristy's laughter.

"Good tip," said Hunter.

"Excuse me, Sinclair," Roger interrupted, his mouth in a frown and a determined look in his eyes. "Can I speak with you—"

Hunter jumped in. "You might want to know—"

"This will only take a moment," said Roger.

"Really?" asked Hunter, brow going up.

Roger nodded.

Hunter anchored Sinclair to his side. "Sinclair has just accepted my marriage proposal."

Roger blinked in confusion, clearly the words were not computing.

"And I'd like to talk to you about a job opportunity for you," said Hunter. "My office? Tomorrow? Sometime in the afternoon."

Roger's brow furrowed. "I don't… You're getting *married?*"

Hunter nodded slowly.

Roger took a step back. "Oh…" Another step. "Well…" A third. "In that case…" He disappeared into the crowd.

"Funny that he didn't congratulate us," said Sinclair.

"He can send a card from Siberia." Hunter smoothly drew her into his arms and picked up the dance.

"Is Chantal going with him?"

"It would only be fair. Who am I to stand in the way of true love?"

"Who, indeed?" asked Sinclair, snuggling close to his broad chest. "And now you and I get to live happily ever after." She sighed.

"Just me, you and the twins."

"You believe the gypsy?"

Hunter nodded. "It has to be true. Jack's probably out there right now losing the family fortune. I just found out the

Castlebay Spa in Hawaii has a golf course. And with your red hair, twins would make it a clean sweep."

She laughed with joy over everything.

"I love you very much," Hunter whispered.

"And I love you," she whispered in return. "Happy Valentine's Day."

He hugged her tightly. "Happy Valentine's Day, sweetheart."

* * * * *

PROPOSITIONED BY THE BILLIONAIRE

BY
LUCY KING

Lucy King spent her formative years lost in the world of Mills & Boon® romance when she really ought to have been paying attention to her teachers. Up against sparkling heroines, gorgeous heroes and the magic of falling in love, trigonometry and absolute ablatives didn't stand a chance.

But as she couldn't live in a dream world for ever she eventually acquired a degree in languages and an eclectic collection of jobs. A stroll to the River Thames one Saturday morning led her to her very own hero. The minute she laid eyes on the hunky rower getting out of a boat, clad only in Lycra and carrying a three-metre oar as if it was a toothpick, she knew she'd met the man she was going to marry. Luckily the rower thought the same.

She will always be grateful to whatever it was that made her stop dithering and actually sit down to type Chapter One, because dreaming up her own sparkling heroines and gorgeous heroes is pretty much her idea of the perfect job.

Originally a Londoner, Lucy now lives in Spain, where she spends much of the time reading, failing to finish cryptic crosswords and trying to convince herself that lying on the beach really is the best way to work. Visit her at www.lucyking.net.

CHAPTER ONE

'MARK, STEP AWAY from the flamingo and get out of the pond. Please.'

Phoebe heard the note of desperation in her voice and prayed it would be enough to penetrate the alcohol-fogged brain of the man who was lurching around the pond and brandishing a bottle of champagne.

'Darling,' slurred Mark as he swung round and threw her a lopsided grin while water lilies slapped around his knees. 'You keep trying to persuade me to get out, but I don't want to.'

He waggled his finger at her and her spirits sank. No amount of cajoling or threatening had had the slightest effect so why on earth had she thought desperation would have worked?

'That much is obvious,' she muttered and racked her brains for a solution. Dealing with problems was part of her job, but right now she was stumped.

'I have a suggestion.' He swayed wildly and Phoebe's heart skipped a beat.

Unless he revealed that he planned to take himself off somewhere quiet and sober up, preferably on the other side of London, she didn't think she wanted to hear it. 'What is it?'

Mark spread his arms wide and grinned. 'Why don't you jump in and join me? The water's great and I'd like to introduce you to my new friend.' He turned and stumbled after the flamingo, which had hopped out of range and was now preening its feathers.

Phoebe shivered and sighed and wondered what she'd done to deserve this. It had clearly been far too much to hope that this evening might remain trouble free, but for a moment everything had been going so well.

So the opulent crimson and silver theme that ran throughout the bar wasn't really to her taste, and the huge chandeliers that sprinkled light over the glittering throng were, in her opinion, totally over the top. And as for allowing birds to wander freely around the gardens six storeys above street level, well, that, as this little episode had proved, was a recipe for disaster, however unique and fashionable.

However, none of that mattered. Not one little bit.

All that mattered was that the San Lorenzo Roof Gardens was the trendiest new venue in town. It was *the* place to hold a pre-launch party for a hip young handbag designer, and it was virtually impossible to book.

But she'd done it. She'd spent weeks flattering the unyielding Mr Bogoni until he'd cracked and agreed to let her hire the venue, and had then poured hours of meticulous planning and endless preparation into ensuring that this would be a party that people would gossip about for months.

Inside the bar buzzed with a subtle air of excitement and expectation, fuelled by exquisite canapés and the finest champagne. Jo's gemstone-encrusted handbags sat high on their individually spotlit pedestals, refracting the light like multicoloured glitter balls, and the star of the show herself was mingling among the one hundred glamorous guests and chatting to the carefully selected journalists as if she'd been doing it for years instead of an hour.

Jo Douglas, Phoebe's first and currently only client, was heading for the stratosphere, and the fledgling Jackson Communications would soar right alongside her.

So she was *not* going to stand back and let Jo's boyfriend ruin an evening she'd worked so hard to put together.

Phoebe's jaw set. There was only one thing for it. She had to get rid of Mark. Discreetly and quickly before someone with a camera decided to step out for a breath of fresh air. And as the bar was getting warmer by the minute, she didn't have any time to lose.

Right. Phoebe broke a twig off an overhanging branch and stuck it between her teeth. She twisted her hair into a thick rope, wound it deftly onto the top of her head and secured it with the twig. Then she slipped out of her shoes and wriggled to hitch her dress up her thighs.

Taking a deep fortifying breath and trying not to think about what might lurk beneath the surface of the water, she gave herself a quick shake, straightened her spine and set her sights on her target.

'Do you need a hand?'

The deep voice came from behind her and Phoebe shrieked, jumped almost a foot into the air and nearly pitched headlong into the pond. She spun round, her hand flying to her throat and her heart thundering as a large shadowy figure leaning against a tree swam into vision. 'Who are you?' she squeaked when she was able to breathe again.

'Someone who thinks you look like you could do with some help.' He pushed himself off the tree and gestured to Mark as he took a step towards her.

Phoebe's hand automatically shot out to stop him coming any closer and then she dropped it, feeling faintly foolish. Wherever he'd sprung from he was hardly likely to be going to attack her. 'If leaping out of nowhere and scaring me witless is your idea of helping, thank you, but no.'

He stopped and tilted his head. 'Sure?'

'Quite sure,' she said, resisting the urge to glance down to check the ground beneath her feet. His lazy drawl was having the oddest effect on her equilibrium. Either that, or London was in the unlikely grip of an earthquake. 'What are you doing out here anyway?'

'Admiring the scenery.'

Somehow she knew he wasn't referring to the landscaping and she felt a kick of something in the pit of her stomach. 'You should be inside admiring the handbags.'

'Not really my thing.'

'Then perhaps you're at the wrong party.' Phoebe frowned. Come to think of it, he hadn't actually answered her question. She'd met and ticked off everyone on the guest list, and none of them had had such an impressive outline. So who the hell was he?

Phoebe ran her gaze over him, momentarily forgetting what was going on behind her, and found herself wondering what he looked like. Part of her longed for him to step into the light so she could get a proper look at him and see if his looks matched up to his voice. The other toyed with the idea of summoning the bouncers.

Because whoever he was, this was a private party and

if he wasn't on the guest list then he was gatecrashing. In fact, she thought, pulling herself together, he could well have sneaked in while she'd been in Mr Bogoni's office, staring at the fuzzy CCTV feed and simultaneously trying to swallow her astonishment, placate the volatile Italian and ignore his mutterings about suing for damages should anything happen to the flamingo.

'I'm at exactly the right party. And it's turned out to be far more interesting than I could possibly have imagined.'

Phoebe frowned and was just about to demand his invitation when she heard a series of splashes behind her. A shower of cool water hit the backs of her legs and she stifled a squeal of shock. Mark must have got bored with the flamingo, thank goodness, and decided to come over and investigate this latest development.

'I suspect the show's nearly over.'

'That's a shame. I was enjoying it.'

Despite the warmth of the night she shivered. 'There's far better entertainment inside. Drinks, music, dancing. Much more exciting.'

'I'm inclined to disagree,' he said softly and her heart thumped. 'Besides, I've spent the past sixteen hours either in a car or on a plane. At this stage of the evening fresh air is a novelty.'

'Plenty of fresh air on the other side of the bar. As you can see, I'm afraid I have things to attend to.'

As soon as Mark stumbled to within reaching distance she'd pull him out and bundle him off herself.

'Do you really think you can handle this on your own?'

If she'd been able to see his face properly she was sure she'd find a patronising smile hovering at his lips and Phoebe bristled. She'd been handling things on her own for years. 'Of course.'

He folded his arms over his chest and shrugged. 'In that case I'll stay out of your way.'

'Thank you,' she said crisply and turned back.

Mark was far closer that she'd thought and was waving the bottle of champagne even more wildly than before. All he had to do was trip and he'd land right on top of her.

It was now or never. Phoebe reached out to grab him but he reeled back, teetering as if balancing on the edge of a precipice and then pitched forward. Flailing around while desperately trying to cling onto his balance, his arm and the hand holding the bottle swung round in her direction. An arc of champagne sprayed through the air. Phoebe let out a little cry and jerked back, her hands flying to her head.

Oh no, not her hair. Please not her hair.

She didn't have time to recover and pull Mark out. A split second later a pair of large hands clamped round her waist and shoved her to one side. She yelped in shock and watched in stunned appal as the shadowy stranger grabbed Mark by the T-shirt and hauled him out of the water.

'Hey, what are you doing?' Mark yelled, splashing frantically as the bottle of champagne landed in the water with a plop.

Good question, thought Phoebe dazedly, her skin beneath her dress burning where his hands had gripped her.

'Taking out the rubbish,' he snarled and leaned in very close. 'Men like you belong behind bars.'

'What are you talking about?' Mark spluttered. 'Get off me. You can't do this. I'll sue.'

'Go right ahead,' he growled.

'You'll be sorry.'

'I doubt it. Wait here,' he snapped at Phoebe, and then dragged Mark, kicking and struggling, across the garden.

Wait here?

For a moment Phoebe had no choice in the matter. She stood frozen to the spot, droplets of icy water clinging to her bare legs, her heart hammering while shock reverberated around her and the outraged sound of Mark's protests and threats rang in her ears.

In dumb stupefaction she watched the two men disappear round the corner and struggled to make sense of what had just gone on. Maybe she'd been hurled into a third-rate action film, because in reality men didn't just leap out of nowhere, elbow their way into the action and then march off leaving chaos trailing in their wake like a brief but devastating tornado. At least, not in her experience.

As her shock receded the potential consequences of this little episode filtered into her head. How dared he barge in like that? When she'd told him in no uncertain terms that she was in control of the situation. Did he have any idea of the damage he could have done?

And then barking at her to wait. What did he expect her to do? Hang around like some sort of obedient minion? Hah, she thought, bending down to pick up her shoes. As if. She had to go and find out whether any journalistic or photographic prying eyes had caught what had just happened and if necessary execute a hasty damage-limitation exercise.

Who did he think he was anyway, creeping up on her like that and scaring the living daylights out of her? And manhandling Mark like some sort of brutish Neanderthal.

Kind of attractive though. That single-mindedness. That decisiveness. That strength…

Phoebe slapped her hand against her forehead. No no no no *no*. That was so wrong on so many levels she didn't know where to start. Focus. That was what she needed. Focus. And her heels.

As she searched for something sturdy to lean against while she put her shoes back on again Phoebe's skin suddenly prickled all over.

Her head shot round and her eyes narrowed in on the man striding in her direction, alone. Tall, broad-shouldered and flexing his hands, he moved in a sort of intensely purposeful way that had her stomach clenching.

In irritation, she decided, straightening and preparing herself for confrontation. Definitely irritation.

As his long strides closed the distance between them she could see that his face was as dark as the suit that moulded to his body. But what he had to glower about she had no idea. If anyone had the right to be furious it was her.

Phoebe's heart began to thud. Forget the shoes. Damage limitation could wait. Adrenalin surged through her. 'You frightened the life out of me,' she said, when he got within hissing distance, her voice low and tight with anger. 'Who are you and what on earth did you think you were doing?'

He didn't reply, merely took her arm and wheeled her off towards the pergola at the bottom of the wide stone steps that led up to the terrace. Phoebe had no option but to stagger after him, shoes dangling from her fingers as panic and shock flooded back into every bone in her body.

'Hang on,' she said, desperately trying to keep her voice down. 'You can't throw me out too. Ow!' The smooth paving stones had turned into sharp gravel, which dug into the soles of her feet.

He stopped, looked down as she hopped madly while trying to put her shoes back on and then, muttering a brief curse under his breath, swept her up into his arms. Phoebe let out a tiny squeal as her shoulder slapped against a rock-hard chest. One of his hands planted itself on the side of her breast, the other wrapped around her bare thigh.

'Put me down!' she whispered furiously, her legs bouncing with every step he took as she tried to tug down her dress in a vain attempt to protect her modesty.

He stopped beneath a lantern and set her on her feet, her body brushing against his in the process. A flurry of tingles whizzed round her and she wobbled. He wound one arm round her waist and clamped her against him.

'I have no intention of throwing you out,' he said roughly, raking his gaze over her face.

'So let me go.'

If anything, his arm tightened and Phoebe felt as if someone had plugged her into a socket. What else could explain the tingles and sparks that zapped through her? What else could account for the searing heat that swept along her veins, making her bones melt and turning her spine to water?

'My name is Alex and you should choose your boyfriends more carefully.'

At the icy restraint lacing his voice, Phoebe's eyes jerked to his and for a moment she forgot how to breathe.

Oh, dear God. His eyes were mesmerising. Grey. No, not just grey. Silver, rapidly darkening to slate, and fringed with the thickest eyelashes she'd ever seen on a man. Set beneath straight dark eyebrows and blazing down at her with fierce concern.

As she dragged her gaze over the planes of his face

in much the same way as he was now doing to her Phoebe's mouth went dry and the blood in her veins grew hot and sluggish. He wasn't just handsome. He was jaw-droppingly gorgeous. But not in the pretty way the men who occupied her world were. This man looked like the sort of man who knew how to do, and probably did, the things that real men were supposed to do.

The little white scar above his right eye and the hint of a broken nose gave him an air of danger that she might have considered to be intoxicating if she'd been in the market for a man. Which she wasn't. But heavens, that mouth. What a mouth…

Her hands, currently curled into fists and jammed between his chest and hers, itched to unfurl themselves, creep their way up the thick white cotton shirt, maybe taking in a quick detour to the V of tanned flesh exposed where his top button was undone, and up, round his neck to wind themselves in his hair so that they could tug that delicious-looking mouth down and weld it to hers.

Phoebe blinked. Agh. What on earth was she thinking? Her body had no business behaving like this, especially without her prior approval. And that would not be forthcoming this evening. Or ever, she reminded herself belatedly, pushing all thoughts of what sort of things a real man might be required to do out of her head.

Giving herself a mental shake, she forced herself to concentrate. What had he been saying? She thought frantically. Boyfriends. That was it. 'What boyfriend?' she managed, squeezing her hands tighter and hauling back some of the self-control that had fled when he'd pulled her against him.

'The jerk in the pond.'

'He's not my boyfriend.' After her last disastrous relationship, she was off men. For ever. Especially ones who crept up on her and nearly gave her a heart attack. However good-looking.

'Did he hurt you?'

'No. Of course not.' What was he talking about? She struggled to pull herself out of the steel circle of his arm, but it was no good. Alex didn't seem inclined to let her go.

Instead he gripped her chin with his long brown fingers and turned her face so that the light fell on her cheek. 'He took a swing at you with the bottle,' he said harshly. 'Where did he hit you?'

Phoebe's skin sizzled beneath the pressure of his fingers. 'Have you lost your mind?' she said, baffled as much by the tingles shooting through her as the direction of the conversation. 'Mark didn't hit me.'

'Are you sure?'

'Of course I'm sure,' she said. 'I think I might have noticed if I'd been thwacked by a bottle of champagne. Particularly vintage.'

His mouth tightened. 'Not funny.'

'I couldn't agree more,' she said sharply. There was absolutely nothing funny about the damage he could have done tonight, possibly the most important night of her and Jo's lives. 'Can I have my chin back?'

He let her chin go as if it were on fire and she swung her head round to glare up at him. For a moment they simply stared at each other and Phoebe became aware that, still locked in his vice-like embrace as she was, every inch of her body pressed up against every hard-muscled inch of his.

Heat pooled in the pit of her stomach and her heart thumped. Her mouth dried and she swallowed. She *had* to get a grip. And not of his biceps. 'Right. So you barged in because you thought my boyfriend had hit me?' A rogue bubble of delight bounced round inside her before she reminded herself that not only did chivalry not exist in her world, she neither needed nor looked for it.

His brows snapped together. 'Where I come from men don't hit women.'

Something warm started to unfurl deep inside her. 'Where I come from no one hits anyone.' The Jacksons employed far more subtle tactics.

'He called you darling. You cried out and jerked back.'

Oh. She felt her cheeks grow warm. 'Well, yes, but only because I didn't want to get splashed,' she said. 'And Mark calls everyone darling.'

His hands sprang off her as if she were a hot coal and he stepped back. 'You didn't want to get splashed,' he echoed softly, his voice suddenly so cold and distant that it sent a chill hurtling down her spine and she automatically rubbed her upper arms.

In the thundering silence that hung between them, a seed of shame took root in her head and the blush on her cheeks deepened. His face was dark, tight and as hard as stone.

The combination of sheer disbelief and icy disdain that replaced the concern in his eyes made her wish she'd kept her mouth shut. If she'd kept her mouth shut she'd still be in his arms, enveloped in his heat and strength, feeling all warm and deliciously quivery instead of feeling as shallow as the pond and utterly rotten.

Then she rallied. Hang on a moment. Why was *she* being made to feel the guilty party in this little melodrama? She hadn't exactly begged him for help. And it was hardly her fault if he'd mistaken her dodging an arc of champagne for something more serious. While a spattering of water turned her sleek mane of hair into a frizzy mess, a carelessly flung spray of champagne would turn it into a frizzy *sticky* mess and she had enough to worry about right at this minute.

Phoebe nipped that seed of shame in the bud. 'This,' she said coolly, pointing at her hair, 'takes hours to straighten and my dress is dry-clean only.'

For a split second Alex looked dumbstruck and then his expression shuttered and his eyes went blank. She cast a glance over his hair, thick, dark and unfairly shiny. Of course he would never understand the struggle she had with her hair, nor the burning need to keep it under control. But what was his problem?

'Look, I didn't ask you to interfere,' she pointed out. 'And I certainly didn't need your help.'

'So I'm beginning to gather.'

'I had the situation totally under control.'

'You were standing barefoot with a twig in your hair and your dress hitched up around your hips—'

'Thighs,' she snapped. 'But wherever my dress was and whatever my hairstyle, you had no business interfering.'

Alex shoved his hands through his hair. 'What did you expect me to do? Stand back and watch you get hurt? Did you really think that he was going to come out willingly?'

Phoebe blinked. 'Well, yes.' With a little persuasion and guidance.

'In case you hadn't noticed, Mark is built like a tank and was totally out of control. Your lack of judgement astonishes me.'

Phoebe flinched. Ouch, that hurt. 'I wasn't in any danger,' she said. 'Mark was incapable of hitting anything. Anyway, what did you do with him?'

'I threw him out.'

Of course. 'Did anyone see you?'

He frowned. 'Does it matter?'

Phoebe gaped. *Did it matter?* She briefly wondered if steam actually whooshed out of her ears. 'Of course it matters.'

Alex let out a harsh incredulous laugh. 'You'd seriously put what other people think before your own safety? Your priorities are unbelievable.'

'My priorities are my own business. You,' she said, glaring at him, 'overreacted.'

Alex looked as if it was taking every ounce of his control not to wrap his hands round her throat and throttle her. 'Do you have *any* idea how volatile someone in that state can be? They can switch from charming to violent in the blink of an eye.' He leaned in so close that she could see her own image reflected in his eyes and snapped his fingers and she jumped. 'Just like that.'

Phoebe stamped down the stab of curiosity that suddenly demanded to know whether his reaction was based on personal experience of something similar and channelled her indignation instead. 'Look,' she said icily, 'this isn't the first time I've come across someone who can't handle his drink. Before you,' she said, stepping forwards, uncurling her fist and jabbing him in the chest with her index finger, 'barged in and started throwing Mark around like some sort of caveman everything was fine. I was dealing with it perfectly well. On my own.'

Phoebe broke off, breathing heavily, suddenly aware that Alex wasn't listening to her. His jaw was rigid. Colour slashed along his cheekbones. He was staring at her mouth, his big frame almost vibrating with an odd sort of electric tension.

She could feel his heart pounding beneath her hand. She could feel the scorching heat of his body burning through his shirt to singe her palm. She could feel his nipple, hot and tight, pressing against her hand.

Appal thundered through her. His heart? His heat? His nipple? *Beneath her hand?*

Her gaze shot down to the finger that had been poking his chest. Only now the jabbing had stopped. Now her hand lay flat against his chest and any minute now her fingers would be clutching at his shirt and yanking him towards her.

Time seemed to judder to a halt. Music drifted towards them, the sultry beat winding through her and whipping up unfamiliar sensations that stretched out and took over her ability to think about anything other than having his mouth hot and demanding on hers.

Phoebe could barely comprehend what was happening to her. No man had ever had this effect on her before. She'd felt attraction, tremors of lust even. Quite often. But never this slow drugging desire humming deep inside her, making her whole body itch with the need to reacquaint itself with his.

She wouldn't even have that far to tug. One centimetre. Maybe two. And they'd be locked together, tumbling down onto the pile of huge cushions that lined the pergola and pulling at each other's clothing.

In the middle of a party that she was supposed to be running.

With a sharp gasp of horror she snatched her hand away and took a hasty step back. Alex's eyes shot back up to hers. Dark, lit with something that made her mouth dry and her pulse hammer. 'No one saw me,' he said, the trace of huskiness in his voice telling her that an identical thought had been running through his head.

'Thank goodness for that,' she managed, although her throat felt like sandpaper. She ran the tip of her tongue over her lips and swallowed hard. 'Now I'd like an apology.'

'I'd like a thank you.'

Phoebe stuck her chin up and gave him a cool smile. 'Then I guess we're both destined to be disappointed.'

Alex reached out to slide his hand round to the small of her back and pulled her against him. 'Not necessarily.'

CHAPTER TWO

As HIS MOUTH slammed down on hers Phoebe instantly lost track of everything except for the flood of heat that rushed straight to the centre of her. He took advantage of her gasp of shock instantly. When their tongues met it was as if someone had lit a firework deep inside her and Phoebe couldn't do anything other than melt against him. Her arms shot up around his neck and his tightened and whether he pulled or she pushed, all she knew was that she was plastered against him and her body thought it had died and gone to heaven.

She ought to pull away. This was utter madness. She was supposed to be working. She'd planned every minute of this party, and at no stage did her plans involve six feet plus of devastating masculinity swooping to her unneeded rescue, kissing her and messing up her mind.

But tingles rippled along her nerve endings and the scent of him wound up her nose, seeped into her brain and fried it. All rational thought vanished.

As the kiss deepened and spiralled into something wildly out of control Phoebe felt the evidence of his arousal press against her and she wanted to writhe against it. Barely aware of what she was doing, she raised herself onto the tips of her toes to feel his hard length better against her, but her dress was too tight, too constricting.

Her breasts felt heavy and swollen and she wanted him to push the bodice down, get rid of her bra and soothe her aching nipples with his hand and mouth. When his hand moved round to cup her breast, lights exploded behind her eyelids and lust thundered through her.

Oh, God, she thought, beginning to tremble uncontrollably. She'd never been kissed like this. Had never kissed anyone like this. And she'd never been swept away by this intensity of…feeling.

'Phoebe?'

They both froze at the sound of Jo's voice. Phoebe let out a tiny moan of protest and Alex jerked back, cursing softly. She hung limply in his embrace and stared up at him in stunned silence. His hair was rumpled from where her fingers had tangled through it and a muscle pounded in his jaw. He seemed to be as shaken as she was. But a moment later he'd let her go and had backed into the shadows.

She blinked and swayed for a second while Jo called her name again, her voice louder and closer, and then reality swooped in and hit her round the head with the force of a fully laden tote bag.

What had she been *thinking?* She was at work. What if Jo hadn't called her name? She'd have come across the two of them practically devouring each other, which was most certainly *not* the sort of professionalism she prided herself on.

Desperately trying to regulate her breathing, Phoebe smoothed her dress and pressed the backs of her hands to her cheeks. As she suspected. Burning. She touched her still tingling mouth, which felt ravaged and bruised, and wondered exactly how bad the damage was.

'Hey, Phoebs, here you are.' Jo came to a halt at the entrance to the pergola and beamed. 'What are you doing out here all on your own?'

Phoebe resisted the urge to glance around to see where Alex had vanished to and cleared her throat. 'Oh, you know,' she said, smiling weakly while searching her imagination for something more sensible to say than an awestruck 'wow, did I just imagine that?'. 'Getting some air.'

Pathetic. She made her living out of manipulating words and spinning situations. Surely she could come up with something better than that?

'Hmm. It is a bit stuffy inside.' Jo frowned. 'What's happened to your hair?'

Oops, she'd forgotten all about that. Her hands shot to her head and she carefully pulled out her makeshift hairpin. She combed her fingers through her hair and thanked God that it appeared to have come through recent events unscathed.

Jo glanced down. 'What on earth is that?'

'A twig.'

'What was it doing in your hair?'

Phoebe tossed it into a flowerbed and waved a vague hand. 'Oh, I was simply experimenting with an idea.'

'Thinking of branching out?'

'Ha ha,' she muttered, and then clamped her lips together to stop a sudden bubble of hysterical laughter escaping.

Jo peered at her closer. 'Are you all right? You look a bit flushed. And flustered.' She paused and tilted her head. 'I've never seen you flustered.'

That was because she took great care never to appear

flustered, even when inside she was a mess. Regardless of the situation, triumph or disaster, she was always the epitome of cool, unflappable collectedness. She never let anything get in the way of her commitment to her job. And she never *ever* lost control.

Well, except for just now…

But that was totally understandable, she assured herself. After all, she'd been flung around like a sack of potatoes and then kissed senseless without any say in the matter whatsoever. Who wouldn't feel a tiny bit on the flustered side?

Phoebe took a deep breath and channelled her inner calm. 'I'm absolutely fine,' she said.

Jo shot her a knowing smile. 'If you weren't out here alone, and if I didn't know that you never mix business with pleasure, I'd have sworn I'd interrupted you in the middle of a clinch.'

Phoebe felt colour hit her cheeks and edged away from the light. It was high time to deflect this line of conversation. 'Hmm. So. You were looking for me?'

'Yes. I came to tell you…' But what Jo had come to tell her never made it out of her mouth.

Phoebe didn't need to look round to know that Alex was standing behind her. The hairs at the nape of her neck had leapt up like an early-warning system and her whole body quivered with awareness.

As Jo's gaze slid over Phoebe's shoulder her smile disappeared, the blood drained from her face and her eyes widened in horror.

'Hello, Jo.' Alex's voice was as cold as ice and Jo seemed to deflate right in front of Phoebe's eyes.

'Oh, no,' Jo said with a deep sigh. 'What are you doing here?'

* * *

Well, that was a relief, thought Alex darkly, thrusting his hands in his pockets and keeping his eyes fixed on his sister. Jo's reaction to his presence at the party was the only thing so far this evening that *had* turned out as he'd expected.

Ever since he'd learned that she'd gone behind his back and hired her own PR representative without his approval, he'd planned to pitch up, demand to know what she thought she was up to and replace whoever she'd hired with his own team.

He'd intended to swoop in and be done within a matter of minutes, and if things had gone according to plan, he'd now be passed out in his penthouse, battling jet lag.

Instead, over the course of the last half an hour he'd fought a drunken idiot in a pond, been thwacked by a deluge of painful memories he'd really rather forget and been forced to face the uncomfortable realisation that for the first time in years he'd been wrong. As if all that weren't enough, it appeared he'd also caught a severe case of lust.

Alex flicked a quick glance at Phoebe, standing there with her dark hair tumbling over her shoulders and looking like a fallen angel, and felt desire whip through him all over again.

Kissing the life out of one of the guests had definitely not been part of the plan. But the moment he'd held her against him he'd been able to think about little else. He could still feel the imprint of her hand on his chest while she'd been ranting about dealing with cavemen or something, her eyes flashing sparks of green and gold at him. When his resistance had finally crumbled she'd fitted against him so perfectly, responded to him so passionately that he hadn't been able to stop. Who knew what might have happened if Jo hadn't interrupted them?

Alex ground his teeth against the urge to drag Phoebe back into the shadows. There'd be plenty of time for that later. Once he'd achieved what he'd come here to do, he'd take her out to dinner. See where a few more of those kisses might end up and maybe find a new way to get over jet lag.

In the meantime, he told himself, blanking Phoebe from his head and training his full attention on Jo, he had work to do.

'Surprised to see me?' he said coolly.

'Somewhat,' Jo muttered. 'But thrilled too, of course,' she added hastily.

She didn't look in the slightest bit thrilled. She looked wary, as if she'd been caught red-handed. Which she should, because she had. If he'd vaguely entertained the idea of giving her the benefit of the doubt over the absence of his invitation, it vanished.

'Of course,' he replied dryly.

'How did you find out?'

'Did you really imagine I wouldn't?'

'I had hoped.'

Alex frowned. Since when had she started keeping secrets from him? That rankled almost as much as the fact that she'd deliberately kept him out of the loop.

'Er, excuse me for interrupting, but would someone mind telling me what's going on?' said Phoebe, edging towards Jo in an oddly protective fashion. 'Because I'm guessing you don't have an invitation, and, if Jo wants, I can have the bouncers here faster than you can say "gatecrasher."'

Alex's gaze swivelled back to his sister. 'Well?' he said in a deadly soft voice.

'There's no need to call the bouncers.' Jo pulled her shoulders back and shot him a defiant look. 'Alex, I'd like you to meet Phoebe Jackson, managing director of Jackson Communications, and my PR.'

Jo's words hit him with the force of a swinging boom and his blood turned to ice in his veins. He glanced at Phoebe, who was staring at him with a determined tilt of her chin and an arched eyebrow.

This was the woman he'd come to fire? The raven-haired goddess in the tight gold dress, who'd piqued his interest the second he'd laid eyes on her sneaking out of a side door? The woman he'd been imagining naked and warm and writhing in his arms? Something curiously like disappointment walloped him in the solar plexus. Alex rubbed his chest and frowned.

Then suspicion began to prickle at the edges of his brain. If she and his sister were working together had she colluded with her to deliberately keep him out of the proceedings? Even taking into account his natural mistrust of anyone and anything that he personally hadn't tested to the limit, it wasn't beyond the realm of possibility.

Whether she had or not, dinner was off. With the ruthless control he'd honed over the years, Alex crushed the lingering flickers of desire and stashed any attraction he felt towards Phoebe behind an unbreachable wall of icy neutrality.

Hmm, thought Phoebe, watching his whole body tense and sort of freeze. For some reason the news of her identity hadn't gone down well at all. Which was odd—she didn't normally incite such a violent reaction in people.

'And, Phoebe, this is Alex Gilbert. My brother.'

She was so busy trying to work out what objection he could possibly have to her that she almost missed Jo's words. But as they filtered into her head Phoebe found herself in the unusual position of being rendered speechless. And then a dozen little facts cascaded into her brain, each one hot on the heels of the other, and she inwardly groaned.

Oh, no.

How typical was that?

Someone really wanted this evening to implode. Because what were the chances that her mysterious, mind-blowingly gorgeous stranger would turn out to be the hotshot venture capitalist who'd injected a huge sum of cash so that Jo could finish and launch her collection? The billionaire who was so busy jetting round the world taking over businesses and entertaining glamorous women that he'd refused the invitation.

She hated it when she was wrong-footed. And not just wrong-footed. Hurled off balance would be a more accurate description. She'd swooned in his arms. Melted against him. Practically devoured him, for heaven's sake. How mortifyingly inappropriate was that?

'I should have guessed,' she said hiding her embarrassment behind a cool façade. 'The family resemblance is uncanny.'

She might be burning up inside, but Alex didn't appear to be the slightest bit fazed. 'Technically I'm her half-brother,' he said with an impersonal little smile. 'We shared a mother and we each take after our fathers.' He held out a hand. Phoebe felt an arc of electricity shoot up her arm when her palm hit his and had to force herself not to snatch it back.

What was he doing here anyway? Jo had said he was quite content to be a silent partner. That he had no interest in what Jo got up to and even less in handbags.

When she'd heard about his supposed lack of fraternal support it hadn't surprised her in the slightest. After all, when had *her* siblings ever supported her? At least he'd shown up at the eleventh hour, which was more than she could expect from any member of her family, all of whom thought her choice of career unbelievably frivolous.

Well, frivolous it might be, but it had given her enough experience to handle any situation with sophistication and aplomb. Even one as awkward as this.

'I thought you were supposed to be in the States,' she said evenly.

'I was.'

'Venturing your capital?'

'Negotiating a deal.'

'Did you win?'

'He always wins,' said Jo grumpily.

'I'm sure you do,' she said smoothly, pulling her hand out of his and surreptitiously flexing her fingers to stop the tingling. 'Anyway, naturally we're delighted to see you.'

'Really?' he said raising an eyebrow. 'In that case, I can only imagine my invitation got lost in the post.'

Phoebe frowned. 'You refused it.'

'Did I?' he said flatly, his expression turning even stonier.

'You were obviously too busy to remember refusing it as well as being too busy to come.'

'Obviously,' he drawled and somehow Phoebe instantly knew that he'd been nothing of the kind.

'So why the change of heart? A hitherto unrecognised fascination for women's accessories?'

A slow smouldering smile curved his lips, and she felt herself heating up. 'This is my little sister's debut. How could I possibly miss it?'

'Then why refuse in the first place?' Something wasn't right here, but for the life of her Phoebe couldn't work out what. Alex had turned her brain to mush.

'All right,' said Jo, throwing her hands up in the air. 'Phoebe, Alex knows perfectly well that I never sent him an invitation.'

Now she was baffled. Phoebe blinked and swung her attention back to Jo. 'So why did you tell me you had?'

'Oh, I really don't remember,' said Jo vaguely, waving a hand.

'Forgetfulness seems to run in the family,' Phoebe said dryly, not believing her for a second. Jo had been very unforthcoming about her brother, despite the fact that he'd contributed so much to her fledgling career, and now that she thought about it Phoebe realised that whenever she'd mentioned the financial generosity of Jo's elusive brother, Jo had deftly changed the subject, which she'd thought odd at the time. However Phoebe had enough experience of tricky sibling relationships to steer well clear of other people's and hadn't probed.

With hindsight, she should have insisted on knowing more. His name at least. That would have saved her a whole lot of trouble.

'Anyway, you two should get to know each other.'

No, they shouldn't. Phoebe already knew far more about Alex than she was comfortable with, and his rigid expression gave her the impression that he wasn't particularly keen on the idea either.

'We met earlier,' she said pleasantly. 'The encounter was brief.'

'But intense,' he said, shooting her a searing look.

'And wet, by the looks of things,' said Jo, frowning as she glanced at the damp patches on Alex's suit.

'I decided to take a stroll round the gardens. It involved an unexpected detour via the pond.' Alex rubbed his chest and Phoebe was instantly transported back to the moments before he'd kissed her. Images flashed into her head. The way he'd stared at her mouth, the hunger in his expression and the fire in his eyes. So different from the cold, controlled man standing in front of her.

Surely he couldn't be that upset about not being sent an invitation? But if it wasn't that, what was it?

'If you're falling into ponds,' said Jo lightly, 'you must be more jet-lagged than usual.'

'I must be,' murmured Alex. His eyes locked with Phoebe's and her stomach flipped.

'Jet lag makes him do the oddest things,' said Jo, clearly thankful that the attention had shifted away from her. 'The last time he had it he shredded a six-figure cheque instead of banking it and stashed his car keys in the fridge.'

Phoebe raised an eyebrow. 'How absolutely fascinating.'

'Don't you just love siblings?' he drawled.

'Simply adore them,' she said, and then thought of her own. 'But I couldn't eat a whole one.'

He didn't even crack a smile and Phoebe felt her hackles shoot up. What was his problem? 'I didn't think international playboys bothered with things like fridges.'

A warning gleam entered his eyes. 'Are you making assumptions about me, Phoebe?'

'Simply making an observation,' she said with an innocent smile.

'Champagne has to be chilled somewhere, don't you think?'

'It certainly does. The colder the better.'

'Especially in this heat.'

Phoebe shivered at the smouldering silvery sparks in his gaze.

'It's not that warm,' said Jo. 'Not for May. And, Phoebs, you've got goose-bumps.'

'Cold?' Alex asked softly, running his gaze over her, and to her irritation her body responded instantly. Her breasts tightened uncomfortably against the close-fitting dress and her nipples hardened while hot flames of desire licked deep inside her.

'No.'

The seconds stretched, and the longer their gazes held, the more it felt as if nothing else existed beyond the sizzling attraction that arced between them. Her gaze dipped to his mouth and the desperate longing to have it on hers again thumped her in the stomach.

And Alex wanted it too, she realised with a jolt. She could tell by the darkening of his eyes and by the way his body seemed to go utterly still. Phoebe shuddered at the desire that suddenly ripped through her and dragged in a shaky breath. Alex frowned and ran a hand through his hair and when he jerked his attention away from her Phoebe felt as if a piece of elastic had snapped her in the face.

She had to stop this. She'd never had trouble controlling her hormones before, so why now?

Jo thankfully seemed oblivious to the electric undercurrents that fizzed between them and was looking round the gardens. 'So what do you think of the venue?' she asked brightly. 'Isn't it heavenly?'

'Quite literally, given that we're six storeys above the streets of central London,' Alex replied. 'The gardens are…' his gaze swung back to Phoebe and her heart practically thudded to a halt '…illuminating.'

'That'll be the clever lighting,' she said, amazed that her voice sounded so steady when her whole body was trembling.

'Not that clever if you're falling into ponds. By the way, have either of you seen Mark?'

Alex tensed. 'Who's Mark?'

'My new boyfriend.' Jo beamed.

Alex's jaw clenched and his face darkened.

'I've been looking all over the place for him but can't find him anywhere. I thought he might have come out here.'

'He did.'

There was a heavy silence. And then eventually Jo swung round, and stared at him. 'Oh no. Have you met him?' She frowned, her expression starting out wary but then when Alex didn't answer immediately, turning to anger. 'What happened? What did you do to him?'

Alex's face was as rigid as stone and Phoebe hoped she'd never give him cause to look at her like that. With all that restrained strength and power, combined with the scar and the bump on his nose, she had a feeling Alex Gilbert could be a dangerous man to cross. 'I poured him into a taxi and sent him home.'

'I don't believe it,' said Jo, her voice tense with frustration. 'Why did you do that?'

'Mark was slightly the worse for wear,' Phoebe interjected. 'I tried to persuade him to cool off but he wasn't really co-operating.'

'Mark was off his head,' Alex corrected sharply, 'and

I was under the brief misapprehension that Phoebe's safety was at stake.'

Jo's mouth dropped open. 'Why would her safety be at stake?

'I thought he'd hit her,' he said flatly.

'Oh,' said Jo in a small voice.

A look passed between Alex and his sister that Phoebe couldn't identify and that nugget of shame threatened to resprout inside her. 'Nevertheless,' said Phoebe, forcing it down, 'you overreacted.'

'We've already been through that,' grated Alex.

'I could put it down to jet lag if you'd like,' said Phoebe helpfully, and then shuddered at the dark scowl that crossed his face.

Jo sighed and her shoulders slumped. 'Was Mark very drunk?'

'As a skunk,' said Phoebe, 'and after some time in the pond he smelt a bit like one too.'

Jo's nose wrinkled. 'What was he doing in the pond?'

'Making friends with the wildlife,' said Alex dryly. 'Someone forgot to put up a fence.'

'No one forgot,' said Phoebe. 'It's deliberate. It's cool. The fencelessness of the San Lorenzo Roof Gardens symbolises the uninhibited harmony between man and nature, and is part of its uber-cool appeal.' At least that was what the website claimed.

'It's absurd,' Alex growled. 'Your boyfriend,' he said, emphasising the word with sharp disdain as his gaze skewered Jo to the spot, 'could have caused serious damage.'

'It's not his fault,' said Jo, her face falling. 'He's up to his ears in debt.'

'Idiot,' muttered Alex.

'Spoken like a true billionaire,' said Phoebe tartly.

Alex's eyes glittered dangerously. 'There you go again,' he said, shaking his head as if in disappointment. 'Jumping to conclusions and making rash assumptions. I haven't always been a billionaire. I know what it's like to have nothing but debts.'

So do I, thought Phoebe, and tried not to think about the enormous loan she'd taken out to set up her business.

'But I didn't drown myself in drink,' Alex added.

'Lucky you.' There were times when Phoebe felt like mainlining vodka, but so far she'd managed to resist.

He turned to Jo. 'I don't think you should see him again.'

'Thanks to you I probably won't,' Jo fired back.

Right. Phoebe had had enough of this. Sibling squabbling had no place here. 'Perhaps you two could continue this discussion another time,' she said in a voice that brooked no argument. 'Jo, you need to go back inside and mingle. Alex, you need to get a drink and relax. And I need to get on with making sure nothing else goes wrong.'

'Ms Jackson?'

Phoebe spun round to see the portly form of Mr Bogoni barrelling towards them, huffing and puffing and looking as if he were on the verge of exploding. Her spirits dipped at the expression on his face. Oh, Lord. What was the matter now? Surely one mishap was quite enough for one evening.

'Ms Jackson,' he said again, smoothing his hair.

'Mr Bogoni,' said Phoebe, flashing him a bright smile that as usual didn't manage to dent the icy demeanour. 'You'll be delighted to know that the flamingo remains unharmed.'

'I am indeed glad to hear that, but unfortunately we have another problem.'

'What sort of problem?'

'I think you'd better come with me.'

CHAPTER THREE

PHOEBE'S MIND RACED as she followed Mr Bogoni across the terrace towards the bar. What could possibly have happened now? And why did Alex have to be following quite so closely? In fact why did he have to be there at all? 'There was no need for you to come too,' Phoebe muttered out of the side of her mouth.

'You think not?' he drawled. 'This is perhaps the most important night of my sister's career. I'm interested in everything that goes on.'

'Whatever it is,' said Jo firmly, 'Phoebe will be able to fix it.'

Phoebe shot Jo a smile of thanks for her vote of confidence and prepared herself for the worst.

But as she stepped into the bar her eyes were drawn up and she froze in absolute horror.

Oh, dear God. This wasn't a problem. This was a disaster of gargantuan proportions, the likes of which nothing in her experience could have prepared her for. Compared to this, the Mark debacle was as insignificant as a tiny sequin on a full-length ball gown.

Phoebe blinked to check she wasn't hallucinating, but no. This was no hallucination.

Every single one of Jo's beautiful handbags was on fire. Multicoloured flames licked at the precious creations and the acrid smell of burning plastic and fabric filled the room. Sparks flew. Metal crackled. Then, as if cremating handbags weren't bad enough, the individual light above each pedestal went out, the localised sprinkler system kicked in and tiny droplets of water rained over the charred remains. Smoke billowed and then whooshed up into the powerful air conditioning vents.

Icy panic flooded through her. How on earth was she going to spin this? All the guests had edged to the sides of the room and every single one of them was staring up at the spectacle in utter amazement. Jo looked as if she was on the verge of tears; Alex's stony expression told her he wasn't amused in the slightest.

The dreadful silence gave way to a rumble of speculation that began to sweep through the room. Gasps of amazement were swiftly followed by murmurs about flammable fabric and toxic materials and Phoebe realised that if she didn't do something in the next few minutes the situation would become unsalvageable and her business would fail barely before it had begun.

But what? For the first time in her life, she didn't have a clue what to say. Terror clawed at her chest and a ball of panic lodged in her throat. Her head went fuzzy and for a moment she thought she was about to start hyperventilating.

No. She didn't have time to hyperventilate. Not when Jo's bags had all just exploded like firecrackers.

Phoebe's heart skipped a beat. Wait a moment… firecrackers…

The idea that popped into her head was so outrageously crazy, so unbelievable, that it might actually work. It was a gamble, but if she showed she believed it, everyone else would too, and she'd have turned a major disaster into a fabulous finale.

Euphoric relief wiped the fuzz from her head and an unstoppable grin spread across her face. 'Don't worry about a thing,' she said, leaning over to whisper in Jo's ear and giving her arm a reassuring squeeze. 'It's all going to be fine.'

So how was she going to wriggle out of this one?

Alex leaned against a pillar and folded his arms over his chest as Phoebe marched across the empty floor, stepped up onto the dais and tapped the microphone. All eyes watched her and the room filled with a sort of morbid excitement that reminded him of birds of prey circling an injured animal.

How could Jo ever have thought that hiring someone of her own accord was a wise thing to do? Especially someone who allowed the evening to descend into chaos.

As far as he was aware his sister knew nothing about PR. Whereas he'd worked with his team for years. So why hadn't she come to him and asked for his advice on something so important? Alex ignored the twinge of hurt and made himself pay attention to what Phoebe was about to say.

'Ladies and gentlemen,' she began, smiling broadly and waiting until every drop of focus was on her. 'Rockets… Catherine wheels… Sparklers… And now handbags.' She paused. 'I think you'll all agree that our grand pyrotechnical finale was much more original than a firework display. A little earlier than planned, perhaps, but no less spectacular.'

Alex's jaw tightened. Hah. She was doomed. As if

anyone was going to believe a story as ridiculous as that. With one ear on the rest of her speech, which continued in the same dubious vein, he surveyed the room with a sceptical eye. She'd never pull this off.

He was just beginning to congratulate himself on having saved Jo from a terrible career move, when to his utter amazement people began to smile and nod and whisper to each other. Surely people couldn't actually be buying her absurd explanation?

'And as that rounds off the evening's events,' Phoebe said finally, 'I'd like to thank you all for coming, and hope you enjoy the upcoming launch of the debut collection of the fabulous Jo Douglas.'

Jo stepped up to her side and gave a little curtsey. Phoebe started clapping and as everyone else joined in the sound grew into a thunderous applause. The pair of them stepped off the dais, basking in glory, and Alex watched through narrowed eyes as a woman in purple cornered Phoebe and a crowd of people flocked around Jo.

OK, so that was a clever wiggle, he grudgingly admitted, still slightly stunned by the fact that everyone had apparently bought into her explanation. Her timing was impeccable, her imagination was extraordinary and she'd had her audience eating out of her hand.

Maybe Phoebe wasn't as incapable as he'd originally thought, but that was tough. To his mind she was an enigma and that made her a liability. And what did Jo really know about her anyway? He'd bet everything he had that she hadn't delved that far into her background and her experience, and had made little effort to see whether she was trustworthy. So it was lucky he'd shown up when he did.

Gradually the guests drifted off and Jo bounded over

to him, grinning like a lunatic. 'You see,' she said trium-phantly. 'I told you Phoebe'd fix it. Isn't she amazing?'

Alex grimaced. Amazing wasn't quite the word he'd use to describe her. Beautiful. That was a good one. Sexy as hell. With a mouth that had been made for kissing and a body that seemed to have been created spe-cially to fit to his.

The kiss they'd shared beneath the pergola slammed into his head and a savage kick of lust thumped him in the gut.

Damn. Burying his attraction to her was going to take far more effort than he'd thought. Still, once he'd got rid of her, desire would fade and in future he'd steer well clear of women who obliterated his self-control and drove him mindless with just a kiss.

'Why didn't you tell me you were planning to hire someone to do your PR?' he said mildly, his voice betraying nothing of the battle raging inside him.

'Because I knew you wouldn't have approved.'

'You're right. I don't. I want you to use my PR people.'

Jo sighed. 'You see. *This* is why I didn't want you here. I knew you were going to do this. Alex, I don't want to use your people.'

'Why not? My team are tried and tested. Reliable.' At least as reliable as anyone other than himself could be.

Jo's expression turn mutinous and Alex wondered where this backbone of steel had sprung from. 'Your team might be excellent at dealing with finance and in-ventions and things, but they wouldn't know one end of a handbag from the other.' Alex felt his jaw tighten. That might be true, but they could learn. 'Phoebe handled the account of a graduate from my college a few years ago when she was working at one of the big PR agencies.

Maria now works in Paris for one of the top fashion houses. Phoebe has incredible contacts and, well, you can see for yourself what she's achieved this evening.'

Alex let out a short burst of incredulous laughter. As far as he could tell, all she'd achieved was a series of disasters.

Jo shifted her weight from one foot to the other, but didn't look as if she intended to back down. 'OK, so I admit that my handbags on fire wasn't exactly in the plans, but would your PR team have come up with such a spectacular excuse?'

Probably not, but that wasn't the point. 'My PR team would never have let it happen in the first place.'

'Phoebe didn't "let" it happen. It was an accident. Not even you can turn it into her fault.'

Hmm. Pity. The implication of her words sank in and Alex winced. He wasn't that unreasonable. If he did come over as heavy-handed occasionally it was only for Jo's benefit. But his sister clearly didn't see it like that. In her eyes Phoebe could do little wrong. Knowing which battles to fight if he wanted to win, Alex decided to switch tactics. 'How well do you know her?'

'Pretty well. I've been working with her for two months.'

Two months was nothing. He'd known Rob for ten years and it hadn't stopped his best friend betraying him. 'And how do you know she won't drop you the moment someone with better prospects comes along?'

Jo sighed. 'At the moment I'm her only client. She needs me as much as I need her so I think that makes her pretty trustworthy, don't you?' She pushed a lock of hair off her face and fixed him with a stare. 'Look, Alex. I know I've been a nightmare and have given you untold cause for worry. And you'll never know how grateful I am for all the help and support you've given me but I really need to start taking responsibility for my own life. Mistakes and all. You can't keep protecting me for ever.'

Couldn't he? He'd been doing exactly that ever since her parents died and he didn't intend to stop now. Especially after the hideous events of five years ago when he'd screwed up so spectacularly. A familiar wave of guilt washed over him and his chest tightened. He didn't intend to screw up again.

'Alex, I really want this. Phoebe and I work well together. She understands what I need. Please don't mess this up for me.'

The quiet pleading in her voice cut right through him and Alex felt his resolve waver. He ran his gaze over her and looked at her properly for the first time this evening. She'd changed in the two months since he'd last seen her. She seemed more confident, more determined, healthier. More like the girl she'd been before she'd met Rob.

Alex sighed and felt his control over her well-being begin to slip away. As harrowing as the prospect of letting Jo find her own way in the world was, maybe she was right. She was twenty-two. He couldn't protect her for ever. Maybe it was time he loosened the reins. A little. But if either of them thought he'd just sit back and hope for the best, they could think again.

CHAPTER FOUR

BY ELEVEN O'CLOCK the following morning Phoebe had spent three hours at her desk, poring over the press, answering calls from potential clients and trying not to wonder where Alex had disappeared to the night before.

Maybe he'd had a date. Maybe he'd succumbed to jet lag and had crashed out in a flowerbed. Maybe he'd been appalled by the haphazard way the party had panned out and left in disgust.

Who knew? Jo certainly hadn't. And Phoebe really oughtn't to care either way; as a silent partner he was unlikely to be popping up all the time, and as her client's brother—and therefore strictly off limits—he could date whoever and pass out wherever he chose. Not that he'd ever been *on* limits, of course.

But to her intense irritation she did care. Because regardless of where Alex had physically got to last night, he was now lodged in her head and she was going slowly out of her mind.

Her memory had become photographic where Alex was concerned. Every detail of his dark handsome face, every inch of his incredible body was as clear as if he were standing in front of her and she just couldn't get rid of the image, no matter how hard she tried.

Phoebe pinched the bridge of her nose and screwed her eyes up. He had no right invading her thoughts like this. It was bad enough that he'd barged into her dreams and had proceeded to do all sorts of deliciously erotic things to her that had woken her up hot and sweating and pulsating with need.

Sleep had whisked her back to the pergola, where he'd kissed her over and over again until she'd been panting and whimpering. Only this time, nothing had interrupted them and Alex had slid down the zip of her dress and peeled it off her and then his hands had stroked over her skin, before pulling her down with him onto the cushions and—

Agh. Phoebe jumped to her feet, utterly disgusted with her lack of control over something so primitive, and marched into the kitchen.

She needed a cup of coffee. So what if she'd already had five? Number six would sort her out. It had to. Otherwise she'd never last the morning.

The phone rang just as she was pouring water into the cafetiere. Her hand jerked and boiling water splashed her skin.

Phoebe howled in pain and frustration. This edginess was so unlike her. Whenever stress threatened to wipe her out, all she usually had to do was take a series of deep breaths and channel the serenity of her office. But today those yoga techniques, the acres of bare white walls and the ordered tranquillity of her surroundings weren't working.

Scowling and rubbing her hand, Phoebe inhaled deeply, closed her eyes and forced herself to pick up the phone slowly and calmly. 'Hello?' Good. Pleasant and polite. That didn't sound bad.

'Phoebs, I have an Alex Gilbert in Reception.'

Phoebe dropped the phone and watched helplessly as it bounced twice and then skidded across the floorboards. So much for inner calm.

What was he doing here? Had her fevered imagination actually conjured him up? What did he want?

'Phoebs? Are you there?'

Oh, to be able to yell 'no!' and go and hide under her desk. But the opportunity to imitate her answer machine and pretend she was out had long gone. 'Just a moment,' she called and dashed across the floor to where her phone lay.

Phoebe picked up the handset. Then she straightened her suit and smoothed her hair and dredged up every ounce of self-possession she had. 'Thanks, Lizzie,' she said serenely. 'You'd better tell him to come up.'

All she had to do was remain steady and in control and everything would be fine.

Alex glanced around Phoebe's office and felt like fishing out his sunglasses. Apart from the woman in the severe black trouser suit perched against the edge of the sparkling glass desk and a few certificates and pictures hanging on the walls everything was blindingly white.

'Good morning, Alex.'

She looked so composed with her poker straight hair and aloof air that for an insane moment he wanted to ruffle her up. 'Good morning, Phoebe.'

'Coffee?'

'No, thank you.'

'Did you have a pleasant evening?'

'Delightful.' And busy. Once he'd reluctantly given in to Jo, he'd gone back to his apartment, had formulated a plan and had wasted no time in setting the wheels in motion.

'I'm so glad.' She gave him a chilly smile and moved round to the other side of her desk. She gestured to the chair on his side. 'Please. Do sit down.'

'Thank you.' Alex folded himself onto the perspex chair and sat back.

'How's the jet lag?'

'Fine.'

'Shredded any cheques?'

Alex grinned. 'Not so far. How are the handbags?'

'Ruined beyond repair.'

'Whose idea was it to put them so close to the lights?'

'That would be mine.'

'Clever.'

She flinched and her eyes flashed. Perhaps she wasn't so composed after all, Alex thought with an odd sense of reassurance. After the heat and passion of last night, this morning's ultra-cool Phoebe had been faintly unnerving.

'I was led to believe that everything would be fine. The three risk assessments I carried out back me up. You can have a look at them if you'd like.'

Alex ignored her sarcasm. 'Any idea what happened?'

'According to the manager, someone had installed the wrong kind of light bulbs, and according to Jo she used highly flammable glue as a sort of quick fix in order to get some samples finished for last night. Normally she stitches everything by hand. A most unfortunate coincidence.'

'So it would seem.'

'Still, it wasn't all bad. Self-igniting accessories are apparently tipped to be the latest craze.'

'Extraordinary.'

Phoebe shrugged. 'Anything's possible in PR.' She picked up a pen and pulled a notepad towards her. 'Anyway,' she said with a bright smile that didn't reach her eyes, 'what do you want?'

Alex stretched his legs out and regarded her carefully. 'I have a proposition for you.'

That surprised her. 'Oh?'

'I'm hosting a party tomorrow night for colleagues and clients and a few friends. I want you to be there.'

Curiosity cracked the glacial façade. 'In what capacity?'

'I want you to raise money for one of the charities I support.'

Phoebe's eyes narrowed. 'That's not really what I do.'

He knew that, and that was the beauty of his test. 'Don't you want the business?' he said shooting her a shrewd glance.

Phoebe frowned. 'Naturally your offer is intriguing, but isn't raising money at a private party a little inappropriate?'

'Highly. There lies the challenge.'

'But why would you want to offer me a challenge?'

Alex regarded her thoughtfully for a while. 'Would you like to know the real reason I was at the party last night?'

Phoebe tensed. 'I'd be fascinated.'

'I came to fire you,' he said lazily.

Outside, traffic rumbled. Horns beeped. People shouted. But inside her office heavy silence descended.

Phoebe blinked and stared at him in disbelief. 'You know, for a moment there I thought you'd said you'd come to fire me.'

'I did.'

Phoebe went white for a second and then that brittle little smile snapped back to her face and Alex was struck by a sudden uncontrollable urge to wipe it away with a kiss. 'That's insane. I don't work for you so how can you fire me?'

He ignored the urge and kept his gaze well away from her mouth. 'I own sixty per cent of Jo's company. I can do whatever I like.'

Phoebe glowered. 'I thought you were supposed to be a silent partner.'

'I was.'

'Your particular brand of silence is deafening.' She paused and total bafflement swept across her face. 'Why would you want to fire me?' Then she frowned. 'Is this about the kiss?'

Alex started. 'Why would this be about the kiss?'

'Well, some might say there was a conflict of interest,' she muttered, taking an intense interest in the papers on her desk as her cheeks went pink.

'I didn't know who you were. Did you know who I was?'

'No. Jo barely mentioned you, and then never by name.'

'There'd only be a conflict of interest were I to kiss you now.'

Her head snapped up and the colour on her cheeks deepened. 'Er, quite.'

'And that's not going to happen.'

'Good,' she said sharply, as if she was trying to convince herself as much as him. 'Excellent.'

Was that disappointment that flared in her eyes? Alex shifted in the chair. 'So in answer to your question, no, my decision to fire you had nothing to do with the kiss.'

'What did it have to do with, then?'

'Your competency.'

Phoebe reeled. Her competency? What on earth was going on?

When Alex had informed her that he'd intended to fire her as casually as if they'd been discussing the weather, she'd thought that nothing more he said could shock her.

She'd been wrong.

'My competency?' He nodded. 'What about it?'

'Based on the…unusual…events of last night, I'm not convinced you're the best person to represent Jo.'

Phoebe gasped. The arrogance of the man. How dared he question her competency when he knew next to nothing about her? 'That's absurd.'

'Is it?' he said in that lazy drawl that made her want to thump him.

'Were you not there last night? Did you not see how I turned a fiasco into a triumph?' Phoebe glared at him, all hope of remaining polite and pleasant a dim and distant memory. 'Last night's party resulted in thirty column inches across six newspapers and four requests for interviews with Jo. Three magazines are going to run features on her and her handbags and the party will appear on the society pages in all of them. This morning I had a call from one of the major high street stores who want her to design a range of accessories for them.'

Phoebe got to her feet, as if standing would somehow stop her anger from brimming over and making her say something she might really regret. 'How, exactly, is that incompetent?'

Alex didn't answer. He merely raised an eyebrow and it shot her anger into incandescence. 'I'm very good at my job, Alex. I have ten years of experience. I've handled million-pound accounts and I've launched products that have turned into best-sellers. I'm also brilliant at breaking up rowing journalists at press conferences, evading difficult questions and managing crises. Winning over disapproving brothers is a new one for me, but I *will* get there in the end.' She paused and gave him an icy smile. 'I've been working with Jo for weeks and we make a great team. She has extraordinary potential and a great career ahead of her. Her launch is in a fortnight and all the plans are in place. I will not let you ruin this for her.'

Long seconds passed before Alex spoke and when he did his voice froze her blood. 'Why don't you tell me about the parts of your career that haven't, I presume, gone quite according to plan?'

The parts of her career that hadn't gone according to plan? His words whipped the wind from her sails and she dragged in a shaky breath. What parts? There weren't any. At least none that he could possibly know about… 'What do you mean?' she hedged, sitting back down and filling with trepidation.

The way he just looked at her, like an animal stalking its prey, turned her even colder. 'I'm talking about the soap, the perfume and the musician.'

Phoebe felt as if he'd pulled the chair out from underneath her. 'How do you know about them?'

Alex's eyes glittered. 'I know an awful lot about you.'

Her stomach fell away and her head went fuzzy. 'Did you have me investigated?'

Alex nodded.

'Why would you do that?'

'Standard due diligence procedures. Why wouldn't I?'

Phoebe rubbed her temples and sank back down into

her chair. Oh, God. He'd had her investigated? What sort of man did something like that? Jo had mentioned that Alex could be a touch on the protective side, but this was madness. Last night he hadn't even known her name. Now, thanks to investigators who must have toiled throughout the night, he probably knew more about her than she did herself.

'Unless you want me to fire you right now, you can start with the soap.' Alex's eyes glittered, as if he was actually relishing the moment.

Phoebe felt as if she were sitting on knives. 'What do you know about the soap?'

He gave her a mocking smile. 'You said that it brought out a rash and made your skin itch. To a journalist.'

'I didn't know he was a journalist. He bought me a drink. And another. And another. I thought he was being friendly.'

His mouth twisted. 'My point precisely.'

Phoebe sighed and rubbed her neck. How lucky she'd had plenty of practice justifying what she did, the decisions she'd taken and the mistakes she'd made. Compared to the grilling her family gave her on a monthly basis, this was a walk in the park.

But then, her family didn't hold her future in their hands.

Phoebe gathered her wits. She needed every drop of strength because right now she had to fight harder than she had in a long time.

'Alex, I was twenty-one. It was right at the beginning of my career. In the second week of my first job. I was naïve. I learnt.' She paused. 'Besides, it *did* give me a rash and make my skin itch. As a result they went back and tweaked the formula.'

'Nevertheless it was hardly a stellar moment.'

'I'm well aware of that.'

'And then what about the perfume?' He paused. 'Falsifying sales figures? I'd say that was verging on criminal.'

Phoebe stiffened. 'It was nothing of the kind. It was simply a mistake. I was given the wrong data.'

'And you didn't think to check?'

'I trusted my team.'

Alex grunted. 'Now *that* was a mistake,' he said more sharply than she would have thought the point warranted.

'Evidently. But you needn't worry. Now I check and double-check everything.'

Alex didn't look as if that information alleviated his concerns in the slightest.

So two blips down, only one remained. Phoebe's heart rate picked up. She'd spent so long in denial over this particular incident that she really didn't want to have to rake through it all over again. But she doubted Alex would let it rest.

'And the musician?'

She sighed and pinched the bridge of her nose and forced back the anguish that clenched her heart. 'Dillon Black was an up and coming musician looking for representation.' She shrugged as if the whole sorry affair had been a mere inconvenience instead of the heart-wrenching nightmare it had become. 'I signed him up with the company I was working for at the time.'

'I thought you specialised in fashion PR.'

Phoebe shifted on the chair and bit her lip. 'I do. That was the trouble. When someone with more experience offered him a better deal he jumped ship faster than you can say "recording label."'

'So why did you sign him up?'

Phoebe closed her eyes briefly. 'It was a blip. A one-off error of judgement.'

A tiny smile hovered over his mouth. 'So it had nothing to do with the fact that you were living together at the time?'

Phoebe's gaze jerked to his and her heart thundered. 'How do you know that?'

'My investigators are very thorough.'

'This is outrageous.'

Alex shrugged. 'Your lack of judgement seems to have been a recurrent theme in the course of your career.'

Phoebe gasped. How did he do that? He hit her where she was most vulnerable and then stuck the knife in, twisting it and slicing her heart open and releasing all the old aches and hurt.

'I wanted to help him,' she said, trying to keep a steady grip on her voice. 'I trusted him. I never imagined he'd turn around and betray me.'

Phoebe's heart hardened. She'd been so besotted by Dillon, had even thought herself in love with him, and he'd just been using her. Infatuation had made her take her eye off the ball, distracted her and screwed up her judgement. She'd very nearly lost her job and she'd vowed then and there that she'd never let herself get in that position again.

'More fool you,' he said flatly.

'Indeed. Anyway,' she said, pulling herself together and giving Alex a cool stare, 'you can be sure that my judgement is now well and truly back on track. The experience taught me, one, to stick with what I'm good at, two, not to allow anyone or anything to deflect my focus.'

So she'd made mistakes. Who hadn't? At least she'd

learned from them. Alex was probably the sort who never admitted to making a mistake. Never admitted to being wrong. Typical, she thought with a little sniff.

'Easy to say,' he said sharply.

Phoebe shot him a questioning glance. 'What's made you so deeply suspicious of people's behaviour?'

Alex's eyelids dropped slightly so she couldn't see the expression in his eyes. 'Experience.'

'Such cynicism in one so young.'

'Not that young.'

'Early thirties?'

'Thirty-two.'

'And in those thirty-two years, have you never made a mistake?'

'We're talking about you.'

Aha. So he had made a mistake. 'What was it, Alex?'

Alex's face darkened. 'For someone who's supposed to be fighting to keep their job, you're veering way off course.'

That was something else that she'd been wondering about. 'Why do you have responsibility over who Jo works with? She's twenty-two. Why can't she make her own decisions?'

His lips thinned. 'She can't be trusted to make her own decisions.'

Phoebe bristled. His arrogance was simply unbeliev-able. 'Why not?'

'Because she's made lousy decisions in the past.'

Haven't we all? thought Phoebe darkly. 'But surely they're her lousy decisions?'

Alex raked a hand through his hair and when he looked at her his expression was so desolate that Phoebe's heart clenched. 'Not when I have to pick up the pieces.'

'Why do you have to pick up the pieces?' Phoebe had always picked up her own pieces. Didn't everyone?

'I'm her brother.'

A tiny dart of envy pierced her chest, but she brushed it aside. 'Does she know you trust her judgement so little?'

'She knows I have her best interests at heart,' he said flatly.

'Her best interests at the moment are me.'

'Then accept the challenge.'

Phoebe sat back and tried to read his expression. But it gave away nothing other than the fact that his position on the matter was totally immutable.

'What if I say no? That I, for one, trust her judgement?'

'I would have no hesitation in replacing you with my own PR team.'

'Yours? Do they have any experience in fashion?'

'Not yet.'

Phoebe stared at him, unable to fathom the emotion in his eyes. 'You'd really do that? Even if it goes against Jo's wishes?'

'I would.'

'And even though I'm the best person for the job?'

She could practically hear his teeth grinding. 'All I want is what's best for her.'

No, he didn't, Phoebe realised with a flash of perception. Well, yes, the chances were he did want what was best for his sister, but that wasn't all. For some reason Alex wanted, needed, to stay in control.

In all probability he'd confronted Jo with his intention, and based on the interaction between the two of them she'd witnessed last night she'd bet her brand new pair of designer heels that Jo had retaliated. That must have frustrated the hell out of him.

Good.

Phoebe itched with the urge to tell him to get lost. But she couldn't. She had no doubt whatsoever that if she chose not to comply he'd have no compunction in batting her to one side and installing his own team. Aside from wrecking Jo's future, it would batter her professional pride and would have devastating consequences on her career.

She really *really* needed to hang onto Jo. If she lost her... Phoebe shuddered at the thought and felt a trickle of cold sweat ripple down her back. The bank would call in the loan, her business would collapse and she'd have failed before she'd barely got started.

Well, that was *not* going to happen. She wouldn't fail. She couldn't fail. Her family didn't do failure. Ever. And she didn't intend to be the one to break the mould.

So she'd accept his challenge, and win.

'I won't let her down,' she said with steely determination.

'Then prove it.'

'Fine. What's the charity?'

He told her and Phoebe jotted down the details. 'What do they do?'

'They help people beat eating disorders.'

She tried and, she suspected, failed to hide her surprise. 'Eating disorders?' What interest could he possibly have in eating disorders?

A muscle twitched in his cheek. 'It's just one of the many charities I'm on the board of.'

'How much do you need to raise?'

Alex named a figure that had Phoebe's head snapping up and her jaw dropping. 'With only twenty-four hours to prepare? That's impossible.'

Alex shrugged. 'If you're as good as Jo seems to think you are, you should have no trouble. If you fail, however, you're fired. Email my secretary for a guest list.' He reached into the breast pocket of his jacket and tossed a card onto her desk.

'This can't be lawful.'

Alex stood up and stared down at her. 'Are you willing to risk it? When did you say Jo's launch was?'

Phoebe's eyes narrowed. How had she ever thought he was gorgeous? The man was ruthless, devious and downright manipulative.

'And if I don't fail?' she said, slowly getting to her feet and clawing back some semblance of control.

'I'll go back to being that silent partner and let you two get on with it.'

Phoebe stuck out her hand and threw him a confident smile. 'In that case, you have a deal.'

CHAPTER FIVE

UGH. WHAT WAS that noise? Phoebe burrowed beneath her duvet and dragged a pillow over her ear while throwing an arm out and taking a swipe in the general direction of her alarm clock. The muffled clatter as it hit the floor and the familiar sound of batteries rolling around the floor-boards filtered into her sleep-sodden head. She waited for a second, and then as heavenly silence reigned snuggled down and drifted back into blissful unconsciousness.

Until the shrill ringing started up again.

It hadn't been the alarm clock. Even in her dopey state she could work that one out. She sat up and clamped her hands over her ears but it was no good. Someone was sitting on her doorbell and clearly had little intention of going away.

With a groan, Phoebe untangled herself from the bedclothes and pushed her eye mask onto the top of her head. She staggered to her feet and stumbled to the window. Lifting the sash, she stuck her head out and yelled, 'All right, I'm coming.'

To her intense relief, the infernal racket stopped in-stantly. She dragged on a silk dressing gown and made her way downstairs, grumbling with every step she took.

Just wait, she thought crossly, marching towards the front door. Whoever was calling at this ungodly hour deserved everything that was coming to them.

'What?' she said heatedly, flinging open the door and getting ready to give the postman a piece of her mind.

But as she glared at the figure standing on her doorstep Phoebe froze. It wasn't the postman. Or the plumber. Or any one of the other possibilities that had vaguely crossed her mind.

It was Alex. Looking good enough to eat in faded jeans and a polo shirt, and a darn sight more together than she was.

'Good morning, Phoebe.'

The bright sunlight burned her retinas and her eyes watered. This really wasn't fair. She lifted her hand to shade her eyes as she stared up at him. 'Uh, morning.'

Alex's leisurely gaze travelled over her and Phoebe bristled at the faint smile that curved his lips. He could laugh all he wanted; he was the one who'd turned up un-announced. If he didn't approve of the state he found her in, he only had himself to blame. 'Can I come in?'

No was the answer on the tip of her tongue. Even though Phoebe suspected she couldn't sink any lower in Alex's estimations, she still had her vanity. She wanted to tell him to go away and come back in an hour. Her current outfit didn't provide much in the way of a defence against a man like him and her hair could probably do with a brush. But as he was already stepping forward there was little she could do to stop him, short of shoving him out and slamming the door behind him, and her head hurt too much for that kind of effort.

'Please do.'

Alex crossed the threshold into the hallway and

Phoebe plastered herself against the wall in an attempt to prevent any kind of contact. Her hall wasn't small but he managed to fill it, and even though he hadn't brushed against her her treacherous body responded as if he had. A rush of heat shot through her and pooled at the juncture of her thighs. Beneath the flimsy layers she could feel her nipples stiffening and with a scowl she wrapped her dressing gown tightly around her and crossed her arms over her chest. 'The kitchen's straight on.'

Phoebe followed him into her kitchen, told herself to ignore the way his T-shirt highlighted the breadth of his shoulders and the muscles beneath, and set about making coffee.

'What are you doing here?' she said, sticking her head in a cupboard and rummaging around for a bag of beans. 'I didn't expect to see you until this evening.'

'I called, but you didn't answer.'

Phoebe pulled out the beans and a cafetiere and shot him an accusatory glare. 'I was asleep.'

He leaned against the counter and looked her up and down again so thoroughly that Phoebe felt as if he'd stripped her naked. 'So I can see. Out partying?'

She wished. Phoebe's hackles shot up. 'I was up until five researching your guests,' she said with as much indignation as she could muster. The last couple of hours of research she'd dedicated to checking him out, but he didn't need to know that.

'Have you come up with a plan?'

'I have.'

'What is it?'

'Oh, no, I'm not telling you that.'

'Why not?'

'You might sabotage it.'

'I'm not that ruthless.'

'Says the man who'd practically blackmailed me into this weekend.'

'You can back out any time.'

Like that was going to happen. Phoebe's head hurt. It was too early for this. She stifled a yawn.

'What time is it?'

'Ten.'

Hmm. Maybe not that early. But still, five hours of sleep on top of the broken night before was not going to have her firing on all cylinders.

A smile flashed across his face. 'Are you always this irascible?'

'Before coffee and short of sleep, always.' Not to mention being caught by him probably looking like something that had been attacked by a pair of pinking shears.

She didn't need a cup of coffee; she needed a tankerful. Flicking the kettle on she lifted her hand to run it through her hair. Oh, heavens. She still sported the eye mask. How attractive. She yanked it off and dropped it on the table.

'Interesting nightwear.'

Phoebe glanced down at the two scarlet hearts. 'A friend gave it to me on a hen night.'

'It suits you. As does the rest of your outfit.'

His gaze slowly slid down her body and Phoebe felt herself growing as scarlet as the eye mask. She poured the beans into the grinder and switched it on. The noise rattled her brain and Phoebe winced. But at least it might stop her from wondering what he wore in bed. Anything at all would be rather a shame. He'd look amazing sprawled out over her sheets, tanned skin against soft white linen, his eyes darkening with desire…

Phoebe swallowed and gave herself a mental slap. She *really* needed to wake up.

Coffee finally made, Phoebe leaned against the opposite counter and regarded him cautiously. 'So?'

Alex set his cup down and folded his arms over his chest. 'It occurred to me that we hadn't talked about the venue of my party.'

What was he? A mind reader? *'Find out party location'* was the only item left on her 'to do' list. 'I assumed it's somewhere in London. I was going to call you later.'

Alex shook his head in mock despair and gave her a smile that made her stomach lurch. 'Didn't I warn you about the dangers of making assumptions?'

'You did. So enlighten me.' She blew on her coffee and took a fortifying sip. 'Where is it?'

'Ilha das Palmeiras.'

Hmm. Phoebe riffled through all the bars, restaurants and clubs that she knew of, but it didn't ring any bells. 'I might need a bit more to go on than that. Where's Ilha das Palmeiras?'

'It's an island in the mid-Atlantic.'

An island in the mid-Atlantic? Phoebe blinked in confusion. He wanted her to go to an island in the mid-Atlantic? Today? For a party? She needed way more caffeine.

'The current temperature is in the mid twenties,' Alex was saying, 'but it gets chilly at night, so you might want to pack something warm.' He glanced at his watch. 'We need to leave in the next half an hour so I suggest you go and get ready.'

Go and get ready? Phoebe could barely get her head around the implications of what he'd told her. It appeared that not only had he set her a challenge way outside her remit, he also intended her to complete it miles out of her comfort zone.

Devious didn't even begin to describe the workings of his mind, she decided darkly. Machiavelli himself would bow down in awe.

She should have guessed he'd pull a trick like this. It wouldn't have surprised her if he'd deliberately kept the location of the party from her just so he could spring it on her when she was least expecting it. Because in her line of work surprises were never welcome and he must know that.

'Chop chop,' he said mildly, looking at her as if surprised to see her still standing there.

Phoebe huffed, shot him a filthy look and stormed out.

Alex took his coffee into the sitting room and, not for the first time since he'd laid eyes on her scantily clad form, wondered if taking Phoebe with him to the island was really such a wise idea.

The challenge that he'd set her would prove her determination and her commitment and would satisfy his promise to Jo without compromising the vow he'd made to himself in the aftermath of losing everything he'd worked so hard to acquire.

However, the glimpses of long tanned leg that he'd got whenever Phoebe's robe slithered open had tested his control to the limit. That ridiculous eye mask perched on top of her mussed-up hair had got him thinking about blindfolds and silk scarves and hours of lazy sensory exploration and he'd nearly stalked over and pinned her against the counter just to see if she felt as warm and soft as she looked.

There was a thump as something hit the floor above, then a yelp of pain and a string of expletives. Alex snapped back to reality and grinned. Phoebe first thing reminded him of a very grumpy, very put out sprite.

He took a look around. Fat cushions sat at random on the two deep sofas that faced each other either side of a coffee table laden with books. Bright splashes of artwork lined the walls. Piles of magazines were stacked high either side of the fireplace. A book lay open face down on the floor beside the sofa.

The room wasn't messy, but compared to her office it was a tip. If he didn't know otherwise he'd have thought that two very different people occupied each space.

But then nothing about Phoebe was quite as it seemed, he realised, making his way over to the bookcase. Was she the cool, efficient PR executive? The whimpering goddess he'd held in his arms, who'd stared up at him with stars in her eyes and passion infused in her face? Or was she a combination of all of them and more?

'I can't imagine you'll find anything there to interest you.'

Alex swung round and his pulse spiked. Phoebe stood in the doorway, dressed in jeans that hugged her legs and a little cardigan that clung to her curves and pulled tight across her breasts. Dark sunglasses held her hair back from her face.

For a moment Alex couldn't decide which version he preferred. The sleepy, tousled Phoebe who smelled of bed or this sleek, fresh-faced Phoebe who smelled of flowers. And then he realised he was expected to say something. 'That was quick.'

'Yup.' She grinned. 'It's amazing what caffeine can do. And I still have five minutes to spare.'

'I'm impressed. Is that it?' he said, glancing at her suitcase.

'Yes.'

'You travel light.'

'You sound surprised.'

'I am.'

'Not all women carry their entire worldly goods whenever they go anywhere, you know. *My* wardrobe is particularly capsular.'

'Unlike your house. This is very different from your office,' he said, indicating the room with a sweep of his arm.

Phoebe frowned. Generally people didn't see both. She shrugged. 'I don't think clients would be too impressed to see this, do you?'

'Do you care that much what people think?'

She smiled. 'I'm in PR. It kind of goes with the territory.'

'Got your passport?'

'Hmm. Good point.' The phone started ringing and Phoebe walked over to answer it. 'Would you mind? It's in the desk. Top drawer.'

Which reminded her, she needed to get it renewed. And not before time. That photo... The hair. Phoebe shuddered. No one apart from herself and a handful of international immigration officers had ever seen it.

And any second now Alex would be sliding open the drawer, taking it out and flicking through the pages...

'No, wait,' she practically shouted. 'On second thoughts, I'll get it.'

Phoebe dropped the phone and hurled herself at him. Her body slammed into his and Alex let out a gruff oomf at the impact. Her hand covered his, their fingers

tangled in the chaos and for a moment she thought the
room had started to spin. Showers of sparks shot up her
arm. His scent engulfed her and she nearly swooned.

Fighting back a blush, Phoebe tugged her passport
out of his grip. 'Sorry about that. Terrible photo.' She
peeled herself off him and walked to the door on very
wobbly legs. 'We—er—should probably get going.'

CHAPTER SIX

WELL, THAT HAD been gruelling, thought Phoebe, pushing her sunglasses up her nose and taking her first lungfuls of Atlantic air. The flight to the capital had been smooth enough and Alex's skill as a pilot during the short hop to their final destination had been impressive. But having to spend close on to four hours in a confined space with him had been a nightmare.

Once on board his jet, she'd hauled out her laptop with the intention of reading up on her notes, but to her intense irritation her usually excellent powers of concentration had gone on strike. Instead, her body had decided to tune itself to Alex's frequency. Every move he made, every frown, every smile, that flitted across his face registered on her conscience.

But if she'd thought *that* had been torturous it was nothing compared to the torment she'd suffered once they'd transferred to the tin pot of a plane that was to carry them to the party venue.

There'd barely been room to breathe. Alex's shoulder had constantly brushed against hers. His denim-clad thigh had sat inches from her hand and her fingers had itched to reach out and find out if it was as firm and muscled as it looked. And then his voice, coming through her headset, deep and sexy, had reached right down inside her, wrapping itself around her insides and twisting them into knots as he pointed out a pod of whales.

Her body ached from the effort of trying to plaster herself against the side of the plane. Her stomach was still churning. The minute they'd landed she'd been so desperate to get out of the plane she'd nearly garrotted herself.

'Welcome to Ilha das Palmeiras,' Alex said, taking her suitcase and throwing it into the back of the Jeep that was parked at the side of the grass runway.

'It's beautiful.'

'I think so.'

'But humid.' Phoebe could already feel her hair beginning to frizz and rummaged around in her handbag for a hair clip.

'The islanders say if you don't like the weather wait ten minutes.'

Phoebe pinned back her hair and then delved back into her bag for her mobile. Hauling it out, she flipped it open and switched it on. Hmm. She frowned. No signal.

Alex glanced up as she waved it around. 'I wouldn't bother. There's no coverage.'

Oh. 'None at all?' She didn't think she'd ever been anywhere where she hadn't been able to pick up a signal.

'Nope. And there's no landline either.'

'What about the Internet?'

'I'm afraid not.'

There was no need for him to look quite so cheery, thought Phoebe darkly. Her phone was like a third limb. She needed to be available every minute of every day, just in case any nasty little surprises popped up.

But there wasn't much she could do about it now.

With a sigh, Phoebe dropped her phone back into her bag and resigned herself to twenty-four hours of being incommunicado. At least weekends tended to be quiet on the PR front.

The island was smaller than she'd imagined, and far more remote. She'd envisaged a buzzing harbour, bright colours and exotic smells. All that had been true of the island that housed the capital, but Ilha das Palmeiras was quiet and peaceful. After a lifetime of living in London Phoebe had imagined she'd have been more freaked out by the absence of noise, but instead she could already feel herself beginning to unwind.

Palm trees swished in the breeze. The sun warmed her skin. The distant sound of waves crashing onto the shore filled her with a sense of wonderful restfulness.

Maybe after the party, when she'd smashed her target and proved she was more than capable of handling Jo's career, she'd do a spot of sunbathing. Relaxing. God knew how long it had been since she'd had a day off.

'Hop in.'

Phoebe's eyes snapped open. Oh, she had to be careful. If she allowed herself to be lulled into a false sense of tranquillity, if she didn't keep her wits firmly about her, she could find herself struggling to pass Alex's test.

She grappled with the handle of the car door that was welded shut and it dawned on her that she would literally have to 'hop in'. Which she'd never manage with any sort of elegance. Alex had vaulted in, but as she hadn't been inside a gym for years if she tried that she'd land in a heap on the grass. Perhaps if she just perched her bottom on the edge and then levered herself up…

'I would offer you a hand, but I can still recall what happened when I last tried that.'

'Try it again,' she said with uncharacteristic sweetness while batting her eyelashes at him in an exaggerated fashion, 'and I can guarantee you'll get a different response.'

Alex grinned, got out of the car and walked over to her side. 'Turn round.'

Phoebe did and he reached down, put his hands on her waist and lifted her so that she could swing her legs round. He dropped her into the seat and Phoebe untangled her legs and arms. 'Thank you,' she said, determinedly ignoring the tingles zapping around her body and her galloping pulse. 'And since you mention it, thank you for your help with Mark the other night.' Hindsight had made her realise that she might not have been able to manage him on her own, and the fact that she'd never got round to thanking Alex had been niggling away at her ever since.

'You're welcome.' He fired up the engine. 'I probably owe you an apology.'

'Oh?'

'I might have overreacted. Just a bit.'

Phoebe sat back and grinned. 'Accepted. It sounds like you're out of practice.'

'Could be,' he said dryly. 'I don't often have reason to apologise.'

'It must be wonderful being right all the time.'

'Most of the time,' he said with a grin and hit the accelerator.

'So this island must be privately owned,' said Phoebe, clinging onto the top of the windscreen in a futile effort to lessen the jarring on her poor battered body as they bounced over the terrain.

'It is.'

She gave up and went with the motion. 'Who by?'

'Me.'

As she'd suspected. 'Of course. What billionaire would be without one?'

'If I'd wanted a status symbol I'd have bought a play-ground in the Caribbean.'

Hmm. 'So what is this deserted peaceful island with no interference from the outside world? An escape?'

'Perhaps.'

'From what?' she asked.

'The city.'

She had the impression the island was an escape from more than just the city because she'd found no mention of it in her research. 'How much time do you spend here?'

'Not enough.'

That seemed a shame, she thought, drinking in the spectacular scenery spreading out before her. The shore-line jutted in and out, shaped by millennia of buffeting winds. After the carefully landscaped gardens of the night before last, the rugged beauty of the island took her breath away.

As did Alex's profile. Phoebe took advantage of the fact that he was staring out of the windscreen to study him. Despite the concentration etched on his face, the lines around his mouth and eyes seemed to have softened, as if the serenity of the place had seeped into him too. The wind ruffled his hair and as she ran her gaze over the hint of the bump on his nose it struck her how much Alex suited this landscape.

'When were you here last?'

'About a year ago.'

'Why so long?'

'Busy. Work.'

'What made you buy a remote island in the middle of the Atlantic?'

'It's a remote island in the middle of the Atlantic,' he said dryly. 'I like my space. I value my privacy.'

That figured. Given the press attention he received she guessed he wasn't a great fan of journalists. Or nosy PRs, judging by the brevity of his answers to her questions. Still, she hadn't got where she had by being deflected by evasiveness.

'No man is an island,' she said solemnly.

'Are you romanticising me, Phoebe?'

Heaven forbid. 'Just thought I'd mention it.'

'It's not completely isolated.'

He'd pointed out the other islands in the archipelago as they'd flown over them. 'Who lives on the other ones?'

'No idea.'

'That's not very neighbourly.'

'Owners of remote islands don't tend to be very neighbourly.'

'What happens if you run out of sugar?'

'My housekeeper makes sure I don't.'

He had answers to everything, thought Phoebe as they headed off the rough land and onto a gravel track. He was wasted in venture capital. He should be in PR.

'If you value your privacy so highly, why host a party for a hundred people?'

'No press. Do you have to keep asking questions?'

'Yup. Sorry. It's my job.'

'Perhaps you should be saving your energies for later.'

'I have plenty of energy,' she said with a grin, and realised with surprise that it was true. Despite her lack of sleep, Phoebe felt oddly invigorated. It was probably the sea air. Or the thrill of a challenge. Or perhaps the exhilaration of the Jeep ride.

It had nothing whatsoever to do with having spent the best part of the day with Alex.

A shower of gravel flew up as Alex pulled up outside the house and yanked on the handbrake. The sooner he could get away from Phoebe, the better.

Her incessant questioning was driving him nuts. He didn't want to have to go into detail about when and why he'd bought the island, but any longer and his resistance would crumble under the sheer weight of her persistence.

'Oh, wow.'

Phoebe was standing up and gazing up at his house, an expression of awe on her face. At least she'd stopped with the bloody questions, he thought grimly, jumping out of the Jeep and striding round to her side. 'Give me your hand.'

'This is amazing,' she said, holding her hands out but still staring up at the house. 'Did you build it?'

Alex helped her out of the Jeep, set her on her feet and took their luggage out. 'I designed it. Someone else built it.'

He glanced up. The two-storey glass and steel construction that stood on the edge on the cliff was very different from the glorified shack that had existed when Jo had been recuperating. He'd bought the island primarily for his sister and he'd worked every second to ensure he could do it before she came out of hospital. However it had taken him another couple of years before he'd recouped enough of his previous fortune to build this house.

Memories clamoured at the edges of his brain and Alex ruthlessly pushed them away.

'It's fabulous. The views must be incredible.'

'Go inside and take a look around. You're staying in the capital with the rest of the guests. They're being ferried over and back. But there's a guest wing here you can use in the meantime to get ready or whatever.'

Phoebe's eyebrows shot up. 'If I'm staying with everyone else, why didn't you leave me there when we passed through earlier?'

Good question, he realised with a start. The thought hadn't even occurred to him. But then that was hardly surprising; the moment they'd boarded his plane rational thought had pretty much given up the ghost and a clamouring awareness of the woman with him had taken over. It had left him feeling unusually on edge. 'I thought you might like to check things out in preparation for later.'

She nodded and gave him a smile that made him think of sunshine. 'I would, thanks.'

Alex had had serious doubts about holding a party here. Despite his determination to avoid a repeat of last year, when the event had been held in London and gatecrashed by an extremely creative journalist, the invasion of his privacy and general disruption to what had always been a haven of tranquillity hadn't appealed in the slightest.

However, right now the hive of activity engulfing the house and gardens was as welcome as the unexpected appearance of a life raft in the wake of a shipwreck, and he had no qualms about clinging to it.

He'd go and see that all the arrangements for this evening were in order. Never mind that Maggie was so efficient he didn't need to check anything; if he didn't head off right now he'd be in danger of doing something rash like suggesting a personal guided tour of the bedrooms. He nodded curtly. 'Then I'll leave you to it.'

CHAPTER SEVEN

THIS WAS THE life, Phoebe thought, rolling onto her stomach and feeling the sun hit the backs of her legs. With the gentle sound of the waves lapping at the shore, the breeze rippling through the palm trees, and the softness of the fine sand beneath her towel, she really was in her own little slice of heaven.

Alex's abrupt departure had left her standing there feeling like a spare part and wondering if she'd said something wrong. But she'd pulled herself together, and, after asking around to see if anyone needed any help and being assured that everything was under control, she'd found her way to the guest wing, changed out of her jeans into a skirt and had headed for the relative calm of the beach.

The file with all the details of the guests and the research she'd done lay beneath her cheek. She'd committed pretty much every detail to memory and she'd honed the strategy she'd come up with the night before. If everything went according to plan, within a few hours her position would be safe and she could get back to her life.

In the meantime she intended to take full advantage

of the calm before the storm. She felt herself drifting off to sleep when the sun went behind a cloud. She shivered and reached for her cardigan.

'Working hard?'

Phoebe jolted, manoeuvred herself into a less vulnerable sitting position and squinted up at him. 'I wish you wouldn't keep doing this.'

'What?' Alex said mildly.

'Creeping up on me.'

'Sand's quiet like that.'

So was he, and looming over her like that he was also rather intimidating. The bright sun behind him cast his face in shadow and sunglasses covered his eyes.

He had changed too, ditching the jeans for a pair of khaki shorts. Phoebe couldn't help running her gaze over his legs: tanned and as muscled as she'd imagined. A vision of them entwined with hers charged into her head and her mouth went dry.

This was ridiculous, she scolded herself, swallowing hard. It was just a pair of legs. Everybody had them. Nevertheless it took every drop of strength she possessed to drag her gaze up his body and reach his face. A tiny smile hovered at his mouth and Phoebe instantly realised that he knew she'd been checking him out.

If he mentioned it she'd attribute the pinking of her cheeks to the sun, she decided, pushing herself to her feet and brushing the sand off her skirt. 'What's up?'

'Nothing's up. I'm going for a sail. You're in my way.'

Phoebe glanced round at the acres of sand that surrounded the spot where she'd been lying. 'It's a big beach. Is that yours?' She pointed to the gleaming white yacht moored up against the jetty that stretched out from the beach into the sea.

'It is.'

'Pretty.'

'I think so.'

'What's it called?'

'*She* is called the *Phoenix Three*.'

'Sounds like a pop group. What happened to the *Phoenix One* and *Two*?'

'They sank.'

'And each one rises from the ashes of the previous?'

'Soggy ashes, but something like that.'

'Can I come?' While she'd learned every possible thing she could about his guests, she'd found out precious little about him. How could she do a proper job this evening without knowing as much as possible? Alex had so far proved remarkably adept at dodging her questions. Trapping him on a boat would be ideal.

'Shouldn't you be working?'

'I've done as much as I can from my notes,' she said. 'The rest I'll just have to pick up as I go along.' She smiled winsomely. 'I promise not to get in the way.'

Alex ran his fingers through his hair in a gesture of frustration. He clearly didn't want her on board his yacht. Well, that was tough. She was coming along for the ride whether he liked it or not.

Phoebe glanced down at the cool box he was carrying and decided that she wasn't above a little manipulation herself.

She stared at it longingly. 'Is that lunch?'

'A very late one, yes.'

She widened her eyes and gave him a doleful look. 'You know, I haven't eaten anything all day.'

Alex frowned. 'Didn't you have something up at the house?'

Phoebe bit on her lip and shook her head forlornly. 'I'm ravenous.' She waited and, when Alex didn't look as if he had any intention of taking her hint, she swayed a little. 'Do you realise that if I pass out this evening as a result of lack of sustenance it'll be entirely your fault?'

'How do you figure that?'

'You didn't give me time for breakfast, so if there's enough in there for two…'

'There's plenty.' He set the box on the ground and took the lid off. 'Help yourself.'

Oh. Phoebe peered into the cool box and her mouth watered. Lunch looked and smelled delicious. But however tempting his suggestion was, nibbling on a chicken leg alone on the beach while Alex did whatever he did on boats had not been the plan at all.

'I'd much rather join you,' she said with a little pout.

Alex's jaw tightened but he remained stonily silent.

'Fine,' she said sadly. 'I understand. I just hope your hosting skills improve by tonight.'

Alex let out a resigned sigh. 'OK. That's enough. You can come.'

Phoebe beamed. 'Great.'

Letting Phoebe on board his boat had been such a bad idea, Alex berated himself for the hundredth time.

He should have thrown her a sandwich and left her on the beach. Better still, he should never have disturbed her in the first place. He wasn't sure why he had.

But even though he'd known perfectly well what she'd been up to with those big eyes and the pout it didn't negate the fact that she was right. The catering staff had gone on a break for a couple of hours before gearing up for tonight. The cool box contained enough lunch to feed an army and he was sick of feeling guilty. What else could he have done?

All he'd wanted was a moment's solitude. To feel the wind in his hair, the tiller beneath his hands, and to fill with the sense of peace that sailing always gave him.

But had he found that solitude? That peace? Nope. Because Phoebe was anything but peaceful and he'd been an idiot to think he could get away with ignoring her.

She might not have hit him with a barrage of questions just yet, but her eyes had locked onto him with the focus of a heat-seeking missile the moment they'd cast off and in the past half an hour they hadn't wavered. Even when he had his back to her he could feel her gaze boring into him. Watching him carefully, as if trying to penetrate right through to the centre of him and fathom him out.

His whole body itched and buzzed as if a swarm of bees had taken up residence inside him. The last thing he wanted or needed was fathoming out, he thought grimly, switching off the engine and releasing the main sail. It unfurled and fluttered in the breeze and Alex hauled and winched the ropes until his muscles burned.

For a while the yacht glided smoothly through water, and as Phoebe turned her face to the sun Alex stared at the horizon, let his thoughts lighten and he finally found an edgy sort of peace.

Until Phoebe's stomach rumbled like a crash of thunder and the flicker of guilt he thought he'd managed to extinguish fanned back into life.

'Uh, sorry about that,' she muttered and rubbed her midriff.

'Lunch?'

'I thought you'd never ask.'

If he hadn't had a conscience he wouldn't have.

Because he had no doubt that as soon as they sat down to eat the questions would come. But he couldn't postpone lunch any longer, so he'd answer them as briefly as possible and if she persisted he'd employ any tactic at his disposal to deflect her.

Ignoring an odd sense of impending doom, Alex steered the yacht towards the coast and dropped the anchor as soon as they reached shallow water.

'How did you get to be so good at sailing?' said Phoebe, finishing off the last piece of cold chicken and thinking lunch had never tasted so delicious.

Alex tensed and she wondered exactly why he was so reluctant to talk about himself. 'I used to race.'

'But not any more?' She set the chicken bone on her plate and licked her fingers.

'I gave up a few years ago.' Alex's gaze dipped to her mouth and her lips tingled as if he'd reached out and touched them. A blaze of heat shot through her and she snatched up a napkin.

'Why?' His strength and agility and obvious skill as he leapt around the yacht had had desire and admiration seeping through her in equal measures.

'Better to stop at the top of your game,' he said, his lazy tone completely at odds with the brief awareness that had flared in his eyes.

'Did you ever win?'

'Yes.'

'Big boats or little boats?'

'Both.'

'Solo or in a team?'

'Both.'

Agh. Trying to get information out of Alex was nigh

on impossible. His defences were so high she'd need crampons and breathing equipment to scale them. And as mountaineering had never appealed, Phoebe decided to switch tactic.

'What made you go into venture capital?'

'The bottom line,' he said dryly.

'Is that all?'

'Isn't that enough?'

'Nope.'

Alex shrugged. 'I'm good at it.'

'Very good at it by all accounts.'

He shot her a quizzical glance. 'Have you been checking me out?'

'A little. Of course *I* didn't have time to hire investigators. *I* simply looked you up on the Internet.'

'What did you find?'

'Surprisingly little for someone who has such a high profile.' She'd found heaps of information about his business and his work, but absolutely nothing about his private life. Or Jo, for that matter.

He grinned. 'I'm not that interesting.'

'I don't know about that.' She might as well admit it. She didn't need to know any of this for this evening. She wanted to know about him for herself. Which wasn't all that surprising, she reasoned weakly. She'd always been interested in other people. OK, so she didn't often burn with this degree of curiosity, but then most people weren't so evasive. 'You help people realise their dreams.'

Alex shook his head. 'It's all about maximising return.'

'You helped Jo realise her dream. What return are you expecting from her?'

'Jo's family.'

'What happened to your father?'

'I never knew him. He died the year after I was born.'

'And your stepfather?'

'He married my mother when I was eight. Jo came along two years later. They died six years ago in an avalanche.'

Phoebe's heart squeezed. Her own family might be tricky but she couldn't imagine life without them. 'I'm sorry to hear that.'

Alex shrugged. 'Don't be. They were cross-country skiing at the time and died doing something they loved. I hope you're not going to ask me how I feel about it.'

'I wouldn't dream of it.' He wouldn't tell her even if she had. 'How did Jo take it?'

The change in him was almost palpable. He tensed and his eyes went blank. 'She was devastated,' he said flatly.

Now what was he hiding? she wondered, watching the familiar stony expression set in. Every inch of him was warning her to back off, not to pry any further. Perhaps Jo wasn't the only one who'd been devastated. Perhaps the deaths of his mother and stepfather had had a greater effect on him than he was willing to admit.

Phoebe took a sip of sparkling water and felt the bubbles fizz down her throat. 'You used to have a partner, but now you work alone. Why is that?'

'It's safer.'

'In what way?'

'Other people have a tendency to let you down.'

She could understand that. Letting people down, especially her fabulous overachieving family, was one of the little insecurities that walloped her from time to time.

'Has anyone ever let you down?' she asked.

'Not recently,' he said bleakly.

'What happened?'

'It was so long ago I can barely remember.'

'I don't believe that for a second.'

'Do you ever give up?'

'Nope. I'm kind of tenacious like that. A PR magazine once described me as "subtly yet ruthlessly efficient".'

'I can see why. Although personally I'd call it nosy.' The ghost of a smile hovered at his mouth as he sat back and regarded her thoughtfully.

Phoebe shrugged and grinned. 'It's a useful trait to have in my line of work.' She tilted her head to one side. 'You won't put me off, you know.' His answers were spare and his face gave absolutely nothing away, but she'd get there eventually.

'I know.'

'And I won't fail this evening.'

'Sure?'

Phoebe threw him a confident smile. 'Absolutely. I've done my research and I'm fully prepared. And besides, I'm a Jackson and Jacksons never fail.'

'Never?'

'Never.'

'That sounds like a lot of pressure.'

'Tell me about it.' She rested her chin on her hand and smiled up at him. Maybe if she opened up a bit he would too. 'Actually, I did fail at something once. I swear the look on my father's face was not something I'd ever like to see again. My mother merely shook her head in disappointment and went off to her study.'

Alex visibly relaxed. 'What was it?'

'My fifty metres underwater swimming badge. I was ten.'

His eyebrows shot up.

'I'd had bronchitis. My lungs weren't up to it. But that was no excuse.'

'Of course not,' he said dryly.

'I used to have nightmares about it. I'd be swimming relentlessly up and down a pool with my lungs bursting. I'd pop up to the surface gasping for air, only there'd be a sea of angry faces staring down at me, yelling at me to get back under the water.' That if she didn't try harder she'd fail and she'd be letting them all down.

'And then?'

'Then I'd wake up drenched in sweat with my heart thundering and my head pounding.'

'What did your parents have to say about that?'

'Nothing.' She shrugged. 'They didn't know. I didn't tell them.'

Eventually she'd conquered it. All by herself. Those three months of nightmares had made her stronger. She was sure of it. As had those little blips in her otherwise flawless career.

'That was brave.'

Warmth spread throughout her body. 'Not really.'

'What happened with the swimming test?'

'I had to redo it the next day.'

'Did you pass?'

'Of course. Now I always pass tests,' she said pointedly.

Alex raised an eyebrow.

'I come from a line of overachievers,' she clarified. 'Didn't your…research…throw that up?'

'Some. It turns out I know your brother.'

Oh? 'How?'

'We recently worked together on an IPO.'

That made sense. Dan worked in corporate finance

and made millions on a daily basis. Privately Phoebe thought her brother was heading straight for burnout, but that was his business. She'd tried to question him about it but he'd told her in no uncertain terms to butt out and she'd given up worrying about him.

'Dan is a case in point,' she said and then tilted her head. 'Let me put it like this. In my family Christmas is treated as a business initiative.'

'In what way?'

Right now Alex sounded intrigued. But as soon as she'd explained he'd think her entire family was insane.

'Every September in her role as project manager my mother sends us all an email to establish what we want out of the event. What our *vision* is.'

'Do you have a vision?'

'Well, I don't generally. I'd be happy with a slice of turkey and a cracker. But not the rest of my family. No. We have to decide on our aim. Do we want to push culinary boundaries? Are we going to use the occasion to innovate and experiment, or do we simply want a day of lazy indulgence? That sort of thing.'

Alex was staring at her as if she'd just landed from another planet. 'I know,' she said nodding. 'Nuts. But it gets worse.'

'How could it possibly get worse?'

'Once the key objective has been identified and agreed on, my mother then itemises what exactly is needed to achieve that particular vision and assigns us each roles. Her list can include anything from strategies to prevent my grandmother hitting the gin too early to calculating the number of Brussels sprouts needed. She then informs us of what she expects in terms of performance.'

'Nice relaxing festivities, I imagine.' Amusement glinted in the depths of his eyes.

'Quite. On the actual day she gives us evaluation updates at regular intervals.'

'What happens if something goes wrong?'

Phoebe gave him a look of mock horror. 'Doesn't happen. Contingencies are built in. Should something go awry, and it hasn't since the memorable incident involving my father and a rolling pin ten years ago, we're to simply remind ourselves of the vision. The experience gets absorbed into the following year's strategy.'

'It's probably not a bad way of handling Christmas,' he said dryly.

'Yes, well, next year I'm boycotting it.'

'The family is revolting.'

Phoebe grinned. 'Not at all. My siblings, rather worryingly, embrace the whole thing with gusto, so technically I'm the only one who's revolting.'

'You're not revolting. You're—' Alex broke off, the humour fading from his eyes.

Phoebe's heart skipped a beat at the sudden shift in his demeanour. I'm what? She suddenly longed to know. What am I? Tell me. 'I'm what?' she said and her breath hitched in her throat as she waited for his answer.

Alex blinked and the stormy look in his eyes vanished. 'Going to burn if you're not careful.'

Oh, how annoying was that? He'd been staring at her face as if trying to commit every inch of it to memory, and the way his eyes had darkened as he'd fixed on her mouth had her thinking that concern for her skin had definitely not been uppermost in his mind.

'I'm always careful,' she said loftily.

'So am I,' he muttered, frowning into the distance and

standing up. Alex stretched and then to her consternation reached round the back of his neck and pulled his T-shirt off.

At the expanse of taut brown skin that hit her eyes, Phoebe nearly passed out. Muscles rippled over his abdomen, a smattering of dark hair covered his chest and narrowed down into a fine line that disappeared into the top of his shorts.

She sat on her hands to stop them from darting out and whipping open the button and sliding down his zip. A primitive longing to run her hands over those muscles, to trace the contours of every inch of him, walloped her in the stomach.

'Did I just hear a whimper?' Alex dropped his T-shirt on a deckchair and turned to her, a tiny smile playing at his lips.

'A whimper?' Phoebe snapped her gaze to the horizon and frowned as if in concentration. 'No. I don't think so. I certainly didn't hear a whimper.'

'I could have sworn I did.'

'It must have been the wind.'

'It must.'

'What are you doing?'

'Going for a swim.'

Thank God for that. Who cared if the Atlantic was supposed to be freezing? Or that swimming after eating was generally considered to be a bad thing? If it removed him from sight and out of temptation's way he could swim to the States and she'd cheer him on with every stroke.

'Want to join me?'

Phoebe shuddered at the thought. 'No, thanks. I'll stay here and look after the boat.' And no doubt drive herself mad speculating about what he might have been going to say.

She tried not to stare at his back as he stepped up onto the guardrail, but then figured that, as he couldn't see her, she could sneak a peak. He twisted and stretched, the muscles of his shoulders and back tensing and flexing, and Phoebe had to clamp her mouth shut to stop another whimper escaping.

Alex dived into the clear blue water and as he disappeared beneath the surface Phoebe let out the breath she hadn't realised she'd been holding. It was only when she started putting the remains of lunch back into the cool box that she saw quite how much she was shaking.

By the time Alex stopped his relentless pace, the boat was a speck in the distance, his muscles burned and his lungs stung. The icy water, however, hadn't had the effect he'd hoped.

His body still ached and he felt as tightly wound as one of the yacht's engine coils. Lunch would have had to consist of food that could only really be eaten with fingers, wouldn't it? All that licking and sucking...

And those whimsical little smiles...

If he'd had a superstitious bone in his body he'd have sworn Phoebe had been sent deliberately to torment him. He'd underestimated the madness of letting her on board his boat. The attraction he'd been doing so well at ignoring was getting harder to resist. He wanted her badly. Maybe more than he'd ever wanted anyone before. Which in the general scheme of things was nothing to worry about. Attraction was, after all, a simple question of compatible pheromones.

What worried him considerably more was that he'd

found himself liking her. Admiring her guts, her tenacity and her ability to have survived growing up with so much pressure.

Searing chemistry and liking were a dangerous combination. He'd spent pretty much the whole of the past hour fighting back the increasingly insistent urge to toss aside the table, bundle her into the cabin and get her naked and hot between his sheets.

On more than one occasion during that seemingly interminable lunch he'd been struck by the hammering urge to open up and tell her everything she wanted to know.

The thought doused the heat in his body more effectively than any quantity of ice-cold water. Spilling his guts out to Phoebe, or to anyone for that matter, was never going to happen.

Alex turned round and started ploughing through the water back to the yacht. As soon as he reached it they'd be heading back to the island and the safety of numbers.

His boat definitely wasn't big enough for both of them. He had the uncomfortable suspicion the island wasn't either.

CHAPTER EIGHT

PHOEBE STOOD IN front of the mirror and assessed her reflection with a critical eye. Outwardly she looked exactly as she'd intended. Immaculate, groomed and unflappable. The dress she'd chosen was a reliable favourite, her make-up was flawless and her hair was poker straight.

But her eyes held a worrying sparkle and her cheeks were tinged with pink and inside her stomach churned and her heart raced. Try as she might to persuade herself otherwise, deep down she knew perfectly well it had nothing to do with the thrill of the challenge she was about to face.

Apart from a curt 'it's getting late, we should be heading back', she and Alex hadn't exchanged a word on the journey back to the island, but the care with which they'd kept well out of touching range and had avoided eye contact had spoken volumes. The tension had reached an unbearable level by the time they'd reached the island and neither of them had been able to get off the yacht fast enough.

The minute they'd reached the house Alex had dashed off muttering something about seeing to any last-minute arrangements. Phoebe had holed up in the safety of the guest wing where she'd spent so long analysing the attraction she seemed to have for Alex and worrying about what might happen if it spiralled out of control that it had given her quite a fright to realise that she only had half an hour to get ready.

But now she was. Armour-plated, prepared for battle and in total command of herself.

It wouldn't get out of control. She simply couldn't let it.

She glanced out of the window and couldn't help smiling at the magical scene that spread out below. In the distance a brightly lit ferry was making its way to the island. Flaming torches lined the path from the jetty up the steps to the house and strings of fairy lights looped from tree to tree. Tables had been set up around the pool and groaned with food. A string quartet had parked themselves in one corner and were busy tuning up.

Whoever had organised all this had done an amazing job, thought Phoebe, idly casting her eyes over the scene. Such a shame that there'd be no press here to witness the results.

Then her gaze snagged on the man striding across the terrace and her breath hitched in her throat. Before she had time to jump back, Alex stopped and turned and looked straight up at her. Her knees wobbled and she felt a shiver race down her spine despite the warmth of the evening air drifting in through the open window.

Alex tilted his head and softly called, 'Show time,' before swinging round to go down and greet the guests who were spilling off the ferry and onto the jetty.

Phoebe took a series of deep fortifying breaths and ordered her stupidly hammering heart to calm down. So he looked devastating in black tie. Big deal. A lot of men did. Not many, though, had such a debilitating effect on her nervous system.

Phoebe pulled her shoulders back. She really didn't need a palpitating pulse and a frazzled brain right now. If she wanted to achieve anything tonight, she thought, smoothing out the non-existent wrinkles in her glittering dress as she made her way downstairs, she'd better avoid Alex at all costs.

Alex knocked back the rest of his champagne and then ran a finger around the inside of his collar.

What was Phoebe playing at?

The rational side of his brain knew exactly what she was doing. He'd been watching her for the past couple of hours, working her way into circles of guests, smiling, chatting and no doubt persuading her targets to part with vast sums of cash.

He ought to be impressed. Delighted that she was devoting so much effort to his challenge. One of his contemporaries had even made a point of coming up to him and telling him he thought Phoebe was smashing and was tempted to hire her himself. Above all, he ought to be relieved that Phoebe was proving herself to be as committed and capable as she and Jo had claimed.

So why, instead, was he irritated beyond belief? Why had he had to grit his teeth to stop himself snapping at his colleague that Phoebe wasn't for hire? And why the hell couldn't he take his eyes off her?

Yes, she looked beautiful. Her skin glowed in the warm light. Her eyes sparkled and her dress clung to her curves like a second skin.

But that was no reason why every move she made

should burn into his head. Nor why every smile, every laugh, every touch she bestowed on his guests should send white-hot needles shooting through him.

It was driving him demented. The food tasted like sawdust. The champagne burned his throat. He'd lost track of conversations he'd started. Had to have questions repeated. He'd even snapped the stem of a glass, he'd been holding it so tightly. Much more of this and people would begin to speculate about *his* competency.

Alex had had enough. He'd tried his damnedest to convince himself that he wasn't attracted to her but he'd been fooling himself. When she'd sidled past him earlier in that slinky golden dress his brain had imploded, and ever since the principle thought hammering round his head was how quickly he could dispatch his guests and get Phoebe on her own.

It would help if she hadn't spent the entire night avoiding him, he thought grimly. Everyone else had managed to come up and at the very least compliment him on the evening. Yet all Phoebe had managed to do was maintain her distance. Was it a coincidence that hordes of people had kept them separate throughout the night? He thought not.

'So who is she?'

At the curiosity-laden voice of the woman threading her arm though his, Alex yanked himself out of his thoughts and glanced down. His eyes narrowed at the knowing little smile on Maggie's face and he forced himself to relax.

'Who is who?' he drawled as if he didn't have the faintest idea who Maggie was talking about.

'The brunette you can't take your eyes off.'

Maggie might have known him a long time but that

didn't mean he had any intention of telling her anything. He stiffened. 'She's business.'

'It's funny,' Maggie said with a casualness that didn't deceive him for a second, 'but no business I've ever been involved in has generated the kind of scorching looks you two have been exchanging all evening. I must be doing something wrong.'

'Your business is thriving.'

'Yes, but it would be so much more fun if Jim and I smouldered at each other like that.'

His gaze swung back to Phoebe and his jaw tightened as he watched one of his friends drop a kiss on her cheek. His hands balled into fists. 'Believe me, it's no fun.' At least not yet. Alex's pulse hammered. There was only one way to find out if she was as at the mercy of this attraction as he was.

'Hmm, perhaps not,' Maggie said, glancing down at his white knuckles and easing her arm out of his. 'Is she coming back on the boat with us?'

To end up in the arms of one of the many men she'd been flirting with all night? Not a chance. 'No,' he said grimly, 'she isn't.'

Oh, God, Alex was coming over.

Phoebe glanced round to try and find someone to latch onto and engage in intense conversation but the crowd of people she'd been using as a shield was thinning out and for the first time in the entire evening she was alone.

She ought to be dashing inside and running up the stairs. Chucking her things into her bag and joining the others and getting off this island as soon as possible.

Because she'd done what she'd set out to achieve.

She'd more than completed Alex's challenge, and, assuming he stuck to his word, she'd secured Jo's and her own future, despite every second of the evening being torture. She had no further reason to stay.

So why wasn't she making a run for it? Why wasn't she seeking out the guest who'd offered her a lift on his private jet and looking forward to being back in London before sunrise? Why did her feet remain rooted to the ground?

Phoebe's heart began to gallop as Alex closed the distance between them. He could have been born to wear black tie. He looked incredible. Dark and brooding and devastatingly handsome. He looked even better without the willowy blonde draped all over him, she thought tartly.

As he strode towards her, grim determination etched into his features, and a wild look in his eye, he pulled off his tie and snapped open the top button of his shirt, and Phoebe's head spun.

An image of her undoing the rest of those buttons and tugging his clothes off him flew into her head and she nearly buckled beneath the force of the desire that whipped though her.

She swallowed hard and tried to ignore it, but it was no use. She couldn't deny it any longer. She wanted Alex. She wanted him so badly that all he'd have to do was switch on the charm and the last vestiges of her resistance would crumble.

Her fingers itched to touch him. Her mouth tingled with the need to feel his lips moving over hers. She didn't care any more. She might have successfully managed to avoid him, but his eyes had been on her all night, burning through the flimsy fabric of her dress and tangling up her insides. When their gazes had locked the hungry fire in his eyes had fanned the flames of desire that swept along her veins and all she wanted now was to assuage this deep craving that consumed her.

Alex stopped in front of her and Phoebe's breath caught.

'You look as if you've been enjoying yourself.'

Enjoying herself wouldn't be quite how she'd describe the torment of trying to concentrate while battling the threat that the constant awareness of where Alex was and who he was with posed to her composure. 'I have,' she answered, inwardly amazed at how steady her voice sounded when inside she was a quivering mass of need. 'It's been a lovely party. Beautifully done.'

He shoved his hands in his pockets and his eyes glittered down at her. 'And my challenge?'

'Completed and detailed here.' She held up a little notebook. 'Impressed?'

A muscle pounded in his jaw. 'I'd be a lot more impressed if you'd managed it without all the flirting.'

What? For a moment Phoebe could do nothing more than gape at him. Then she snapped her mouth shut and told herself to hang on before leaping to the wrong conclusion. 'If you'd wanted to draw up conditions about how I raised the money,' she said with a calmness she really didn't feel, 'you should have mentioned them before.'

'I would have had I thought you'd resort to such obvious measures.'

That was it. The disdain in his voice tipped her over and a sudden explosion of anger erupted inside her. She'd done everything he'd demanded of her and for him to then turn round and accuse her of flirting... A swirling mass of incandescence and hurt and something strangely like disappointment boiled in her veins. How could he even *think* that was what she'd been doing? Hadn't he learnt *anything* about her?

'I wasn't flirting,' she said icily. 'It's called taking an interest. Conversation. The exchange of information. Not that you'd know much about that.'

Alex let out a humourless laugh. 'So the people you set your sights on just doled out the cash in a sudden fit of generosity?'

His voice dripped with sarcasm and Phoebe just wanted to get as far away from him as possible. 'No, they didn't. They offered things. Jewellery. Holidays. Wine.'

'I bet they did. To you?'

'No, of course, not to me,' she snapped witheringly. 'For the auction you're going to have at your charity event. So good luck with that.'

Alex went very still. Good. She hoped he froze to the spot. She slapped her notebook against his chest barely noticing it fall to the ground. She didn't care if she never saw him again, the arrogant, patronising jerk.

She turned on her heel but then stopped suddenly and whipped back. 'And just for the record, those donations? Three quarters of them came from women.'

Oh, *hell.*

Alex watched Phoebe storm off into the house and called himself every name under the sun. He wanted to hit something. Hard. Preferably himself.

He bent down to pick up the notebook and flicked through it as he straightened. Page after page of handwriting detailed each donation, the estimated value and the contact details of the donor.

He totted up the total. Phoebe hadn't just completed

his challenge. She'd raised double the original target. Dammit, he *was* impressed. So what on earth had prompted him to attack her like that?

Alex thrust the notebook into his pocket and strode after her. He took the stairs two at a time and found her in the guest wing, whirling round the room like a dervish, flinging things into her bag and muttering furiously under her breath.

He stopped in the doorway. 'Phoebe.'

Phoebe spun round. Her cheeks were red and her chest was heaving, but she didn't stop moving. 'Go away.'

Alex had no intention of going anywhere. The need to finish what had started beneath the pergola clawed at his stomach. 'I'm sorry,' he said. 'I shouldn't have implied that you'd sell yourself to bring in business. It was a careless thing to say and totally unfounded.'

'No,' she said. 'You shouldn't. So why did you?'

He ran his hands through his hair. 'I was angry.'

'About what?'

'That dress would tempt a saint.'

That stopped her in her tracks. She stuck her hands on her hips and glared at him. 'So now it's *my* fault?'

He frowned. 'Were you aware of the looks you were attracting?'

'The only looks I noticed were the filthy ones you kept flinging in my direction.'

'You smiled at and talked to everyone yet you avoided me. All night,' he ground out.

Phoebe's lip curled. 'You sound jealous.'

Alex blinked and felt faintly stunned. He'd never experienced jealousy, but it certainly explained a lot. 'You're right. I was.'

Her eyes flashed. 'Again, not my fault.'

'Why were you avoiding me?'

'I wasn't,' she snapped, but her gaze slid away and he knew she'd been doing exactly that. 'I had little time and a long list of people to talk to. I couldn't afford to waste a second.'

'Is that the only reason?'

'What other reason would there be?'

'Perhaps I distract you.'

'Don't flatter yourself.' She swivelled round and stuffed the rest of her things into her bag.

'Where are you going?'

'To catch the boat.'

'Don't.'

'What?'

'Stay here,' he said. 'With me.'

Phoebe froze. 'Why would I want to do an insane thing like that?'

Alex took a deep breath and started towards her. 'Because I think you want me as much as I want you. If I'm right then it's tearing you up as much as it's tearing me up. I don't know about you, but I can't take it much longer.'

For several long seconds absolute silence hit the room and then the air began to vibrate with electricity. Phoebe stared at him, her eyes darkening and her breathing quickening. For a moment Alex thought she was going to hurl herself into his arms and adrenalin and lust surged through him.

But her face suddenly went blank and the shock of it nearly winded him. 'If you're after a bit of attention I suggest you cuddle up to the blonde,' she said acidly.

Bewilderment sliced through the heavy beat of desire. 'What blonde?'

'The one surgically attached to your arm.'

The penny dropped and Alex felt like punching the air with relief. Phoebe was jealous, which meant he'd been right. She did want him. 'You mean Maggie?'

Phoebe frowned. '*That* was Maggie? Your house-keeper, Maggie?'

'She's more than just a housekeeper. She organised this evening. She used to plan events in London.'

'Good for her,' she said tartly.

'We go back a long way. I was in a solo race once and hit a storm. My mast broke and I capsized just off the coast. She picked up my distress signal and towed me in.'

'Kind of her.'

'I thought so, especially since I'd broken a leg, an arm and a couple of ribs.' If he'd blinked he'd have missed the wince that flashed across her features. 'We've been friends ever since.'

Phoebe stuck her chin up. 'I really don't know why you're telling me all this.'

'Would it interest you to know that she and Jim, her husband, run a chandler's over in the capital?'

Something flickered in the depths of her eyes. 'Not in the slightest.'

'Liar,' he said softly and pulled her into his arms.

CHAPTER NINE

THE MINUTE HE reached for her, Phoebe was lost. What was left of her resistance fled. Crushing disappointment and excoriating anger switched to thumping relief and scorching desire. As Alex wrapped her tightly in his embrace Phoebe flung her arms around his neck. His mouth met hers. Teeth clashed and tongues duelled and as they kissed the heat that spun through her made her melt against him.

As the kiss softened and deepened Phoebe clutched at Alex's jacket, desperate to be able to slide her hands beneath his shirt and feel the warm skin of his back.

Her breasts swelled, nipples tightening and pushing painfully against the bodice of her dress. She could feel the thick, hard length of his erection pulsing against her stomach and she filled with a desperate ache to have him filling her, pounding into her, sending her into oblivion.

While his mouth continued to devour her, Alex's hands slid down her back, over the curve of her bottom, and pulled her tight against him and Phoebe moaned. She'd never felt anything like this before. This primitive craving. This total abandonment. The throbbing conviction that if she didn't have him deep inside her she'd die.

As their kisses grew more ravenous Alex slid the zip of her dress down and it fell in a pool of shimmering silk at her feet. Phoebe shoved his jacket off and tugged at his shirt, dismayed by the number of studs there were to undo. But Alex pulled it over his head, and got rid of the rest of his clothes and hers, and then they were tumbling onto the bed.

Their hands roamed over each other, stroking and rubbing and caressing slick hot skin until they were both shaking with need.

'Please tell me you have a condom somewhere,' Alex groaned against her mouth.

Phoebe froze and felt like wailing. 'Of course I don't have a condom with me. I didn't come here for sex.'

He pulled back and stared down at her, his eyes blazing with frustration. 'Damn. Neither did I.'

The ferocity of the disappointment that thundered through her took her breath away. But then Alex gave her a wicked smile that had all sorts of delicious thoughts running through her head. 'But that doesn't mean we can't still have a heck of a lot of fun.' He began kissing his way down her neck.

Phoebe fell back and let herself drown in the sensations pulsating through her and tried to ignore her disappointment. Part of her wished she were irresponsible enough to tell Alex she didn't care about protection. But then look what had happened as a result of exactly that to the friend whose hen night she'd been to. Furious parents and a shotgun wedding. Not her idea of fun. Although...

'Stop. Wait.'

Alex lifted his head and stared at her in disbelief. 'Are you serious?'

'I do have condoms. A pack of six.' Handed out by her friend with the solemn warning to always take care.

'Where?' he said hoarsely.

'My suitcase. Front pocket.'

Alex rolled off her and was back within seconds ripping away the plastic with his teeth and emptying the box onto the bedside table.

'Always prepared?' he said.

'A hen weekend,' she said, her voice suddenly husky.

'Sounds like an interesting weekend.'

'We learned to pole dance. I can show you later if you—'

Phoebe didn't get to finish her sentence. Alex came down on top of her and crashed his mouth down on hers. Desire slammed straight into her as his lips and tongue embarked on a devastating assault that ravaged her senses. Her pulse galloped. Her legs trembled. She kissed him back greedily, seeking more of him and getting it as the kiss deepened. Her body softened. Her fingers twisted in his hair and she pressed herself even closer to him.

The heat of his mouth, the hardness of his body threatened to send her hurtling out of control. Phoebe's head began to spin with the deep yearning to have him inside her. She itched and throbbed and ached. His erection pressed against her and her thighs fell apart.

Her chest was heaving with the effort of struggling to breathe. 'Now,' she whispered, half crazed with need, her fingers digging into his shoulders.

It must have been the desperate pleading in her voice that broke the grip on his control. Because a second later Alex had rolled the condom on, and she could feel the tip of his penis nudging at her entrance and let out a soft low moan.

'You're very beautiful,' he murmured, bending his head and kissing her slowly and thoroughly.

Delight flooded through her and, just when she thought she was about to pass out from the anticipation, Alex thrust into her. Her inner muscles instantly clamped round him as if never wanting to let him go.

The tightness was back in the pit of her stomach, drawing all her attention to it, sucking her into a black hole of aching need. Phoebe wrenched her mouth from his and panted. Alex groaned and went still, as if the merest movement would send him over the edge.

He felt so incredibly good, deep inside her. Better than anything she could have possibly imagined. Her pulse started to race, her breathing shallowed and she couldn't prevent her hips from arching up. Her hands found their way to his back, and she pressed and traced his muscles, biting on her lip to stop herself from crying out at the incredible sensations that rolled through her, stronger and wilder than anything she'd ever felt before.

Phoebe's insides started to unravel and she felt the beginnings of an earth-shattering climax roll towards her.

And then it was as if Alex lost the thread on his control. He began to move, pulling out of her and then driving in deeper and harder and faster until they were both spiralling towards a peak that they hit at the same time. With a tiny cry, Phoebe broke apart and heard Alex's hoarse groan as he collapsed on top of her.

Long seconds passed during which the only sounds she could hear were her tiny gasps for breath and the thundering of her heart.

'I can't believe that just happened,' she said shakily.

Alex gently pulled away from her and rolled onto his back. 'Can't you? I can't believe it didn't happen before.'

'If I'd known it was going to be like that, I'd have suggested it earlier.'

'No, you wouldn't. Any more than I would have.'

'Well, I'm glad I've finally found out what the fuss is about,' she said feeling a drowsy smile spread across her face.

'What?'

Phoebe stilled. Oh, heavens, had she actually said that out loud? 'Er—nothing.'

Alex propped himself up on his elbow and frowned down at her. 'Please don't tell me you were a virgin.'

If only it were that simple. 'Oh, no,' she said, aiming for breezy nonchalance and failing dismally. 'I've had sex. Loads of it. Well, not that much,' she amended, seeing his raised eyebrow. And probably not nearly as much as he had, judging by his skill. 'But I've never…' Her gaze slid over his shoulder and focused on the white gauzy curtain fluttering in the breeze. She could scarcely believe she was about to tell him this. 'You know…enjoyed it that much.'

'You've never had an orgasm?' Alex sounded stunned.

'No. Well, I mean, not really.'

'What on earth do you mean? Either you have or you haven't.'

Phoebe felt her cheeks flame. 'I've always managed perfectly well on my own, but never, er, with anyone else.'

'Much more fun with someone else, don't you think?' he said, smiling down at her.

'Heaps.' She grinned. 'You look pleased with yourself.'

'I gave you your first orgasm. What man wouldn't be pleased about that?'

'And, hallelujah, it proves I'm not frigid after all.'

'Why would you think you're frigid?'

Phoebe's grin faded and she shrugged as if it hadn't bothered her in the slightest. 'I've been told so. On various occasions.'

Alex curled a lock of hair around his finger and tugged her head forwards for a scorching kiss. 'I think we've dispelled that myth,' he said when he eventually came up for air.

'If you get told something often enough you end up believing it. So I decided it probably wasn't worth the bother. You know how I feel about failure. Jacksons tend to avoid things they're not particularly good at.'

'It's not your failure. It's the failure of the men you've slept with.'

Phoebe grinned and glanced up at him. 'I like that.' She ran a finger over his scar and he flinched. 'How did you get this?'

'The same way I got this,' he said, tapping the slight bump on his nose.

'Sailing?'

'A fight.'

Phoebe's eyebrows shot up. 'About what?'

Alex lay back and stared up at the ceiling. 'It was so long ago I can't remember.'

'Was it over a woman?'

'I think it may well have been.'

'Did you win?'

'Yes.'

Phoebe smiled. Of course he won. 'Would you like to see mine?'

Alex rolled onto his side and looked down at her. 'You have a scar?'

'I do.'

'What from?'

'I once fell out of a tree.'

'What were you doing up a tree?'

'Rescuing a scarf.'

His brows snapped together. 'Are you mad?'

'The most beautiful cashmere scarf. I was sixteen.'

'You fell from a tree when you were sixteen and all you ended up with was a scar? You were lucky not to have been killed.'

'So they told me. I was a clumsy teenager.'

'Where is it?'

'Hanging up in my wardrobe at home, I think.'

'Very funny. I was talking about the scar.'

'Didn't you see it earlier?'

Alex shook his head. 'My mind must have been on other things.'

'Well,' she said, batting her eyelashes and throwing him a sultry smile, 'why don't you try looking for it?'

CHAPTER TEN

THE SUNLIGHT FILTERING through the curtains gradually roused Phoebe from her sleep. For a split second she couldn't work out where she was, but as the events of the night before rolled through her head she grinned and stretched and felt like purring.

She shifted onto her side and opened one eye to double check she hadn't been dreaming. At the empty space beside her, Phoebe's heart plummeted. Then she saw the indent on the pillow and felt the lingering heat of Alex's body on the sheet and her spirits soared.

Her body ached deliciously. Alex had seemed set on making up for all those years of mediocre sex and she'd decided it would be churlish to stop him. The argument about who suffered the least from jealousy had been resolved in a highly satisfactory manner.

But as the sounds of people clearing up outside dragged her into the day the implications of what she'd done began to set in and the doubts she'd managed to keep at bay throughout the long hot night crowded at the edges of her brain.

However inevitable and incredible the night had been, one thing was undeniable. She'd gone to bed with her client's brother. The man who still had the power to ruin her, despite her success at the party.

What would happen now?

A cold film of sweat broke out all over her skin as her mind raced through a variety of different scenarios, none of which allayed her worries in the slightest.

Her thoughts were still a mess when she heard foot-steps on the landing. Phoebe pulled the sheet up to her chin as if it might provide some sort of defence against what he might have to say about her conduct.

Alex appeared at the doorway looking all gorgeous and rumpled, carrying two cups of coffee and wearing nothing but jeans and, despite her concerns, desire surged through her.

'Good morning,' he said, walking over to the bed where Phoebe lay quivering beneath the sheets. He didn't look as if he had a problem with her behaviour last night, she thought as he set the cups down on the bedside table. But who knew? He could be lulling her into a false sense of security. Getting her all languid and pliable before, bam, he hit her with the news that he'd decided to install his own team after all.

His own team, who probably wouldn't jump into bed with him at the first available opportunity.

He sat down and planted his hands either side of her. Phoebe felt like groaning and burying her face in the pillow. 'Uh, morning.'

Alex leaned down and kissed her. He'd brushed his teeth. That really wasn't fair.

'Phoebe?' he said, pulling back and looking down at her with concern.

'Uh-huh.'

'What's the matter?'

'Nothing.'

He frowned. 'Do you regret last night?'

'No. Yes. Maybe.' Her gaze slid over his shoulder and she bit on her lip. 'Do you?'

'Not at all.'

'Oh,' she said, slightly disconcerted by the gleam in his eye. 'Good.'

'So what is it?'

'I was just wondering where I stand with regard to the job.'

He visibly relaxed. 'Is that all?'

'All?' She glared at him. 'Don't you realise how important it is to me?'

'I have some idea.'

'I'd do pretty much anything to hang onto it.'

'Anything?' He arched an eyebrow.

Phoebe blushed. 'Well, not anything exactly.' She paused. 'I hope you don't think I went to bed with you to secure it or something.'

'I don't think that. At least I didn't.' He frowned slightly. '*Did* you go to bed with me to secure it?'

'Of course I didn't,' she said heatedly. 'I went to bed with you because it had got to the stage when I couldn't not. You were right. This...' How could she begin to describe it?

'Chemistry.'

'Yes, chemistry...has been tearing me apart.'

Alex grinned. 'Well, I'm glad that's cleared up.'

'It's not cleared up.'

Alex ran a hand through his hair. 'Is this conversation ever going to make sense?'

'Agh.' She batted him on the arm. 'Just tell me. Do I or do I not have the job?'

'You do.'

Phoebe flopped back onto the pillows as relief flooded through her. Then a thought struck her and she froze. 'Not because of last night?'

'Of course because of last night, but not the part you're thinking of. I think the strategy you came up with to raise the money was inspired and executed brilliantly.'

Phoebe beamed. Thank heavens for that. 'So just to make sure I've got this right, I continue working with Jo and you go back to being a silent partner?'

Alex grimaced as if the thought of taking a step back was hard to swallow. 'Something like that.'

'Can I have it in writing?'

'Don't push your luck.'

Phoebe grinned and levered herself upright to plant a kiss on his mouth. 'The thought of relinquishing control drives you nuts, doesn't it?'

He shot her a thoughtful glance. 'Not as much as I anticipated. And I dare say I'll get used to it.'

Then he looked over her hair and a faint smile hovered at his mouth. 'I like this.'

Phoebe's heart skipped a beat. She dreaded to think what sort of state her hair was in. In the middle of the night Alex had carried her into the shower and had made love to her so thoroughly she hadn't given it a moment's thought. Now, though, she wished she'd at least run a brush through it while it had still been wet. 'Don't mock. It's a sore point.'

'I'm not mocking,' he said mildly, shooting her a quick smouldering smile. 'It suits you.'

'Huh?'

'It goes with the rest of you.'

Phoebe frowned. 'Springy?'

'Curvy.'

Curvy? What woman wanted to be described as curvy? 'I'm not sure I like curvy.'

'I do,' said Alex, running a hand up her body and cupping her breast.

Phoebe bit on her lip to stop herself from moaning and tried to concentrate. 'I always wanted to be a sleek blonde.'

To her great disappointment Alex removed his hand and tilted his head. She should have kept quiet and moaned after all. 'Why?'

'My sister is a sleek blonde. I peroxided my hair once but it went green, so I decided to stick to being a sleek brunette instead.'

'I prefer brunettes. And I prefer ruffled.'

Ruffled was good. Ruffled sounded seductive in a sort of louche sex-kitten kind of way. 'You do?'

Alex's eyes gleamed. 'Uh-huh. And right now, I don't think you're ruffled enough.'

'So what are you going to do about it?'

'Hmm, let me see… Where shall I start?' He ran his eyes over her as if assessing every inch of skin. 'How about here?' He bent his head and dropped a kiss at the base of her neck. Phoebe shivered. 'No?' He hooked a finger over the top of the sheet and pulled it down. 'All right, how about here?' He ran a trail of kisses down the slope of her breast and flicked his tongue over her nipple. Phoebe's back arched and she gasped.

'Feeling ruffled yet?' He lifted his head and looked into her eyes. It felt as if he could see right into her soul and Phoebe had the sudden premonition that Alex could turn out to be very bad for her indeed.

'Getting there,' she said huskily.

The sound of a phone ringing somewhere downstairs

jolted her out of the haze of desire. 'I thought you didn't have a phone.'

'There's a satellite phone,' he murmured against her skin.

'Shouldn't you go and answer it?'

'Too late.'

The ringing stopped as the answer machine kicked in.

Phoebe grinned and stretched back. 'Don't you just love civilisation?'

'Where would we be without it?'

'The Stone Age?' she said softly. 'In fact I can just see you in a loin cloth, hunting and gathering.'

Alex lifted his head and his eyes gleamed. 'I can see you lying on the floor of my cave waiting to be ravished on my return.'

'I wouldn't,' said Phoebe indignantly, thinking how wonderfully wanton that sounded. 'I'd be decorating. Doing something creative with shells. Drawing on the walls. Or alternatively I'd be sitting with the other cave-women and listening to how they sent their men out for some leaves and roots for supper and they came back with a woolly mammoth.'

Alex laughed and the sound of it rumbled right through her making every nerve ending tingle.

'Besides, it would be *our* cave, not just yours.'

Alex pulled back a little and Phoebe wondered what she'd said. 'Alex?'

'Phoebe.' The cool tone of his voice sent an involuntary shiver down her spine. 'Before we go any further, you should know I'm not looking for a cave with anyone.'

No. In the past five years he hadn't been photographed with the same woman twice. 'You're the one who mentioned me lying in your cave.'

'Yes, but I didn't have you decorating.'

If he hadn't been lying half on top of her, she'd have kicked herself. 'My mistake. I don't really like decorating anyway. The decorative arts were shunned in the Jackson household in favour of academia, so I'd probably have to get someone in.'

He frowned. 'You're missing my point.'

'No, I'm not. I understand perfectly well what you mean. You needn't worry. I'm not going to get all clingy and needy. The last thing I need at this stage in my career is anything serious or heavy.' She shot him a smouldering smile. 'But the hot sex is kind of nice.'

'Nice?' he murmured. 'I must be out of practice.'

Yeah right. 'I guess you have it a lot,' she said lightly. 'What with being an international playboy and things.'

'Not as often as you might imagine. And don't tell anyone, but I'm not much of a playboy either.'

A kick of something resembling delirious relief punched her in the stomach and alarm bells rang in her ears. Oh, if she wasn't careful she could find herself careering down such a slippery slope.

'Ever been in love?'

'Phoebe…'

'OK, OK,' she said, grinning. Neither had she, and frankly the idea of being at the mercy of rampaging emotions made her feel sick just thinking about it. 'So all those photos… all that arm candy…?'

'Just arm candy.' He paused and lifted an eyebrow. 'Is there anything else you'd like to know?'

Everything, she thought, feeling unaccountably pleased at his answer. She wanted to know everything about him. But not right now… 'About that hot sex,' she said, throwing him a coquettish smile. 'Any chance of some more?'

Alex listened to the soft sound of Phoebe's breathing as she dozed. Her head lay on his chest, and her arm was flung across his stomach. Sleep, however, eluded him completely. He'd never felt more awake or more alert.

The way Phoebe had responded to him over and over again astounded him. Once she'd had her eyes opened, she'd been insatiable. And he'd been more than willing to help her make up for lost time. But if he wasn't careful this could get way out of hand. By now, he'd have expected the itch to have gone away. That after the night they'd just had, desire would have faded. But it hadn't. Quite the opposite. Even now, he could feel himself stirring again.

What was it about her? He stared down at Phoebe's face and felt a weight shift in his chest. Something bordering on panic gripped his insides and he suddenly felt an odd desperation to escape. He gently lifted her arm and eased himself from beneath her.

Phoebe stirred and made a little sound of protest. 'Where are you going?' she said sleepily.

'To see who that was on the phone. Don't go anywhere.'

Oh, good Lord. Phoebe stood in the bathroom and stared at her reflection in absolute horror.

When Alex had said he liked her hair like this he had to be lying. Frizzy didn't even begin to describe the mess. Her hair stuck out at bizarre angles, as a result of her going to sleep with it wet and Alex's fingers tangling through it all night. Her poor overworked straighteners would never be able to tame this. She needed an industrial tool kit, the likes of which she'd only ever found in a handful of London salons. She'd head to the nearest one just as soon as they landed back on British soil.

And then what? Would Alex suggest dinner? Should she suggest a drink? Nervous excitement fizzled around her stomach. Or might that be too clingy for something which was only about hot sex? She was sailing into uncharted territory here, she realised, frowning at her reflection. She'd better figure out the rules. Maybe she'd ask Alex. He was bound to have a whole string of them.

'Phoebe.'

The sound of his voice jerked her out of her thoughts. She couldn't let him see her like this. Horizontal, with her hair spread out over a pillow or his chest was one thing. Vertical was quite another.

'Just a minute.'

He flung the bathroom door open and as she swung round every niggle about her hair and rules flew from her head. Alex looked absolutely terrible. His face was white. His eyes were stormy grey and filled with concern.

Phoebe's heart lurched. 'What's happened?'

'We need to leave.'

'Now?'

'Immediately.'

'Why?'

'That was Jo on the phone.'

Fear gripped her stomach and she clutched at the basin. 'Is she all right?'

'Physically she's fine. Mentally I'm not sure. The press have got hold of a story about her.'

Oh, no. Phoebe went very still. 'What about?'

'How much has she told you about her life before design college?'

'Not a lot. I guess I'd imagined she'd been at school.'

'She was. While she was there she became anorexic and ended up in a psychiatric hospital.'

Her stomach churned. 'How long for?'

'A year.'

God, how awful. Phoebe could barely begin to imagine what Jo must have gone through. 'And that's the story?'

'In a nutshell.'

So much for her rash assumption that weekends in PR were quiet. She should never have tempted fate like that. Feeling as if the walls were closing in on her Phoebe dragged in a shaky breath. 'Can I use the phone? I'd like to check my messages.'

Alex nodded briefly. 'It's in the study. As soon as you're ready we'll leave.'

Thirty-five missed calls.

Fifteen messages before the time had run out.

Messages from Jo. Growing increasingly frantic. From the fashion house wondering what the hell was going on. From journalists asking for comments and verification of the facts. From potential clients cancelling meetings and postponing lunches.

All wanting to know where Phoebe was and why she wasn't answering her phone.

As realisation dawned her heart began to thud and panic clawed at her stomach. Her palms went damp and a ball of dread lodged in her throat. A bolt of sheer terror gripped her insides and squeezed. Her vision went fuzzy as a wave of nausea reared up from her stomach to her throat. Blindly Phoebe stumbled to the window, threw it open and sucked in great gulps of air.

Everything she'd ever worked for, everything Jo had

ever worked for, hung in the balance. She knew the field she worked in well. If she was there, on the scene, she'd be able to reassure people that she was in full control and handling the crisis. If she was there she'd be able to divert disaster.

Instead where was she? Miles away. And what had she been doing while Jo was falling to pieces and her whole life was threatening to implode? Laughing and talking and exploring the new-found delights of sexual ecstasy with Alex.

Phoebe felt like banging her head against the desk as a tidal wave of guilt flooded through her. She'd allowed herself to get distracted and taken her eye off the ball. How could she have been so stupid?

And the principle thought running round and round her head on the tense and fraught journey back to London was that it had happened again.

Phoebe read the story for the third time, then closed the newspaper and tried to rally her spirits, but it was as bad as she'd imagined.

According to the report, Jo had once had a boyfriend who'd bullied her, nagged her about her weight and introduced her to diet pills, which had led to addiction, extreme anorexia and the subsequent hospitalisation.

She could scarcely believe that the girl described in the article and the girl sitting next to her on the sofa were one and the same.

'Is all of this true?' Phoebe said, more to break the taut silence than out of any necessity to know the answer. Whether it was true or not, the damage had already been done, as the messages on her mobile and in her inbox testified.

'Pretty much.' Jo sniffed. Her eyes were red and puffy, but she was holding up remarkably well given the circumstances.

'Is there any more?'

'No.'

Thank goodness for that. 'Why didn't I know about this?'

'No one does,' said Alex flatly.

Phoebe glanced over at him and steeled herself against the effect Alex had on her brain. She really needed a clear head at the moment. 'Well, someone clearly does… A source close to Ms Douglas…' She turned to Jo. 'Can you think of anyone that might be? Someone who worked at the hospital perhaps?'

Jo sighed. 'I suspect it might have been Mark.'

A stunned hush fell over the room.

'Mark?' Alex's voice sliced through the silence like a whip.

Jo slumped back against her worktable. 'I might have mentioned that I once had problems with my weight and I haven't been able to get hold of him since the party.'

Phoebe's brain raced. 'If he was broke, then he may well have sold what he knew to the papers. Once a journalist gets the sniff of a story it usually doesn't take much digging to uncover the rest.'

The memory of Mark's drunken threats flashed into her head and she cast a quick glance at Alex. The haggard look on his face told her that he'd come to a similar conclusion.

'I'm sorry I wasn't here when you called.'

Jo gave her a wan smile. 'It doesn't matter. You're here now. But where were you? I've never not been able to get hold of you before.'

Jo sounded more curious than accusatory, but that didn't stop guilt washing over her. 'I was away,' said Phoebe. 'On business. Last minute. It won't happen again.'

She shot a quick look at Alex, whose face had turned even stonier. 'I'll organise a press conference as soon as possible and we'll sort this out. Jo,' she said with more confidence than she felt, 'you've come a long way since then. It'll be OK.'

Alex had barely been able to resist the urge to hurl the paper against the wall when he'd read the article. The only part they'd left out was that Jo's ex-boyfriend had been his business partner. A man he thought he'd known inside out. His best friend. Who'd nearly destroyed Jo and had nearly ruined him.

He kept his gaze fixed on his sister and battled the shock that she'd so casually let slip to Mark something he'd taken such pains to keep buried. Hadn't she learned from him? Hadn't he warned her about the dangers of trusting people? About what happened if you let someone get near you?

Alex's hands clenched into fists and he had to stamp down on the urge to hunt Mark down and beat him to a pulp. The night of the pre-launch party slammed into his head. The threats and the warnings as he'd dragged Mark out of the pond that he'd dismissed as drunken ramblings. The debts. All tiny little clues that Mark might be a danger. And he'd ignored them.

The moment he'd seen the headlines, guilt had started attacking him on all sides. Firstly for failing to protect Jo. Again. A second blast had struck him when he'd realised that Jo had needed him and he hadn't been there. As if that hadn't been enough for one man in one lifetime, guilt also prickled that he'd lured Phoebe away for the weekend when she ought to have been here for his sister.

He glanced over at her and there it was again, another arrow of guilt piercing his chest. Because despite the torment his sister was suffering, the main thought rattling round his brain was how soon he could get Phoebe back into his bed.

A wave of weariness swept through him. He'd been carrying around the burden of guilt for five years now. It had clung to his shoulders like a heavy mantle, dragging him down, and he was so tired of it.

His gaze flickered over to his sister. She was listening to Phoebe outlining the strategy for sorting out the mess, and it struck him that she seemed a lot calmer and more confident than he'd have imagined in the circumstances. In fact she appeared to be more concerned with the effect that Mark's revelations might have on her career rather than on her personally.

Phoebe was right, he realised with something of a shock. Jo had come a long way since then. She didn't need him to pick up the pieces any longer. So why was he still beating himself up over something that Jo had clearly decided to get over?

Would it really be so bad if he dispensed with the guilt? Jo had told him time and time again that she didn't hold him in any way responsible for what had happened to her, but up until now he had resolutely resisted the temptation to forgive himself. And what good was that doing anyone?

Jo might have come a long way, but he hadn't, he acknowledged reluctantly. If his sister was able to get over what had happened and get on with things, why shouldn't he?

CHAPTER ELEVEN

JO AND THE last of the journalists left the room where the press conference had been held and Phoebe slumped back into her chair.

Thank God. It was over and she never wanted to go through anything like it again. She could scarcely believe how close she'd come to losing everything. She felt dizzy just thinking about it.

But she'd pulled it off. She'd spent the last twenty-four hours working like a demon with her phone permanently glued to her ear while she slowly repaired their reputations. And it had paid off. Jo had been brilliant and the fashion house deal was back on.

Phoebe herself was back in control and she didn't intend to lose it again. Ever. If that meant no more hot sex with Alex, then so be it.

She ignored the little voice in her head telling her she was a fool to let something so fantastic go. But it was only sex, and she couldn't afford to slip up again. The way she'd been so out of control on Saturday night, so at the mercy of her body's needs, terrified her and she wanted no more of it.

She might not be able to avoid Alex altogether, she

thought, folding her arms on the table and resting her forehead on them, but she could certainly make sure she never slept with him again.

Alex strode back into the hotel conference room and cleared his throat. Phoebe jumped and jerked back. 'You look like you could do with this,' he said, placing a cup of coffee in front of her.

That was an understatement. Phoebe looked awful. Dark circles ringed her eyes and her face was pale.

'Oh. Er, thanks. I didn't see you earlier.'

He sat on the edge of the table and watched her carefully. 'I was lurking at the back. Congratulations.'

'Thank you.' She gave him a wan smile. 'And thank you for keeping out of things.'

Alex lifted a shoulder. 'It was part of the deal. Have you missed me?'

Phoebe's gaze snapped to his face. 'No,' she said quickly, and then began to shuffle the papers on the table.

Alex grinned. 'What are you doing for the rest of the afternoon?'

'Work, I imagine.'

'You ought to get some rest.' Preferably in his bed.

'I ought to get going.'

'Do you ever stop?'

'At the moment I can't afford to stop,' she said with a brief humourless smile that made him frown. 'You've been involved with new businesses. You must know that they require attention every hour of the day and night.'

True. And investing in new businesses meant a similar kind of commitment. But Alex recognised the signs of exhaustion and the way Phoebe was going she'd collapse before long.

'Would you like a lift?'

A startled look of horror crossed her face. Surely his suggestion wasn't that bad? But if that was her reaction to a lift, maybe he'd wait until she was in a more relaxed frame of mind before putting forward his proposal that they continue to see each other. 'No. It's fine. I can get a taxi.'

'You'll never find one. It's pouring outside.'

'Or a bus or a train or something.'

Her cool tone and the way she deliberately avoided eye contact was beginning to irritate him. As was the incessant shuffling of papers. What was the matter with her? Alex crossed his arms over his chest. 'Is something wrong?'

'Wrong?' Her gaze flicked to his for a second and then darted away. 'The press conference went well and Jo's career is back on track. What could possibly be wrong?'

The ball of baffled frustration that had been ricocheting around his chest stopped and burst. To hell with waiting. 'How about the fact that only a couple of days ago you were writhing in my arms, gasping with pleasure and begging me for more, yet now you can't wait to see the back of me?'

Colour stained her cheeks and her gaze slid to the table. 'That was then.'

'What's changed?'

'What happened on the island was a one off.' She sighed and when she did finally deign to look at him her eyes were unfathomable and Alex found he didn't like it one little bit. 'A momentary lapse of reason. It was a mistake.' She plucked her jacket off the back of her chair.

'So I guess an affair's out of the question,' he drawled.

Phoebe went very still. 'An affair?'

'You and me and the hot sex you were so keen on on Saturday night.'

She threaded her arms through her jacket and did the buttons up. 'You're right. Totally out of the question. I'm not interested in an affair.'

Disappointment far greater than it should have been thwacked him in the stomach. Then just before she twisted away he saw that her hands were trembling and it made him wonder. 'So you don't want me?'

'No, I don't. Not any more.'

He slid off the table and moved closer. 'And you don't want me to pull you into my arms right now and kiss you until you're shaking with desire? You don't want me to peel that little suit off you and spread you over the table and trail my mouth over every inch of your body?'

'No.' Her voice cracked.

'In that case you definitely won't want me doing this.'

Alex spun her round and brought his mouth down on hers. His arms snapped round her and he pulled her tight against him. He plunged his tongue into her mouth and desire flared inside him. His heart hammered. But Phoebe remained rigid in his punishing embrace.

He broke off, breathing raggedly, and stared down at her. 'Kiss me back,' he muttered hoarsely.

'No,' she said, glaring at him, fury written all over her face.

God, why was she denying this? Did she really not want him? The thought made him dizzy for a second. It was an uncomfortable sensation. But maybe she didn't. Maybe he'd read it all wrong and Saturday night had just been about high-running tempers. If that was the case then he had no business hauling her about, however much he might want to.

He was just about to let her go when he saw something flicker in the depths of her eyes. His heart skidded to a halt. She did want him. Triumph and relief pummelled through him.

He'd make her respond, make her see that an affair was an excellent idea, if it was the last thing he did. He loosened his grip on her and slid one hand slowly up her back to her neck and buried his fingers in her hair.

Alex felt her tense as if in preparation for another onslaught, but when he lowered his head this time he brushed his lips against hers and then dropped feather light kisses along her jaw.

Phoebe's head dropped back and he smiled against her skin. He explored the creamy smoothness of her neck and then found her mouth again and this time when he kissed her he found no resistance. Just warm, wet sweetness.

'If you don't want me,' he murmured, 'then this is the moment when you would slap me.'

Phoebe jerked back and without warning her hand flew up. She was quick but Alex's instincts were quicker. With a sharp curse he blocked her hand and wrapped his fingers around her wrist.

'What was that for?' he said, his eyes blazing.

'You suggested it.'

Alex stared at her, stunned. He'd felt less at sea in the middle of the ocean in the throes of a force-twelve hurricane. 'You want me.'

'No, I don't.'

He'd had enough. 'I thought *I* was good at denial but you're a master. You'd drive a man to drink.'

'All right,' yelled Phoebe. 'I do want you. You're right. Saturday night was amazing. I do want a repeat. But it's not going to happen.'

Alex shoved his hands through his hair. 'Why the hell not?'

She gaped. 'How can you even ask that? While I was in your bed, papers were going to print with that story. I should have been here.'

Alex froze. Was that what this was all about? Guilt? It was lucky he was an expert on the subject. 'That wasn't your fault. It was mine. I shouldn't have dragged you off to the island in the first place.'

'I could have got on that boat. I *should* have got on that boat.'

Alex frowned. 'It wouldn't have made any difference. We were due to leave at lunchtime.'

Phoebe threw her hands up in a gesture of anguish. 'I'd planned to hitch a lift with one of your colleagues who was leaving that night. If I'd done that, if I'd had the strength to stick to the plan I would have been here for Jo.' She laughed bitterly. 'But no. What did I do? Leap into bed with you.'

He winced at the disgust in her voice even though he knew it was directed more at herself than at him. 'Guilt doesn't do anyone any good. It's a complete waste of time.'

'Hah. What would you know about guilt? I bet you've never suffered a moment's guilt in your entire life.'

Alex felt as if she'd thumped him in the gut. 'Is that what you think? Then let me set you straight. I've spent the last five years riddled with guilt. Over what happened to Jo. Over whether I could have done something to prevent it. And you know what? Maybe I could have done more. Who knows? But one thing I've come to realise recently is that beating yourself up about something that can't be undone is utterly pointless.'

'It isn't pointless,' she said sharply. 'It can stop you making the same mistake again.'

'Can it? Does it stop *you* making the same mistakes again?'

Phoebe glared at him. 'It'll stop me jumping into bed with you again.'

Alex reeled. 'I didn't realise you found it so unpleasant the first time.'

Her shoulders dropped and she ran a hand through her hair. 'I didn't. You know I didn't. But you make me lose control. You distort my focus. My judgement does derail when I get distracted and I can't risk that.' Her voice cracked. 'Honestly, sometimes I feel like my finger is hovering over my self-destruct button and it's only sheer will power that stops me from jabbing at it and watching my life unravel with some sort of morbidly fascinating relief. I nearly just lost everything. My business, my career, everything I've ever worked for.' She pulled her shoulders back and shot him a look of calm finality. 'I won't compromise that for a brief fling with you. It's just not worth it.'

Something deep inside Alex suddenly exploded. 'That's utter rubbish.'

'*What?*' Phoebe gasped but he carried on regardless.

'You're good at your job. You know you are. You spent long enough telling me about it. You might not have been available the instant the story hit the papers, but you salvaged the situation regardless.'

'By the skin of my teeth.'

'But you did it. And if you're so terrified of your precious life unravelling, why set up your own business when nine out of ten start-ups fail within the first year? Now I have no idea where this sudden misguided lack of confidence comes from, or even if it *is* a sudden misguided lack of confidence, but whatever it is, for some reason I can't work out, you're using it to hide behind.'

'I'm not hiding behind anything. Is it really so difficult to believe that I just don't want to have an affair with you?'

'Frankly, yes. Because your body still craves mine as much as mine craves yours.'

Phoebe shrugged as if electrifying sexual chemistry was nothing more than a minor inconvenience in her life. 'That's just biology.'

Alex felt the energy drain out of him. Why was he fighting so hard for this? It wasn't as if Phoebe were the only woman on the planet. 'Fine.' He stepped back and shot her a humourless smile. 'You know something? I really don't need the hassle. I just thought a fling might be fun.'

And with that he turned on his heel and stormed out.

CHAPTER TWELVE

THE MINUTE PHOEBE got home, the strain of holding herself together snapped. The door slammed behind her and her bag landed on the hall floor with a thud. Her raincoat fell into a crumpled heap a foot further on and she stumbled into the sitting room. Her legs gave way and she collapsed on the sofa shaking uncontrollably.

The taunts and accusations Alex had hurled at her spun round and round inside her head so relentlessly that she wished she could reach in and yank them out.

Because he didn't know her. He couldn't know the effect her upbringing had had on her. Nor the power of the rigid principles that her parents had instilled in her. He couldn't possibly understand the stress of living with the fear that of all the siblings she was the one most likely to let everyone down. Unless she kept a firm grip on her emotions that could happen all too easily.

So Alex was wrong. She wasn't hiding. It was all about self-preservation, mainly saving herself from herself. He had no right to have a go at her like that.

And yet…

The little voice that had been hammering away at

her conscience throughout the Tube journey refused to be silenced.

What if Alex was right?

Phoebe sat up, crossed her legs and pulled a cushion onto her lap. What if she *was* using her insecurities as an excuse and hiding behind a wall of guilt?

She'd survived the past couple of days, hadn't she? She hadn't let anyone down, least of all her family.

And actually guilt didn't stop the same mistakes happening over again, did it? Not when other emotions came into play and corrupted your ability to think rationally.

Guilt certainly didn't prevent problems and tricky situations sprouting up all over the place. And what was she going to do when they did? Torment herself with 'what if's and 'if only's and 'should have's? Or just get on and deal with them?

Frankly she was always going to fret about any course of action she took and wonder whether things might have turned out better had she done something differently. It was the way she was built and had been for the last twenty-nine years. She might as well get used to it.

Phoebe chewed on her lip. She tentatively ran her mind back over the conversation with Alex in the conference room and tried to look at it from his point of view. All he'd done was suggest an affair and she'd completely overreacted. Her cheeks burned and she buried her face in the cushion.

What was so scary about an affair anyway? People had them all the time without going to pieces. After all, it wasn't even as if Alex had been proposing a proper relationship. Just sex to unwind after a long day at work. Stringless, emotionless but scorching nonetheless.

Fun, he'd said. An affair with Alex wouldn't just be

fun. It would be amazing. Exhilarating. And probably about time. She'd worked hard, but it had been at the expense of playing, and didn't she deserve some fun?

Surely she'd be able to keep her focus clear. She was a very different person from the infatuated fool she'd been when Dillon had betrayed her three years ago. And what was she going to do? Steer clear of men and messy emotion for ever?

As her brain adjusted to the possibility of an affair with Alex Phoebe felt excitement flicker in her breast. She had no plans for the afternoon and she was far too wound up to settle down to work. She ought to dash over to his office right now and tell him of her change of mind.

Hmm. In all likelihood he'd never want to see her again. She'd resisted him. Rejected him. She'd nearly slapped him, for heaven's sake. Shame hit her square in the chest. That had been particularly appalling. She owed him an apology for that at the very least.

Because she *had* wanted him. He'd definitely been right about that. She'd wanted him with an urgency that confounded her but had her heart thundering just thinking about it now. When he'd described what he'd like to do to her on the table in the conference room she'd nearly passed out at the thrill.

Phoebe jumped up as the glimmer of an idea crept into her head. Maybe there was a way she could let him know she'd changed her mind without actually having to suffer the embarrassment of admitting that maybe, just maybe, he was right and she'd been wrong.

After all, didn't actions speak louder than words?

Alex sat back in his chair and tried to concentrate on the meeting going on around him. Negotiations with his latest investment opportunity were at a delicate stage. He ought to be dedicating his full attention to it.

But all he could think of was Phoebe's flat refusal to have an affair with him. The disdain in her voice, the look of horror on her face… It grated more than it should have. He never usually had any trouble persuading women into his bed.

Although there hadn't been too many of those lately. Maybe that was why her rejection stung.

'Alex?'

The voice of one of his finance department snapped him out of his thoughts. 'What?'

'They're pushing for twenty-five percent. I know we originally wanted a fifty-percent stake, but I think we should drop it.'

'Settle at forty,' Alex said and suddenly got to his feet.

This was driving him insane. And dammit, there was no reason he should feel like this. His scowl deepened with every stride towards his office. Where was his address book? He threw himself into his chair and pulled out the drawers of his desk. Aha.

Alex brushed off the dust and flicked through yellowing pages filled with the phone numbers of women he'd dated over the years. One of the numbers was bound to still be valid. He didn't particularly care which one. Any of them would do to prove to himself he didn't need Phoebe.

His phone rang and he snatched it up. 'What?' he barked and then told himself to calm down. Whatever his frustrations, they had nothing to do with his secretary.

'I have a Ms Jackson to see you.'

Alex nearly dropped the phone. Then his eyes narrowed and he felt himself grow cold. What was she here for? Wasn't rejecting him bad enough? Was she now planning to slap a sexual harassment charge on him as well?

He had every intention of telling his secretary to tell Phoebe to get lost, so he was utterly stunned to hear the words, 'Show her in,' coming out of his mouth.

Alex clenched his fists and moved round to stand in front of his desk where he reckoned he'd look more intimidating and more in control. And if ever he needed to be in control, now, with his brain behaving like a loose cannon, was it.

The firm rap at his door made his pulse spike.

'Come in,' he said curtly.

The door swung open slowly and Phoebe sidled in. Something about the way she moved had every one of his senses springing to attention.

Unable to help himself, he let his gaze travel over her. Her hair was tied back but she'd done something to her eyes. They seemed bigger than he recalled, more slumberous somehow. Her mouth seemed…poutier.

Alex swallowed and dragged his gaze over the rest of her. She was wearing the knee-length raincoat she'd had on earlier—with the collar turned up and the belt tightly tied around her waist—but she'd changed her shoes. If she'd been wearing those black patent heels at the press conference he'd have remembered. As he'd have remembered the inches of leg enclosed in sheer black nylon.

'You'll have to be quick,' he said, hauling his gaze back up to her face. 'I'm in the middle of a meeting.'

'So your secretary said. I don't mind waiting.'

Was it his imagination or had her voice dropped a couple of notes? 'Fine. What can I do for you?'

A slow smile curved her lips. 'It's really more a question of what I can do for you.'

Alex's mouth went dry and his body temperature shot up as an image of exactly what she could do for him slammed into his head. So much for thinking he was in control. He needed to sit down before the effect she was having on him became too obvious. Deliberately taking his time, he levered himself off the edge of his desk and moved to sit behind it. At least her legs were now out of sight, not that that offered much comfort to his aching body.

'And what is that?' He picked up a pencil and began to twirl it around his fingers as if he couldn't be less bothered by her presence in his office.

'I've come to apologise.'

Alex's brain had clearly disintegrated because he hadn't the faintest idea of what she was talking about. 'What for?'

'Slapping you.'

'You didn't.'

'I wanted to.'

'Why?'

'You suggested an affair.'

'You turned me down.'

She reached up and pulled the band from her hair. Glossy curls tumbled over her shoulders. 'I've changed my mind.'

Alex's pulse leapt. 'How predictable,' he drawled.

Phoebe's smile faltered for a split second but she didn't take her eyes off him. 'I thought you might say that.'

She took her hands out of her pockets and unknotted her belt. Then she started to undo the buttons. Achingly slowly. The lapels fell open revealing a V of skin and a tantalising glimpse of black lace.

The scorching heat of her gaze trapped him where he sat. Alex couldn't move. He could barely breathe.

'I also wanted to say that I've had time to reflect on the points you mentioned and have come to the conclusion you might be right.'

'About what?' He cleared his throat.

'A number of things, but mainly the futility of guilt.'

'I see,' he said hoarsely, thinking that that was utter rubbish. All he could see was Phoebe.

'Did you really feel that guilty about what happened to Jo?'

Alex blinked. 'It consumed me day and night.'

'Past tense?'

'Absolutely.'

'Good, because she doesn't blame you, you know.'

'I know.'

'So blaming yourself is pointless.'

'I know.'

'Based on that reasoning I now see I may have been a bit hasty in rejecting your proposal.'

The pencil snapped.

Her smile deepened and she walked round the desk. 'If you're still open to the idea, I don't see any reason why we shouldn't have an affair.'

His chair swivelled as he followed her every move. Hunger and desire roared along his veins and his erection strained and ached. 'I'm still open to the idea.'

Then she was standing in front of him, her coat hanging open, baring soft skin and black lace and those shoes, and Alex's vision blurred. 'Earlier this afternoon you mentioned something about peeling my clothes off, spreading me out over a table and trailing your mouth over every inch of my body.'

Had he? That sounded like the best idea he'd had in a long time.

Phoebe sat on his lap and leaned forward to whisper in his ear. 'I've done the first bit. How about you helping me with the rest?'

Her scent spun through his head and the last vestige of control snapped. He clamped one arm around her waist to keep her where she was and reached for the phone with the other. He pressed the button that connected to his secretary's desk. 'Cancel my appointments for the rest of the day and take the afternoon off,' he said when she answered. 'Something's come up.'

Alex hung up and Phoebe let out a soft laugh. 'Thank goodness for that. I thought you were going to call Security.'

He raised an eyebrow and smiled. 'Why would I want to do a thing like that when you're apologising so nicely?'

Phoebe gripped the back of his chair, lowered her mouth to his and kissed him so slowly and thoroughly that Alex's head swam. As her tongue slid along his, his hands delved beneath the lapels of her coat and gently pushed it down her arms. She shrugged it off and then wound her arms around his neck and pressed her pelvis against his. She moaned into his mouth and Alex lost it.

With one quick move he wiped the papers and pens and things off his desk and lifted her onto it. Her coat fell to the floor. Phoebe untangled her hands from his hair and eased herself back onto the leather.

Alex stared down at her and thought he'd never seen anything so beautiful. The bra she was wearing was a strapless concoction of lace and silk that pushed her breasts up and out. Further down, she wore a matching suspender belt and the tiniest excuse for knickers he'd ever come across.

The blood roared in his ears and then he found he could barely think. Only act. He unclipped her bra and slipped it off her and her breasts spilled free. He ran his hands over the rounded flesh and rubbed his thumbs over her nipples. Phoebe gasped sharply and arched her back as if begging him to take them in his mouth. Alex leaned down and trailed a string of feather light kisses over the sensitive skin of her chest before flicking his tongue over the straining nub.

'Oh, God, don't stop,' she whispered raggedly. 'Don't ever stop.'

Alex didn't plan on stopping. He lifted his head for a second to gaze down into her face. Her cheeks were flushed and she was biting into her lip as if trying to stop herself from crying out.

He kissed his way down the soft skin of her stomach and pressed his mouth to the hot wet heat of her. Phoebe jerked as if he'd branded her.

Alex's fingers shook as he hooked them under the thin lace at her hips and pulled her panties down her legs. His hands circled her ankles, slid up her shins, swept up her inner thighs and her legs fell apart.

His hands moved round to cup her bottom, then lifted her to his mouth. Her hips automatically tried to twist but he held them down. He pressed his thumb against her clitoris and she groaned.

Then his mouth was on her, licking and sucking and tasting with just enough pressure to drive her wild. He felt her tremble, heard her breathing shallow and, as he licked deeper inside her, felt her tense and then shatter. His mouth pressed against her, absorbing every tremor shuddering through her, milking every drop of her desire. Eventually, when the aftershocks subsided, he kissed his way up her body, feeling every tiny nerve ending of her skin jumping as he did so.

Alex planted his hands either side of her and leaned over her. Her face was flushed, and her eyes a dark shimmering green. A satisfied grin spread across her face and Alex felt something shift deep inside him. 'This was supposed to be about what I could do for you,' Phoebe murmured.

'Too late. Every time I sit at this desk,' he said hoarsely, 'I'm going to see you. Like this. It's going to be agony.'

She pushed herself up on her elbows and gave him a slow smile. 'Well, we can't have that, can we?'

Her eyes dropped to the huge bulge in his trousers and widened. He was so hard he ached and he was seconds away from unzipping his fly and plunging straight into her without a thought for the consequences.

Stunned by the ferocity of his desire Alex jerked back and removed himself from temptation. The taste of her on his tongue had addled his brain.

Phoebe slithered off the desk and reached for her coat. 'Is this what you're looking for?' she said, delving into the pocket and pulling out a condom.

Too right. He lunged for her but she dodged him, instead backing away in the direction of the sofa, a come-hither look in her eye that he couldn't have resisted even if he'd wanted to.

Alex matched her pace for pace, not breaking eye contact with her for a second. He ripped his clothes off and tossed them to the floor. Phoebe slipped out of her shoes and suspender belt and rolled down her stockings, her teeth digging into her lower lip and her steps becoming more and more languid until she stopped altogether.

Alex didn't stop. He'd never seen anything lovelier. Taking the condom out of her trembling hands, he shoved one hand in her hair and kissed her hard, twisting her around and pulling her down with him onto the sofa.

Phoebe sprawled on top of him, her breasts crushing against his chest. His hands stroked over the backs of her thighs and up over her bottom and she moaned into his mouth.

In one quick powerful move, he tipped her off the sofa and onto the rug. As his hands and mouth roamed over her Phoebe's soft, stunned laughter soon turned to moans of pleasure. Slipping a finger deep inside her, he watched her writhe and gasp and arch her back. And when she was convulsing around him, crying out his name Alex lifted himself over her and drove into her.

A fever raged inside him as he saw her eyes widen and felt her muscles clamp around his length. Her legs wound round his waist as if she never wanted to let him go. Her nails raked his back as between pants she told him exactly how he was making her feel.

Her hips rose to meet every thrust in perfect synchronicity. Alex's heart hammered. The blood thundered around his body and pleasure pounded along his veins. No one had ever made him lose control like this. As his head went blank of everything except pure need Alex gave in and let his body take over. His thrusts quickened, intensified, became harder and faster. He felt her tense and then shatter in his arms, and as waves of ecstasy slammed through him Alex plunged deep inside her, buried his face in her neck and with a great groan hit the strongest, most intense climax of his life.

They lay there together for a few moments while their breathing slowed then Alex rolled onto his back and pulled Phoebe with him.

'Have dinner with me tonight.'

She rested her chin on his chest. 'I can't.' She sighed and he felt it reverberate through him. 'My parents are having a party. They have it every year. For the great and good of the city. It's a nightmare.'

Alex waited for her to ask him to go with her and wondered how he'd say no. When she didn't it annoyed him. Which irritated him even more. He ought to be delighted that she understood the no-strings rule, but bizarrely he found himself wanting to know what her family was like. What sort of people had shaped the woman she was. 'Some other time perhaps.'

'That would be nice.'

If she wasn't going to invite him he'd have to get there some other way. 'What time do you have to be there?'

Phoebe picked up his wrist and glanced at his watch. 'In a couple of hours. I ought to go.'

She started to wriggle away, but Alex flung an arm around her to stop her going anywhere. He felt himself stirring inside her and her eyes widened. 'I'm not sure you're done apologising,' he said and tugged her head down for a kiss.

CHAPTER THIRTEEN

PHOEBE STEPPED OUT of the taxi and looked up at her parents' house with a familiar feeling of misgiving. Even the afterglow of this afternoon couldn't wipe out the ribbon of trepidation that wound through her.

And what an afternoon… How she'd ever plucked up the courage to turn up at Alex's office dressed like that she'd never know. Throughout the taxi ride she'd been convinced the driver had known exactly what she was up to. But it had certainly paid off. Phoebe went dizzy for a second as a flush swept up through her body and she had to clutch onto the railing for balance.

It had been on the tip of her tongue to invite him tonight, but she'd thought about the definition and general properties of a fling just in time and had bitten back the words. So she was on her own. As usual. It had never bothered her before, so why was it bothering her now?

Taking a deep breath and telling herself not to be so idiotic, she pulled her shoulders back and walked up the steps. The glossy black door swung open and a wall of warmth and chatter hit her. She smiled at the waiter and handed him her coat then wandered into the drawing room and started to squeeze her way through the guests.

With any luck she could say a speedy hello to her parents, avoid her siblings and leave after half an hour.

She'd start with her mother. Phoebe spied her by the fireplace and made her way over, feeling tension seep into her with every step.

'Hi, Mum,' she said, giving her mother a quick kiss on the cheek and bracing herself for an attack.

'You're late.'

'You look nice.'

'Thank you. So do you.' Her mother cast a critical eye over her outfit and nodded with approval. 'Good. There's someone I'd like you to meet.'

Oh, no. Not another one of her mother's attempts to get her to switch careers. Other people's mothers engaged in not-so-subtle efforts to marry off their daughters. But not her mother. She'd apparently made it her lifelong mission to rescue her daughter from the clutches of the frothy world of PR by any means possible. 'He's a friend of Dan's. Try and be nice.'

Phoebe fought the urge to stamp her foot like a petulant child and bleat that she didn't want to be nice and she didn't need to meet another man who thought he could whip her off the PR track and set her on the straight and narrow. But her mother had a firm grip on her arm and Phoebe was left with no choice but to follow.

Five minutes. That was all she'd give whoever her mother had lined up for her, and then she'd leave. She'd shown her face and that would have to do. All she wanted was to go home and flop into bed and relive the glorious hours she'd spent in Alex's office.

Phoebe fixed a bland smile to her face and rummaged around in her head for her stash of stock responses.

'Here we are.'

She glanced round to where her mother was looking and her jaw dropped. She'd recognise that back anywhere. Only an hour ago she'd been raking her nails all over it.

Alex turned and a bubble of delight started bouncing around inside her. What on earth was he doing here?

'Phoebe, this is Alex Gilbert. He's a venture capitalist. Alex, this is my daughter Phoebe. She's in PR.' Her mother scrunched her nose up. 'But I'm hoping you might be able to make her see the light.'

'I'm delighted to meet you,' he said softly, a smile hovering at his lips. He dropped a kiss on her cheek and she swayed as she breathed in his scent.

'Me too.' Her voice sounded husky and she cleared her throat.

'Perhaps some of you will rub off on her.'

'I'll try and make sure that it does.'

Phoebe felt her cheeks flame. God, he was gorgeous. Dressed in a navy suit and pale blue shirt he looked dark and dishevelled and Phoebe felt her heart lurch.

'Remember. Rub.' Her mother patted him on the arm and made a little circular movement with her hand.

'How could I forget?'

Her mother blushed and giggled, then dashed off muttering, 'Charming. Quite charming.'

Phoebe stood there stunned. Since when had her mother blushed and giggled? 'Alex,' she said, when she eventually managed to find her voice. 'Gatecrashing again?'

Alex grinned. 'Why do you automatically assume that I receive so few invitations that I have to gatecrash parties?'

'You mean you actually have an invitation?'

'I do.'

'Who from?'

'Your brother.'

'Why didn't you mention it earlier when we—?' She broke off and went red.

'I didn't have it then. I rang your brother after I dropped you home.'

'Why?'

Alex shrugged and frowned slightly as if he couldn't work it out either. 'I was intrigued.'

'By what?'

'Your family. They sounded interesting.'

'You think?' she said, her eyebrows shooting up.

'Perhaps "interesting" isn't the right word. Your mother I'd describe as a force to be reckoned with.'

He sounded as if he thought that was a good thing. 'She's a Rottweiler in couture.'

Alex laughed. 'She's been telling me all about you.'

That really didn't sound good.

'Would you like to know what she said?'

Alex was standing so close she could feel the warmth coming off his body and she swayed involuntarily towards him. His gaze roamed over her face as if he was trying to memorise every millimetre. Phoebe's mouth went dry and her surroundings faded until all that she was aware of was a hot flame of desire burning deep inside her and a desperate need to kiss him.

'Not really,' she breathed, staring at his mouth. 'I'd much rather—'

'Hello, Ditz, darling.'

Phoebe jumped as the strident voice of her sister pierced the bubble that had enveloped them. She blinked as if coming out of a trance and caught the amused quizzical expression on his face. 'Ditz?' he murmured.

Phoebe couldn't believe it. Why now? After all these years?

'Family nickname,' she mumbled. 'A very, very *old* family nickname,' she added, swinging round and glaring at Camilla.

'Now that's something your mother didn't mention,' Alex said with a grin.

'Probably because most of us have forgotten about it. Haven't we?' she said pointedly to her sister.

But Camilla wasn't paying any attention. Instead she was staring at Alex with undisguised admiration. 'Who's this?'

Phoebe performed the introductions and watched as her sister gave Alex one of her most dazzling smiles before turning back to Phoebe.

'So how's the fluffy world of PR?'

Ah, how long had that taken? Thirty seconds? Camilla was slipping.

'Still fluffy.' She'd long since given up trying to justify what she did to her family. 'How's the matter-of-life-and-death world of cardiac surgery?'

'Busy. They're making me Head of Department.'

'Wow, congratulations.'

Camilla grinned. 'Thanks. Of course, it's going to be mad. So much pressure.' She laughed and shrugged and batted her eyelids in Alex's direction. 'You know sometimes I wish I had a job like Phoebe's. All glamour and long lunches. Parties and celebrities and gorgeous shoes.'

Phoebe felt the old familiar feeling of hurt swell up inside her. Calm down, she told herself. She doesn't mean it. She forced herself to smile and opened her mouth to mumble some sort of agreement.

'Actually, it's not all long lunches and parties, is it,

Phoebe?' Alex's voice sounded mild but she cast a quick astonished glance at him, and saw that his jaw had tightened and if anything he looked even bigger and taller than she remembered.

'What? Oh—er—no.'

'Are you in the same field?' asked Camilla.

'No. But I've seen her in action. And it's extremely hard work. Everyone only sees the results. They don't see the hours of effort put in. The constant juggling, the management, the organisation.' He smiled lazily but the look in his eye was razor sharp. 'It might not look like life and death, but reputations can hang in the balance and the way the balance goes can have a serious impact on those involved.'

Crikey. Even Phoebe was now seriously impressed by what she did.

His eyes pinned Camilla to the spot as he continued his ruthless attack. 'And who do you think it is who comes to the rescue of hospitals when a story appears about a patient dying on the operating table, or some misdemeanour during routine surgery?'

Was her ice-cool sister actually blushing?

'Yes—er—I see what you mean.'

'From my own experience Phoebe has been first class.' He shot her a look that curled her toes. Which particular experience was he talking about?

'My sister was about to lose everything.'

Good, the professional one. Not the personal one. Not the hot and steamy and fiery one. Excellent. Wasn't it?

Phoebe gave up trying to work out what she thought she ought to be thinking and decided to just wallow in his praise. Who knew when she'd get another chance?

'Phoebe worked her guts out to protect her reputation and restore her confidence and fix the problem. She pulled off an incredible piece of damage limitation when I wouldn't have had a clue what to do. And as the balance tipping the wrong way could well have sent my sister spiralling down into hell, I do rather consider it to be a matter of life and death.'

'Yes, well, she's always been the brightest one in the family.'

Phoebe's jaw dropped.

'Well, you are,' said Camilla tetchily. 'Oh, the rest of us might have the doctorates or the string of letters after our names, but you're the creative one, the only one who has any sort of emotional intelligence. To tell you the truth I'm rather envious.'

Whatever next? Would her father renounce all things capitalist and take up yoga?

'Right, who'd like a drink?' said Alex.

'God, yes, please,' said Phoebe with more haste than decorum.

Alex nodded and gave her a scorching smile. 'I'll be right back.' Then he turned on his heel.

'Wow,' said Camilla, staring at him with an unusually dazed expression on her face. 'I wouldn't mind having him on my side. He's quite something.'

'I wouldn't get too carried away,' Phoebe muttered, swirling with confusion and feeling all topsy-turvy inside. 'He probably bites the heads off Jelly Babies.'

As Alex stopped, turned and shot her a wicked grin Phoebe added 'hearing of a bat' to his list of talents. 'Actually,' he said, 'I swallow them whole.'

'Is she always like that?' asked Alex, thrusting a glass of champagne into Phoebe's hand and steering her through the French doors and into the relative peace of the garden.

'She doesn't mean it like it sounds,' said Phoebe, shrugging and following him into the shadows. 'I guess when you're doing something that saves lives, public relations does seem a little shallow.'

'Rubbish.'

'Well, I know that and you know that, but they're not as enlightened as we are.'

Alex dropped a swift hard kiss on her mouth that left her reeling. 'You are beautiful and brilliant. You look incredible in that dress, and you'd look even better out of it.'

Phoebe's heart thumped. 'Someone should bottle you.'

She took a sip of champagne. Did it really matter what her family thought of her job anyway? She'd been doing it for years. She was good at it and she loved it. If she'd been truly concerned she'd have given into the pressure and become a corporate lawyer years ago. She wasn't going to give up her career, so it was high time she got over her fear of letting them down.

'What happens to the people whose businesses fail, Alex?'

'Those that are determined enough pick themselves up and start again.'

'As simple as that?'

'It's far from simple, but it's what I did.'

'Really?' He'd lost everything? 'When?'

'A while ago. In the early days.'

'What happened?'

'I made a bad judgement call.'

'Nice to know it happens to you too.'

He gave her a small smile. 'Only once. That was enough. How about that dinner?'

'Sounds great.'

CHAPTER FOURTEEN

'ARE YOU GOING to sit behind that paper *all* morning?' Jo prodded the pages of Alex's paper and made reading the rest of the article on the new piece of technology launched by the latest company he'd invested in impossible.

'That was my plan.'

'I've hardly seen you all week.'

'I've been working.'

Her eyes held a mischievous light he didn't entirely trust. 'Evenings too?'

No. Alex had spent every evening since her parents' party with Phoebe. Most lunchtimes too. He couldn't seem to get enough of her. 'Some.'

'But you must have found time to eat? Take the air?'

He frowned. What was Jo talking about? He scoured her face but couldn't find anything other than mild curiosity in her expression. His sister obviously wanted to chat. Presumably that was why she'd suggested breakfast. And as he'd been keen to find out what spending time with his sister without being racked with guilt might be like, he'd agreed. So it was high time he started doing exactly that.

Suddenly realising he felt lighter than he had in

years, Alex grinned, folded the paper and set it on the table. 'Sorry. Bad habit. How are things coming along for the launch?'

'Brilliantly.' Jo beamed. 'I've finally finished the collection and there's not a drop of glue in sight.'

'Thank heavens for that.'

'I can't believe it's only a week away.'

'I'm very proud of you, you know.'

'I know. I'm kind of proud of me too. Although I couldn't have done it without Phoebe.'

'Probably not.'

'Hah,' said Jo triumphantly. 'You see. I told you she'd be brilliant. It's odd, though,' she added after a little pause, spooning sugar into the cup and idly stirring her coffee.

Alex waited for her to continue but Jo appeared to have gone off into her own little world. The relentless clink of her spoon against the side of the cup started to set his teeth on edge. 'What's odd?'

Jo blinked and looked up at him. 'She's different.'

Alex already knew that. Why else would he have broken the vow he'd made years ago never to see the same woman more than a couple of times? The fact that he'd not only broken it but hadn't wasted a moment agonising over it should have scared the living daylights out of him.

Instead, while he wasn't exactly shouting it from the rooftops, the idea of having Phoebe around a bit longer didn't have him running for the hills. In fact it made him feel warm and remarkably content. Especially when he thought about the delightful manner in which she'd woken him up this morning before telling him he ought to go home before she forgot where it was.

'Different in what way?' he said, taking care not to appear too interested in Jo's answer.

'She has a sort of spring in her step.'

'Does she?'

'I wonder what put it there.'

Alex's eyes narrowed in suspicion. This was no innocent conversation. 'What are you implying?'

'Me?' she said with breezy nonchalance. 'Nothing. But now that you mention it, I was wondering if it could have anything to do with this.'

Jo reached into her bag and dropped a magazine onto the table.

Alex raised an eyebrow and wondered where his sister was heading with this. 'A gossip magazine? I wouldn't have thought that was your sort of thing.'

'It wouldn't be normally. But when I hear that my brother is splashed all over it I suddenly find it essential reading. Pages six, seven, eight and nine.' Jo took a sip of coffee and grinned. 'Just for the record, because I know you don't need it, I approve.'

As he drew the magazine towards him wariness gripped him, and every one of his muscles tensed.

He flicked to the relevant section and as he began to read he felt the blood chill in his veins.

The headlines insinuating that the City's most eligible bachelor might finally have been snared by the current darling of the PR world swam before his eyes.

His heart pounding, he scanned the text and by the time he'd reached the final word the last flicker of warmth inside him died. Quotes littered the article. Phoebe was well aware of what he thought of journalists yet she'd obviously spoken to this one.

Alex knew his expression hadn't altered an inch. He'd perfected it to see him win out during the toughest negotiations. He'd never have thought he'd need to use it to conceal the winding effect of the crushing weight of betrayal.

A cold sweat broke out all over his skin as disillusionment and searing disappointment engulfed him. He pushed his chair back, not caring that all eyes in the cafe swivelled round at the grating sound of metal against stone.

'Alex?' Jo stared up at him in surprise, but he barely noticed.

Numbness started spreading through him, reaching out to wind itself around every cell of his body and gradually he began to feel absolutely nothing. 'I have to go.'

The last three days had been fabulous, Phoebe thought, taking the stack of papers and a steaming cup of coffee into the garden. A long delicious lazy dream and one she hoped she'd never have to wake up from. She'd signed up three new clients. She'd finalised the arrangements for Jo's launch. And she'd had more dynamite sex than she'd ever thought possible. She felt as if she were floating, which for a five foot nine generously proportioned woman was an unusual experience.

See, she told herself, aware that she was smiling smugly and not caring one little bit. Combining a fling with her career *was* possible. All it took was discipline and an ability to compartmentalise.

And the right man.

Alex, in fact.

Phoebe stopped suddenly in the middle of the patio and coffee slopped onto the stone. Uh oh. That didn't sound good. She put the papers and the mug on a table beside the sun lounger and tried to imagine not seeing Alex ever again. Not kissing him, not being able to stroke that magnificent body, not talking and laughing late into the night. Not having him deep inside her and sending her soaring.

Pain gripped her chest and her brain actually ached.

Oh, God, she had to watch it. She gave herself a quick shake and told herself not to be so stupid. There were bound to be hundreds of 'right' men out there. Thousands, even. What was the global population these days? Billions?

Phew. She had nothing to worry about. Alex was simply the right man for this particular stage in her life. That was all.

She'd barely finished the first article when the doorbell rang. With a sigh she dropped the newspaper on the grass and levered herself to her feet. How typical was that? Just when she'd been hoping for a stretch of uninterrupted peace and quiet in which to digest the papers and then gear herself up for meeting Alex later.

She padded through her house to the front door and peered through the spyhole. At the sight of Alex on her doorstep, her heart lurched and then galloped with delight. Had he not been able to wait until tonight?

Phoebe threw the door open and knew she ought to be playing it cool, but the idiotic smile she could feel curving her lips wasn't cool in the slightest.

However as she took in his dark, tight expression her smile faded and a flicker of alarm sprinted down her spine. Because the man looming on her doorstep with a thunderous look on his face and a fierce glint in his eyes bore little resemblance to the man who'd made love to her so thoroughly this morning.

'Alex? What's wrong?' When she'd left him, he'd been going to have breakfast with Jo. What could possibly have happened in the couple of hours since she'd last seen him?

Alex didn't answer, just barged his way into the hall and disappeared into the sitting room. Utterly bewildered, Phoebe raced after him and then slammed to a halt when she saw him standing, feet apart, with his back to the window, his massive frame radiating tension and fury.

'This is what's wrong,' he snarled and tossed a magazine on the table.

Phoebe stared at it as if it were a bomb he'd just dropped. Her heart sank. Oh, no. Please let it not be another story about Jo.

'It starts on page six.'

With trembling fingers Phoebe picked it up and swallowed back a surge of nausea. She didn't think Jo's career would survive another salacious story.

The pages were stuck together. Or maybe she was shaking so much it just seemed that way. But eventually she got to page six.

Her heart thumping with apprehension, Phoebe scanned the headline and her initial reaction was one of relief. Thank goodness. The story had nothing to do with Jo.

But as she read further the apprehension flooded back. The article was a dodgy blend of fact and supposition. About her and Alex. It detailed the times and location of their dates and hinted at the possible professional benefits such a relationship might give her. Indignation spiked through her alarm. As if she'd ever take advantage of their affair like that, even assuming that the supposed 'benefits' did exist.

Nevertheless it was awful. No wonder Alex was in such a foul mood. He hated any invasion of his privacy.

And those photos… Phoebe shuddered at the thought that someone had been watching them. As they kissed beneath the pergola at the roof gardens. While they were walking in the park during lunch a couple of days ago. In the middle of dinner at that cosy little Italian round the corner from his flat.

But even so, she thought, Alex must be used to seeing himself in the press, so why was he reacting so strongly about something that was so clearly fabricated and badly patched together?

'Nothing to say?'

Phoebe blinked and jumped in shock at the icy steel in his voice. 'Why would I have anything to say?'

'What? No hint of shame? No apology?'

She went very still. Confusion swilled around her head. 'What do I have to be ashamed of and what do I have to apologise for?' she said carefully.

Alex shoved his hands through his hair and let out a bitter laugh. 'You really are unbelievable.'

Phoebe gaped. What the hell was going on? 'Alex, I know how you feel about your privacy and I can imagine you're not particularly pleased about this—'

'Not particularly pleased?' he echoed, in a dangerously soft voice.

An inexplicable sense of dread seeped into her. 'Now you're scaring me.'

His eyes glittered and turned as dark and hard as granite. 'You tip the press off about our…' he paused as if searching for the right word '…our liaison,' he said eventually, 'and you accuse me of scaring you.'

'Is that what you think?' she said in horrified disbelief.

'It does seem a logical conclusion.'

'Why would I tip off the press about us?'

Alex's jaw tightened. 'I have no idea. Publicity? It wouldn't be the first time someone's used my name to bring in business.'

Phoebe felt the blood drain from her face. Her legs shook and she stumbled back, not stopping until she hit the bookcase. She gripped the edges and could feel her knuckles turning white with the effort of keeping herself upright. 'You arrogant bastard,' she breathed, scarcely unable to believe what was going on. 'Firstly, I don't need to use your name to bring in business. I'm doing exceptionally well by myself. And secondly, are you honestly suggesting I'd be capable of stooping that low?'

Alex glowered. 'You said yourself you'd do anything for your career.'

'Not this. Never something like this.'

'Read it again, Phoebe,' he said, picking up the magazine and thrusting it at her. 'You're quoted.'

How could she possibly be quoted? She hadn't spoken to anyone about her relationship with Alex, let alone a tabloid journalist.

She read it again, the words swimming before her eyes. And suddenly her shock gave way to anger. 'No, I'm not, you jerk. "A source close to Ms Jackson" does not mean me. It means they've made it up.'

'Right,' he said, his sarcasm striking her straight in the chest. 'And they'd do that because they're not worried about libel.'

Her anger turned into incandescence. 'This is a scandal sheet. They couldn't care less about libel. Their fabrications sell so many extra copies that they simply pay the injured parties off.'

'Do you seriously expect me to believe that?'

What? 'You should. It's the truth. But I suppose you think I lined the photographer up too.'

'It wouldn't surprise me.'

As Phoebe realised that Alex genuinely believed what he was saying she felt as if he'd thumped her in the stomach. Surely he must know she'd never go to the press with any information about him or their affair. So why was he doing this? And why did it hurt quite so much? The backs of her eyes stung and she swallowed back the lump in her throat. 'Don't you trust me at all?'

The look on Alex's face darkened and Phoebe felt her legs give way.

'Oh, my God,' she breathed in horror as she sank into an armchair. 'You don't, do you? You don't trust me an inch.'

A muscle throbbed in his jaw. 'It's nothing personal. I don't trust anyone.'

Nothing personal? *Nothing personal?* So why was her heart splintering? Why did she feel as if she were cracking open? She wanted to pummel him in the chest. Scratch his eyes out and pull him to pieces and hurt him as much as he was hurting her. 'Why not? What happened? Did an ex-girlfriend run to the press with a kiss and tell?'

'My ex-business partner ran to Bermuda with the contents of the company's bank account.'

Oh. Phoebe went very still.

'You once asked me about why I now work alone,' he bit out. 'Well, that's why.'

She could see that. But still… 'Alex, I'm not going to run off with your fortune.'

He raked his hands through his hair and his features suddenly twisted with such pain that Phoebe thought he was ill. And then his anger seemed to drain away and he looked wearier than she'd ever seen him. He slumped into a chair and rubbed a hand over his face.

'Rob was the boyfriend the article in the paper mentioned,' he said bleakly. 'The one who bullied Jo and put her into hospital.'

Oh, God. 'What happened?'

'We made a lot of money very quickly. I invested in property and other things. He spent a fortune on drugs and gambling.'

Alex's voice was flat, as if he were reciting the weather forecast. But his face was white and tight and she'd never seen such turmoil in his eyes.

'He met Jo and they started dating behind my back.'

Phoebe's heart squeezed and there wasn't a thing she could do to stop it. 'Why?'

Alex shrugged. 'She was sixteen. Rob was twenty-six. I guess they knew I wouldn't have approved. They went out for a year.' His voice cracked. 'A whole year and I didn't have a clue.'

Phoebe didn't know what to say. There was nothing she could say.

'The business was going through a rapid expansion and I was too engrossed to notice. Too focused on making money. I didn't notice how thin she was getting. And I didn't pay enough attention to Rob's increasingly erratic behaviour.'

No wonder he'd spent the last five years racked with guilt. Part of her wanted to jump up and take him in her arms. But the pain of his accusations was still too raw and she made herself stay where she was.

'I caught him slapping her once.'

Phoebe's hands flew to her mouth. 'What did you do?'

'I acquired a scar and the bump on my nose. Rob came off worse. He ended up in Casualty. A week later he disappeared and I discovered he'd cleared out our accounts.' He shrugged. 'I thought I knew him inside out. Turns out I didn't know him at all. So if I do have an issue with trust I think it's kind of understandable, don't you?'

Phoebe's heart wrenched. 'Absolutely. Five years ago. But now? Still?'

'It doesn't go away.'

'The guilt has.'

Alex frowned. 'Maybe.'

'I'm not Rob. I would never betray you, nor intentionally let you down.'

'You can't know that. I can't know that.'

Frustration suddenly flared inside her. Why was he being so stubborn about this? 'Well, like it or not, I think you do trust me.'

Alex tensed. 'I don't. I can't.'

'You can and you do. Why else would you have allowed me to work with Jo when all your instincts fought against it?'

'Because you were the best person for the job.'

'Has that ever influenced you in the past?'

'I don't allow my personal feelings to get in the way of business.'

Phoebe let out a hollow laugh. 'Really? I bet you've let that sense of betrayal influence every single decision you've made since.'

'I wouldn't be so short-sighted.'

'Yet you were so quick to think the worst of me.'

Alex went very still.

'You know,' Phoebe continued, chewing on her lip,

'I've made mistakes—plenty of them—but I've learned from them. Made myself stronger. You've let yours eat away at you. You once accused me of hiding, but who's hiding now?'

'I'm not hiding from anything.'

'Are you sure about that?'

'Absolutely.' Alex got to his feet and shrugged. 'Like I said, it's nothing personal.'

The cool indifference of his tone sliced through her and Phoebe felt as if a steel band had suddenly wrapped around her chest and were slowly crushing the air out of her lungs.

She'd thought she could handle this, that a casual fling was exactly what she wanted. But the power he had to wound her, the depth of the cut, told her more clearly than any number of words that she'd been fooling herself. She didn't want a mere fling. She wanted a proper relationship and she was convinced they'd been heading in that direction. But Alex clearly didn't.

Phoebe felt her heart harden. What an utter idiot she'd been. Well, not any more. 'If it's nothing personal,' she said quietly, 'then I think you should leave.'

Alex leaned back against the front door, closed his eyes and waited for relief to pour over him.

Because Phoebe was wrong. Utterly wrong. About everything. He didn't trust her. Or anyone. And so what if he *had* let the events of five years ago influence pretty much every decision he'd ever made? Look at the way Jo had turned out. And look at the way he'd picked himself up and rebuilt his fortune. Neither of those things would have happened if he'd allowed himself to trust anyone other than himself.

Even getting round to trusting himself, when he'd screwed up so spectacularly, had taken a heck of a lot of work. He'd had to shut himself off, hurl himself into some sort of emotional Siberia. Which was just fine. He was perfectly happy with that. Emotions were messy and he didn't need mess in his life ever again.

Alex pushed himself off the door and strode down the path. He couldn't afford to trust anyone. He'd never stand back and give anyone one hundred per cent autonomy. Never had and never would.

Except Phoebe.

He stopped, his hand on the gate, his heart suddenly pounding.

She'd been right. He did trust her. The realisation thundered into his head and with it came another flash of insight.

Maybe it was more than that.

One of the photos that accompanied the article flew into his head. He'd met Phoebe for lunch. They'd gone for a walk in the park. He'd slung his arm round her shoulders and they'd been laughing about something.

But it had been the look on his face and in his eyes that had put the fear of God into him. And then when he'd thought she'd betrayed him, he'd felt as if he'd been punched with such force he'd reeled back and crashed against the wall.

Suddenly something inside him collapsed. He was so tired of being cold, of not allowing himself to feel. He was tired of empty, meaningless flings. What he had with Phoebe wasn't empty or meaningless. He'd shared more with her in the past week both emotionally and physically than he had with anyone ever before.

And he'd just thrown it back in her face. He'd seen

the hurt in her eyes when he'd hurled his accusations at her, and he'd ignored it. Too consumed by his own torment to think clearly.

Alex's heart thumped. The knowledge that he'd made the most horrendous mistake tore at his gut. A dreadful feeling of panic spread through him and a tight knot formed in his chest.

He had to undo the damage he'd done.

He swung back and rang the doorbell. When there was no answer he knelt down and pushed open the letter box.

'Phoebe?'

'Go away!'

He guessed he deserved that but she wasn't getting rid of him that easily. 'I want to talk to you.'

'There's nothing left to say.'

He hammered on the door. 'Open the door.'

'No.'

'Please. I'm on my knees. I feel like an idiot.'

'Good.'

'I'll sit on the doorbell if I have to.'

Silence. Then the door flung open and the relief that he'd been waiting for earlier finally came.

'Fine. What?'

Phoebe's face was white and drawn, her eyes were huge and glassy and his heart wrenched at the realisation that it was all because of him.

'I'm sorry I accused you of going to the press. I know you'd never have done that.'

'So why did you?'

'Instinct. Habit. You're right. I *have* let mistrust influence my decisions over the years. But apparently not any more.'

'Apparently?'

The lack of emotion in her voice rocked his confidence and sent a chill running down his spine. 'I think I do trust you. And it *is* personal. You're the only person I've ever not worried about letting me down.'

A faint light flickered in her eyes. 'And?'

Alex frowned. 'And what?' If he was being honest, he'd been expecting her to fall into his arms, draw him back inside and let him prove to her how sorry he was for being such an idiot. 'Doesn't it make any difference?'

'To what?'

Fear clawed at his stomach and a sense of panic began to spread through him. 'Well, to us. Our affair.'

'Not really.' She sighed deeply. 'Alex. Look. Please go. I don't want this and I don't want to see you any more. So please. Just go.'

The door clicked shut and Alex reeled. For a moment he just stared at it in shock. Then a searing pain began to burn in his chest as he realised that whatever had existed between them, whatever it might have turned into, he'd destroyed it.

CHAPTER FIFTEEN

PHOEBE SPENT THE rest of the weekend wandering around listlessly, her head filled with thoughts of Alex. Every second of every minute, day and night. Where he was, what he might be doing, who he might be seeing.

So much for thinking she didn't want him. Didn't need him. She felt as if she'd suddenly lost a vital organ. She shouldn't have shut the door on him. She should have taken what she thought he might have been offering: the chance to resume their relationship and get back to the hot sex.

So why hadn't she? Why had no-strings-attached sex suddenly seemed so meaningless? When had it become not enough?

Over the course of the weekend Phoebe drove herself slowly mental with self-analysis and self recrimination. Tormenting herself with those annoying 'what if's and 'if only's.

By Sunday evening she was in such a state that she had no idea why or how she ended up standing on the doorstep of her parents' house. All she knew was that she was climbing the walls of her own place and she had nowhere else to go.

Her mother opened the door, her father standing just behind her, and for a second they both stared at her in surprise. 'Phoebe?' said her mother, recovering first and peering at her closely. 'Are you all right?'

'Fine,' Phoebe said, then promptly burst into tears.

Unable to stop the torrent that streamed down her cheeks and the racking sobs that shook her body, Phoebe let herself be pulled into the house and ushered into the kitchen. In the midst of her misery, she felt her mother gently push her down into a chair and wait while she bawled her eyes out.

'Sorry about that,' she said with a watery smile once she'd cried herself out and could actually find her voice. 'Where did Dad go?'

'His study. Tears aren't really his thing.'

'Nor yours.' She pulled a string of tissues out of the box her mother had thrust in front of her.

Her mother frowned. 'Well, no. But I've never seen you cry. Not even when you fell out of that tree. I was worried.'

Worried? Phoebe hiccupped and blew her nose. Her eyes stung and her throat was raw. 'I don't really know why I'm here,' she said hoarsely.

Her mother sat down on the opposite side of the kitchen table. 'Phoebe, I know I'm not the most…demonstrative…of mothers, but if you tell me what's wrong, I might be able to help.'

'I don't know what's wrong.'

'Is it work?'

'No. Work's fine.'

'Is it a man?'

'Yes. No.' She wailed in frustration and dropped her head on the kitchen table. 'I don't know.'

'The man in the magazine?'

Her head shot up. 'Don't tell me you saw that as well?'

'Your sister told me I might like to see a copy. Especially since I'd introduced you to him at our party.'

Phoebe groaned and buried her face in her hands. 'I met him before that. I work with his sister.'

'Is she in venture capital too?'

She glanced up and couldn't help smiling at the hope in her mother's voice. 'I'm afraid she designs handbags.'

'Oh well, never mind. Is any of the article true?'

'Some. Mum, what do I do? I can't eat. I can't sleep. I'm a wreck and I'm worried it's going to affect my work.'

'I can't pretend to understand PR, and you know it's not what we'd have chosen for you, but we brought you up to have belief in yourself. That whatever course of action you take, you have the confidence that it's the right one because you've given it thought. Weighed up the pros and cons.'

How could she weigh up any pros or cons when she didn't have a clue about anything?

'I'm very proud of everything you've achieved, you know.'

'Really?' she sniffed.

Her mother nodded thoughtfully. 'I don't worry about you nearly as much as I worry about the other two.'

'Why?'

'I always knew you'd be all right. Your siblings, on the other hand, are harder.'

Bewilderment muddled her brain. 'I always thought you admired their ruthlessness. The way they don't let emotion dictate to them.'

Her mother shook her head gently. 'Emotion isn't a bad thing.'

Wasn't it? 'It scares me. Alex scares me. He distorts my judgement and wipes away my self-control.'

'That's not his fault. He seems like a nice man.'

Huh. 'Nice isn't the word. He's manipulative and arrogant and annoying and…' Gorgeous, protective, passionate.

'Yet you love him anyway.'

Phoebe froze. 'No, I don't.'

Her mother shot her a shrewd look and Phoebe blinked. She couldn't be in love with Alex. Could she? Her mind raced. 'Oh, God. I think I do.'

'You think?'

'I don't know. I mean… I've never been in love before. How do I know if that's what this…thing… is?'

'How does he make you feel?'

'Like I could rule the world.'

'So what are you doing here?'

'I told him I never wanted to see him again.'

'Oh dear,' said her mother. 'I can't imagine that would have gone down very well.'

'It was his fault. He accused me of using our relationship to further my business.'

'Oh.' Her mother frowned.

'Quite.'

'Then you need to talk. Communication is the thing. Give him the chance to explain. To apologise.'

'I did and he did.'

'And you still turned him away? I'm lost.'

'So am I,' Phoebe wailed. 'Totally and utterly lost. I hate that my mental stability depends on him. I hate that he can do this to me.'

'Phoebe, darling, have faith in yourself. Loving someone and marrying them doesn't mean you have to give up your independence. And so what if it does?

At times, you'll have to rely on him. At others he'll rely on you.'

Phoebe hiccupped. What would it be like to have someone to lean on from time to time? Someone strong and dependable. Someone to protect you when you were attacked, to pick you up when you fell. Someone like Alex. Her heart began to thud.

'If he's The One, it doesn't make you vulnerable and it doesn't mean you're any weaker.'

Phoebe gave a shaky laugh. 'I can't believe you're talking about "The One".'

'What do you think your father is?'

Her jaw dropped.

'Don't look so surprised. I wouldn't have given up my own independence for anyone else. Is Alex The One?'

'I think he might be.' Her heart leapt and then plummeted. 'But I'm not sure I am.'

Her mother tilted her head. 'Did you ever look at the pictures in that magazine?'

'Of course.'

'Properly?'

'Not that closely.'

Her mother got up and rummaged around in the stack of papers on the counter. 'Look again,' she said, opening the magazine and putting it in front of Phoebe.

Phoebe ignored the grainy photo that had been taken while she and Alex had been kissing beneath the pergola and concentrated on the picture in the restaurant.

An empty bottle of wine sat on the red and white checked tablecloth. They'd been talking and laughing and desperately trying to keep their hands off each other. The way they hadn't been able to hold back any longer and had rushed back to his house for a night of passion made her breathless just thinking about it. The dreamy expression on her face… The light in her eye… It was obvious to anyone with half a brain cell that she was nuts about him. Up until now, she'd clearly been lacking even that half a brain cell.

'What am I looking for?'

'Just look.'

She huffed and switched to the picture of the two of them strolling in the park. Alex's arm was around her shoulders, pulling her into him and she was smiling up at him.

She leaned closer. Oh, goodness. Phoebe's heart began to thump crazily. The expression on his face…the look in his eyes… Exactly the same as hers had been in the restaurant.

'He adores you.'

Phoebe went very cold. The image of his face, white and stunned, when she'd told him to go away for good flashed into her head. Maybe he'd have told her if she'd let him. But she hadn't given him the chance. She'd just pushed him away.

She began to shake uncontrollably. What had she done? *What had she done?*

'You'd better go and find him.'

Finding Alex was easier said than done. He seemed to have disappeared off the face of the earth.

Phoebe staked out his house but he didn't show up. His secretary must have known where he'd gone, but if she did she was keeping the information to herself, despite Phoebe's best attempts at trying to wheedle it out of her. And Jo was as much in the dark as she was.

It was driving Phoebe demented.

Now she'd acknowledged that she was in fact in love with Alex all she wanted to do was tell him. Get down on her knees and grovel. Persuade him to admit he loved her too and see if they couldn't make something of whatever they'd had before.

Simple. Or it would be if she only knew where he was.

Maybe she could hire an investigator. Whoever Alex had used to check her out had produced incredible results in a breathtakingly short period of time. She could do the same.

Or perhaps she'd resort to desperate measures and contact each and every one of the people who'd attended his party on the island. Someone was bound to know where he was.

What the hell. She was desperate. This was no time for dignity. She'd beg if she had to. She opened the relevant file on her computer and then went very still.

A flashbulb went off in her head. Her heart pounded and she felt more alive than she had in days. That was where Alex was.

He'd escaped. To the Ilha das Palmeiras.

CHAPTER SIXTEEN

PHOEBE WATCHED JIM'S boat as it grew smaller and smaller and felt sicker now than at any point in her journey to Alex's island. And that was despite the turbulent flight and the even choppier boat ride.

Her stomach was churning and adrenalin pounded through her veins. With her nerves rocketing, Phoebe turned and stared up at the house. Her heart thumped. Alex was in there. Her future happiness was in there. Hopefully.

But what sort of mood would she find him in? Would he be pleased to see her? Or horrified? Would he even be prepared to listen to her when she'd so recklessly pushed him away?

Doubts began to assail her from all sides. Maybe she should have called Maggie and established that Alex was in fact on the island. Maybe she should have waited until he got back to London, as he surely would have had to have done at some point.

Oh God. She hadn't weighed up the pros and cons of this course of action at all. She'd never acted so rashly. But then she'd never needed to.

Phoebe swallowed back the nerves and told herself that a faint heart had never achieved anything.

The spatter of great fat raindrops galvanised her into action. She hauled her bag onto her shoulder and raced up the steps to the house. She reached the front door just as the heavens opened.

Her heart thundered with anticipation and exertion. She was so close. Just a few more minutes and she'd know her fate one way or another.

She turned the handle and pulled, but nothing happened. She tried again, rattling it back and forth, but it was locked. Panic swept through her. She bashed on the door with her fist and shouted Alex's name. But there was no answer and no sound of footsteps striding towards the door.

Alex wasn't there. So where was he? *Where was he?* Could she have got it wrong? Was he in fact back in London? In the arms of another woman, one who wouldn't blow hot and cold and push him away. Her heart clenched. No, she wouldn't believe that. Alex wouldn't do that. Not if he loved her.

But supposing she'd read too much into that photo? Fancied she'd seen something that didn't exist simply because that was what she wanted to see? Or what if he *had* felt something for her but as she'd rejected him had decided that that was that and had moved on?

Wind lashed at the palm trees. The rain turned torrential and plastered her clothes to her body. Phoebe shivered and rubbed her arms. Her knees shook. Her heart twisted. No. She wouldn't let that happen. If that was the case, she'd just have to do everything in her power to get him to love her again. She was *not* going to fail.

She cupped her hands to the glass to see if there were any signs he'd been there. But she could see nothing except the blurred outline of the Jeep on the other side of the house.

Phoebe's heart leapt with encouragement. Alex *was* here. Somewhere. And it was up to her to find him.

Thunder crackled above her and lightning sliced through the sky. She dropped her bag and raced across the terrace. She tore along the paths, searching desperately, hoping wildly, not caring that rain sluiced over her, drenching her clothes, her skin, her hair. She stumbled to the top of the steps that led down to the sea and frantically scoured the beach. She looked for him until her body ached inside and out. But with every passing minute, hope faded.

Because there was no sign of him.

Wherever he was, Alex didn't want to be found.

As the realisation dawned Phoebe's energy drained and her heart broke. Utterly defeated and exhausted, she felt a flood of emotion crash over her. Despair, misery, hopelessness all piled in on top of each other and she knew she'd never felt pain like it. Tears mingled with the rain and she dashed them away with the backs of her hands.

She'd been so sure she'd find him. So sure she'd be able to fix the mess she'd made of things. And the knowledge that she'd failed was agonising.

The dark stormy grey of the huge waves rolling towards the shore reminded her of Alex's eyes the last time she'd seen him, and as memories cascaded into her head she felt yet more misery well up inside her.

Oh, God, would it ever end?

She felt as weak and vulnerable as a little boat being battered by the waves, completely at the mercy of something far too powerful to comprehend.

And then her heart skipped a beat.

Hang on.

She snapped her gaze to the jetty.

Alex's yacht was gone.

She'd been in such a state when she'd got off Jim's boat that she hadn't noticed, but it wasn't there.

Hope flared in her chest. And then her heart began to pound. He must be out there. Somewhere in the vastness of the ocean. In the middle of this raging storm.

Fear clutched at her breast and obliterated the relief. What if something happened to him? He was out there because of her. She started to shake as pure terror began to flood through her. She hadn't even told him she loved him.

Phoebe tore down the steps and charged onto the jetty. She scanned the sea, but the visibility was getting worse and she could see nothing but great mountains of water.

Her mind began to race. Her imagination went into overdrive. Scenario after scenario ripped through her head and she filled with the agonising awareness that she could well have lost him.

As wretchedness scythed through her and a wave washed over her Phoebe's legs gave way and she crumpled into a heap.

Even the weather had turned against him, thought Alex grimly, dredging up every ounce of strength he possessed to keep the yacht upright.

He'd been out in worse, but not much. He braced himself for yet another wave that bore down on him. A whoosh of water crashed over the stern and as the boat groaned and creaked Alex staggered beneath the force of it. His muscles stung with the effort of holding the tiller steady. Every bone in his body was battered and bruised and he could feel a cut on his cheek.

He should have checked the forecast. He should have turned back at the first hint of rain. He should have been watching the wave patterns and paying attention to the darkening of the skies. He should have remembered that storms in this part of the world tended to set in in a matter of minutes.

But then there were lots of things he should have done over the past week.

He should have realised the depths of his feelings for Phoebe sooner, and he should have stayed in London and insisted on hammering things out with her instead of running off to lick his wounds here.

Because what good had that done him? None at all. All he'd done here was sit and brood and ache for her. At least, he thought as adrenalin coursed through his veins, it proved he could still feel something.

If he ever got back to the island alive, and right now the chances of that happening were looking pretty slim, he'd head straight back to London. He'd wine and dine Phoebe and woo her properly until her resistance buckled under the relentless pressure. Once he'd got her back into his bed and rendered her all soft and warm and amenable, he'd set about making her love him as much as he'd realised he loved her. However long it took. He didn't care. He was fully prepared to devote the rest of his life to the endeavour.

And as that was the case, he thought determinedly, he would not be consigning himself to a watery grave any time soon. His heart pumping wildly with renewed energy, Alex hoisted the storm sail, set the stern to the of which stood an array of humming computers. Five screens flickered with constantly changing CCTV feeds of the school's corridors and fenceline. A guard in the all-black uniform of Talos Security sat in front of them, his eyes moving from one image to the next. Over his shoulder, Gray could see busy corridors and the common room, crowded with students. That switched suddenly, replaced by the dining hall where the staff were preparing for dinner, draping white linen cloths over the tables.

More guards sat in front of other computers or gathered in small groups, talking quietly. One wore headphones, and talked steadily into a microphone.

"This is Gold Command," Julia announced. "The new headquarters for security at Cimmeria Academy. Raj sent a crew down this morning to upgrade the security system. They've been installing more tech all day. More equipment is coming this evening. By tomorrow, we'll have every inch covered."

Gray watched the images flickering on the screen. Someone was playing the piano in the common room, then the screen flickered and showed the busy main hallway, with students walking in groups, laughing and talking.

"I wanted you to see this so you could understand that last night won't happen again." Julia's voice was firm. "We are all working as hard as we can to make sure of that."

At the far end of the room, Allie and Carter stood talking to Zoe Glass and two guards. Allie waved them over.

"Welcome to our new HQ, Gray," the headmistress said, before turning to Julia. "Jules, there's someone here who wants to speak with you."

The two guards turned around.

"Hey," Riley said, his broad, tanned face breaking into a grin. "It's been a while."

"Bloody hell." Julia stared at the man who had been her Talos partner before she left London. "When did you get here?"

"Twenty minutes ago," he said. "Heard you could use some spare hands."

The two of them exchanged a quick, awkward hug, patting each other's shoulders a little too hard.

Riley turned to Gray and held out his hand. "It's nice to see you looking so well. Settling in OK?"

She nodded, shaking his hand a bit stiffly. She didn't know Riley as well as Julia, but she liked him. He'd always been there when she needed him although she got the impression he didn't always approve of her.

"It's great," she said. "Thank you."

"Except for last night, I guess?" he said.

Her smile faded. "Yeah. Except for that."

"Well, that's why we're here." He winked at Julia. "They've called in the real guards at last, eh?"

She rolled her eyes, but Gray could tell she was glad to see him.

"Once you're settled in we should have a coffee," Julia told him. "I'll bring you up to speed."

The guard next to him was listening to this exchange with amused interest. She had a curvy figure, thick dark hair, and animated brown eyes.

"Oh, hey, I forgot." Riley turned to her. "This is Cameron Perez. We worked together on the investigation in London. Raj sent her to help out."

"I've heard a lot about you," Cameron told Julia. "Riley and Raj are big fans of yours."

"It's a lie," Riley deadpanned.

When Cameron smiled, deep dimples appeared in her cheeks, giving her an impish look that Gray instantly liked.

"Well, I hope I don't disappoint." Julia said it mildly, but Gray could tell she was flattered.

Cameron turned her attention to Gray. "I've heard a lot about you, too. I'm going to do my best to help get the guys who are after you."

"OK," Allie interrupted, drawing them back to the matter at hand. "The security is in place. We have fresh recruits. We've been throwing around a lot of ideas – whether we should keep the school open or close it down. If we keep it open, should we have business as usual, or change things up?" She glanced around the circle of faces. "I think we're all agreed that the school should stay open, and classes should continue as usual?"

Everyone nodded.

"Winter Break starts in just a few days," Allie explained to Julia and Gray. "After that we have a long break when we can take a look at security and make sure we're doing everything we can to keep the students safe. It doesn't make sense to shut down before then." She drew a breath. "The other big issue, though, is what to do about the Winter Ball. After what happened last night, I propose we cancel it."

"I agree," Julia said. "Security will be a nightmare."

Riley and Cameron looked between the two of them. "OK, fill us in," Riley said. "What's a Winter Ball?"

C J DAUGHERTY

"It's a big fundraiser held every year on the last day of the term," Julia explained. "Alumni come back for it. Lots of bigwigs. It raises a lot of money for the school and the charities it supports."

"How many people?" Cameron asked.

"We're expecting a hundred and fifty this year," Allie said.

Riley gave a low whistle. "That would be a lot of people to watch."

"It's not just how many people," Julia told him. "It's which people. The prime minister is invited, members of Parliament, junior royalty, lots of CEOs. It's a big deal."

"And it's happening next week?" Cameron looked doubtful.

"I think we should cancel it," Carter said, decisively. "Too risky."

"You don't want to be obvious, though. People would ask questions," Riley said. "We're trying to keep all of this low key. Has it ever been cancelled before?"

"I don't know." Allie glanced at Carter, who gave a slight shrug. "We could come up with an excuse. Problems with the heating or something."

Gray listened as they talked through the different ways they could cancel it, how they would handle it. It was odd – until this moment, she hadn't thought much about the ball. She hadn't even thought she would go, though her mother had made her bring a dress just in case. Now the thought of cancelling it made her unbearably sad.

It was mostly an adult affair – only senior students got to go, and it was a big privilege. They'd all been looking forward to

Alex tilted his head and stared at her for what seemed like hours. 'No,' he said eventually.

'No?' Phoebe suddenly felt very cold. Oh, God. Maybe she *had* got it all wrong. Maybe it was way too late.

'I don't want an affair.'

Phoebe thought she might break apart. 'Alex, please—' She didn't care that she was begging.

He pushed himself off the wall and walked slowly towards her. 'It's a good thing you're here.'

No, it wasn't. It was heartbreaking. She should never have come. She took a step back and swallowed down the aching lump in her throat. 'Is it?'

Alex nodded. 'Saves me a bumpy ride back to London,' he said, a faint smile appearing on his lips.

Phoebe jerked to a halt and her heart began to bang around so wildly she feared it might leap out of her chest. 'You were going to come back?' Was it too much to hope that he'd been planning to return for her? 'Why?' she said shakily.

'I came here to escape. It hasn't worked.'

He stopped in front of her and Phoebe began to tremble. 'Escape from what?'

'The way I feel about you.'

'How do you feel about me?' she breathed, and time seemed to stand still as if aware of how much hung on his answer.

He searched her features and brushed a clump of hair from her face. 'I love you. So I don't just want an affair. I want everything.'

For a moment Phoebe went dizzy and then her chest filled with such happiness that she didn't think she'd be able to contain it. Without warning tears sprang up from nowhere and began to spill down her cheeks.

'Why are you crying?' he murmured, gently wiping them away with his thumbs. 'Is the fact that I love you really that appalling?'

'It's not appalling at all.' She sniffed, giving him a watery smile. 'It's the loveliest thing I've ever heard.'

'That's better.'

'You really love me?'

'I do.'

'Even like this?' She pointed to her red-nosed, puffy-eyed, bedraggled self.

Alex laughed softly. 'Any way you come. I should have told you I loved you the last time I saw you.' The laughter faded from his eyes. 'I just want you, Phoebe. All of you. For ever.'

Phoebe closed the gap between them and ran her hands up his chest to hold his face. 'You have me. Everything I have, everything I am, it's yours. I love you too. So much. When I think about you… Out there…'

She shook and Alex wrapped her in his arms. 'Don't think,' he said, capturing her mouth in a sizzling kiss filled with love and promise. His heart beat in time with hers, and as she felt a smile spread throughout her body Phoebe wondered what she'd done to deserve this much happiness.

'You're still thinking,' he said, lifting his head a fraction and arching an eyebrow.

'I am. Want to know what about?' she murmured as the familiar beat of desire began to unfurl inside her.

'What?'

Phoebe wound her arms around his neck and smiled up at him. 'I'm thinking we should get out of these wet things.'

MILLS & BOON®

Sparkling Christmas sensations!

This fantastic Christmas collection is fit to burst with billionaire businessmen, Regency rakes, festive families and smouldering encounters.

Set your pulse racing with this festive bundle of 24 stories, plus get a fantastic 40% OFF!

Visit the Mills & Boon website today to take advantage of this spectacular offer!

www.millsandboon.co.uk/Xmasbundle

MILLS & BOON®

Want to get more from Mills & Boon?

Here's what's available to you if you join the exclusive **Mills & Boon eBook Club** today:

✦ *Convenience – choose your books each month*
✦ *Exclusive – receive your books a month before anywhere else*
✦ *Flexibility – change your subscription at any time*
✦ *Variety – gain access to eBook-only series*
✦ *Value – subscriptions from just £1.99 a month*

So visit **www.millsandboon.co.uk/esubs** today to be a part of this exclusive eBook Club!